BAGGAGE IN A B CUP

SHIRLEY GOODRUM

A NOVEL

Shirley Goodrum

DEDICATION

To my husband, Rodney, for pouring me endless cups of apple tea and encouraging every word, my late mother, Patricia, for leaving this story in the deed box, and my children who believed I could write it.

1

Music blared from Pam Richards' Alfa Giulietta. It was parked in the driveway, the radio tuned to fourteen-year-old Brian's favourite early-morning station.

"Turn it down," she shouted, but her son, smart in his high school uniform, his tennis kit stashed in the boot ready for this afternoon's match, seemed not to hear, and drummed his fingers on the dashboard in time to the heavy beat. Wrung out after last night's trip to the ER and worried about Alex's chest pains, she didn't have the energy to shout again. She shrugged, picked up her keys, Brian's forgotten lunch-box and headed for the front-door. The phone rang. A quick glance at her watch told her it was seven-thirty. They were running late; no time to take the call.

It might be one of the hospitals.

She grabbed the receiver.

"Hello."

"Is that Mrs. Richards?"

"Yes, it is."

"Mrs. Richards, I don't know how to tell you this."

Oh, God, Kelly's pneumonia has come back. No. Doctor Frank, the paediatrician, would phone her himself. Alex, it must be Alex. The doctors were wrong. Last night they said it wasn't a heart attack, but it was. He's had another one.

"Toni's in Hillbrow."

Relief made her giddy. It wasn't either of the hospitals and Toni was on tour with the Art School, nowhere near Johannesburg's most dangerous suburb. She smiled into the receiver.

"You've got the wrong Toni. Bye."

"She's with Stelios."

Brian's lunch-box fell from her fingers.

STELIOS WAS *persona non-grata* in the Richard's house. Twelve years Toni's senior, he had no respect for her curfew or their parental role. His couldn't-care-less attitude had rubbed off on Toni. She'd changed; become a law unto herself, turning their home into a battlefield, bunking school, possibly failing Matric.

"WHAT'S THE BIG DEAL?" Stelios had shrugged. "I don't have Matric, and hey, I'm never short of money. She was with me and my friends."

Grabbing the collar of Stelios' body-fitting shirt, Alex had lifted him off the couch and swung a punch.

"DAD!"

Pushing her aside, Alex had landed another punch.

"Get the hell out of my house and stay the fuck away from my daughter."

Brian's lunch-box landed under the telephone table.

"Mrs. Richards, are you there?"

Pam held the receiver close to her ear.

"Yes, yes I am. Who are you?"

"An old girlfriend, one of the many he's cheated on. I've got an address for you. He's rubbish, believe me."

"I know that, but Toni…"

"Toni's in danger. Big time."

Pam shivered. "What's the address?"

"17 Avalon Heights, Kotze Street."

Pam scribbled on the jotter next to the phone.

"How do you know this?" she asked, but the line buzzed in her ear.

"Hello? Hello?"

She jabbed the keypad, desperate to hear the girl's voice. Nothing. She tore off the page, slammed the door on Brian's lunch and raced to the car.

"Slow down, Ma. School won't run away."

"But Toni has."

She swerved past Frans, their live-in gardener of seven years, ignored his waving rake and shouts for compost and zipped into the morning traffic. Brian didn't say a word as she leaned forward, hands on the steering wheel, knuckles white and sped right on past his school.

PAM'S FEAR STANK. It soaked her armpits, stained her blouse, made knots in her stomach and pushed her foot hard on the accelerator pedal. Hitting the outskirts of Hillbrow, she slowed down, smoothed out the scrap of paper clutched in her wet hand, checked the address and turned into Kotze Street. Avalon Heights was on the right and five youths loitered on the steps of the half-tiled, half-bricked entrance, their clothes screaming anti-rules-anti-establishment. Thick chains threaded through belt-loops of frayed, skin-tight jeans, grubby tank tops, scuffed, black boots, heads shaved, ears and noses pierced, they watched her drive two buildings further up the street, find an empty parallel parking bay and reverse in. The angle was sharp. She clipped the curb. They smirked and nudged each other, bouncing the morning sunlight off the studded dog-collars buckled around their necks.

"SHIT. SHIT. SHIT." She forced the gears, screeched them into first, straightened up the car, cut the engine and wiped her hands on her pencil skirt.

"Stay here, Brian. Lock the doors," she said, pulling the keys from the ignition.

"I'm coming with you." Her son's adolescent voice was high-pitched.

"I said LOCK THE DOORS. Dammit, I should have dropped you off at school."

"But you didn't, Ma."

They both climbed out of the car.

"GET BACK IN."

Brian shook his head and pulled on his blue, school blazer. "You can't waltz around Hillbrow on your own."

"For God's sake, I am not waltzing around Hillbrow. I'm looking for Toni."

"Me too, Ma, me too."

Pam looked at her son's gangly body and set jaw. Blocks of flats, tall and neglected, lined both sides of the road; rubbish clogged the gutters and dammed the flow of last night's rain. The car offered little safety in this neighbourhood. She locked it and dropped the key into her handbag, ignoring the mocking wolf-whistles coming from Avalon Heights.

"Okay, come; walk fast, but don't run."

Pulling himself up to his full five-foot-ten-inches, Brian adjusted his tie and smiled down at her. "Don't worry, Ma, I'll be cool."

. . .

HE MANAGED a swagger and Pam's high-heeled, sling-back sandals assaulted the pavement. Chins up and looking straight ahead, they strode up to the leering grins, but their bravado didn't fool the layabouts who gave them the middle-finger, didn't move an inch, and forced them to detour around their unsavoury bodies to enter the block.

INSIDE THE LOBBY, Pam and Brian scanned the dull, brass numbers of the mailboxes built into the wall. Number 17 was on the second floor. Graffiti stained the walls and the smell of urine seeped from the cement that crumbled between the bricks.

I don't care what the place looks like. Please let the girl on the phone be right; let me find Toni here. Please.

THE ONLY WAY UP TO number 17 was via the narrow stairway to the left of the entrance. Grime of dubious origin coated the handrail. Pam hugged her arms around herself, took the first step and turned to face Brian. His face was level with hers, his foot ready to follow hers, his eyes wide. He held a hanky over his nose and mouth.

"Don't touch anything," she said.

He sighed.

"Don't give me that look, just do as I say."

He rolled his eyes. "Honestly, Ma, this place reeks. You know I'm a health freak, do you think I'd touch anything?"

She shook her head. "Of course, not. I'm just not thinking straight."

"At least that's normal," he teased, but Pam heard the tremor in his voice. He was frightened, and he had every right to be. This was not his place; it was her husband's. *Damn him.*

HER ANGER TOOK her by surprise, but rushing Alex into the ER last night, for the third time in as many weeks, and getting nothing concrete from the doctors, was frustrating. These middle-of-the-night trips were not fun and, if she was truth-ful, Alex was not fun anymore. She was getting fed up and last night's episode had been scary for Brian. Alex was not the dynamic husband she was used to and loved. *What were the doctors missing? What was wrong with him? Why had he been shutting himself off, retreating to his bed? She'd always looked to him as her pillar of support, now it seemed like she was coping with everything on her own, and the nightmarish pains in his chest scared her. What the hell was happening?*

SHE CURSED UNDER HER BREATH. "Follow me, Brian," she said, marching them up to the second floor and hurrying them down a dank corridor.

"We've gone past it, Ma."

She rounded on Brian. He put his hands up in the air, surren-der-style. "*Jeez*, don't get mad. It's not my fault, look, this is number 18." He pointed to a door.

She let it out as a sigh. "I'm not mad, Brian."

"Well, your eyes are popping out at me and you've got that red face."

She touched his arm. "Okay, I'm mad, but not with you."

"Toni?"

"She's a good fit, that's for sure."

And Alex and his chest pains and my helplessness.

"She doesn't mean to hurt you, Ma. She's not a bad person. Stelios has some kind of hold over her."

"Don't make excuses for your sister."

"I'm not, I'm just telling you the truth. She'll do anything for him."

"Why? He's an arsehole extraordinaire."

Brian shrugged. "Don't know, but she says she loves him."

"Well I don't and I'm ready to kill him."

"I see that."

THEY TURNED and walked back to number 17. Pam rapped on the door. "Toni? Toni, are you in there?"

Silence.

"Answer me Antoinette."

She pounded harder, bruising her fists.

"Open up. Get out here. Now," she shouted and kicked a hole in the cheap wood.

"Wow. Ma, have you tried the handle?"

Brian turned the doorknob and the door swung open.

. . .

A MATTRESS LAY on the floor in the middle of the room, the black sheets and pillows a crumpled mess. The palm of a purple ceramic-hand chopped off at the wrist, and filled with cigarette butts, sat on top of Toni's school jersey, covering the gold, embroidered school badge and dribbling ash on the sleeve. Pam fought to stay calm, to keep her fear, her terror, from Brian. She pointed to some sticks poking out of the neck of a brandy bottle.

"Are those incense? Something smells in here, like wet paint and sweet."

Brian picked up the purple hand, handed Pam the jersey, and rummaged through the ash.

"It's not incense, it's *zol*," he said. "See these small bits."

"What's *zol*?"

"Marijuana. Pot."

"Oh my God." Pam sank onto a small couch and clutched her hands together to stop them from shaking. Kapok popped through the broken cushion seams and rough tweed scratched the back of her knees.

"I'm going to have a look around," said Brian.

PAM BIT her lip and forced back her tears. She mustn't show Brian how afraid she was. She closed her eyes and focused on the breathing technique, learnt years ago in yoga classes and often practised when Kelly took sick. Restoring a smidgen of calm, she picked up the sounds of running water and clattering dishes. Brian touched her shoulder and handed her one of two glasses. "Here, Ma, it's flat Coke. I found an open bottle on the kitchen table. Don't worry, I've washed the glasses."

"Thanks." The liquid stuck half-way down her throat, she forced a swallow and walked over to the window. Staring at the street below, the tears stung the back of her eyes. She fought for control. She must not cry in front of Brian.

"Ma, bring me the jersey," he called. She counted to ten before following his voice to the kitchen. He spread the jersey on the cracked lino floor. Collecting Toni's skirt and blouse off the chairs, her black shoes and white ankle socks from under the Formica table, he piled them on top and, tying the sleeves together, he made a neat Dick Whittington parcel and pulled Pam's heart into a tight ball.

"Leave it here," she whispered." Go and check if she's left anything else."

PAM CIRCLED THE SMALL KITCHEN. She touched the kettle; it was cold. She leaned forward and pulled off Toni's special notepaper from the splashback. Tiny yellow butterflies adorned the edges; her daughter's writing filled the middle.

LOADS OF CAT *food under the sink. Don't worry about the dog, we're taking her with us. Use the milk in the fridge. Thanks for letting us stay in your flat. T & S. xxx*

. . .

SHE SCRUNCHED and pocketed the paper and wrenched open the fridge door. There was no milk. Someone had obeyed Toni's instructions.

"HEY, MA, COME AND SEE THIS."

Swinging the fridge shut, Pam caught sight of her face in the handle. It was a distorted mess. A tear had escaped and run down her cheek. She pulled a tissue from her bag, gave thanks to Revlon for its smudge and waterproof mascara, dabbed at her lash line, and wiped away all visible signs of the turmoil raging inside.

BRIAN WAS SQUATTING on the floor, looking at a painting balanced against the wall. She knelt next to him and gasped. There, in the right-hand corner, was Toni's signature and a date that shocked her. It was the very day she'd taken Toni to school early, to catch the tour bus. On the way, they'd chatted about what fun it would be, how grateful she was to Pam and Alex for paying for it and letting her go.

SHE'D LIED through her teenage, Stelios-besotted teeth; she'd never intended boarding the school bus. She'd come back here, to this filthy flat, for three days before running off with him to lord-knows-where.

PAM PUSHED HERSELF UP, stumbled and knocked over a tin mug. Dirty brushes and turpentine fell across the floor, soaking into a paint-smeared piece of mutton cloth and make-shift cardboard palette. Her fingers reached out to the painting and touched the thick, raised strokes and bright abstract forms. The oil paint was tacky; drying while her child went missing with that rat-rubbish man. Fear and anger collided and exploded. Pam hurled the empty mug.

"RIGHT. That's it. I've had enough. Bring her stuff. Let's go."

"Where to?"

"You're going to school."

"Ah, Ma, come on, it's too late, I've missed two periods already."

"Don't argue, Brian," she snapped. "Just do as I say. I can't deal with another delinquent this morning."

Brian's lips drew tight. She pulled him into a rough hug, squashing the clothes parcel between them. His stiff body saddened her. She wished she could take back her harsh words; instead, she ruffled his auburn hair.

"I'm sorry, you know I didn't mean that, don't you? You've been a star and deserve the day off. I'll take you home."

She picked up Toni's painting.

"What are you doing with that?" asked Brian.

"I'm taking it to the police."

"Now?"

"No, after I've dropped you at home and been to the hospital."

"Which hospital?"

"The one your father's in."

2

Pam hurried down the carpet-tiled passage, past the breakfast trolleys, the sluice-room and the nurses' workstation and stopped outside semi-private ward C11. Taking a deep breath, and composing her thoughts, she hoped that Alex would be the only occupant.

"Mrs. Richards. Hello. Mrs. Richards." The ward sister, in danger of bisecting her large bosom, leaned over the workstation counter, flashed Pam a wide smile and waved a green card. "Mrs. Richards," she called again.

Pam retraced her steps.

"Hi, I'm Sister Bennett. No need to look so worried, my dear. Your husband's just fine and he's been discharged. Please take this to admissions on the ground floor." Sister Bennett checked her wristwatch. "If you get it in by twelve o'clock they won't charge you for another day."

"Discharged? Who discharged him?"

"Dr Gordon. He's with him now."

Pam ignored the green card, headed back to C11 and opened the door.

THE PHYSICIAN BEAMED AT HER. It seemed as if everyone smiled around here. Everyone that is, except Alex. He sat on the edge of the high hospital bed, shoulders slumped, head hanging down, feet dangling in mid-air. A small plaster, stuck in the crook of his right elbow, almost covered the blown-vein bruise, and hid the evidence of their trip to the ER last night.

"Good morning, Mrs. Richards," said Dr Gordon.

Alex lifted his head, his blue eyes flat and expressionless.

"Hi," he said. His voice matched the death in his eyes. A slight hand movement and offered cheek acknowledged her arrival, but she did not respond with her customary kiss and a frown furrowed his brow before his head dropped and he went back to staring at his feet. *Sister Bennett said he's been discharged. Why? He looked dreadful; in no fit state to go home.* Pam noted his skew parting, unlike Alex, and the increase of grey hair nestled amongst the black alarmed her. Dr. Gordon waved her to a visitor's chair.

"Sit, please, sit."

Pam sat. Dr Gordon puffed out his chest and proceeded to deliver his news.

"I've been chatting to your husband; going through the results of his tests. Definitely no sign of a heart attack."

Pam crossed her arms over her chest. Dr. Gordon's smile flashed perfect, white teeth and a slither of pink, upper gums.

"He can go home. Everything's normal."

Normal? Was he mad?

"Like hell it is."

The doctor stepped back from Pam, his smile faded.

"Pam, please," whispered Alex. She ignored him.

"Look at him." Pam jabbed her finger in Alex's direction. "Obviously, there must be something wrong."

Dr. Gordon handed her the laboratory reports. "See for yourself," he said.

Standing up, she grabbed the sheath of papers from his hands and shook them under his nose.

"Throw these away. Can't you see that they're useless?"

Alex touched her arm. She shrugged him off.

Doctor Gordon cleared his throat and peered at her over the top of his glasses.

"Mrs. Richards, those results confirm the tests I did the last time Alex was admitted. Everything has come back negative."

Pam flung the papers onto starched sheets. "Forget these. Open your eyes. Look at this man; really look at him. See his dead eyes. Use your ears. Can't you hear the flatness in his voice? He's sick, I tell you. What kind of doctor are you?"

Dr. Gordon plunged his hands into the pockets of his white coat. "Young woman, I will not have you talk to me this way."

"Yes, oh yes, you will. I'm not taking him home. Not again." Pam sat down, pushing her legs together to stop her knees knocking. "Not until you find out what's wrong with him."

Dr. Gordon stared at her; she looked him straight in the eye. He nodded. "Right then, get him a pair of running shoes," he said. Alex's movements were wooden and slow, but he stood up. "Let's go, Pam," he said.

"Get back on that bed," she said, pushing his shoulder. "We're not going anywhere. And as for you," she turned to the doctor, "running shoes, you say? You saw him get up, saw that he can barely stand, yet you suggest running shoes. What's he supposed to do, swallow them?"

"Please, Mrs. Richards. Calm down."

"Don't you 'Mrs. Richards' me. I've rushed him into the emergency rooms three times. I will not calm down."

"I understand how you feel."

"No, you don't." Pam's eyes filled with tears. "You wouldn't prescribe running shoes if you did."

"Please, don't cry." Dr. Gordon fumbled in his pocket and handed her a Gary Player tissue. "Here. Please. I think his problem is stress-related and regular exercise will help."

"Really? Regular exercise?" Pam blew her nose. "He can't function at home; he struggles at work. You're crazy if you think he'll run."

"Forget the shoes," said Alex. "I'm telling you it's my heart."

The physician shook his head. "It's not your heart, Mr. Richards. These tests and the ones I've conducted previously, prove conclusively that there's nothing physically wrong with you."

Pam tossed the used tissue in the bin and scooped up the

reports. "Then what do you think is wrong with him?" she asked.

"Stress, as I said. Last night's 'heart attack' was a panic attack."

Alex grimaced. "I had pains in my chest. I couldn't breathe, and my arm was lame." He stood up. "I'm leaving. I've heard enough."

The doctor addressed Pam. "He needs a psychiatrist."

Alex gripped the edge of the bed. "What I need is a decent doctor."

Pam put her hand over his. "Let's hear what Dr Gordon has to say."

"Why? Do you think I'm mad?" Alex scowled at them.

"You're not mad, but you are stressed," said Dr. Gordon

"For Pete's sake, I run a bloody company. Of course, I'm stressed. Have been for years. I do not need a shrink."

"Your stress is out of control. You are having panic attacks and I suspect that you have depression."

"Crap. Let's go, Pam."

Pam turned to Dr. Gordon. "Will you excuse us, please?"

"Of course." Dr Gordon switched his smile back on. "I'll finish my rounds and see you later."

THE DOOR CLOSED. Pam didn't move. Her lips were pressed tight. Alex glared. "Do you want to tell me why we're still here?" he asked. Tears sprang into her eyes again and she dashed them away with the back of her hand.

Alex reached for her, but she stiffened. "What's wrong? Why are you nearly crying? Is it Kelly? Isn't she coming home today?"

"It's not Kelly. She's fine. When I dropped Brian at home, Dr Frank phoned to say that he'll discharge her later."

"Then what is it and why did you drop Brian at home? Why isn't he at school? What's going on?" Irritation shifted in his dull eyes.

"Do you know where I've been today?" she asked.

He shrugged his shoulders. "It sounds like you didn't go to work."

"I went to Hillbrow and Brian came with me."

"What? Why? Hillbrow? It's 1986 not the bloody Sixties, Pam. It's dangerous." The muscle in Alex's jaw worked overtime. "You don't go there, no one goes there, and you sure as hell don't take your kid there. *Jesus*, Pam, that was a stupid thing to do."

"Don't you think I know that?" Pam's anger flared. She felt her cheeks go red. She had to calm down. She busied herself, straightening the medical reports, making them neat and tidy, slotting them into the metal file hanging at foot of his bed.

"I got a phone call from one of Stelios's old girlfriends. She said Toni was in Hillbrow with him, and she gave me an address."

"That's a lie. Toni's on tour. I'll bet that bastard…"

"Toni never got on the bus. The flat was empty, but she had been there three days ago."

Alex pulled open the pedestal drawer, grabbed his toothbrush and comb. "Give me the address."

"What for?"

"To find her and to kill that son of a bitch." Alex zipped the toiletry bag.

"You're not going anywhere." Pam snatched the bag and flung it back into the drawer.

"Says who?"

"Me." Her face was an inch from his. "I'm serious, Alex. I'm tired of these heart attacks or whatever they are. You're always exhausted and going to bed. You don't want to talk to me about it and I can't count on you anymore."

"Rubbish. I haven't been well lately, but…"

Pam grabbed his shoulders. "Try six months, Alex. Since Brian turned fourteen."

"You're exaggerating."

"I wish I was, but remember when I went to the kitchen to fetch Brian's birthday cake and found you there and asked you to carry the side plates to the table?"

"No, I don't."

"Well, I do. You said you couldn't go back to the party, the noise was too loud, you felt trapped; claustrophobic and were going to lie down."

Alex fidgeted. "I wasn't lying."

Pam shrugged. "Anyway, you didn't come back to the party, even though our families had come all the way from Cape Town and East London. Ask them, they'll tell you that I managed the rest of the day and their visit by myself and, what's more to the point, I've been managing by myself ever since."

"I'm not discussing this." He reached for his trousers. "Toni's missing and I'm not staying here."

"You were missing this morning, Alex. I don't need another child. Next time I go looking for one of them I want my husband, not my son, there."

Alex grabbed her wrists. "That was below the belt, Pam."

"No, it's not, it's the truth and I'm tired of this. I agree with Dr Gordon. You do need help." He released his grip and she scooped up her bag.

"Get it." She opened the door and strode out.

ALEX DRAGGED his navy trousers onto the bed. Pam ran her own business; she knew the stress levels were constantly high. *Why was she acting like a first-class bitch?* Heavy legs and clammy hands slowed his dressing. He gave up trying to button his shirt. He pushed the tail into his pants, pulled in his stomach and zipped his fly. Running shoes. What a bloody stupid idea. The doctor was an idiot. His belt refused to buckle; he left it hanging. Sitting on the chair vacated by Pam, he rolled his socks and bent over to put them on. Bugger Pam and Dr Gordon; he'd take a taxi to the police station, hopefully get there before she did, and report Toni missing. His breathing quickened, pins and needles numbed his mouth and cheeks. His heart took off and thundered in his chest. He dropped the socks and leaned against the back of the chair. Pain gripped his chest.

DR GORDON STOOD in the doorway, stethoscope cradled in his hands.

"Another attack?" His eyes, peering over the reading glasses balanced on the tip of his nose, were neutral.

Alex nodded. The doctor placed his hand below Alex's rib cage.

"Breathe to the count of eight. Lift my hand with your diaphragm."

"I can't."

"You can. Now, do as I say. Breathe in, slowly; hold it. That's it. Now, breathe out. Slower. Five - six - seven - eight. And again."

Too scared to do anything else, Alex obeyed and, as Dr. Gordon counted and Alex breathed to order, his heart slowed, and the numbness disappeared, but exhaustion chained him to the chair.

Dr. Gordon smiled. "See, you can control it. It's not a heart attack."

"But... I can't do this all the time." Alex buried his head in his hands.

"No, you can't. You must fix the cause. We've just treated the symptoms. It's a good trick to learn, but it's not the answer to your problem."

"So, what is?"

"Are you willing to see a psychiatrist?"

Alex raised his head, his muscles heavy, trapped in fatigue. Dr Gordon held his gaze, but his brown eyes were kind.

"Can't say I'm happy to, but yes, I will," sighed Alex.

"Good. Is your wife still here?"

"No."

"Will she be back later?"

"I hope so."

"Quite a woman you have there."

"You mean cheeky?"

"No, I mean strong and most protective of you."

"Not when you left."

Dr Gordon smiled. "Gave you a hard time, did she?"

Alex nodded. "You could say that."

"I'll have Sister Bennett arrange an appointment with Dr De Bruin. He's a brilliant psychiatrist; got a reputation for treating post-traumatic stress in the military. I can recommend him. Meanwhile I'll prescribe a sleeping pill. Take it. You need the rest."

"Can I still go home today?"

"Ask your wife."

3

A t the police station, Pam itched to deliver a well-placed clout to the head of the young policeman who sucked his HB pencil like a lollipop. Charcoal bled onto his yellow, smoker's tongue. "Listen, lady, I've told you, you have to wait forty-eight hours. I can't open a missing person's until then."

Pam glared at him. "What about abduction? If you take a minor away from her home without her parents' permission is that abduction?"

A slow shrug. "*Ja.*"

"Then I want to report her abducted and I want her boyfriend arrested."

"I can't open a warrant of abduction for nothing."

Pam's neck and cheeks flamed. "For nothing? You think abduction is nothing? Well I think it's serious. I'm not leaving here till you open a case and issue a warrant. So, save us both some time, take that pencil out of your mouth and fill out the forms."

"No need to be rude, lady, I'm just doing my job. As you say, abduction is a serious charge."

"So is my daughter's disappearance."

"But what happens when she comes back, hey? Then you'll drop the charges against the boyfriend and leave us with all the paperwork."

"I swear to God I won't do that. Wait a minute, you can file my daughter as a missing person. She has been missing for longer than forty-eight hours."

"How do you know?" He tapped the pencil rubber and arched his ginger eyebrows.

Pam dumped Toni's painting on the counter. "I found this in the flat. She painted it three days ago. See the date."

"That doesn't mean she's missing."

"Of course, it does. We thought she got on the tour bus and went to Cape Town on this day, but she didn't and the flat's empty. She is missing."

"Maybe she was at the shops when you arrived at the flat this morning."

"Not according to this note." Pam handed over the butterfly-edged paper. The policeman smoothed it out and mouthed the words as he read them to himself. "I don't think that this proves anything."

"I don't care what you think." Pam stopped herself from ripping the pencil from his hand. "She's seventeen, underage, and no one gave anyone permission for her to be there. I do not know where she is. I want to report her missing. Failing that, I want to lay a charge of abduction against her boyfriend. Today. Right now."

"Sorry. You can't do that."

"What is your name?"

"Sergeant Coetzee."

"Well, Sergeant Coetzee, get me the officer in charge."

"He can do nothing," said Coetzee, sticking the pencil behind his ear and folding his arms. "The law says you must wait, and you must just wait."

The tears came; she could not hold them back. They shook her and intimidated Coetzee, his impudence turned to horror. "Oh, please, lady, don't cry." She tried to stop. She sucked in her breath and gagged. Coetzee's face paled, his freckles stood to attention.

"I'll get some water," he said and hurried off.

THE TEARS RAN down her cheeks and fell onto the blank report sheet. She was exhausted. She rested her arms on the wooden counter, buried her face in them, and wept.

"HERE, LADY." Sergeant Coetzee offered her a glass of iced water. The hairs on the back of his hands were pale gold. Like a car pulling off in third gear, her sobs shuddered to a halt. "Thank you," she said, rummaging in her bag for a tissue. She was fresh out and she pinched her nose to stop it dripping.

Coetzee ran and fetched a piece of toilet paper from the men's room. Embarrassed, she took it and blew her nose. He pulled the forms towards him.

"What's your daughter's name?"

"Antoinette Richards."

His tongue moved as he filled in the squares.

"Age?"

"Seventeen."

"When did you last see her?"

"Three days ago."

"What did you say her boyfriend's name was?"

"I didn't, but it's Stelios Panos."

The policeman ran a hand over his ginger brush-cut. "A tall Greek? Always wears white shoes?"

"Yes. Why?"

Cupping his hand so that she could not see, he wrote on the form. "I think I know him. I think he's got to report here every week. He's out on bail."

Pam's legs threatened to give way. The anonymous caller had told her Toni was in danger, but, oh my God, bail?

"Why? What's he done?"

"I'm not allowed to tell you, but his bail's R5000. That's heavy, so it's serious, but I might be wrong. The guy I'm talking about lives in Lanseria, not Hillbrow. Let me go check."

· · ·

LEFT ALONE, Pam turned the report around and read what the policeman had written.

DRUG-DEALER- GUILTY - LSD. SKIPPED BAIL???

SHE READ and re-read the pencilled words. They lifted off the page. A ringing filled her ears, her hands shook, her legs crumbled, and her body slid onto the concrete floor.

FROM A FAR DISTANCE, Coetzee's voice sounded like it was strained through a wet dog's blanket.

"Jeez, she's passed out."

"Sit her on that bench and put her head on her knees."

Obeying the guttural voice of authority, Coetzee hooked his hands under her armpits, pulled her unresponsive body upright and settled it on the bench, head on knees, as instructed.

"I'm sure it's the same guy, *Meneer.*"

"Okay, Coetzee, get hold of central office. Tell them to check out the Hillbrow address."

"*Ja Meneer.*"

Coetzee's hands left her. With each click of the telephone's dialling wheel, the dog blanket dried and lifted. Her brain cleared. She heard him speaking to an official on the other end of the line and replace the receiver.

"Man, if it's him, her daughter's in real trouble. Shit," said the voice of authority. "He's a hardened bastard and we're for it if he's skipped."

"He always comes in with a pretty chick, *Meneer*, maybe her daughter's been in here too."

"Do we know what she looks like? Have we got a photo?"

"No, but I think she'll be hot. Her *ma* looks okay."

Pam's choking ended her unintended eavesdropping.

"Are you okay?" The voice of authority belonged to a heavy-set, tall man with a proud moustache. Pam nodded.

"I'm Inspector Bezuidenhout."

Pam shook his offered hand.

"Coetzee here has asked our central office to…"

"I heard. Please just issue the warrant. I want this man arrested. My daughter is in danger."

"We must first wait for central to report back." The Inspector hitched up the waist of his pants. They rode back to his hips and the overhang of his belly buried his belt.

Pam shook her head. "How long will that take? You're wasting time; when are you going to do something?"

"As soon as they phone back. Believe me, we're as worried as you are."

"I don't think so."

.   .   .

CENTRAL OFFICE WAS EFFICIENT, but each waiting second was an eternity for Pam.

"*Meneer*, they say the Hillbrow place belongs to his friend, Costa Tournavitis."

The Inspector checked his holster, patted his gun, and shouted down the passage. "Danny, come take charge here. Coetzee, let's go to Lanseria."

"I'm coming with you." Pam smoothed her skirt, tucked her bob behind her ears.

"Sorry, lady. This is police business."

"You're wrong. My daughter is with him. This is my business."

The inspector let out a sigh. The space between his shirt buttons gaped and soft knobs of fat pushed through.

"Call your husband. Have him take you home. I promise we'll get back to you as soon as we can."

Pam shook her head, her fingers tugging at the sodden toilet paper. "He's in hospital. I can't go and just wait. Please, let me come."

"Let her, sir. She looks like she's going to cry again." Her fainting spell had sharpened Sergeant Coetzee's powers of observation.

Inspector Bezuidenhout stood tall and pulled in his stomach. The shirtfronts closed, and his belly disappeared from view.

"Okay. Come."

· · ·

IN LANSERIA the plots were measured in hectares. Miles of untouched rolling *veld* separated one neighbour from another. In the back of the police van, Pam opened the window. The smell of yesterday's thunderstorm seeped from the soil and swelled in the summer heat. It was a smell she loved but today, images of the last few days trampled its fragrance. They filled her mind and jostled for prime position: Kelly going into hospital, her fluffy toys packed with her pyjamas; Toni, surrounded by her school friends, waving goodbye at the bus stop; Hillbrow's clogged gutters and sullen stares; Alex's comfortable ward and reams of useless reports; Stelios, his little dog, his white shoes. She stared out of the window. *How did we get here?* she thought. *Yesterday we were an ordinary family, now we're involved with a criminal, have a missing daughter, and belong on the back page of the Sunday papers.*

Sergeant Coetzee caught her eye in the rear-view mirror and pointed to a small-holding on the right.

"That's it," he said. "The Spanish-style one."

TWO ALSATIANS RAN the length of the wire fence, barking at the police van as it bounced down the rutted driveway, turned into a cleared patch behind the house and parked in front of the collapsing veranda of the converted servants' quarters.

"This is his cottage."

The policemen climbed out and Sergeant Coetzee opened the van's back door for Pam. The Inspector walked around the building. "Looks deserted," he said. "Come, let's see if it is."

4

The policemen pulled on gloves, checked their guns and knocked on the cottage's stable-door. The Alsatians barked louder, but Pam felt light-headed, her body heavy and the barks sounded far away. She wanted a back-track button, she wanted to go back to before Stelios strutted into their lives: she wanted to peep into Toni's room and find her asleep in her bed and never drop her off for the school tour. Sergeant Coetzee's polished boot kicked the door open. It was a large boot. She wondered how heavy it was, if it was a size 11 and if he spat on his boots to make them shine like that. Her feet followed Inspector Bezuidenhout's into a large room that combined a bedroom, lounge and kitchen. Red dust, driven under the gap at the bottom of the door, crunched underfoot and crept into her sandals. Her index finger trailed over the television, leaving a clean, thin, black road in the dust on top. Housekeeping was long overdue.

THE SAME SWEET smell of the Hillbrow flat filled her lungs.

Zol. Looks and nods passed between the policemen as they stirred ashtrays with their state-issue, yellow, Bic pens.

"Naughty bastard. *Dagga.* I'll bet he's still dealing," said Bezuidenhout. He pointed to a bank of cupboards covering the far windowless wall. "Open those, Coetzee."

"But, *Meneer*, we haven't got a search warrant." The young Sergeant's freckles danced on his bobbing Adam's apple.

The Inspector pulled himself up to his full six foot four, expanded his chest and gripped his solid love handles with spade-square hands.

"I said open it. Now."

Pam was glad that she wasn't Coetzee. He fumbled with the door's rounded knobs and flimsy locks and did as he was told. Inspector Bezuidenhout thrust the hanging clothes to one side. Pam watched as he worked through each item, examining pockets, linings and turn-ups, finding cash, handkerchiefs, chewing gum, packaged condoms and, what he called, marijuana joints. He took his time, sliding each searched piece back along the rail. He pushed his hand into the pocket of a pair of white linen pants and pulled a government-stamped buff envelope, slipped a gloved finger under the flap and shook out a passport. Pressed into the green leather cover, a yellow crest and bright gold letters proclaimed The Republic of South Africa in English, Afrikaans and French. He flipped the pages, paused at the identifying photograph and showed it to Pam.

"Is this your daughter?" he asked.

Toni's face stared back at her. Pam squeezed her eyes shut.

Now is a good time for this nightmare to end.

She opened her eyes. Toni's head and shoulders photo, and the name Antionette Panos, had not disappeared.

"Here, take it," he said.

No. Never.

She hugged her arms to her body, holding tight to her dream of her daughter's innocence. Toni's passport was locked in the middle drawer of the filing-cabinet at home, safe with other important documents. This was a forgery

Toni lied and faked a signature to get it.

This was proof of Toni's deceit.

"Is this your child?" The Inspector splayed the pages. Betrayal cut deep, and Pam prayed not to faint again. She searched the photo for a remnant of the child she'd reared and loved. She stared at it for a long time, and there, in the eyes full of mischief and the much-kissed button nose, she found the little girl who had trailed enchantment and magic.

"Yes." She whispered, her tears blurring Toni's oval face. She cleared her throat and picked up her chin. "Yes, that's my daughter, Antoinette Richards."

"You know she helped get this, don't you? Do you still want to press charges?"

Pam sucked in air and collected her unravelled self. "Yes. More than ever, I do. I want her back."

Inspector Bezuidenhout closed the passport, rubbed his thumb over the cover and put it back where he found it. "We'll fetch it when we officially come to investigate," he said, spreading the hanging clothes back in place and closing the wardrobes.

"Take us back to the station, Coetzee."

RUNNING and kicking up clouds of red dust, the dogs barked as the van drove back to the tar road. Pam fidgeted on the hard seat, crossing and uncrossing her legs, reliving the horror of discovery. The pain of deception scrambled thoughts. Fetch Kelly from hospital. Toni the delightful child. Shop for supper. Toni the talented artist. Check in on Alex. Toni the liar. Toni with Stelios. Huge drops of rain fell from the sunlit sky. A 'Monkey's wedding' bombed the windscreen and pelted the *veld*. Coetzee switched on the windscreen-wipers. Toni loved running in the sunshine-rain. Coetzee didn't noticed Pam wipe away a tear, but Bezuidenhout offered her a clean, white hanky, folded small enough to fit into his shirt pocket. She waved it away.

"It's okay, really, I'm fine." Pam blinked and held back another flood. *No, Not again.*

"Take it." Bezuidenhout shook out the folds, holding a corner between his thumb and forefinger. The working cells of Pam's addled brain registered the blue embroidered double lines, the letter 'I' and the curved, feminine arch of the Inspector's little finger. Manic giggles threatened to push pass the lump in her throat.

Sergeant Coetzee caught her eye in the rear-view mirror, "I'm sorry for you, lady," he said. The simmering hysteria turned to tears. She grabbed Bezuidenhout's handkerchief, soaking and soiling it as she cried and blew her nose over and over again. The policemen concentrated on the wet road ahead, but the effort it took to ignore her waterworks in the back seat stiffened their necks and shoulders.

Back at the station, her face blotchy, her eyes puffy and her body untrustworthy, Pam clutched the sodden hanky and gave Inspector Bezuidenhout a wan smile. "I'll wash and return it," she said.

"That's okay," his big hand dismissed her offer. "Keep it."

"I feel like such a big baby. Please excuse me."

"*Ag*, you're just a *ma* whose kid's in trouble." Bezuidenhout's voice was kind. "*Kom*. Run. The rain is heavy, let's get inside."

DANNY HANDED over some messages and went back to his own office. Coetzee found an old towel and they dried off. "I'll get some coffee," he said. Bezuidenhout took a pile of sandwiches out of a plastic lunch-box, unfolded the wax paper and offered them to Pam.

"Apricot jam. Have one," he said. It was nearly midday and Pam hadn't eaten since breakfast, before the anonymous caller had thrown her into a nightmare. Her hunger surprised her, and her mouth watered. She bit into the soft, white bread, licking the squashed jam from the corners of her lips. Inspector Bezuidenhout ate the rest, one gulp per slice.

"What does the 'I' on the hanky stand for?" asked Pam.

"Ignatius. It's a family name." His deep voice was shy. "I hate it. My friends call me Ig."

Coetzee came back with a tray holding three mugs of coffee and passed one to Pam.

"Hope you like condensed milk," he said.

She nodded and her fatigued body mopped up the instant energy. Coetzee completed the forms and she signed the report and pulled her car-keys from her handbag. Next stop; Kelly. Poor child, stranded at the hospital, waiting, since her discharge this morning, to be collected and taken home.

"*Baie dankie*, Ig," she said, in her best, second-language Afrikaans.

Inspector Bezuidenhout placed a square hand on her shoulder.

"Try not to worry. We'll find her."

Pam managed a smile, but she'd been at the cottage and she was no longer naïve. Toni had deceived them. Toni was with a drug-dealer, a man who was used to dodging the cops; Toni was in danger.

INSPECTOR BEZUIDENHOUT'S words helped control her fear as she drove to Johannesburg General Hospital, took the lift to the eighth floor of orange block 'H' and found Kelly staring out of the window at the jacaranda trees below. A toy mouse sat in the palm of her hand, his once furry body was bald, and he only had one ear. Mouse, as Kelly called him, had gone with her, ten years earlier, to America.

5

I t was 1976 when the National Institute of Health in Washington had invited Kelly to Bethesda. They had, accommodated her, Pam, Alex and Mouse in a private *en suite* ward. It had two beds and a pull-out sleeper-chair and Kelly's eyes had sparkled when she saw the big screen TV.

"Oh, Mouse, we don't have that at home, but Granny Hilda and Grandpa Peter do, and Toni and Brian are staying with them while we are here. They said they were going to be so spoilt and lucky because they could watch *The Brady Bunch*, and I could not, and now, look, we have a TV too."

Alex had laughed. "And it has lots and lots of channels, Kelly, and it's on all day and all night. Granny Hilda and Grandpa Peter's only has one channel for a few hours a day. Let's cuddle up and find something to watch."

"Imagine how jealous they are going to be when I tell them, Mouse."

. . .

FATHER AND DAUGHTER loved the cartoons and were glued to the Sunday night *Bugs Bunny Show* when the Professor of Immunology paid his first visit.

"Hi, I'm Prof Wilson; Patrick to you guys. Excuse my clothes," he said waving at his jeans, checked shirt and boots. "I've just got back from my farm in Virginia where I grow grapes. Wine making is a hobby of mine. My wife says I'm a lousy wine maker, but I'm getting better. Have you settled in okay?"

"Oh yes, thank you," said Pam, putting aside her book.

"Nice to meet you, Patrick," Alex stood and shook his hand. "We've been treated like royalty by everyone, haven't we, Pam?"

"Yes, we have. Doctor Frank told us your research programme was big, but he was wrong - it's huge; we're very impressed."

"I guess we are well-funded, it makes life interesting and we get to see many rare cases like Kelly. Have you met Jane Stanley, the paediatric nurse, Kelly?"

Kelly nodded, her eyes flitting back to the screen and *Bugs Bunny.*

"What's that you have there?"

"My mouse."

"Okay and what's your mouse called?"

"Mouse."

"Okay. Well you tell Jane that I said Mouse can go everywhere with you, okay?"

"She said she's my very own nurse, is that true?"

"Yes, Kelly."

"But, at home I don't need my own nurse."

Patrick sat down on his haunches, bringing his eyes level with hers.

"Does that make you nervous?"

She nodded again.

"Don't be. You're a very special patient and Jane wants to take care of you, and only you, until you go home to South Africa. Okay?"

Kelly's scalp was a patchwork of dry skin and turfs of curly hair. The curls bounced in agreement.

"Okay. Tomorrow she'll take you to school on the 3rd floor and show you around. Okay?"

"Yes."

"Now, what do you think is wrong with you?"

"Well, my Doctor Frank says it's two things. My blood cells are lazy and he says sometimes they don't work properly, and then I get pneumonia, and he also says my body doesn't know I have this stuff," Kelly opened her mouth wide and pointed to the white coating on the inside of her cheeks and gums, "and the patches on my head, so it doesn't fix it."

"Okay. You're pretty clever for a six-year old. That stuff in your mouth and on your head, is called thrush and the grown-up name for the blood cell thing is Lazy Leucocyte Syndrome. The thrush won't go away because a piece of what we call your immune system – that's the bit that fights the bad guys – is missing."

Kelly giggled. "Yes, that's what I just said."

"Okay. Well, Doctor Frank told us about you and we asked you to come here because we want to do some more tests and see if we can help you. Okay?"

"You say okay a lot, but yes, okay."

KELLY CREPT into Jane Stanley's heart as they ran from the ward to the escalator, from building to building, criss-crossing the lawns to the X-ray department, the laboratories and physicians' rooms where phials of Kelly's blood, skin shavings, urine and stool samples were collected. Some of the procedures made Jane cringe, but Kelly didn't cry, not once and Jane gave her a hug when she heard her whisper "I'm scared, Mouse."

ON EASTER MORNING Kelly's hushed, excited voice woke Pam. Alex, lying on the pull-out sleeper-chair, put a finger to his lips and pointed to a huge cellophane-wrapped basket sitting on Kelly's locker. It crackled as she hauled it onto her bed, untied the ribbon and spilt chocolate eggs, sweets, biscuits, chickens and bunnies all over the white sheet.

"Wow, look at this, Mouse. Let's eat the biggest first. Mmmm, yummy, have a bite. Good, hey? I'm going to give these two to Daddy to take home to Brian and Toni. He's going tomorrow, don't you wish we were going with him?"

• • •

PAM AND KELLY waved and waved until they couldn't see Alex's taxi anymore. Brushing the tears from hers and Kelly's cheeks, Pam hugged her child close. "Just a few more tests and things to go, Snoogums, then we can go home too. Let's get ice cream, and feed nuts to the squirrels outside the hospital canteen."

"Would you like that, Mouse? Okay. How long will they take, Ma?"

"The tests? You are half-way through; so maybe three weeks and Jane's taking us to her house for the weekend and to supper, at a place called a 4by4."

"What's a 4by4?"

"I'm not sure, but she said it's fun. You'll get a bib, a hammer and a pile of crabs."

"Will they be alive?"

"Of course, not. Hammering them makes a mess and Jane says the meat inside is delicious."

THEY LOVED SMASHING CRAB, but they loved Tubob, Jane's St Bernard, more. The dog sniffed at Mouse, bowled Kelly over by way of a greeting, allowed her to ride on his back and brush his hair, and raced her to the red post-box at the end of the drive. While Kelly rested on a real feather bed that belonged to Jane's great granddad, Pam took Tubob for a long walk through the silent, dogwood forest. She sat with him, on a carpet of crushed leaves, buried her face in his soft coat, and opened her heart.

"I can't watch them prod and poke Kelly anymore, Tubob. I'm a goddamn mess. What am I going to do? Kelly's so brave; she says it's okay, but I know it's not and I want to scream at the doctors, tell them to STOP. I hate not being able to help her. I hate it. I hate it. I hate it. I want a miracle. She deserves a miracle." Tubob's wet nose nudged her. He let her cry for her child, whose pain was her pain, whose bravery shamed her. The leaves grew cold, the forest damp and Tubob's long tongue licked and licked her tears, glued her back together and made her stronger for Kelly.

THE PHOTOGRAPHERS CAME ON MONDAY. They stretched Kelly's mouth, forced a small camera inside, and took pictures of the white thrush.

"You're going to be famous, Kelly," they said. "We're writing about you and putting these pictures in *The Lancet Medical Journal*."

"I can taste blood, Ma."

They've split the corners of her mouth.

Pam spat onto a tissue, dabbed Kelly's lips "There you go, and here's a kiss to make it better. We're done for today."

"Not yet, Mrs Richards, we have just one…"

"No." Pam raised hand and the resolve in her eyes stopped the keen photographers. She pulled Kelly close, wrapped her arms like a shield around her daughter's little body, and kissed the curls on her head. "It's okay, Snoogums, no more tests today, I promise."

"I want to go home now, Ma, so does Mouse, don't you, Mouse?"

PROFESSOR PATRICK WILSON came with the results at suppertime.

"Those burgers look good."

Pam nodded and swallowed. "They're from the canteen and are delicious."

"Great. Okay, Kelly, we're nearly ready to send you home. You've been a very brave girl. We've taken lots of tests and you've answered lots and lots of questions. Now, do you have any questions for me?"

Kelly wiped her mouth and whispered in Pam's ear. "Can I ask him anything at all?"

Pam nodded and the buttons on Kelly's red shoes clicked as she crossed her feet, one over the other, and looked at the Professor. "Can you fix me?"

The question turned them into statues.

Pam's throat tightened. *Please, please, please say yes.*

Patrick straightened his tie and shoved his hands into his pockets. "Doctor Frank is a very good doctor, Kelly, and he's done everything that we would do. You're in excellent hands."

Kelly looked at the floor, her feet still, the buttons on her shoes silent. A tear fell onto her pyjamas; she knew the answer. It was no. Pam scooped up her daughter and rocked her back and forth. "There, there, Snoogums."

Patrick shuffled his feet. "Look, we're investigating horse serum. We've got our first trial underway, but the injections are very sore and you…"

Kelly wiped her cheeks and wriggled on Pam's lap. "How sore?" she asked.

"Extremely."

"Can I meet the other kids?"

"What other kids?"

"The kids having the injections."

"All the trial patients are adults, Kelly. You'd be the first kid."

"Will the horse serum help me?"

The Professor shrugged. "I don't know, but we have nothing else to offer "

Kelly chewed her thumb nail. "What do you think, Ma?"

"I honestly don't know, Snoogums." Pam turned to the Professor. "How often must she have the injections and for how long? Are there any side effects?"

"None that we know of, but it is experimental, so we can't say. You'd have to give permission and sign a contract. The injections are given once a month, for three months."

"Must I stay here for another three months?" asked Kelly.

"No, we'll give you the first shot, then you can go home, and Doctor Frank will manage the rest."

Kelly offered her arm. "Okay then."

"We have to do it in your bottom, Kelly. I'll see you in the lab and we'll start tomorrow."

KELLY CLIMBED onto the narrow bed and pulled down her cotton panties.

"Okay, Kelly?" asked Patrick.

"Okay."

Pam patted one of Kelly's exposed bum cheeks. "Ready, Snoogums?"

"Yes." said Kelly, holding Mouse with both hands. Aimed like a dart, the needle plunged into her skin. The horse serum hit its mark and her little body arched backwards. She screamed, sank her teeth into Mouse's ear, and bit it off.

THREE MONTHS later Doctor Frank spoke to Professor Wilson. Kelly's condition remained the same and the treatment was stopped, but they stayed in touch, and when immunogobulin became available to boost the immune systems of AIDS patients, they'd organised for Kelly to have shots in Ward 309.

SHE WAS Ward 309's darling. They'd zipped her into many oxygen tents, tucked Mouse next to her pillow and watched her grow into the sixteen-year old who stood at the window, ready to go home.

"Where's Ma?" she asked, touching her nose to the mouse's bald one.

"Right here." Pam stepped into the ward, her bright smile forced and firmly in place.

"Hi, Ma, where've you been? I've been waiting for ages; long enough to get my discharge medicine."

"Sorry, Snoogums, I know I'm late," Pam kissed Kelly's hollow cheek, "glad you're ready, let's go home."

Kelly wedged Mouse into the pink bag between school textbooks, and puzzles. "Your eyes are red, Ma. Have you been crying?"

"Is that everything?" asked Pam, avoiding Kelly's question. She scanned the stainless-steel locker, checked under the bed, shouldered the pink bag and picked up the portable TV.

"Yes," Kelly hooked two plastic bags of pills and ointments over her arm. "But what's wrong?"

"Nothing. Let's get you out of here."

"Ma." Kelly rolled her eyes as if to say any an idiot could see there was something wrong.

Pam sighed. She didn't think it was the right time or place, but Kelly wasn't going to stop asking.

"Toni's missing. She's run away with Stelios. The police are looking for her and there's a warrant out for his arrest."

"*Jeez*, Ma." Kelly's blue eyes opened wide. "Where's Dad? Is he looking for her? Is he at the police station?"

"Nope, he's in hospital."

"In hospital? Why? What's wrong? Is he okay?"

"He's fine, just a bit stressed." Pam sugar-coated the truth.

"How long's he going to be there?" Kelly was concerned and Pam wished she could give her a reassuring answer, but she couldn't.

"I'm not sure. I'm going to see him later."

"Can I come with you?"

"No, I think you've had enough of hospitals." Pam touched her hand and gave her a smile. "Dad's going to be okay. He might even come home tonight."

"And what do the police say about Toni?"

"The Inspector promised to phone as soon as he has some news."

"Gee, I hope they find her soon."

"Me too." Pam turned away so that Kelly couldn't see how terrified she was. "Now let's say goodbye to Sister Armstrong."

ON THE WAY HOME, they stopped in at the supermarket. "After three weeks in hospital, pushing the trolley is exciting."

"Good, you can do a big shop tomorrow while I take Brian to his tennis lesson," teased Pam. She dropped potatoes into the cart and juggled chores in her head, but thoughts of Toni wriggled into all of them. *Where was she?* There was no way to know; no way to think straight. It was too soon to phone the police, but she had to. She'd do it as soon as she got home. *No, go to Alex first and then phone. No, wait for Bezuidenhout to call. Stay calm, don't be neurotic. If I saw Toni now I'd wring her bloody neck.*

"Ma, the cashier's waiting."

"Oh, sorry, I'm lost in thought." Pam parked the trolley and piled her purchases next to the till. She paid and pushed the shopping to the car.

I'm going to phone. I am neurotic; my child's missing.

MICKEY PICKED UP HIS EARS. Kelly was home. The black and white dog sprang off Brian's bed and ran as fast as his short legs could carry him, hurrying to his mistress, running circles around her feet, dancing on his back legs, jumping into her arms, covering her face with fast, wet licks. Brian ran behind him.

"Back again?" he said, squashing them both into a bear hug. Kelly laughed and Mickey licked his way to freedom. Pam caught her son's eye; he read her question and shook his head.

"No one's phoned, Ma," he said.

Torrents of conflicting emotions tied Pam's stomach into knots. Relief. Kelly had beaten another bout of pneumonia and was home. Fear. *Where was Toni?* Guilt and confusion. *What was wrong with Alex? He was obviously sick, but she couldn't stop being angry with him. Stop. Keep busy. Unpack the groceries.*

SHE GRABBED packets and hurried past the children into the

kitchen. Brian pulled Kelly's stuff from the car. "Do you know about Toni?"

"Ma said she's run away with Stelios."

"We went to Hillbrow to look for her. Man, Kelly, I was *poep*-scared." Brian dumped the bags in Kelly's bedroom.

"Why Hillbrow? Doesn't Stelios live in Lanseria?"

"Some old girlfriend of his phoned Ma and told her where Toni was, except she wasn't there, and you should have seen Ma's red face. They're in big trouble."

Kelly unpacked and sat Mouse on her desk. Mickey bounced across the pillows, rolled on his back for a tummy tickle. Brian tuned the TV, adjusting the position to give Kelly a clear view from her bed. She looked tired. She'd be in bed early and he'd come and watch the movie of the week with her.

"Ma's really upset. And what's wrong with Dad?"

"I don't know," Brian shrugged. "Ma took him to hospital last night. She said he thought he was having a heart attack."

"Do you think he's okay?"

"He must be. Ma wouldn't have left him otherwise."

"She's been crying."

"I know. I hate that, don't you?"

"Yes. What can we do?"

"Nothing."

. . .

IN THE KITCHEN, Pam cut a few potatoes into chips. *Busy, keep busy. Stop thinking.*

She rinsed the chips and shivered as she remembered the butterfly boarder of Toni's note paper stuck to a dirty splashback. She cut lemon wedges and trimmed the lamb chops, allowing two for Alex. Would he be home to eat them? Without his strength, she was floundering. She'd never complain about her A-Type personality husband again. She wanted him back, but not the way he was lately. *What am I to do with him if he hasn't taken the doctor's advice? Bring him home?* No, she couldn't cope with a repeat of last night.

"WE'LL SEE TO SUPPER," Kelly's voice made her jump. "You go and see Dad."

"You sure?"

"Brian can fry the chips and I'll do the chops; slosh them with lemon juice and smother them in celery salt, just like you do."

"I do not smother them," said Pam, handing over the sharp knife and wiping her hands with a paper towel.

"You do, ask Brian."

"No question," he said. "You smother them."

"Cheeky bugger." Pam balled the towel and threw it at him. He caught it in mid-air and laughed.

She picked up her bag and car keys. "Thanks, you two. If the police phone..."

"Don't worry, Ma," said Brian, "we can take a message."

"Right." She paused, unwilling to go and miss the possible call. "Should be back by seven-thirty."

"You and Dad?" asked Kelly.

"Maybe."

ALEX SPOTTED the little red Alfa turning into the private hospital grounds and hurried to meet it. Pam parked, stepped out of the car, adjusted the strap of her shoulder-bag, turned and looked straight into his eyes.

"Didn't mean to make you jump," he said.

"What're you doing in the parking-lot?"

"Waiting for you of course. You didn't give me a kiss this morning, am I going to get one now?"

Her lips barely touched his cheek. "Did you discharge yourself?"

He frowned. "Did you go to the police?"

She nodded and steadied her breathing.

"And?"

"They know Stelios."

"What do you mean, they 'know' Stelios?"

"He's supposed to report there every week. He's out on bail."

"What the hell for?"

"He's a convicted drug-dealer."

"Jesus Christ."

"They found a forged passport for Toni in his house in Lanseria."

"I'll kill that fucking bastard."

"The police have opened a warrant for abduction." Pam's lip trembled. "Oh, Alex, Toni's in real trouble. Stelios is a very dangerous person."

In the lengthening shadows of the public parking-lot, Alex pulled her into his arms and held her close. His touch turned her fear for Toni down a notch and she hated drawing away from him, but he'd ignored her question. He'd made no mention of any further medical appointments and dammit, she wasn't kidding when she'd told him to get help.

"Do I need to go to the police station to sign anything?" asked Alex.

"No, everything's done. The Inspector promised to call as soon as he has some news."

"Kelly?"

"Home with Brian."

"Let's go then."

Pam swallowed. "Well, did you discharge yourself?"

"Yes, I did."

"Didn't you hear what I said earlier? I mean it, Alex. I... you... we can't go on like this, you have to …"

"I heard you." Alex's tight voice clipped every word, he

waved an appointment card under her nose. "See this? It's my ticket home. I'm going to see a shrink tomorrow."

A sledgehammer of mixed emotions hit Pam. She felt a right shit, an elated right shit.

"Thank you," she whispered.

"Can we go now?"

6

Her pen poised and forgotten, Pam stared at the office phone sitting at Maggie Williams' end of their shared desk. Each time it rang she panicked. Was it Inspector Bezuidenhout? Had they found Toni? Was she safe? Everyone had phoned in the last few days, the family all over South Africa, her gran in the UK, their friends; but not him. The support kept her sane, the anxiety drove her mad, she lived in turmoil and exhaustion. Every cell in her body willed him to call, but the beige phone remained stubbornly silent. She tore her eyes away from the phone, walked over to the window and gazed outside. She listened for the sharp ring, but it stayed silent. Summer blazed in the garden. Purple bougainvillea, yellow hibiscus and red cannas, framed the Williams' swimming pool. The mid-morning sun shone on the chlorinated water, reflecting and sashaying it on the ceiling of the Williams' converted family room. It was now an office for Direct Technologies, importers of electronic components, and a testament to recycling and Eric Williams' DIY skills.

. . .

HE HAD BRACKETED two rejected doors to the wall and screwed planks above them, creating a work space for Pam and Maggie. Direct Technologies' stock was stored on the opposite wall in three rescued and resprayed metal cupboards, and an L-shaped counter next to them served as the receiving and despatch department. Lastly, Eric had hauled in a second-hand wooden desk and executive chair for himself, placed with its back to the window where he could survey the success of his handiwork.

THE PHONE RANG and Pam's heart raced. She hoped against hope that it was Inspector Bezuidenhout or one of Toni's friends, or anyone who knew where she was.

Maggie gave her a look and snatched up the receiver, setting her silver charm bracelet jingling. "Direct Technologies. Good morning," she said, her Welsh accent a little rushed, as she tucked dark-brown, almost-black curls behind her ears. "Ah, Mr. Abbott, how can we help you?" Maggie shook her head and Pam's hope collapsed. She went back to waiting for the policeman's call and decided that, back home later, she would thumb through the telephone index, and phone all of Toni's contacts again. She wasn't sure if she should believe those who said they didn't know where she was, but she'd checked out every lead that had come her way and found nothing so far. She was exhausted; her despair so deep that she wanted to run away too.

SHE TURNED BACK to writing up figures in the 14-column analysis book, but her thoughts refused to focus. They jumped from Alex to Toni and back to Alex. He wasn't happy about going to the psychiatrist. Would he chicken out? What was the time? Could she phone Inspector Bezuidenhout?

It was ten-thirty. No; he'd promised to contact her. Give him a chance.

THE SMELL of fresh lawn clippings and dug-in compost floated in through the window and mingled with Eric's aftershave. He tapped her shoulder. "Go home, Pam," he said.

She shook her head; she did not dare turn to look at him. "I'll go mad if I don't keep busy, Eric. Besides, we need this information. I'll have it ready by lunchtime."

"Okay, but look, if we can help in any way, with Toni or Alex, – what I'm trying to say is, I'm sure the police will find her soon and, look, we're here, and... well... you know…" Eric's compassion chipped at Pam's brittle composure.

"Thanks, Eric." Her grip tightened on the clutch pencil, she took a deep breath and pressed her lips together. She was not going to cry.

"What time is Alex's appointment?" Eric spoke to Pam's stiff back.

"One o'clock." She tapped the calculator keys.

"Do you know anything about this shrink he's going to?"

"Only that Doctor Gordon says he's the best. He's specialised in post-traumatic stress with the army and is now in private practice. I'm counting on him." Pam's voice cracked. "If he can't help Alex, I think we're sunk," she said.

"Ah, come on, Pam. You and Alex are forever, man," said Eric.

"Look, I know he's not himself. He hasn't flown with me for ages, but he'll come right and Toni... she'll be home soon, you'll see."

Pam doodled on her message pad. She wanted to believe Eric, but Toni hadn't run off with a regular guy, she'd run off with a bloody drug-dealer who could outwit the police and Alex hadn't picked up a model aeroplane in ages. He'd lost all interest in life, including his passion for flying that brought him and Eric together.

THEY'D MET IN A NEWS-AGENCY. Alex had been picking up his monthly subscription of *RC Modeller*, when he had overheard a man placing a back order for the July issue.

"It'll take three months," the clerk had said.

"Why so long?" the tall bearded man had asked.

The assistant had shrugged. "Don't know."

"Can't you get it sooner? There's a slope soaring article in it and I need it like yesterday."

The assistant had consulted his magazine list. "No. It says three months, sorry."

The bearded man had sighed, turning to go.

"I couldn't help overhearing you," Alex had said." I've got the July issue at home and could lend it to you."

"Thanks, man. You sure?"

"Sure. What do you fly?"

"An Ugly Stik, but it's broken. And you?"

"I've got a Graupner K10. My wife gave it to me when we first got married."

"A glider. Gee, I love gliders. How does it fly?"

"I don't know. We had three kids and I've never been able to afford a radio. I'm Alex Richards by the way." Alex had extended his hand.

"Eric Williams. Nice to meet you, and hey, I've got a radio."

THEY HAD POOLED their equipment and driven to Harrismith with Pam and her divorced friend, Maggie, to slope soar. Their enthusiasm had outstripped their experience and they had launched the K10 from the mountain slopes in all conditions. Taking turns to fly, they had crashed, fixed and flown the glider and, by the end of the weekend, yards of duct tape had held the plane together, Pratley's Five Minute Epoxy had sealed their friendship and Eric was in love with Maggie.

PAM'S MESSAGE pad was full of scribbles. Slope soaring and Saturday afternoons at the local flying field were no longer part of Alex's life. She shuddered and stared at the pad, the drawings of her troubled mind and sleep-deprived body had no meaning. Maggie placed a mug of coffee and a buttermilk rusk next to her elbow and covered her hand with her own. "We've been friends since Toni was born, Pam. Too long for you to act like superwoman here," she said. Her touch was gentle, her blue-grey eyes soft. "Go ahead and have a good cry."

Maggie's empathy smashed Pam's flimsy self-control to smithereens. Her tears blurred and fuzzed the columns, the figures swam. She pushed back her chair and dashed across the passage to the second bathroom.

Good God, you look awful, she told her reflection in the mirror. *Stop this stupid crying, it's not going to help any.* Cupping cool water in her hands, she splashed her face, pulled down the toilet seat and sat on it. She blew her nose on blue double-ply paper. *Now, pull yourself together.* She took a deep breath. Pine air-freshener and Harpic filled her lungs. Her chest ached and burned. She'd read somewhere that eye exercises could help to reduce the effects of stress. She exhaled and gazed at the patterned wall tiles, making herself cross-eyed. Grooved into the white tiles, navy diamonds shifted, touched, drifted apart. Five minutes of crossing and uncrossing her eyes made her giddy, but it slowed her heartbeat. When it was slow enough to count, she walked across the carpeted passage and back to the polished slasto floor of Direct Technologies.

Maggie and Eric stopped talking in midsentence. "You okay?" asked Maggie. Pam nodded, pulling the analysis book closer and raking her fingers through her hair.

"You look a mess, you need your hair done," said Maggie. "Take yourself off to Raymond."

"Do you remember saying that seventeen years ago, when Antoinette was born and deposits from empty Coke bottles put bread on the table at the end of the month?"

Back then, the Richard's medical aid had barely covered Pam's spot in the eight-bed maternity ward and Margaret

Jones, whose face had recently adorned the latest cover of Ms Magazine, had occupied the bed next to hers. Maggie, as she had introduced herself, was a knock-out, but the birthing process bestows milk-swollen breasts and sagging, spongy stomachs on all mothers - photographic models included - and Maggie's good-looking husband hadn't fancied nature's transformation. He had avoided visiting hours and had set their marriage on the course of divorce. The rest of the women in the ward already had other children at home and, from their beds and experienced positions, they had guided Maggie and Pam through the first feed, first bath and first crying jag of unnerving motherhood.

EVERY FOUR HOURS, pink and blue papoose-parcels of hungry babies had arrived. The mothers had fed, changed, burped, counted fingers and toes, cuddled and cooed at their offspring, until efficient nurses bustled in and took them away, leaving the women to swab Savlon onto their fannies and rub antiseptic cream into cracked nipples. Their sharp intakes of pain had become long ooohs and aaahs when Maggie had emptied the contents of her make-up bag onto her bed. Giggling like school girls, they had blushed on high cheekbones, painted pouting lips, shadowed and pencilled eyes. Pam had played with the powder and paints but had really wanted to change her hair from mouse to sun-kissed, honey blonde, just like Maggie's.

"There's easy," Maggie had said. "We'll have it sorted by visiting hours at seven. I've got a tube of magic stuff. You'd never know my hair was dark brown, nearly black, now would you? Had to go blonde for my last shoot but I'm not going to keep it up, I'm not a blonde at heart."

. . .

THE WARD HAD WATCHED as she had set to work, mixing
packets of ReadiBlonde Extra Strong for Dark Hair in a
kidney dish and brushing it onto Pam's head. She had
combed it through and covered it with an empty plastic
packet from maternity-size sanitary towels.

PAM'S BREASTS HAD TINGLED, and the milk had rushed in for
Antoinette's six o'clock feed.

"Ten minutes each side," the nurse had instructed.

Pam had popped a left breast out of her new feeding bra and
guided Toni's seeking mouth to a milk-spraying nipple. Her
daughter had sucked it for five minutes before spitting it out
and no amount of kissing, tickling and undressing had woken
Toni's rag-doll-relaxed body and she had returned to the
nursery, leaving Pam with fifteen minutes of untouched milk
and lopsided breasts.

MAGGIE HAD GLANCED at her watch. "Time to wash that off
and get your hair set and dried before visitors come."

At five-to-seven Maggie had given Pam's hair a last blast
from the hairdryer and taken out the curlers. The ward had
gasped, and Maggie had groaned and clapped a hand over
her mouth.

"Dear Lord."

Pam had grabbed a mirror. She had looked like her father-in-
law's prize canary. Every hair on her head had turned bright

yellow. Shampoo in hand she had run to the bathroom. She had wanted her nondescript mousy hair back. Right now.

Maggie had grimaced. "It won't come out. It's permanent."

Pam's slippers had skidded to a halt. "What do you mean permanent?"

"It won't wash out." Maggie's eyes had remained glued to Pam's head.

"Oh God I can't go around with hair like this."

"I'll cover it up. Put it in a turban. They're very fashionable right now and you'll look glam in two ticks. Don't panic. We're going home tomorrow, and I'll take you to Raymond. He's the model agency's hairdresser. He can fix anything."

"Promise?"

"Yes, and you'll just love him. He'll keep you beautifully blonde for as long as you want."

MAGGIE NODDED. "Yes, I remember it like yesterday. Just a mo, Raymond's checking his diary." She nodded and covered the mouthpiece with her hand. "He can do the whole works next Saturday, or a quick cut today?" Her arched brow asked the question.

"I'll wait," said Pam. A quick cut wasn't the heavy-duty pick-me-up that a woman needed when her daughter was missing and her husband was depressed.

"Next Saturday," Maggie relayed the answer and laughed as she put down the phone. "He told me, as always, to keep my hands away from your head."

Pam smiled, but her eyes strayed to the digital display on Eric's radio clock. It flashed two minutes past eleven. Two hours to go before Alex's first appointment with the psychiatrist and over a day since she'd reported Toni missing. Not a word from the police. Images of her runaway daughter and mentally unstable husband filtered the news bulletin.

Stop this. Concentrate. Finish the damn cash flow.

SHE SCOWLED when it was finished. It painted a bleak picture. She handed the page to Eric.

"I warn you, we look sick," she said. "We break even for the next three months and then we dive into overdraft and we're dead in six months."

Eric studied the bottom line and tugged at his beard. "Have you included the connector sales?" he asked.

"Yep." She pointed to the figures under the second month. "Booked out and collected."

"You sure this is correct?" asked Eric.

"Unfortunately, yes, I've double-checked," said Pam.

"Shit."

Maggie leaned across Eric, her ample boobs straining against her top and catching his eye.

"None of that," she said smiling at him and tucking dark curls behind her ear. Her long, red nail tapped the "Assembly Costs" column. "We could save this if we made the connectors ourselves," she said.

"What, make them here? At the office?" Eric chewed the arm of his glasses.

"Why not? And if you teach us girls how to solder, we can save labour costs on these printed circuit boards too." She tapped the page again. "What do you think?" she asked them.

"Sounds feasible," nodded Pam. "Let me take them out and rework this." She moved back to her space at the long desk and adjusted the figures while Maggie and Eric sketched floor-plans on recycled paper, making space at the receiving and despatch counter for the proposed assembly line. They'd be a bit squashed, but they could manage. Pam gave a thumbs-up. "You've just bought us another six months, Maggie," she said.

"Fantastic." Eric clapped. "Okay then, I'll get a 3M Punch, a solder pot and a couple of soldering irons," he said. "But you two are going to be really busy."

Maggie tweaked his beard. "You can't count, can you, my love? There are three of us here, all equal partners. You'll be soldering too."

"Okay, okay." Eric rescued his whiskers. "You've made your point."

Maggie planted a kiss on her slender fingertips and transferred it to his forehead.

"We'll still need to increase the turnover," said Pam.

"I'll get that gas arrestor order," said Eric.

"You sure?"

"Ninety-nine percent. It's a big deal and the profit's excellent. The capacitor order is almost in the bag too."

"When will we know for sure?" asked Pam.

Maggie consulted her A4 diary. "Our samples are in for approval at the client and their board meets at the end of this month," she said.

"Let me worry about the turnover, Pam," said Eric. "Cash-flows aren't real. Next month you can do another one. Then it'll look great and it'll make you feel better."

"What if our samples aren't approved?"

Eric grinned. "Stop fretting. I'm the best electronics salesman in the country. That's why you're in business with me. Remember?"

His boasting was rewarded with a wry smile.

Direct Technologies could cut costs. Eric would nail the new orders and their little company would survive. She looked at the radio clock. Twelve fifteen; forty-five minutes to Alex's appointment with Doctor Pieter De Bruin; zero minutes before her phone call to Ignatius Bezuidenhout.

THE INSPECTOR WAS VERY SORRY; he had no news, but they were working on a lead. Stelios and Toni might be in the Transkei. Unfortunately, it was difficult to communicate with the Independent Homeland, but, as soon as he had something concrete he'd get back to her. He promised.

"Thanks. Thanks very much." Pam was shaking as she replaced the receiver. She buried her head in her hands. Eric's broad hand warmed her shoulder.

"Give them time, Pam."

"Nag them," said Maggie. "They expect you to be neurotic. Hell, I'm just 'Aunty Maggie' and I'm a basket-case. I'd be phoning every five minutes."

"Maggie." Eric gave her a sharp look.

"Well, I would be. Let's be honest here, I can't bear not knowing where Toni is." Maggie's hooped ear-rings swung as she shook her head. "And she's run off with a drug-dealer."

"Okay, Maggs, that's enough," said Eric. "Pam's worried enough and Toni's a good kid."

"Exactly, she is a good kid, but she's missing." The steel in her grey eyes silenced Eric. "And she's no match for that rotten bastard Stelios"

Pam lifted her head to look at her friends. "They think she might be in the Transkei," she whispered.

"What? The Native Homeland?" Maggie's eyes were wide and Eric wiped his hand across his beard. His friends didn't deserve this shit. He had no children and he thanked God that Maggie's sports-mad son was safe in boarding-school in Natal. Toni was in real trouble. The Transkei people, mostly black, weren't happy with their so-called independent state and their relationship with the South African Government was not good. Getting her back into the country would be difficult and being on the run with a drug-dealer did not increase her chances.

Alex scanned the tender for the third time, but the words did not sink in and his body was a dead weight. He was jeopardising Powertronics' chance of landing the lucrative contract. Unlike Pam's, his company was not new, but was experiencing adolescent growth, outstripping available cash reserves, demanding long hours and one hundred per cent commitment from its young, professional staff and two directors. It couldn't afford the luxury of his exhaustion.

ELEVEN YEARS AGO, Alex and his friend, Steve Dixon, had taken on the business; worked like hell to pay off its debt and were rightly proud of their vibrant company. They were a winning pair. Steve, a brilliant design engineer, excelled at problem-solving and inventing new electronic products and Alex, an entrepreneurial catalyst, saw opportunities in the marketplace and married them to Steve's expertise. Although they no longer had to share a car and plan family outings on alternate weekends, they continued to share an office. It facilitated an easy flow of information, kept them abreast of each other and did away with memos or time spent in meetings, but it afforded no privacy in terms of their personal lives. Steve worked and played hard, often crawling home in the early hours of the morning, somewhat pickled. His frequent spells in the dog-box had failed to turn him into a devoted husband and hands-on dad, and Jean, his wife of ten years, had consulted their lawyer and friend, James Griffiths, and was filing for a divorce. Steve moved out, upped his smoking, drank more beers, stayed out later and said he was cool with his new life, but Alex saw his loneliness and Steve wasn't blind to Alex's emergency trips to the hospital and the tests that proved nothing was wrong. Alex's shit worried Steve. The more Alex retreated into himself, the more Steve puffed up a smokescreen, but it didn't hide his friend's pinched face and forced, mechanical movements.

ALEX STIFLED A YAWN. "I have to leave at lunchtime." He felt like a real bastard. He'd given zero per cent to the company today and Steve must be getting pissed off. "But I'll be in early tomorrow."

"No sweat," said Steve, lighting up a new cigarette with the glowing tip of another. "Going anywhere special?"

"I'm... er... I'm well... I'm going to see a shrink."

Steve gagged. "You're what?"

"Pam so decreed."

"And what? You said fine?"

"Let's just say that it wasn't up for debate. Doctor Gordon

convinced her that it's my head not my heart that needs fixing."

"No shit? I always said you were crazy."

Steve's smile didn't quite reach his eyes, but his weak joke helped Alex lift his guilty butt off the chair, get it into the car and drive to the appointment with the psychiatrist.

HE ARRIVED EARLY, at ten to one, to find an empty reception area. No one, sane or insane, occupied a single burgundy seat or the chair at the reception desk. Side tables held stacks of well-thumbed magazines, mandatory potted plants filled the corners and piped classical music grated on his nerves. He walked across the room and checked the name on the closed door. Doctor Pieter De Bruin, Suite 114. He was on the right floor and in the place where Pam wanted him to be.

"DE BRUIN'S waiting list is three weeks long," Doctor Gordon had said when he'd handed him his discharge form and the appointment card. "But I gave him a brief history and he's agreed to see you in his lunch hour tomorrow."

WHAT HAD Gordon told the shrink? How mad did he think he was? Why was he getting such urgent attention? Alex swallowed and took a seat across from the door. He stood up. He paced. He returned to his chair, drummed his fingers on the chrome arm, crossed and uncrossed his legs. The hum of the air-conditioner hauled him to his feet and he walked to the window. It overlooked the shaded car-park. A breeze was nipping flowers from the branches of old Tipuana trees and dropping their yellow blossoms on the car roofs and tarmac. Clouds were building up, billowing, promising rain later. Alex returned to his seat and looked at his watch. Eight minutes past one. His appointment was for one o'clock; the shrink was running late. Shit, what was he doing here flipping through the pages of last month's *Reader's Digest*? He dumped the book, rummaged through the pile on the table next to him and pulled out a copy of *Engineering News*. He opened it, then slapped it closed. His hands were sweating. To hell with what Doctor Gordon and Pam wanted him to do, he was leaving; he had better things to do, like swinging by the police station and checking in with Bezuidenhout. Pam had asked him not to do that; saying that the Inspector had promised that he would phone as soon as he had any news of Toni; well, stuff that. This morning he'd resisted the urge to go there but surely, they would have something by now.

TEN MINUTES PAST ONE. He stood up. That's it; he wasn't waiting any longer.

The door to suite 114 opened.

Damn.

A YOUNG MAN WALKED OUT. He was tall, Alex's height, but he had to look up to the man behind him.

"*Dankie Doktor*," he said, offering an outstretched hand. His jeans were faded and tight-fitting, his belt fastened at the waist by a silver skull buckle, a white T-shirt clung to his chest and shoulder muscles. His pink scalp showed through his short haircut. Alex guessed that the patient was an army guy, one of thousands of young men conscripted to the South African Defence Force who lived for their weekend passes, thumbed lifts home from camps scattered throughout the country and returned to anxious waiting mothers, girlfriends and wives.

"Goodbye, Dawid." De Bruin's wide grin and vigorous hand-shake wrung a wry smile from the closed face that caught Alex's eye and looked away, before heading for the stairs. His takkies squeaked as he ran down.

The psychiatrist offered his hand. "Welcome. You must be Alex Richards. I am Pieter De Bruin." His Afrikaans accent was thick, his English precise. "I am delighted to meet you. Please do come in." A grin, a bow, a theatrical sweep of an arm; more an elaborate invitation to join a dinner party than to enter his consulting room. Alex hesitated.

Another flourish. "Come."

THE ROOM WAS COMFORTING. Alex guessed that the furniture had either been inherited or collected and purchased at select auctions, where lesser bidders might have run covetous fingers over the well-placed, timeless pieces. Plump cushions invited a lowering of the guard, a chance to talk, while daring salmon-pink walls hinted at the hand of an interior decorator and provided a warm backdrop. Framed University certifi-cates and a tastefully-framed, large, oil painting of purple swirling clouds, Karoo-cracked fields and a whitewashed farmhouse hung on the walls. Above the desk, the loud tick of a railway clock kept track of time.

·   ·   ·

"PLEASE, SIT," De Bruin gestured to the brown couch at the window and settled himself into the overstuffed armchair that faced it. Alex obeyed, sitting ramrod-straight on the piped edge of the soft leather. Pulling a fountain pen from his shirt pocket, the psychiatrist picked up a small clip-board from the coffee table and straightened the form attached to it.

"Please bear with me," he said. "Lyzette, my assistant, normally takes care of these details, but she has gone for lunch."

"I can come back another time."

"No need." A hint of mischief flickered in the eyes behind John Lennon glasses. "I am

confident that I will manage. Now, may I have your full name?"

"Alex Paul Richards."

De Bruin wrote fast and Alex's name vanished in scrawl.

"Age?"

"42."

"Married?"

"Yes."

"Children?"

Alex stiffened.

Yes. One's a runaway and I'm sitting here doing sweet stuff-all to find her.

He forced his voice to stay calm. "Three teenagers. Two girls and a boy," he said.

"Ever divorced? Widowed?"

"No, never."

"Medical Aid?"

"Yes, here's the card." Alex dug it out of his pants pocket. De Bruin recorded the number and handed it back.

"Thank you," he said. "Lyzette will contact you if she has any queries."

Unable to read the tightly-packed squiggles, Alex expected her call.

The shrink stretched his legs out straight, crossed them at the ankles, letting the heels of his shoes rest on a faded Persian carpet.

"May I call you Alex?"

"Yes."

Kind brown eyes examined Alex's strained face and straight back. "You are not happy to be here?"

Alex shrugged.

"So why did you come?" De Bruin stoked his trimmed moustache.

"My wife insisted."

"Ahh. Did she say why?"

"She said I need help."

"Do you agree?"

"No."

"I see." De Bruin leaned back into his chair.

Tick, tick, tick, tick, tick. The railway clock struck each second. Alex glanced from it to De Bruin. *Jesus, he should have left before that guy Dawid opened the door.*

The shrink's hands were still and his face expressionless.

Tick, tick, tick, tick, tick. The second hand hammered in the silent room.

Alex's back ached. The edge of the seat dug into the top of his legs. He licked his dry lips and longed to pour a glass of water from the full jug on the coffee table.

The minute hand clunked. De Bruin didn't move.

"This is a mistake," blurted Alex.

"How so?"

"It just is."

"Doctor Gordon sent me your file. I have studied it and his extensive tests found no physical cause for your chest pains."

"And he thinks that I imagined them? Well I didn't. You can ask my wife. They woke me up in the middle of the night and then my arm went lame. I don't care what he says I'm sure it's my heart."

De Bruin shook his head. "It is panic; one of the many gifts of depression."

"Depression? But I'm not depressed. He said I was stressed, and maybe I am. I run my own business and times are tough, but... "

"When last did you laugh or sleep well?"

Alex shrugged. "I don't know."

"Would you describe yourself as happy? Sad?"

Another shrug.

"Flat?"

"Maybe."

"As though life has lost its sparkle?"

The shrink's accurate description belly-punched him.

"Do you have thoughts of dying or suicide?"

Dear God, these were his secret thoughts. Vomit rose in his throat and his nails dug into the leather couch. De Bruin's stark question hung between them.

"Often?"

Alex looked away from the compassion in De Bruin's eyes. His jaw ached. These thoughts woke him up at three every morning, crept into his soul; took him to an abyss of nothingness; whispered death and suicide.

"Am I mad?" he asked, his voice strained.

"No, Alex, you are not mad; not crazy, but you are suffering from depression, a treatable illness. It is not your heart; you are having panic attacks. Today, I will teach you a breathing technique that will help you to control them."

Alex was terrified, he closed his eyes. He was ill. Mentally. *Was that different from being mad?*

"Please slip off your shoes and make yourself comfortable."

"You mean lie down? On the couch?"

"Yes," said De Bruin, humour creeping into his voice. "I am sure you have seen it done in the movies."

Alex took off his shoes, laid back, arms folded tightly across his chest, legs stiff and straight, eyes fixed on the ceiling. It was his best shot at being comfortable, and, behind his John Lennon glasses, Pieter's eyes looked amused.

"Try putting your arms at your sides and relaxing your hands," he suggested. "That's better. Close your eyes. Now, breathe in and out, slowly."

Alex obeyed. It was simple. The same as Doctor Gordon had told him to do.

"Slower, Alex. To the count of six. In… two, three, four, five, six… hold… three, four, five six, and out… good, four, five, six. Again. And again."

Following De Bruin's rhythmic instructions, Alex breathed. The lulling Afrikaans accent calmed him and took him to a place free of thudding fear. Far from suicidal thoughts, his mind floated free and he basked in peace.

THE VOICE FADED INTO SILENCE. Awareness crept back; his toes wriggled in his socks, his shirt stuck to the leather couch and he opened his eyes. The railway clock struck the hour. His appointment time was up, and his mentally imbalanced world returned, but the shrink had taught him to breathe and had given him a smidgen of hope, enough to hold the abyss at bay, but it was as fragile as hollow Easter eggs and his next appointment was a long week away. Could he make it until then? As sure as hell, he would try.

8

Brian paused at the school gates and rolled up his white sleeves. He shoved them above his elbows, opened his collar and dragged his tie knot down to the third button on his shirt. He hooked his blue blazar, edged with the school's academic ribbon, onto his index finger and slung it over his shoulder. Today's tennis match was important for the school team, they wanted revenge on Maxwell High for the beating received last round, and he hoped his mom was waiting. She was always on time, but if the police had found Toni, she could be anywhere, and he wanted them to find Toni more than anything. He was worried about her, it made him feel wired up. It was not the same type of worry that he felt when Kelly got sick and he chewed his fingernails; it was a sharper fear and it frightened him.

THE WHOLE FAMILY WAS STRESSED, he couldn't sleep, and his great-grandmother, Big Gran, had even phoned from the UK, using precious pounds from her government pension.

"I know just how you feel, my luv," she'd said to his mother. "Your father up and ran away, joined the Royal Navy, he did, when he was thirteen. Landed up after the war in South Africa, and just look at him now; a successful business man. Your Toni's a good kid too. She'll be okay, you'll see."

Brian had not understood how that information helped, but his mother had dried her eyes, thanked Big Gran for understanding, promised to keep in touch, and even managed a smile when she put down the receiver.

HE SPOTTED PAM'S CAR, parked in the shade across the road from the school, she waved, and he sauntered over.

"Here comes Mr Cool himself," said Kelly. She'd come out of school a few minutes earlier, climbed in and claimed the front seat on the basis of first-come, first-take. Her sassy humour and Brian's swagger wriggled into Pam's never-ending worry of Toni and Alex. His heart attacks. Toni trapped in the Transkei. Alex needing a psychiatrist. Toni sleeping who knows where. Alex grey-faced. Toni sleeping with Stelios. Alex, Toni. Toni, Alex. God, her brain was fried.

FLASHING PAM A SMILE, Brian swung his blazer off his shoulder and stashed it with his heavy, canvas school case in the boot of the car and took out his tennis tog-bag.

"He thinks he's God's gift to mankind," said Kelly. The comical face she pulled and the roll of her eyes stemmed the flow of dark thoughts that raged around Pam's mind.

"I'd say he's working on it," she smiled.

Brian eased his gangly body into the backseat. "What's so funny?" he asked. Kelly and Pam exchanged glances. "Nothing," they said.

"Women," said Brian with a shake of his head.

"That's us; the superior sex," said Kelly.

Brian groaned. "Give me strength; the women's libber is home."

Their banter washed over Pam as she pulled away from the curb and into traffic.

Brian pulled the lid off a Tupperware lunch-box and bit into a bacon sandwich. "Any news of Toni, Ma?" he asked.

She tried to keep the fear from her voice. "The police think she could be in the Transkei."

"*Jeez*, that's even more dangerous than Hillbrow," said Brian.

Pam's hand gripped the gear lever and Kelly glared at her brother.

"Shut up, Brian. Just shut up," she said. "Can't you see how worried Ma is? Sometimes you say the most stupid things."

"Okay, okay." Brian yanked off his tie and shirt, pulled on his tennis top and unlaced his shoes.

"Argh, Brian's taking off his socks," said Kelly, holding her nose closed.

"Ah come on; my feet don't smell. At least not half as bad as Toni's."

"You just can't help yourself, can you?" snapped Kelly.

"Sorry," mumbled Brian and an awkwardness silence filled the car. Pam caught his eye and sheepish expression in the rear-view mirror. She was the mother here, not Kelly, and protection was her job, not her daughter's.

"Listen," she said. "I'm not going to pretend that I am not worried about Toni. I am, and so is Dad."

"Me too," said Brian. "I had no problem with Stelios, he was just a boyfriend of Toni's that you guys didn't like, but now that I know what he is, I'm really scared for Toni and didn't sleep last night."

Kelly's funky glasses framed her concern; she reached for Pam's hand and squeezed it. "Me too," she said.

"We're all scared, but not talking about her isn't going to help, neither will avoiding the subject or bottling up your feelings; just be yourselves."

"I didn't mean to make you feel bad," said Brian.

"I know that."

Mischief snuck into his eyes. "But it's true; Toni has got stinky feet."

Pam and Kelly laughed.

"Indeed she does, but those socks of yours are pretty ripe too, Brian."

PAM PULLED up at the main entrance of the supermarket and Kelly hopped out of the car, taking the blank cheque, grocery list and cash from Pam's hand.

"I've underlined the main things. If you get tired, stop and leave the rest and grab a milkshake and something to eat at the Do-nut Bar. We'll pick you up after tennis."

With a wave of the list, Kelly disappeared into the shopping centre, her denim jeans hanging from thin hips and her cropped top from skeletal shoulders. Yet again, pneumonia had reduced her bodyweight and halted her womanhood. Pam judged that she'd dropped two sizes while in hospital and made a mental note to have the chemist deliver a food supplement - chocolate flavoured, Kelly's favourite.

"She's real skinny," Brian voiced her thoughts. "Got to fatten her up, Ma."

"I'm working on it. Now, let's get you to Maxwell High before they start the match without you."

BRIAN WAS THRILLED. He had done his bit for the team, winning his singles match, but his opponent had fought hard and the games had been tight. Focusing on the match had taken his mind off Toni and he zinged with energy. He drummed his fingers on the dashboard, rummaged in the cubbyhole, fiddled with the radio. He got on Pam's nerves. She'd watched the match, but worries had distracted her and her mind whirled in an unrelenting circle. Alex, Toni, Direct Technologies' cash flow, Kelly's skinny hips, plans for supper, and back to Alex. She could not remember the points Brian had won or the final score and her shoulders were tense as she drove back to the shopping centre to pick up Kelly.

BRIAN RETUNED THE RADIO, a blast of disco pierced her eardrum.

"For Pete's sake, Brian, turn it down," she snapped, but her bad humour did not dent the generous winner's smile that he gave her and his sister. "Hi, Kell," he said, jumping out of the parked car. "I see you bought the shop?"

Kelly elbowed him, connecting his ribs; he clutched his stomach, feigning injury. "Ah, Germaine Greer strikes again."

She shoved the trolley at him, slipped into the car and took over the favoured seat.

"I'm sitting in the front," she jeered.

"Be my guest," he grinned.

The corners of Kelly's mouth turned down and Pam smiled. "He won," she said.

"I guessed," said Kelly. "It's all over his face and he needs a bigger hat for his fat head."

Their sibling rivalry tugged at Pam. She felt sick. She was a child short. *Where was Toni? Was she safe?* Helplessness engulfed her. *Please, please, protect her*, she prayed, over and over again. She swung into the traffic. She had to get home, to the phone. *Please let Bezuidenhout call.*

lex's first session with the psychiatrist was over and he felt the same, but different. Lighter. He decided that it had gone well and that he liked Pieter De Bruin. The shrink had smudged the edges of the emptiness and had dulled the gnawing anxiety. He'd done a pretty good job. Alex stopped for the red traffic light. A hawker ran in and out of the cars, his hands full of roses. He smiled at Alex. His teeth, unlike the four wilted bunches of flowers that he waved in front of Alex's windscreen, were perfect. Under the shade of a faded umbrella, empty galvanized buckets declared that he had had a successful day. Alex glanced at the sun-sapped flowers and the salesman pushed them through the open driver's window.

"Last ones, *baas*." Dark brown fingers clutched long, thorn-stripped stems. "Cheap, very cheap. Ten rand for four."

Their fragrance flooded the car and sealed the deal. Pam loved scented roses.

Behind him an impatient taxi-driver hooted and Alex

grabbed the flowers.

"Thanks, *baas*." The flower seller jumped onto the dirt verge, pocketed the green note and waved to the taxi. Overloaded, it was taking its cargo of passengers from their jobs in the white Sandton suburbs to their homes in the black township of Alexandra. The drooping roses needed water; the traffic was heavy. His heart and lungs were behaving and his palms were dry. His fingers felt in his shirt pocket, fingering De Bruin's prescription for anti-depressants and tranquilisers, but he wanted to get home; he felt good. A stop at the chemist could wait until tomorrow.

PAM'S CAR wasn't in the garage when he parked and killed the engine. He heard Kelly's dog, Mickey, barking. An Alsatian trapped in the body of a Maltese poodle, Mickey was a fearless watchdog who gave his all, and, as Alex let himself into the house, the little dog danced around his feet, wagging his tail in vigorous greeting.

"Hello, Mickey boy." Alex tickled him behind his black-tipped ears. "You happy now that that your mistress is out of hospital?" Mickey peeped out of the open door, head tilting from side to the side.

"Where is she? Not home yet? Come on then, let's get some water for these roses and find a titbit for you."

SHOVED into a sink full of cold water, the roses perfumed the kitchen and he imagined Pam's delight when she saw them. He wasn't going to tell her, but he was relieved she'd insisted he see a shrink. De Bruin was an okay guy, and, better yet, he now had a name for the bloody heavy blanket of dread that stifled him and filled him with terror. Depression. It was called depression. Not insanity. He could lick depression. The breathing exercises had helped. For a second, a very short second in the session, he'd felt 'normal'. He couldn't explain it, couldn't say what had changed, but he craved more of the same, more of himself. He would keep next Thursday's appointment.

"And, between you and me, Mickey, it's not to keep the wife happy. I'm looking forward to it," he said. Mickey wolfed down the leftover chicken, danced on his haunches, waved his paws and begged for more. Alex stroked him and refilled his dish. "That's it for now, Mick. Kelly will be cross if you don't eat your supper and I'm off to grab a cup of tea."

PAM'S NOTE was propped against the kettle. *Be home by 6.30. Police think Toni maybe in the Transkei. P*

THE BLOODY TRANSKEI. Jesus. He should have gone to the police station on his way home. He fumbled with the telephone book, thumbing the pages. N, O, P. Police. Police.

Where the hell is it?

There.

POLICE SERVICE. He ran his finger down the column; found the local station. His fingers shook as he dialed the number. It rang once; twice.

Hurry up.

Three, four.

Answer, dammit, answer.

Five, six.

I'm going to drive there.

Seven.

"Police."

Alex's couldn't speak.

"Police." Abrupt, official, no invitation to chat. "Who is this?"

Alex swallowed, cleared his throat, and unstuck his tongue.

"Inspector Bezuidenhout, please," he said.

"Not in, sir. Can someone else help you?"

"My wife – my daughter. Sorry, I mean... Look, yesterday my wife came in there and reported my daughter missing..."

"Stelios Panos's girlfriend?"

"Yes. No. My daughter, Antoinette Richards."

"*Ja,* Panos's girl. Young, about seventeen. The Inspector will get back to you."

"But I need to speak to someone now."

"Sorry, Sir. Panos's case is confidential."

"To hell with Panos," shouted Alex. "I don't give a damn about him. I'm Toni's father, I'm phoning about her."

"But she's tied in with his case, Sir. She's run off with him and he's violated bail. I'll make sure the Inspector gets back to you."

The line went dead.

Alex slammed down the handset and marched into Toni's bedroom. "Fucking imbeciles. I'll find you myself."

MICKEY JUMPED onto Toni's bed and barked for another pat, but Alex didn't respond. He opened the wardrobe, flinging the doors wide. He rifled through everything; the shelves, the detailed drawings and vivid paintings of the child who had enchanted him, the clothing, books, records and tapes; he scoured them all. He found nothing to help him find her. Her sheet music, bought with her own pocket money and played for him on Sunday mornings, pulled him up short. He felt like a creep, going through her things like this, but he had no choice. He loved her, she'd run away; she was missing and in danger. He had to find her.

"Where are you, Toni? Give me a clue." He spoke out loud and Mickey wagged his tail, rolling over, exposing his soft, white, furry tummy, but Alex moved on to Toni's dressing-table. Make-up, curlers, hairspray, perfume, the trappings of a teenage girl, filled the drawers. On his knees, he looked under the bed. Mickey joined him on the floor and licked his face.

"Not now, Mickey." Alex pushed him away, catching his hand between the wall and the bed leg, he touched her first school case. It was small, wedged in. Hidden. He remembered stenciling her name on it. She'd insisted on him writing her name in full because she was big, she was six and she was going to proper school. He'd squashed in the letters and returned her tightest hug and soppy kiss.

HER NAME WAS FADED NOW, the handle long gone. He pulled

out the case and sat on her bed. Mickey snuggled against his thigh. The worn latch opened easily. What the hell? Cigarettes, lighter, school reports, his signature forged in the parents' block, shocking marks. A membership card to Idols, the notorious nightclub. He stared at the laminated photo, the heavy make-up, sleeked-back hair and seductive pout. What the fuck? Who was Antoinette Panos?

"Oh my God. He wiped his hands over his face, pressed the heels of his palms to his eyes. His nose prickled. "Toni."

Her deception stunned him. This was not his enchanting daughter. Mickey mewed, cocking his head to one side.

The truth assaulted him. This was Toni. Insanity drummed in his head. Dagger-sharp, Toni's lies and deceit plunged into his heart and the abyss yawned.

You can end this agony. Take a hosepipe and run it from the car's exhaust into the car. It will be quick, painless. Peaceful. Come.

Jesus Christ, pull back, pull back. Concentrate. Concentrate.

Tyres crunched on the gravel driveway. Mickey yelped, jumped off the bed, and raced to meet Kelly. Pam was home.

"Hello, boy." Kelly dropped her parcels, picked up Mickey, and was rewarded with his usual face-washing. She laughed and cuddled him close. Pam smelt roses. Funny, she hadn't noticed new blooms on the garden bushes and she hadn't picked any for the house since before Kelly went into hospital. She took a deep breath. Definitely roses. Brian carried heavy packets to the kitchen. "The sink's full of red flowers," he called. "Must be from Dad, is he in the dog-box or something?"

Pulling them from the water, Pam buried her nose in the petals. "None of your business, young man," she smiled. "Bring in the rest of the groceries while I arrange these." She trimmed the stems, placing them in a tall, clear glass vase. "Alex," she called out. "Where'd you get the roses?"

Alex didn't answer.

"They're a bit floppy but they smell wonderful. I'm making tea. Come and have a cup." She set a tray and filled the teapot, but Alex didn't come. Had he had another of those awful attacks or done something stupid like cancel his first psychiatrist's appointment? Were the roses a peace offering for doing so?

Well, if they were, they bloody well weren't going to work.

She left the children to sort out the shopping and marched into the main bedroom. It was empty, the bed and *en suite* bathroom undisturbed. She felt the urge to laugh out loud. Her daughter was missing and, now she couldn't find her husband. Her mind whirled. *Was she about to lose her mind too?* Hysteria bubbled up her throat; she heard herself laugh and clapped her hand over her mouth. Alex's car was in the garage. He must be here somewhere, maybe in the garden. She turned and retraced her steps down the passage.

THE GASP CAME from Toni's room. The door was ajar and she tapped it open. Alex sat slumped on the edge of Toni's bed. His face was ashen. Dark rings circled his blue eyes and Toni's room was turned upside down. Pam stared at the chaos. He respected the children's privacy and never went into their rooms. Had he disturbed a robber? Was he hurt? He seemed not to know that she was there. She couldn't see any blood. His hand clutched a yellow, laminated card.

"Alex?" He stared at the carpet. "What happened?" she asked.

No response. Pam shook his shoulders. "Alex, look at me." His eyes were slow to focus, lifeless.

"Did you go to the psychiatrist?" she asked. He nodded. *Thank God.*

"Did he give you something?" Was this a bizarre reaction to medication?

"Yes, but I haven't filled the script yet." He bit his lip. "I can't help her," he said.

"What do you mean? What are you talking about?"

"I did this." Alex indicated the jumble mess. "I went through her stuff, Pam, violated her space. I needed a clue. I wanted to find her." He squeezed his eyes shut. Pam pulled his head towards her body and rested it on the slight mound of her belly. She rocked him slightly but had no words of comfort to offer. She was locked in the same terrifying place.

"Did you one?" she whispered.

He waved to the little, upturned school case, the contents spewed across the pale pink duvet.

"No, but I found a stranger," he said and handed her the laminated card. Pam stared at Toni's kohled eyes. She remembered the smiling face in the forged passport Bezuidenhout unearthed.

"I found one too," she whispered.

10

D e Bruin's prescription for antidepressants, tranquillisers and sleeping pills came with an order to stay off work for a week. Super effective, the medication not only severed him from gnawing anxiety and the ever-waiting abyss, it also ironed his emotions flat, buttoned him into detachment and presented Pam with a packaged zombie. She itched to shake life into him and yet she could only blame herself for her frustration. She'd forced him to get help; see a psychiatrist and this was the numbing result. He stayed home on Friday, popped pills over the weekend, discarded the rest of De Bruin's order to take a week off and got into her car with Kelly and Brian on Monday morning. Giving her a drug-drenched smile, he asked her to drive him to Powertronics. Ignatius Bezuidenhout had confirmed that Toni was somewhere in the Transkei. He said he was confident they'd find her soon, but, when pressed, admitted that progress with the authorities in the Homeland was difficult. She must stay calm and be patient.

. . .

SHE HADN'T SLEPT PROPERLY since the anonymous phone call. She didn't have the energy to argue with Alex. "You really want to go to work?"

He nodded. She shrugged. She'd taxi him for a few days, but Eric was setting up the assembly line at Direct Technologies and next week she'd be making connectors and knocking off work later than usual. *How was she going to fit him in then? How long was he going to be like this?* She needed Toni, Alex and her life back. Staying calm and patient was impossible. She needed help. It was time to call Doctor De Bruin.

HE WAS polite and his English was just as Alex had described. His pronunciation was precise, his grammar correct and his words Afrikaans flavoured, but he would not discuss Alex's case with her. He upheld the patient-doctor confidentiality code he said. She was glad of it, she replied. In fact, she counted on it and hoped he extended it to the patient's spouse, as she didn't want Alex to know about this call, but please, he had to do something; anything. Alex, the walking dead, was unfit to drive, but was hell-bent on going to work. Her to-do schedule was overflowing, and it was stressful fitting him in. The doctor was charming and assured her that he would look into her concerns at Alex's next appointment on Thursday; perhaps an adjustment in medication would help. Grateful, she thanked him and hung up. She hoped he was as good as Dr Gordon had said he was; there was no one else who could help her.

IT WAS mid-afternoon and mid-week and Pam was between lifts. Having a few moments of free time was driving her crazy. She had to keep busy; busy kept the worry from boiling over. She would go and check on Frans. She'd seen him working on the pavement garden. He tended it often, turning it into a living testament to his social skills as he dug up local news, sifted truth from fiction, raked over disagreements and shared seeds of friendship with all who passed by. His flowers on the pavement grew in abundance, but a quick inspection of the rose-beds inside the garden walls told Pam that he hadn't clipped off the old flowers or trimmed the dead wood in a while. She'd have to speak to him about it, but first, she had to touch base with Inspector Bezuidenhout.

SHE SWALLOWED HARD when the Inspector apologised and told her he could offer nothing new. Her fear flared but she forced it from her voice as she rang the extended family. A quick chat with Gran, because she kept telling her 'it's costing you a lot of money to phone all the way to London, my luv', and then calming both sets of Toni's grandparents and declining offers from both her siblings, Linda and Kevin, to come to Johannesburg. *What on earth would be the use of that?* She loved them dearly and they wanted to help but coming here would not change the situation and she was incapable of putting on a brave face for them. Besides, Linda had her own family to see to in East London and Kevin was studying at university in Cape Town. Her fingers shook as she zipped open a can of Coke, poured it over ice cubes and added a slice of lemon. Frans and the pavement seemed too far away, but she had twenty minutes to fill. She would dead-head the roses herself. Mickey followed her back to the garden, but the sleepless nights dragged at her bare feet and she put her clippers aside and sat down on the garden bench.

· · ·

THE NIGHTS WERE BAD. Alex, cocooned in chemical oblivion, slept, while she tossed and turned, clutched sodden tissues and cried. Fear simmered as she counted the dark hours and the illuminated hands of the bedside clock ticked it to the boil. By first light she was done in and Alex's drugged sleep irritated her. *Why had she insisted that he go to a psychiatrist?* Now she had a husband who passed out ten minutes after swallowing his sleeping pill, leaving her more alone than ever. Perhaps having Linda or Kevin around would help. Dawn was tardy. It gave definition to the bedroom shadows and her irrational thoughts of shaking Alex until his teeth rattled in his head and chased her from their marital bed.

MICKEY LICKED her face and put an end to Pam's napping. Startled, she opened her eyes, wiped the slurp from her forehead and checked her wrist-watch. No time to do the roses before she had to leave and fetch Kelly from her extra maths lesson, Alex from the centre of town and Brian from school. Fat clouds puffed up in a brilliant blue sky promising an afternoon thunder-storm. A light breeze caressed her skin and Mickey's wet nose nudged her hand; she ran her fingers through his coat. In a minute or two she'd start the round-up.

The phone rang.

Pam was running before Mickey barked. She grabbed the receiver.

"Is this Richards' residence?"

"Yes, it is." The line crackled.

"Will you accept a collect call from Antoinette Richards?"

"Yes."

Pam's hands were clammy, her heart pounded. She heard the operator speak. She heard Toni's voice. Dear God, she was alive. Thank you.

"You're connected to your party," the exchange operator said to Toni. "Speak up, please."

Pam didn't give her a chance.

"Toni? Toni is that you?"

"Hi, Ma."

"Are you okay? Where are you?"

"I'm fine. I'm with Stelios in a caravan park."

"What caravan park?"

"I can't tell you."

"Why not?"

"I can't."

"Listen, Toni, we're sick with worry. Just tell me where you are."

"I'm sorry, Ma. I should have phoned sooner."

"No, Toni. You've got it wrong. You shouldn't have run away in the first place."

Pam could hear muffled voices on the other end.

"Is that Stelios? Is he there with you?"

"Ma...."

"Let me speak to him."

"He's not here."

"I heard him. Don't lie to me, young lady, you've done enough of that. Have you any idea how worried we are? How much you've hurt us?"

"I don't know what to say, Ma. I know you won't believe me, but I love you."

Pam ran out of steam. She'd prayed for this call, waited for it every second for more than a week. Toni was alive and safe enough to speak. That was the important thing.

"Are you there, Ma?"

Tears stung Pam's eyes; she sucked them back. Now was not the time for such luxuries. Get her back home.

"I'm here. Do you have any money?"

"No. We used my pocket money for petrol, but Stelios has a job here. He gets paid at the end of the month, but he's asked for an advance. I'll be okay."

"Toni, listen to me. You're not okay. He's a convicted drug-dealer. Do you know that? He's out on bail awaiting his appeal."

"They framed him, Ma, he's innocent."

"So you knew about his bail?"

"Yes."

"And you still ran away with him? Are you crazy?"

"But he didn't do anything."

"Don't be stupid. He's no angel, believe me."

"I went to the court. I heard his case."

"WHAT?"

"I didn't tell you because I knew you'd be mad."

"For shit's sake, Toni, when last were you straight with us?"

"See, I knew you'd be mad."

"Damn right. You've lied and lied to us."

"I had to. You stopped me seeing him."

"Just listen here, Toni, you're seventeen, still at school and he's twenty-seven. We stopped you seeing him when we caught him helping you sneak in at four in the morning and he told us we were cramping his style…"

"Ma, please, slow down."

"Don't you dare tell me to slow down. This man's dangerous."

"His friends sent him a message. They said you've set the police on him."

"That's right. I reported you missing. There's an open warrant of abduction."

"Please call them off. You're making things difficult for him."

"Excuse me."

"Ma, please. Stelios thought I'd asked you if I could go with him."

"He's not stupid enough to believe that. I know he's there. Let me talk to him."

"You don't understand. He loves me."

"Crap. He's looking after himself. This isn't love, Toni. Put him on the line."

"You're spoiling it for us."

"Tell that spineless creep, from me, that he'd better find a way, and quickly, to get you home."

"Ma, please."

"I'm hanging up and phoning the police. Tell him that."

"Ma."

"Get your arse back here. *Pronto*."

11

P am drove Alex to his second appointment with the psychiatrist. Dropping him at the door to the building, she popped into the nearest shops, picked up a newspaper, along with steak and salad for a quick supper and returned to wait for him. Parked under one of the tipuanas, she flipped the pages of the magazine she'd bought the day before the anonymous phone call and dismissed the urge to write a 'to-do' list or fly up the stairs and remind Pieter De Bruin to speak to Alex about his medication. It was her third attempt to read the magazine. The glossy pages failed to block out the flashing images of Alex, the proud father, beaming at the sleeping baby girl; the stumbling toddler; the Grade One ballerina; the schoolgirl with a missing front tooth; the teenager winning the fashion design contest; Alex in hospital, his eyes dead, his voice lifeless; Antoinette Panos's membership card to Idols; her black and white photo in the false passport. Fear crawled into her chest and goosebumps rose on her arms and neck. She stared at the magazine page, but there was no escape hidden in the print, the photos or between the covers.

. . .

ALEX SAW the devastation in Pam's eyes. Toni's disappearance and his inability to do anything, especially drive, was destroying them. He felt anaesthetised - in a haze; a voyeur at arm's length from himself. He was going to speak to De Bruin about it. His steps were uncertain as he climbed the stairs to the first floor and approached the reception desk. *Could De Bruin wipe out the fuzziness without the panic attacks coming back?* He had to. Alex might be chemically numb, but he wasn't dumb, and he'd been married to Pam for twenty years. Her forced smiles didn't fool him. Tight and thin, they never reached her eyes and she wasn't about to drive him around forever. His dependency was getting to her; he heard the veiled irritation in her voice. She needed a strong, independent, capable husband; a husband who could help her find their missing child. She needed the man he used to be, she needed the impossible.

BEHIND THE RECEPTION DESK, a tailored woman pushed stray curls into the tight, dark bun at the nape of her neck.

"Good afternoon," she said.

"Hi, I'm Alex Richards, I have an appointment." Did his voice really sound like he was holding his hand across his mouth?

"I'm Lyzette," the woman smiled, crinkling her light-brown eyes. She popped on square glasses and found his name in the diary, pencilled in in Doctor De Bruin's scrawl.

"You're his last patient of the day," she said. "Please take a seat at the table and complete this questionnaire." She handed Alex a wad of stapled A4 sheets and a pen.

"But you phoned me and checked all the details I'd given to the doctor last week," Alex heard himself protest.

"I did and I've opened your file, but all new patients fill in Doctor's questionnaire."

Alex flipped the pages. The questions covered twenty pages. "What? All of this?"

"It looks worse than it is, you'll see. It's multiple choice."

Alex took the papers to the desk. He pulled them close, his back shielding them from Lyzette and he read the first question.

Do you feel happy?

a) Often. b) Sometimes. c) Never.

What the hell?

His daughter had run away, he was taking pills to get through the day. He was having imaginary heart attacks. He circled 'c'. Never.

Next question: Do you feel helpless?

Hell yes. Pam had to ferry him everywhere. Circle 'a'. Often.

What's the point of all this?

Do you think of suicide?

Shit, he was heading for the loony-bin. De Bruin already knew his answer to that, no point circling anything but 'a'. Often.

He looked over his shoulder. Lyzette nodded. "Go on," she said. "It will help you and Doctor."

Alex bloody well hoped so.

• • •

THIRTY AGONISING minutes later he was done. Question by question the answers had peeled away 'let's pretend everything's okay' and he felt like he'd lost a game of strip-poker and was standing in just his underpants and too-tight-to-get-off wedding ring. Shaken, he gave the sheets to Lyzette and was relieved when she did not read them before putting them into an envelope and handing it back to him.

"Come this way."

THE PSYCHIATRIST STOOD up as they entered the room. "*Dankie, Lyzette,*" he said. She smiled and left them. De Bruin took the envelope from Alex. "Ahh, Alex, please sit. I see you have completed my questionnaire." He placed it on the coffee table next to a box of tissues and a soapstone sculpture of a kneeling bushman. Alex couldn't take his eyes off the envelope. The answers inside scared him and tugged at his underpants. He didn't have the balls to play this round and his hand reached out. He was walking out of here, taking the bloody questionnaire with him and shredding it.

De Bruin leaned forward and stayed his hand. "It will tell me many things. Did you answer truthfully?"

Alex nodded.

"That takes courage. See, I already know that you are brave."

Alex hesitated. "Who marks it?" he asked.

"I evaluate it myself," empathy softened de Bruin's Afrikaans accent.

"What about Lyzette?"

"No. I promise." De Bruin's direct look reassured Alex. He sat back in the couch, leaving the darkness of his mind lying in the envelope on the table.

"Good," said Pieter. "We will discuss the results at your next appointment."

"Why not now?" Those wretched answers would haunt him for seven days and turn him into an incurable basket case.

De Bruin smiled. "It takes a few hours to assess."

"It's multiple choice. A computer would spit out the results immediately."

"An intriguing idea, but I know nothing about computers."

"You don't need to; all you need is a good program and I know just the guy to write one. He works for me. I'll have him contact you and get you sorted out."

"Thank you. I would appreciate being sorted out," laughed Pieter. "You are the first patient who has offered to do so."

"Sorry, I didn't mean it like it sounded," said Alex. "But you need to speed things up for your patients. Waiting to be evaluated and get started is the pits."

De Bruin pointed to the sealed envelope. "In answering, you have already started," he said. "Did you find it difficult?"

"Yes." Alex shifted in his seat.

"Examining one's psyche is difficult. It is also painful and, I must warn you, a lengthy process. Do you want to carry on?"

Alex nodded. Circling the answers had opened Pandora's Box and scared him. He was dead inside. He had no choice.

"Good. Has the medication helped?"

Alex shrugged. "I feel like I'm covered by a thick blanket. Everything's fuzzy; far away."

"It's been a week since you started the tranquilisers. Try halving them. You may feel on edge. Unfortunately, finding the correct dosage takes time."

"Can I drive?"

"See how you feel tomorrow."

I'll be fine.

STOPPED AT THE INTERSECTION, Pam rode the clutch, faced an endless stream of cars and waited for a polite driver to let her in. Alex spied a half-car gap between a blue Audi and yellow Toyota.

"Go."

Pam ignored him. The cars whizzed by. Alex rolled his eyes. "*Jeez,* we're going to be here forever."

Anger stroked Pam's neck.

For the last half hour she'd waited in the parking-lot for him, her mind a jumble, her nerves shot, hoping that De Bruin was performing a miracle in his rooms and restoring Alex to Alex, or at least reducing the zombie quotient that had arrived with last week's prescription. Toni was in the Transkei with a criminal and Pam needed her good old, supportive husband, but Alex had emerged from the building, fumbled with the car handle, pulled open the door, muttered that multiple choice was no bloody choice and scowled through the windscreen.

· · ·

THREE MORE CARS flashed passed and Alex grimaced. "You've missed another gap."

"Want to drive?" hissed Pam.

"You know I can't, but I will tomorrow. De Bruin's cut down the pills."

"Hoo bloody ray." Her sarcasm pulled his attention from the traffic and to her face; it was beetroot red. "Now shut up or get out."

Alex took the first option.

BRIAN WAS WAITING at the front door. "Some guy called about Toni."

Pam held her breath. Alex stiffened.

"Said he was Stelios's landlord and that Toni will be home tomorrow."

"Thank God," Pam's chin quivered, but she held back the tears.

"Did he leave a number?" asked Alex.

"No. He just said Stelios had phoned him and asked him to tell you to fetch Toni from the bus station in Jo'burg."

"He's not bringing her home himself?" Pam shook her head in disbelief and rubbed the knots of muscle pulling tight at the base of her neck.

"Bastard," spat Alex. "He's not a man's backside; doesn't even have the guts to phone us himself. Did this landlord tell you what time her bus arrives?"

"At five o'clock in the morning," said Brian.

Pam glanced at her watch; it was ten past six. They had ten hours and fifty minutes to wait.

THE FAMILY NEEDED distraction and settled on an early movie and supper at Mario's. Maybe the movie deserved an Oscar, maybe the food was sublime, but their blunted appetites appreciated neither. They put on happy faces, pretended to enjoy themselves and filled awkward silences with forced laughter. They tried to be jolly, but their jokes fell flat. They could not fool themselves. They were home before nine, weary, and in bed by ten, but no one slept well.

WITHOUT THE MAGIC of a sleeping pill, Alex woke at 3 o'clock. His tossing and turning put Pam's nerves on edge and she tried in vain to switch off her thoughts of Toni as she watched the minute hand of the bedside clock creep to four o'clock. Alex pushed back the duvet and Pam pulled on her dressing-gown.

"Like some coffee?"

"I'll get it," he said.

Her muscles screamed for action. "Don't worry, I'm already up," she said.

Trying not to make a noise she hurried past the children's rooms to the kitchen, but Kelly and Brian had beaten her to it. Both in pyjamas, they were dunking Ouma rusks into mugs of hot chocolate.

"Want one?' asked Kelly.

Pam nodded. "And a coffee for Dad."

"Can we come to the bus stop?" asked Brian.

"No. Dad and I are going alone."

"But, Ma, what about Dad? His sleeping pill…" Kelly handed Pam the steaming cups.

"He didn't take one last night. He's wide awake. Now go back to bed."

"You sure?" Brian arched his eyebrow. "What if Dad has one of those turns?"

"Dad will be fine."

Pam wished she was as certain as she hoped she sounded. The kids were worried; they weren't blind to his imagined heart attacks or his trips to a psychiatrist. They were all having a tough time, battling to keep strong and look out for each other.

"We'll both be fine," she said. Catching sight of her bed-ruffled hair in the wall oven's glass door reminded Pam that she had an eight-thirty appointment with Raymond today. She scribbled his number on the kitchen notepad, tore off the page and gave it to Kelly.

"Please phone and cancel my hairdressing appointment, and don't worry, we'll all be back before you know it."

Kelly looked doubtful.

"Now, shoo." Pam gave her a peck on the cheek and tapped her bottom. "Go back to bed."

· · ·

Pam turned and stared at her reflection in the glass oven door. She looked normal but she knew she wasn't.

Who are you? How come you are going out at the crack of dawn on a Saturday to fetch a daughter who ran away with a man who sells drugs? Her reflection had no answers. *What had gone wrong? What had happened to her and her family and their dreams? Was this nightmare real?* The hair on the back of her neck stood up. Oh yes, the nightmare was real. She shivered and carried the mugs to the bedroom. *How will we survive? Can we ever be what we were, or was that an illusion?*

This Saturday promised frustrated shopping, household chores, energetic sport and decadent leisure to all, except the terrified parents of Antoinette Richards. For them, it delivered a trip to the Johannesburg Central Bus Station. As the father of a runaway daughter, Alex gripped the steering-wheel and drove like the devil to bring her home. He made the journey in record time, wiping wet palms on his trouser legs, not once, but many times, and Pam told herself that his actions had nothing to do with halving the dosage of his tranquilisers. He was anxious to see Toni, not about to fly into a panic attack, but she didn't convince her stomach, which tied itself into a million knots. They drove through the noisy crowds spilling out of the luxury air-conditioned coaches, the mainstream Putco buses, the rundown taxis and headed to the Transkei stop at the far side of the terminus.

Dawn tickled the dew on top of the grey metal guardrails. It squirmed and fell onto the cracked concrete pavement. Alex and Pam had arrived early, but the meagre sheltered space under the tin roof of the Transkei stop was full of people. Sitting on paint-peeled benches, or the cement floor with legs stretched out straight in front of them, they shared loud conversations as they waited for the bus; their suitcases, zipped bags and string-tied bundles scattered among them. The Richards, feeling uncomfortable in their white skins, parked across the road from the bus-stop. They sat quietly, holding hands, their thoughts too fragile for the weight of words.

Five o'clock came, delivering the early morning heat of a sweltering day, but not the Transkei bus. It arrived an agonising hour later. Hooting and scattering curb-sitters, it shuddered to a halt amid Xhosas cheers. Potholes and a flat tyre had caused the delay, but no matter, it was here and the embarking passengers collected their luggage and readied themselves to board. Colliding with those getting off, they exchanged exuberant greetings and complicated handshakes. Pam and Alex scrutinised the black crowd, but there was no sign of Toni's pale skin and straight brown hair. "Where the hell is she?" Alex dropped Pam's hand, shifted in his seat, sat forward and looked through the windscreen. Pam willed her to appear. Alex's fingers drummed a tattoo on the steering-wheel. "Damn it. That bastard's making fools of us and Toni's playing along with him," said Alex.

"Nonsense, she'll be here," said Pam, but the bus was almost empty and she tasted bitter doubt. *Please. Please. Please. Please. Please.*

"Jesus what're they up to? More bloody lies, that's what."

"She'll be here." Pam prayed harder. *Please. I'll do anything. Anything. Please bring her home today. Please.*

• • •

THE LAST PASSENGERS, all women, grouped and descended the stairs. Barefoot, wearing loose dresses and matching tribal headgear, they moved as one along the pavement. Alex spotted the white toes keeping pace in the middle of the brown feet and pink soles.

"There she is," he shouted. They jumped out of the car and ran towards her.

"Toni," Pam yelled and waved her arms. "Here, over here."

The circle tightened, hemming in the white girl.

"Let her go." shouted Alex. "Let her go, now."

Toni broke free. "It's okay, Dad. I'm fine."

She was safe. She was home.

"Dad, I'm sorry, I didn't…"

She'd deceived them. Anger swept aside his relief. She was Antoinette Panos and she had an Idols Membership card to prove it.

"I don't want to hear anything from you Toni," he said. "You're a bloody liar. Your mother has been out of her mind with worry. Just keep your mouth shut. Keep your fucking lies to yourself."

She stood still. She wiped her tears and nose with her fist.

She was his little girl.

Her deception locked his arms at his side, but every cell of his body ached to hold her.

"Mom?" Toni's voice caught in her throat.

"You're grounded forever, young lady," said Pam, but she pulled them together, enfolding her man and her child in her arms. Their tears ran unchecked and wet their faces.

Thank you, God.

Alex was the first to pull back. "Get in the car," he said.

"I must say goodbye," said Toni.

"Who to?" asked Pam.

Toni pointed to the women. Nattering, shifting hips, picking up parcels and balancing them on their heads, they were preparing to depart.

"But they crowded in on you," said Pam.

"They were protecting me, Ma. When I got on the bus some of the men gave me a hard time." Toni looked at her feet. Alex and Pam locked eyes.

"And those ladies pushed them away. They gave me food and sat with me all the way home."

"For Christ's sake," groaned Alex. They'd probably saved her from rape, maybe even death. He felt small. He could never repay the Xhosa women's generous protection. Money was too easy; a pittance, an insult, but it was all they could give.

"Got any money in your bag, Pam?" he whispered, pulling out his wallet.

Pam and Alex raided the cubbyhole, pockets, purse and wallet. Embarrassed, they held out all the cash they had. The women's chatter died.

"Please. Take it, please," said Pam.

Clap, clap. Thanks, thanks. Arms outstretched, palms cupped, one on top of the other, Toni's guardian angels accepted the woefully, inadequate sum. The women smiled, pocketed the coins, divided the notes, folding them into small squares and tucking them under worn shirts and into bras.

"I'll never forget you," said Toni.

The Xhosa women had never learned English, but Toni hugged each one and they hugged her back, and they understood.

12

Inspector Ignatius Bezuidenhout never told his wife, Hettie, that he volunteered for Sunday duty at the station. She was a staunch member of the Dutch Reformed Church and she loved seeing him dressed in his bottle-green, double-breasted suit with the flared pants. Pulling the station's Sunday shift provided him with a perfect excuse not to squeeze his big body into the uncomfortable polyester blend, clip a broad tie to his matching striped shirt and be a hypocrite at the ten o'clock service. Eight years of police work had stripped him of belief in a good God and had exposed his fellow man as His irredeemable flawed work. The evil he'd seen, often committed by practising Christians, sickened him and no amount of going to church would restore his faith. It had gone forever and his job was now his religion. Police work wasn't joyous, but it was his calling. Not a well-paid or appreciated calling, but one he embraced without complaint.

SEATED opposite him and flanked by her parents, Antoinette

Richards fidgeted on the beige vinyl and chrome chair. A pretty girl, somewhat on the skinny side, he thought, but, at seventeen, she still had time to fill out. The high collar of her pastel-checked blouse curled on her neck. Straight-legged, tight denim jeans set off her slender hips and a trio of thin leather belts and flat 'ballet' pumps pulled her style together. Gleaming brown hair, cut with a full fringe, framed her oval face and hung to the middle of her back. Pale freckles kissed a cute, upturned nose and her full lips and heavy, arched brows and thick lashes reminded him of that model, somebody Hemmingway. Hettie disapproved of her and scorned the glossy magazines whose covers she adorned, but he thought she was okay.

Antoinette struck a pose. She aimed for nonchalance, but the barren police station spooked her, and she missed her mark. Looking uncomfortable, even frightened, she scuffed her shoes on the peel 'n stick carpet tiles. Her eyes remained glued to the open file on his desk.

HE FELT sorry for her parents. Decent people they were. Mr. Richards had shaken his hand, thanked him for putting strong police pressure on Stelios and forcing Antoinette's return, and Mrs. Richards had brought a Tupperware box filled with homemade shortbread for the station staff and returned his initialled hanky. She'd washed her tears and ironed her distress from the folded cotton and it lay next to Toni's docket on the green desk-blotter. She looked done in. Her hair was scraped back and secured at the base of her neck in an elastic band and red streaked her blue eyes. She sat quiet and erect, but her hands, clasped tight in her lap, betrayed her inner turmoil as she listened to Antoinette.

· · ·

"I LIED TO STELIOS," said Toni. "I told him my parents had said I could go with him." She twisted a signet ring on her little finger. It was a christening present from Alex's mother; a small engraved bird holding a heart in its beak. The letter 'A' was just visible in the 9ct gold. Bezuidenhout's face mirrored her father's frustration. He shook his head in disbelief, sighed and rested his elbows on the desk.

"Stelios is supposed to report here every week, Antoinette," his gruff Afrikaans accent added weight to his words. "He skipped bail. Now that's a serious offence, but taking a minor to the Transkei without permission, that's even worse; that's called abduction."

Toni's hair swung in denial.

"I told you. He thought I'd asked them."

"He knows your parents wouldn't let you go with him."

"But he believed me."

"*Ag* man, Antoinette, he is not a child or stupid, he knows the score. Don't make excuses for him. He's not worth it."

"You don't understand." Toni's body stiffened. "None of you do. He just wanted me to be with him. It was supposed to be a holiday for us. He loves me."

"Really? You think about that. He put you on a 'black' bus, in the Transkei, a very dangerous place right now given our political situation and sent you home. All alone." Toni winced. Ignatius wanted to nail Stelios, make him pay for the pain he'd caused these good people, help this lovesick kid. "Do you call that love?"

"He heard about the warrant and it spoilt everything." Toni's eyes were wide; tears glistened. "He had no choice. He had to send me home."

"No, no, no," Bezuidenhout's fat finger punched the stale air. "Listen, Antoinette, a decent man would have brought you home himself, not put you in danger. You are lucky that those women helped you. He was in big trouble, so he got rid of you. Simple. Don't you see that?"

"You're wrong. You made it impossible for him."

"Listen carefully, this is important. I know he's up to no good. I hear he's catching crayfish illegally. He skipped bail and took you with him. You know where he is but you won't tell me. He has made you an accessory."

"He didn't mean to. It was my own fault." Shrill hysteria crept into Toni's voice. "How many times must I tell you that I lied to him? You don't know him like I do."

She was defending him and Bezuidenhout felt the case slipping away. He hunted for a new angle.

Muscles twitched in Alex's clenched jaw. "For God's sake, Toni, Stelios is no fool; he knew what he was doing."

"No, he's not to blame," Toni shook her head. "You don't like him. You never did. You stopped me seeing him."

"Oh, come on, Toni." Anger flashed in Pam Richards' eyes as she ditched her quiet poise. "He's a first-class jerk and I'm sick to death of listening to you stick up for him. We caught him helping you to sneak out at night; you were bunking school and failing exams. What did you expect us to do? Stand by? Let him ruin your life?"

"It's my life." Toni met her mother's anger head-on. "And you're destroying it."

"No. Toni. I don't need to. Stelios is doing a great job. He's rubbish, do you hear me? Rubbish."

ANTOINETTE STARTED to cry and Inspector Bezuidenhout handed her the initialled hanky.

"*Kom* now, don't cry. We all just want to help you."

The hanky soaked up Antoinette's tears, as it had her mother's on the trip back from Lanseria.

"You say that he loves you?" Perhaps a kinder approach would lead to a conviction.

Toni nodded.

"You say you lied to him? Did he threaten to break up with you if you didn't go?"

Toni's face gave him the answer. Bingo. He baited the hook. "He did. So, tell me, on the day you ran away, did he fetch you from home or from school?"

The lure wasn't subtle enough. Stelios had taught her street sense.

"He's not to blame. He didn't abduct me." Toni blew her nose on his hanky, blowing his case right out of the barred window.

• • •

BEZUIDENHOUT TYPED up her statement and Toni signed it. The docket was useless. He could not charge Stelios with abduction and his disappointment tasted vile. Antoinette Richards loved the bastard. The kid and her family were heading for heartache and, as a policeman, he could do nothing to protect them, but Dirk Swanepoel, his old friend at Child Welfare could.

"I'M OBLIGED to report this case to the Social Services," he said, addressing the parents. "Antoinette is a runaway and is involved with a criminal. He's skipped bail and she knows his whereabouts; she's withholding information in a criminal investigation."

Toni shot a look at Pam; her bottom lip quivered and she reached for her mother's hand.

Leaning back in his chair, the Inspector studied the 1986 wall calendar and wished this moment away.

"They'll assess the situation and make recommendations to keep Antoinette safe."

"Such as?" Alex sat forward in his seat.

"They could make her a ward of the court. Put her in a place of safety." Bezuidenhout's words exploded in the room.

"You mean, take her away from us?" Pam stared at him and squeezed Toni's hand. The Inspector nodded.

Alex slammed his fist on the desk. "No one is taking her away. Find Stelios, lock him up and throw away the key. We're out of here."

· · ·

INSPECTOR IGNATIUS BEZUIDENHOUT watched them leave the Station. Mr. Richards was angry; he had every right to be. Hell, if Antoinette was his kid Stelios would be dead by now. Grabbing a red marker from the pens and pencils in the chipped coffee cup, he wrote *Phone Dirk Swanepoel* at the top of Monday's page of his diary. He pressed a rubber stamp into the inkpad and slammed it onto the buff file cover, 'CLOSED'. Blazoned from corner to corner the letters dried and he wished he'd worn the tight suit and gone to church with Hettie today. He felt powerless and the feeling ate into his soul. Being a hypocrite had never felt this bad.

13

P am and Alex entered the 5th floor chambers of their friend and lawyer, James Griffiths. The diehard advocate of childless marriages waved them to a dralon sofa. Curt and unsmiling as always, he wasted no energy in greeting them.

"Do you know if Steve's read the terms of divorce?" he asked Alex.

"No, but he said you're representing both of them. Isn't that a bit difficult?"

"No. Jean came to me first, then Steve. They know they'll not find a better lawyer in Johannesburg and that I'm capable of looking after both of their interests. Now, on to the matter at hand."

He fired sentences like bullets from a gun. Encapsulated in an accent reminiscent of colonial Natal, the word 'fuck' or variants thereof, rifled his conversation. He claimed that it was an expressive word, understood worldwide and was therefore an excellent communication tool.

"Per your instructions of last week, I contacted Dirk Swanepoel at the Department of Health and Welfare," he picked up a thick document, held together with heavy-duty staples, and paced the large room. His black court robe flowed from wide shoulders and added menace to the jabs he aimed at the heavens.

"I also called for this. It is the full transcript of the trial of one Stelios Dimitri Panos." He paused, fanned the pages and handed them to Pam, but addressed Alex. "Strictly off the record, let us say that if Toni was my daughter, I would, without hesitation, dispose of this Stelios."

Shock registered on Alex's face. Pam gasped.

"Shit, James. Don't you think that's a bit drastic?"

"It does not matter what I think, Alex. I'm speaking here, not as your lawyer, but as your friend and I'm telling you not to fuck with this. Toni's life is in dire danger. She knows the people in Stelios Dimitri Panos's life. Criminals, drug-traf-fickers and he's one fucking guilty dealer. He was caught red-handed by an undercover cop selling LSD. Large quantities of LSD. The case against him is airtight. He can't win his appeal and he knows it." James paused, the seriousness of the crime and the guilt of the perpetrator sank in. "If you are to beat this fucking bastard you have to think like him. He has no inten-tion of going to jail."

"But surely there's something else we can do rather than… dispose of him?"

James shrugged. "We could try an interdict, but I don't think it would suffice."

Pam was stunned. What were they talking about? A contract,

like actors in *The Godfather*? But they weren't movie stars, and this was no movie set. In her world, contracts bound business partners, formed the basis of marriage, set out terms of employment, locked the clasp of debt, but didn't kill or maim anyone. Case Number 26/689/85 lay heavy in her lap. It creased her skirt and its contents stripped her of ignorance and placed Toni in the underworld of criminals. James pressed on.

"Let me tell you, this mother-fucker plans to skip the country and that passport Pam found at his house tells me that he will take Toni with him."

Alex and Pam exchanged stunned looks. Traffic noises from the street below snuck through the closed window.

"Believe me I'm not fucking exaggerating. He's scum of the worst kind, a big, bloody drug-dealer, connected to a dangerous mob and, if Toni gets to Greece, I doubt you will see her again."

"This is crazy. We can't talk like this." Pam looked to Alex. His silence panicked her. *For God's sake was he entertaining the notion? It was absurd.* James pulled a typed sheet from an official-looking buff envelope and flicked the page straight. This time he directed his attention to Pam.

"Swanepoel from the Welfare department has also read the trial record. This is his reply and instructions. I shall read it to you." James cleared his throat, dropped his tone. "You are to report to the department of Health and Welfare at 77 Main Street with your daughter, Antoinette Richards. She will be placed in a Place of Safety pending the outcome of a hearing before the Children's Court."

"Jesus Christ."

James ignored Alex's interruption. "Should your child be found to be in need of care, this placement will be permanent, and she will stay there until she is 21."

A strangled moan escaped Pam and she pushed a fist against her mouth. Alex touched her arm, but she shrugged it off and stood up, the transcript crashing to the floor.

"Toni doesn't belong in a reformatory." Fear coiled in Pam's stomach. Vomit was a millisecond away. She refused the glass of water James offered.

"I agree," said James. "I anticipated your response, Pam, and have already dispatched our reply. I suggested an acceptable alternative. We seek an interdict."

Pam swallowed. Acid hit the back of her throat. "But you just said that an interdict wouldn't work."

"Not with Stelios. But our action will keep the Welfare Department happy and Toni out of their 'place of safety'."

"What then?"

"Toni will have to co-operate fully."

Pam retrieved the fallen papers, hugging them close to her chest. "I think she will. She was frightened by Bezuidenhout."

James swept her opinion aside. "Swanepoel led me to believe that she defended Stelios fiercely. Hardly the action of a docile daughter."

Alex sighed, rubbed the back of his neck, felt in his pocket and patted his pills. Pam saw the tremor in his hands. James turned to him.

"And you are satisfied that you can control her?"

"Truthfully? No," Alex replied. "But we have no option, we can't put her at the mercy of the courts. We'll ground her. Keep her locked up. Whatever it takes."

"You do realise that by taking the interdict route as your only action you are also taking the chance of losing her to Greece?" James raised his eyebrows again.

Alex looked at Pam. Toni's safety dangled before their eyes, reducing them to animals protecting their young. Dust motes hung in the sun shafting through the venetian blinds.

"We can't kill him," whispered Pam.

"I thought not," said James, adjusting his robe and disturbing the floating patterns. They whirled and whirled, dizzily, like the inside of Pam's head.

"The police are still looking for Stelios. In my opinion he'll play it safe and stay away from Johannesburg for as long as possible, take this time to reconsider, Pam."

HE OPENED THE DOOR. "Fucking hell, this is one unholy fuckup. Give me the Dixons' divorce over this shit any time. I'm glad Beatrice and I never had kids."

14

With each completed connector, Direct Technologies saved a little money, improved its bottom line and kept the doors open. Eric did his share in the evenings, cutting 12 cm lengths of flexible two-inch wide cable, joining plugs, sockets and headers to the ends. Pam and Maggie took up their new tasks, doubling their office hours, sitting side by side each morning at the new assembly-line counter. Pam crimped and soldered the parts. Maggie kept her long nails clear of the tools, but her silver charm bracelet set up a soft rhythm as she tested the completed connectors and packed them in boxes of ten. It was monotonous, repetitive work and Pam's thoughts clambered aboard the worry merry-go-round. Never leaving their posts, her anxious thoughts slid up and down the poles, following each other nose to tail, circling around and around in her mind. Alex, Toni, Kelly, Brian, Stelios, Bezuidenhout, Swanepoel, James, back to Alex. The relentless ride nauseated Pam but she was powerless to stop it.

•   •   •

MAGGIE'S FIST punched the air. "Yippee."

Pam jumped, scattering connector parts across the slasto floor.

"Sorry, Pam, I didn't mean to startle you, but that's ten boxes finished and it's time for a break." Maggie's Welsh lilt was as soft as the clunk of her charms as they crawled on the floor and picked up the pieces. "Same old thoughts, Pam?"

"Yep, and I'm out of my depth, Maggs."

Maggie dusted herself off and finished labelling the boxes, sealing them with packaging tape. "Didn't your meeting with James help?"

Pam gazed out at the garden. Thanks to the summer rain, the bougainvillea's branches had sprouted skyward and were in dire need of trimming. She sighed, not sure whether she should tell Maggie the truth.

"Remember how he drew up our partnership agreement?"

"God yes," laughed Maggie. "He kept referring to 'Eric with a c' and 'let us say this' and 'let us say that' and he was so cynical. He took our trust in each other, seventeen years, mind, and tried to smash it to bits."

Pam turned to her friend. "He warned us of the pitfalls of partnerships and forced us to make some heavy decisions, Maggs."

"It was like a dose of bad medicine."

"But we landed up with a fair and watertight contract," said Pam.

Maggie grinned. "A twenty-eight-page gospel is what he gave

us. I think his words were that Direct Technologies would survive any 'fucking eventuality'. Anyway, what did he say about Toni?"

"He said Stelios is dangerous and he thinks he plans to skip the country and take her with him."

Maggie covered her mouth, her grey eyes wide. "Oh my God. What're you going to do?"

"Serve Stelios with an interdict. Stop him from having anything to do with Toni."

"Do you think that'll work? Stelios is a law unto himself; a hard nut."

"It will stop the Welfare Department taking Toni from us and putting her in reform school."

"Reform school? Are they bloody mad?"

"I read Stelios's court case and they did too. It's their way of protecting her."

"And what keeps Stelios away from her?"

"James said, if Toni was his kid, he'd 'dispose' of Stelios."

"What do you mean, like take him out? Surely he didn't mean it?" Maggie whistled and picked up their empty mugs.

"I think he did."

"Jesus. What did Alex say?"

Pam fiddled with the connector cable and chewed her bottom lip. "Alex hasn't really said anything. He's crept into himself and looks exhausted, but he'll do anything to keep Toni safe."

The clock-radio played Billy Joel's 'Uptown Girl' and Maggie fiddled with her charms.

"God's truth, you must speak to his shrink, Pam. He'll go over the edge if he gets someone killed and you guys can't handle that."

Good advice; but Pam hesitated to approach the psychiatrist. He'd addressed her issue of the medication and Alex's zombiness and, except for telling her about the breathing and relaxation exercises, Alex had volunteered no further information on his Thursday sessions with De Bruin. She didn't feel that she could butt in. She sidestepped Maggie's concern.

"I'm praying that the interdict works," she said.

Fading out the song, the DJ announced the eleven-thirty news.

"Shit." Maggie's grip tightened on the mug handles, long Revlon Red nails cut into her palms as she crossed the stone floor. The rat-a-tat of her four-inch heels stopped as she paused in the doorway, her head cocked to one side, a fan earring dangling in the curve of her slender neck. "I'm going to make us a bit of lunch and coffee," she said. "Brandy, vodka or whiskey with yours, Pam?"

"None, thanks, I'm fetching the kids from school."

"One vodka coffee won't hurt." Maggie turned into the passage, muffling the tattoo of her sling-backs as she hurried, via the bar, to the kitchen.

PAM COULDN'T FACE another boring connector. The smell of popcorn wafted through the house. She moved her chair from the assembly counter, parked it at her desk space and opened the cashbook. She put her mind to recording the cheques and deposits.

Ping.

The microwave hijacked her logic and threw her mind into turmoil. Anxiety stretched her nerves to breaking point. She was giddy and she couldn't think straight. The ringing phone slammed on the brakes.

She picked up the receiver. *Please let it be Bezuidenhout with good news.*

"Direct Technologies, good afternoon."

"*Howzit*, Pam. You owe me six grand." Stelios's greeting riveted her to her seat.

"What the hell are you talking about? Where are you?"

"Here, in Jo'burg and I lent Toni five hundred rand to get home."

Oh God, he's back. Pam struggled to breathe. She heard him pull on a cigarette,

imagined the smoke curling from his lips and nostrils, sifting through the hairs of his dark moustache. Maggie placed a tray on top of the connector boxes, added sugar and poured a tot of vodka into each coffee and handed Pam a mug.

"Who's it?" she whispered.

"Stelios," mouthed Pam.

"Thanks to you, the police arrested me. They confiscated my van and took my crayfish. They fined me five hundred rand and I had to pay another five thousand to reinstate my bail.

I'm broke and I don't have any transport so when can you give me the money?"

Pam choked on her rage. He hadn't asked if Toni was okay, didn't give a damn about her. Oh how she loathed him. She longed to rip out his heart, cut off his balls and shove them down his throat. He was bloody lucky that he was on the other end of a telephone line. It saved his life and his manhood. It transmitted his arrogance. "How about tomorrow?"

"Fuck off." She slammed down the receiver and took a swig of the laced coffee. Maggie and James Griffiths were right. Vodka coffee didn't hurt and fuck was a very expressive word.

15

Pam swirled the coffee, hugging the cup with both hands. "He's back home, here in Jo'burg. He says I owe him money."

"Does he now?" Maggie offered the popcorn, filling her own cheeks with a handful of the salted, buttered puffs.

"Says he lent Toni money to get home, was caught in possession of crayfish, had to find money for a fine and to reinstate his bail. He figures I'm to blame and must cough up."

"He's can't be serious," said Maggie.

"Oh, he is. Shit, Maggs, I'm scared."

Maggie added another slug of vodka to their mugs, picked up an HB pencil, dialled a

telephone number with the rubber end and held the receiver to Pam's ear.

"Here, speak to James. Do whatever he tells you to do."

"But, Maggie, what if he… Hello, James?"

"Pam." Curt, no invitation to dally.

"Stelios phoned."

"When?"

"Now."

"Where from?"

"Jo'burg. He wants...."

"Fuck what he wants. Where's Toni?"

"At school."

"Fetch her. Don't let her out of your sight. Have you told Alex?"

"Not yet."

"Good. Don't phone him until you've collected Toni. I don't want him to panic."

"Not to panic? Listen, James you've just frightened the life out of me."

"But you're not seeing a shrink, he is."

"Who told you that?" asked Pam. Alex needed psychiatric help. He had now accepted the fact and they weren't ashamed of it but they hadn't exactly sung it from the rooftops.

"He did. Let's not alarm him unnecessarily."

Pam detected a smidgen of gentleness in James's clipped words.

"Should I get hold of Inspector Bezuidenhout?"

"No, leave him to me. We'll arrange a visit to Stelios and serve the fucking interdict."

"What if…" But James had rung off. Pam replaced the receiver.

"So?" demanded Maggie.

"He said I must fetch Toni immediately."

"So go." Maggie flapped her hands, clanking charms and flashing red nails.

"Thanks."

"For what?"

"This." Pam drained the remains of her doctored coffee, hugged her friend and left for Toni's school.

STICKING to the speed limit was out of the question and luck deserted her. She swore when a hidden camera flashed the Alfa doing 93 km in a 60km zone. Too bloody bad. She didn't slow down; this was an emergency. She'd pay a dozen speeding-fines if need be. Stelios was back; James had frightened her and confirmed the bad feeling in her gut. If only she hadn't ignored it when she'd first met Stelios, she wouldn't be tearing around Parktown today.

IT WAS the love he had shown his little dog that had fooled her. Bella was a moth-eaten, pavement special; the result of a sexual liaison between a randy miniature Doberman Pinscher and a hot Pomeranian. She had huge bat ears, a jutting-out bottom jaw and a heart-melting, 'poor me' expression in her large black eyes. She was so ugly that she was cute, and Mickey loved playing with her. Stelios had talked to her like a baby and had taken her everywhere on his motorbike. Pam had seen his affection for the scrappy dog and had found herself sticking up for him.

"I don't like this guy, Stelios. He's way too old for Antoinette," Alex had said.

"I know, but he can't help that now, can he?"

"He doesn't have a regular job."

"But he gets by."

"I wonder how." Alex was suspicious. "I don't trust him. He's full of himself. A slimy bugger. What does Toni see in him?"

Pam had shrugged. "He can't be all bad, look how well he treats his dog. Give him a chance before you judge him."

Alex had softened but had laid down some rules: dating only on weekends, and a midnight curfew.

Pam had breathed a sigh of relief when Stelios had played ball, bringing Toni home on time and towing the line.

"See, Alex? They're trustworthy after all."

It had been Doris Jeffrey who had busted them.

EIGHT YEARS AGO, the Jeffreys family had welcomed Alex and Pam to the neighbourhood with tea and chocolate cake. They had become good friends; sharing lift schemes, borrowing the odd cup of whatever ran out in their households from each other and baby-sitting each other's children.

• • •

Doris, standing at the waist-high privet fence, tugging leaves off the branches, had waved Pam over.

"Hi, Doris, are you back to your running?"

"Not yet, I'm still sneezing, but I hope to get back on the road next week, there's a

race coming up."

"Wish I had your energy."

"I don't want to upset you," Doris had said, letting the leaves drop to the grass, "and my girls didn't want me to tell you, but I feel I must. They went clubbing last night and, when they came in, they saw Toni's boyfriend's car parked around the corner. Toni was getting out of it."

The colour had drained from Pam's face. Jodie and Linda were in college, but they'd gone to primary school with Toni and they often linked up at local parties.

"Oh God. What time was that?"

"About two-thirty in the morning. I'm sorry, Pam, but I thought you should know."

"That's it. She's grounded, and his arse is out of here. I don't care how much she shouts and screams and hates us."

Fat lot of good it had done them, thought Pam as she pulled into the school grounds. She was done with fighting. She was ready for war. Stelios's demand for payment and his casual disregard for her daughter's safety had hardened her heart. He treated his dog better than Toni. He'd better take that interdict seriously and stay the hell away from her daughter.

His life depended on it. How do you hire a killer, was it easy? No matter, she was ready kill him herself.

THE PLAYGROUND WAS EMPTY; second break was over and the scholars of the School of Arts were in class. Pam hurried in the direction of the pottery studio. Young musicians occupied the assembly hall and the haunting strains of a classical guitar trailed her steps down the passage, fading away as she walked fast, past the ballet studio with its wall of mirror reflecting graceful bodies balanced on blocked black pumps, their fluid movements directed by a straight-backed, duck-footed teacher and a frustrated pianist. Fear hurried her feet and she half-ran to the row of black bins, marked earthen-ware, stoneware and porcelain, stored next to the long wedging table under the wide roof overhang. She didn't greet the dust-coated student who was cutting wet clay on the canvas-covered surface as she strode towards the open studio door.

"Hi, Mrs. R. You looking for Toni?" he asked.

She knew many of Toni's classmates, but it took her a second to recognise the student with the peroxided white curls, as Valentino, otherwise known by everyone as Aunty Val.

"Yes, I am, but what on earth have you done to your beautiful black hair, Aunty Val?"

His brown-black eyes crinkled. He loved his nickname.

"My boyfriend, Thomas, likes blondes," he said. "But Toni isn't here."

Pam's hand grabbed the table for support. Stelios had beaten her to it. *Where are they?* Valentino patted the clay into shape.

"She's in the sick-room."

"Oh, thank God."

His black eyebrows pulled together. "Pardon, what do you mean?"

"Nothing. Everything." Pam turned to go.

"Okay. Hey, Mrs. Richards, we all freaked when she ran away. I wanted to phone you, but… You know…"

Pam looked at the lovely child. *What a pity he was a queer, if only he and Toni… oh, stop thinking such rubbish.*

"Thanks Aunty Val."

"Sure." Valentino picked up the wet, grey ball and carried it into the studio. "Nice seeing you Mrs. Richards."

PAM RETRACED HER STEPS. Clicking castanets and twirling bright skirts had transformed the refined ballerinas into fiery Spanish dancers. In the hall, the guitars lay in their cases as trombones, trumpets and drums delivered a rousing march. Unfortunately, the talent, imagination and creativity that flowed through the classrooms and studios of the school stopped short of the sickroom. It was decorated in varying degrees of bleak, serviceable brown and faded curtains hung at the narrow window, too skimpy to close. Sunlight wriggled through the gap and fell onto the chocolate tiled floor.

TONI LAY on the only narrow bed with her knees drawn up, her face turned to the wall, a thin blanket pulled up to her ears. Her blazer hung from the back of a straight chair that was also used as a table for a glass of water and a box of tissues. Pam stroked her daughter's pale cheek. She turned and looked at her.

"Hi, Ma. What are you doing here?"

"More to the point, what are you doing here?"

"I've been vomiting."

"Migraine?"

"No, just nauseous."

"Do you feel okay now?"

"So-so, but how'd you know I was here?"

"The school phoned me," Pam lied.

"When? I've only been here for ten minutes," Toni swung her legs off the bed and reached under it for her buckled shoes.

"Actually, I came to see the headmaster." Pam's cheeks felt hot. Lying was not one of her strengths.

Toni kept her eyes on Pam as she pushed her feet into the shoes. "And, did you see him?" she asked.

Pam ran her tongue over her lip. "Well, yes, he told me you were here."

Toni stood up. "He's not at school today; the deputy-head took assembly this morning. Why are you lying to me?"

"Stelios is back."

Toni looked away. Pam reached for her, but she pulled back, leaving Pam's arms empty.

"I'm sorry I lied, but James Griffiths thinks he's planning to skip the country and that he'll take you with him."

Toni bit her lip and stopped it trembling, but her eyes filled with tears. "He won't do that. He dumped me."

"Ah, Toni." Pam hugged her daughter's slim body to hers. She stroked her hair, smoothed it off her face and kissed her forehead, but she could not take away her daughter's pain. It was locked deep inside Toni, stiffening her back, robbing the sparkle from her eyes and leaving them full of sadness. *Dear God, that bastard was going to pay.*

16

M ost days Alex's medication kept the depression and panic at a distance, far enough for him to scrape himself together and shoulder his share of the responsibilities at Powertronics, but they were no match for Pam's phone call. When she'd said, "Stelios is back" his heart had shot into overdrive and, when she had added, "But I've got Toni, she's safe," it had thundered on. His afternoon tranquilizers screamed for back-up ; panic rammed his chemical drawbridge. He shoved his chair away from his desk, wiped his hands and fumbled in his pocket for more pills. Steve looked up. "Anything wrong?"

"Stelios is back." Alex repeated Pam's words.

"Shit." Steve took a long drag on a Marlboro.

Alex threw a pill down his throat and dry-swallowed it. The phone on his desk rang four times before he was calm enough to answer it.

"Alex Richards," he said.

"I understand from Pam that the object of your daughter's affection is back in town."

"Hello James."

"I endeavoured to have the bastard detained, to serve him with the interdict, but I failed. Bezuidenhout and I did not find him at his recorded place of work or home and I consulted the court calendar. It seems that Panos's appeal is scheduled for a week hence. I'm bloody sure the fucker's making a run for it."

Alex couldn't breathe.

"Alex?"

"I'm here." A vice squeezed his chest.

"Did you hear what I said? On my instruction, Pam fetched Toni from school and, as we speak, Bezuidenhout is looking for Panos, but he thinks we've spooked him."

"How do we keep him from getting to Toni and Pam? What can we do?"

"Fuck-all."

Alex's mind went into a tailspin. Pam and Toni were in serious danger.

"Bezuidenhout impressed me," said James. "He's good; but Panos has connections and believe me they are powerful. You want Toni and Pam safe, correct?"

Alex closed his eyes. "Correct, I need to find someone..." he whispered.

"You sure?"

"No, I'm not fucking sure, but I can't let him grab her from Pam and take her to fucking Greece. What the hell else can I do?"

"Nothing."

Click.

"James? James?" He stared at the dead receiver, his every nerve stretched to full alert. He had to get out. He dropped the phone, ran to the old Otis Elevator and wrenched open the expanding grille gate. Steve caught up with him as he stepped inside.

"You okay? You're as white as a sheet."

"I need some air."

"Me too." Steve cupped his hands, lit up and inhaled deeply. They rode the three floors to the roof in silence and clouds of cigarette smoke.

POWERTRONICS USED the flat roof-top for staff socialising. A wrought-iron railing secured the perimeter and a stretched canvas, strung between four upright steel poles, provided protection from the whims of the sky. Steve unlocked the padlocked door fitted into a massive wooden packing crate left by a previous tenant, swung it open and stepped inside. In the corner, a Fuchs fridge stood next to a rubbish bin, a pile of fold-up chairs and a sideboard, salvaged from a junk yard, stored glasses, bottles of whiskey, brandy, gin and boxed wine. Steve pulled two beers from the fridge, but Alex waved his away. "Taking drugs, can't drink," he said. Steve found him a Coke, unzipped the cans and killed his cigarette in a bucket of sand. "Cheers." The partners chinked cans, leaned against the railing gazing out across the jagged Johannesburg skyline and drank in silence.

FINISHING HIS BEER, Steve nudged a cigarette from the packet, lit up and smoked; tapping the ash into the empty beer can. Alex picked out the Carlton Building in the cityscape. In another life he'd taken Pam and the kids there and taught them how to skate at the ice-rink. Pam had fallen about on the ice, clutching the sides and stumbling to the benches to nurse her bruises. Wet, cold and giggling, the children had teased her all the way home, begging for a repeat trip.

"WHAT'S IT ALL ABOUT, STEVE?" asked Alex.

"Fucked if I know, man, just hang in there"

"Bad choice of word - hang."

Steve sucked on the filter. "How's that?"

Alex gripped the railing. "I'm 'disposing' of Stelios."

Steve snorted smoke.

"I could hang for that."

"Holy Shit. Does Pam know about this?"

"She knows that James is doing the lawyer thing and serving Stelios with an interdict, but the police couldn't find the bastard today and James thinks he's skipping the country and taking Toni with him."

"Fucking bloody unbelievable. Are you going to update Pam?"

"No."

From the rooftop, Alex watched the comings and goings of the car-park below. He propped his elbows on the secured railing and dropped his head in his hands. He'd made the decision, he had no option but to get rid of Stelios, but it plagued him. He knew it would secure Toni's safety and keep his family together, but it plunged his soul into turmoil.

"She's better off not knowing," sighed Alex.

"For her own protection?"

Alex nodded. Below, a wide pavement separated the office block from the tarred

parking-lot. *If he jumped, his body would land there, on the cement. Was the drop high enough? Would he die outright?*

STEVE LIT ANOTHER CIGARETTE, smoked and blew rings. They drifted upwards, growing bigger and breaking up; fodder for a polluted sky.

"So, what happens now?" Steve dropped a second filter into the beer can and tossed it into the rubbish bin.

Alex faced Steve. "I don't know. Frankly, I don't want to know."

"Me neither," said Steve.

It hit Alex. Stupid fool. He'd confided in Steve. Did that make him an accomplice?

"Hell, Steve, I'm sorry. I should have kept my big trap shut. This isn't your problem. Hell, man, you've got a divorce to deal with."

"It's okay. Jean's being gentle with me. Just don't tell me any more disposal stuff, and believe me, I won't tell anyone."

ALEX AND STEVE closed the crate's door, clicked the padlock and pocketed the key. Silence amplified the secret. Back in the office they buried it in avoidance, but it turned the pages of Alex's detailed tender, tapped Steve's pencil on the latest circuit diagrams and shot adrenaline bullets through their veins each time the phone rang. At five-thirty Steve rattled his car keys.

"I'm done for the day. You okay to drive home?" he asked.

Alex nodded. "Listen, Steve, I shouldn't have..."

"Sorted," Steve grabbed his briefcase. "See you tomorrow."

Alex stared at his friend's retreating back and wished that he was right, but this shit could never be sorted. Like a gangster in a movie he was going to get Stelios killed. *Fuck. Who did that?* This whole episode with Toni had bludgeoned him, slamming him into an extreme and violent decision. He couldn't tell Pam. He'd put enough crap onto her plate with this bloody depression. It weighted all his problems tenfold. He was seeing De Bruin twice a week, but the sessions weren't producing speedy results. It seemed that he was leaving the doctor's room much as he arrived. He was a man who couldn't share his wife's dreams, laughter, or life, and now he was on the way to being a murderer. She'd be better off without him. The rooftop waited. One jump and he'd set her free.

STEVE STRODE BACK into the room.

"My car won't start," he said. "I think it's a flat battery. Can you give me a jump?"

Again, Steve's words were choice, but this time Alex kept his mouth shut. He parked his car nose to nose with Steve's. They propped up the bonnets and Alex got the jump leads from the sauna in his boot. The hot, plastic-covered handles burnt his hands as he forced the jaws open and clipped them into position." Try it," he shouted.

Steve turned his car's ignition; the engine came to life. Alex disconnected the leads, dropped the hoods and patted Steve's car. "Cheers," he said. Steve signed okay, waved and drove out of the parking-lot. Alex looked up at the rooftop. He'd burn in hell and Pam would curse him forever. He climbed into his car, switched on the air-conditioner, pulled away from the building and slid into peak hour traffic.

Toni didn't speak as they drove away from the Art School. Clipping her seat-belt into position, she looked out of the side passenger window. Her refection in the glass showed not only her closed face, but also the haunting sadness in her eyes. Longing to comfort her, and searching for the right words, Pam discarded sentence after sentence. In truth, her sympathy and true feelings collided, and she was relieved that Stelios had dumped her daughter.

HAVING COLLECTED Toni as instructed by James, Pam was heading back to the office, planning to put in an hour of work before fetching Kelly from school and taking her to the hospital for her monthly injections. James was adamant about policing Toni, but it was gruelling and impractical. *What about tonight? Should she sleep in Toni's room? And tomorrow? Must she keep her out of school, take her to the office? How could they manage this impossible task?* She would phone James again; tell him that Toni and Stelios had broken up. Maybe he would reassess the situation, find it less dangerous, tone down the paranoia and let Toni go to school.

"MA, STOP THE CAR." Toni's hand held her mouth closed, her face was chalk-white. Pam pulled over. Toni flung the door open and heaved into the gutter.

"Sure you didn't eat anything at school?" Pam knelt next to Toni and held her forehead and wiped a tissue over her lips. Toni shook her head. "No. Nothing."

"Okay now?" Toni nodded. Pam laid her back against the seat, closed the door

and climbed back into the car. She glanced at her watch.

"We've got time to get you to the doctor."

"Stop fussing, Ma. It's probably a twenty-four-hour bug."

Pam's tired body and limp brain settled for that. She'd deal with Toni's puking tomorrow if it hadn't stopped by then.

"But can we stop for a flat Coke?"

Pam nodded and, ditching the idea of going back to work, they stopped at the nearest

coffee shop.

A TEASPOON of sugar de-fizzed the Coke and restored faint colour to Toni's cheeks,

but unhappiness hung in her eyes and chatting was not on the menu. The window display of the shop across the way caught Pam's eye. Glamorous negligees draped lithe female dummies and a bordello of delicate bras and panties nestled on the red satin of a raised platform. Nothing lifts a woman's spirits like luxurious underwear and without doubt, Pam and Toni qualified in the low spirits department. She decided they were a worthy challenge for the sensuous slinky goods beckoning in Loretta's Lingerie Shoppe.

A DISCREET TINKLE announced their entry and summoned help.

"Hello, be with you in a moment." From the back of the shop the upper-class vowels rolled off a tongue. "Feel free to browse." Racks and drawers of bras, panties, slips and negligees filled the intimate space between them and the voice. No need for Pam and Toni to look at the 'lift and divide' or 'heavy support' for their under-endowed chests so they examined the bras on the front hangers, small in number and cup size, light, lacy or padded.

EMISSIONS OF REVLON'S PERFUME, 'You're the Fire,' preceded the appearance of the owner of the voice. Pam and Toni were holding the magic inserts of a white Wonder Bra when she found them. She tossed back her long grey locks. "I'm Loretta," she said, as she offered a hand.

Pam wasn't sure whether she was expected to shake or kiss it and offered a smile in return. Clasped behind a creased neck, a long gold chain slid off large breasts and dangled a medallion in mid-air. Screaming pink nail polish clashed wildly with brown age spots and a caftan fell to thick ankles and feet strapped in Jesus sandals. "Mother and daughter?" she asked.

Pam handed over the magic pads and nodded. "My dears you are so lucky. Small bosoms are high fashion right now and I have lots to show you. Come, let me measure you both." Loretta gestured to a large change-room. Pam's mouth went dry. She wanted to flee. She never measured up. She'd been waiting since her twelfth birthday to take delivery of a cleavage, but it had never arrived. Loretta took command.

"Mother first."

Cornered, Pam lifted her arms.

"Top off."

The tape was reversible. Inches on one side, centimetres on the other. It measured Pam above, below and across her boobs. The measurements changed little, and Loretta recorded them on a stylised card. She pulled at Pam's bra straps, walked around her and checked the back fit. Pam waited for the customary "You don't need a bra" or "Why don't you go braless?" comment, but Loretta simply smiled and turned to Toni. "Your turn, sweetie."

Toni shook her head. "I don't like bras. I only wear them to school because of PT."

"Cooper's Droop." The vowels were voluptuous.

"Pardon?"

"Look at your mother's breasts. They are beautiful." Pam loved this woman. She decided, then and there that for the rest of her life she would buy her bras here. Loretta pointed to Pam's chest. "Small, but firm. If she'd left them unsupported, they'd be little hanging marble bags called Coopers Droop, by now."

Toni's graphic mind needed no further encouragement and she lifted her arms.

"Top off."

Toni pulled her shirt over her head. Loretta measured, nodded and went to fetch an armful of bras.

SHE WAS AN EXPERT FITTER. "Slip your arms through here," she said, anchoring the straps on Pam's shoulders. "Bend forward. Let your boobs drop into the cups. I'll fasten the hooks. Scoop them in. That's it. Now, stand up straight." She adjusted the shoulder straps and tutted. "We can do better." Seeking perfection, she fastened and unhooked bra after bra. Many fittings later she stepped back, satisfied. "There," she smiled. "Divine."

THE INCREDIBLE CURVES cupped in the black French lace triangles, were Pam's and the matching bikini panties flattered her fuller bottom. Alex's depression had changed their sex life, taking it from 'anytime Pam was willing' to 'if I really have to', and Pam found herself missing her randy husband, and for the first time since they'd married twenty years ago, she felt undesirable. If her new purchase didn't get Alex going, nothing would.

TONI LOVED the navy and white gingham set.

"Anything else I can help you with?" asked Loretta.

"A camisole for a sixteen-year-old, please."

"Small-breasted, too?"

Pam nodded. Kelly was less than that. Moods and bosoms lifted, mother and daughter left the shop, fetched Kelly and, on the way to the hospital for the injections, Toni did a good imitation of Loretta. Miming the measuring and fitting of their small assets, she had the three of them laughing all the way.

18

The nurses in Ward 385 hated giving Kelly her monthly injections and they drew straws for the lousy job. Kelly sat straight-legged on the hospital bed, pulled up her school skirt and tucked it into the leg elastic of her panties. Unlucky Beth Hall pulled back the plunger, sucked 10ml of Hoechst Beriglobulin into the syringe, clipped on a thick needle and wiped the top of Kelly's leg with an alcohol swab. Toni turned away. She couldn't watch the needle puncture Kelly's thigh, but she held her sister's hand.

"Sorry, pet," said Beth, her thumb knuckle whitening as she forced the plunger. Viscous fluid crept under the surface of the skin, stretching and raising it to breaking point. The sticky liquid oozed from the lump and Pam blotted it with a cotton wool ball.

"One down, one to go," Beth tapped two brown glass phials, scored off the tops, drew up the next 10ml. "Sorry, again. Wish I didn't have to do this to you."

"It's okay. I'm used to it," said Kelly, but Pam heard her sharp intake of breath as the second needle plunged in, forming a matching bump on her other leg as the immune-boosting medication was forced into her body.

"There; finished." Beth patted Kelly's arm and disposed of the used medical supplies. Kelly couldn't bend her legs.

"You know the drill," said Beth. "Thirty minutes before you hop off the bed. I'll organise some tea."

" Don't worry," said Pam, "I'll collect it from the kitchen on my way back from the loo."

"HEY, Toni, you can look at my golf balls now," said Kelly.

"No thanks." Toni swallowed. "Pull down your skirt."

"Can't, it'll get all sticky." Kelly grinned at the distaste on Toni's face. "You're such a big baby. How come you're here?"

"Ma picked me up early from school and she hasn't let me out of her sight."

"Why?"

"Stelios is back in town."

"Shucks. Panic stations."

Toni turned away, but not before Kelly saw the tears. "Hey, you know Mom and Dad, they'll come around. Eventually. Or maybe not, now that they know he deals in drugs."

Toni gulped back the tears. "He broke up with me. Said he's had enough of this family."

"Gee, Toni, I don't know what to say but I hate to see you cry."
Kelly held out her arms. "Come here. Let me give you a hug."

Toni bent down, her long hair brushed the leaking bulges on
Kelly's legs and she jerked back. "Yuck. It's in my hair."

"What's in your hair?" asked Pam, setting the tray of tea
down on the locker.

"That stuff coming out of Kelly's legs." Toni squirmed and
held up the contaminated tresses. "Look. Argh."

Kelly giggled.

"It'll wash off," smiled Pam.

"Ah, Ma, please," Toni flapped. "Do something. I can't
touch it."

"Okay, okay. Bend over the basin."

A FEW SQUIRTS of pink liquid soap and a flush of hot water
sorted out Toni's hair neurosis but not the sadness in her eyes.
She refused the strong hospital tea and Kelly teased her about
her squeamish stomach. Pam stirred her cup and listened
with half an ear, but her mind had latched onto the reflection
of Toni's nipples in Loretta's Lingerie Shoppe. Something was
wrong with them, but she couldn't figure out what.

THE THIRTY-MINUTE WAIT WAS OVER. Kelly's body had absorbed
the Berigobulin and the swellings on her legs were reduced to
half their previous size. After a quick wipe and pat dry of the
bumps, Pam helped her climb off the high bed and took the

tea tray to the sluice-room, leaving Toni to put an arm around her sister's waist and, matching her step to Kelly's slow, stiff-legged one, to guide her out of the ward. As she rinsed the cup, Pam realised what was wrong with Toni's nipples. They were the wrong colour; they should be pink not dark brown.

PAM ARRIVED at the third-floor lifts and pressed the down arrow. Her daughters tried to hurry, but Kelly stumbled and Toni caught her by the elbow. Pam held up her hand. "Don't rush. These hospital lifts take forever," she said, her finger pointing to the closed doors, her mind bringing her own nipples, and their change of colour, to the fore. She gasped; hers had gone from pale rose to brown during her first preg-nancy. *Dear Lord, she's just a school kid. She can't be pregnant. But was she?* The lift doors slid open and Pam stopped them closing while the girls caught up and hobbled in. "We're prac-tising to be old ladies," giggled Kelly.

"You're giving a sterling performance." Pam forced a smile and her daughters stifled giggles as the passengers in the lift shifted and made room for them. Pam pushed 'P2'. No one spoke as the lift descended to the parking-lot leaving Pam at the mercy of her thoughts.

HAD TONI MISSED A PERIOD? Should she ask her? No, not today; find a moment tomorrow. No, don't do that. Take her to the doctor, have her 'twenty-four-hour bug' checked out. Keep quiet and don't tell Alex. She might not be pregnant. Dear God, if she is, then Stelios Panos, drug-dealer and man of no morals, would be the father of their grandchild, and be part of the Richards' family tree.

• • •

T<small>ONI TAPPED HER ARM</small>. "P2," she said. Pam and the girls, no longer giggling but looking tired, exited the lift. Pam was anxious to get them home and cursed the architects who'd built a hospital fit for athletes not patients. Why had they connected the three buildings, each eight storeys high, with miles of marathon passages, and separated the lifts from the pay booth on level P2 with another relay length of concrete flooring?

"W<small>AIT HERE</small>," she said. "I'll bring the car and pick you up." There was nowhere for Kelly to sit. Toni spread her school jersey on the filthy floor, sat on it, propped her back against the wall and tapped her knees. Kelly accepted the bent-legs seat and Pam ran to the kiosk.

S<small>HE WAS FIRST</small> in the queue; it shouldn't take her long to get an exit card. Catching her breath, she passed her ticket through the gap under the glass window.

The faint movement of lips wobbled a set of double chins. "One Rand."

Pam rummaged in her purse and handed over a two-rand note. The woman looked at the money.

"Can't clock you out."

"Excuse me?" said Pam.

"Got no change to give you."

"Then please keep it."

Podgy fingers opened the cash-drawer, rings, welded in puffed-up skin, flashed as the note was placed into the correct slot and patted straight.

"Please hurry," said Pam. "My daughter can't walk properly, and I've left her waiting at the lifts."

Her plea slowed the process. A furtive trace of pleasure flitted across the face behind the glass and the ringed fingers shuffled dog-eared cardboard tokens like a deck of cards, but dealt none, as pig-eyes looked at and through Pam. Obscenities dammed up behind Pam's teeth, but she held them back, remained calm and shut down the game. Boredom shrugged huge shoulders and tossed a token on the counter. Pam grabbed it and exploded.

"You evil, fat bitch."

The woman's lips twitched "fuck you" and she threw a zap sign. Pam returned the sign, threw in another one for good measure, ran for her car, picked up the girls and headed home.

ALEX TOOK A LEFT off the highway, swinging into Main Road and there, three cars up, was Pam's red Alfa. He caught up with her, hooted and waved as he overtook it. The girls waved back. *They were safe and he'd fixed it so they would stay that way*. He caught Pam's eye in his rear-view mirror, she smiled at him and pierced the blackness of his deed. Like sugar syrup poured on hot tipsy tart, his love for her soaked into his being. He had to hang in there, get through this crap and be the husband she deserved.

. . .

HE PARKED and left the garage door open for Pam, but Pam parked as close to the front door as possible for Kelly to get out. Yapping and shaking with pleasure, Mickey scooted out.

"Stay," said Kelly. Mickey braked, but Bella, Stelios's mongrel, wriggled and squirmed out of Brian's arms and dashed to Toni.

"What the hell?" Stelios was never far from his dog. "Is that bastard here?"

"No, Dad. Mrs. Jeffreys came over with Bella when I got home from school. She said that Toni's boyfriend asked her to make sure Toni got the dog."

"When was that?" Alex held his breath.

"About eleven. She'd seen him and another guy sitting in a strange car outside our house and came to see what was going on. He told her that he was waiting for Toni, and in a hurry. Said he had a plane to catch at lunchtime."

Just like James had warned them, Stelios had done a duck, and Alex could let out his breath. He'd phoned James in the middle of the afternoon, long after Stelios had skipped. *Thank God.* Alex relaxed. Toni held Bella close to her chest, tears rolling down her cheeks.

"Oh no. He's gone."

"Believe me, my girl," said Alex, "it's for the best. He's trouble; he'll always be trouble. You, me, all of us, are lucky to be rid of him."

"You don't understand," sobbed Toni. "He broke up with me, but I thought he'd come back. He knows I'm pregnant."

Whack. A blow behind the knees, but Alex didn't sag. Toni was carrying his grandchild and he was going to be a grandfather and a damn good one at that. Timing, just a couple of hours, had saved him from the heinous crime of murder. He was a lucky man.

19

T he officials at Johannesburg International would have detained Stelios Panos, but his flight to Lusaka flew out from Lanseria, the countryside airport near Randburg, where they glanced at his face, checked it against the photo in Carlos Dimitri's passport and waved him aboard the flight. Long glasses of frosted beer killed the two-hour stopover in the humid Zambian transit lounge. He licked the white foam from his moustache, wiped away the residue with the back of his hand and raised his glass in silent thanks to his uncle, George Panos, who, back in Johannesburg, had organised his escape, the tickets to Zambia, those onward to Greece and the two false passports. One was for Toni but he'd broken it off with her. She was sexy and she adored him, but she was heavy going right now; freaking out in the Transkei when she'd found out that she was pregnant, begging him not to put her on the bus alone. *What the hell did she expect?* Her parents were to blame for the abduction warrant. It was their fault she had to go back home before his crayfish job was finished. Besides, after escaping a jail sentence, he wasn't about to get locked up in a marriage. She'd cried when he'd told her it was over, but she understood that her trouble-making parents were the cause and that they should deal with her and her pregnancy. Anyway, without paternity tests he couldn't be sure that the kid was his, but, if it landed up looking like him, Uncle George would make a plan to get it out of South Africa and maybe Toni too.

HE DRAINED the beer and joined the short queue for the Olympic Airways flight to Athens, found his seat in economy class and made eye contact with the airhostess. She stretched over him, stowing hand luggage and he enjoyed the boob show. Picking her up was easy and he had secured a date before tipping back a couple of miniature ouzos and ordering moussaka with red wine for supper. He slipped off his white shoes, swapped them for cabin slippers, slept under the airline's blue and grey blanket and arrived in Athens well-fed, rested and ready to party. The pretty airhostess gave him a lift into the smog-clogged city and her kiss promised him a great evening.

BRIAN AND TONI took over Kelly's share of kitchen duty as she hobbled from the dinner table. "Have fun," she grinned. Brian aimed a wet dishcloth at her head. "Shirker," he said, but she ducked, and it hit Toni smack on the tummy.

"Now, you're in trouble," she laughed as she left the room. "You've just hit Toni's baby."

Brian patted the wet splodge on Toni's skirt. "Sorry, Toni's baby, Uncle Brian won't do it again, I promise."

He returned to the sink full of dirty dishes, washing and

passing them to Toni to dry. "Mmmm, I think Uncle Brian sounds pretty cool," he said.

"You're pleased? You think I should keep the baby?" Toni packed the clean plates into the cupboard.

"For sure. Why?"

"Well, for one thing, I won't be married."

"So?"

"And the baby won't have a dad. We'll be all alone." Toni's eyes glistened.

"Never." Brian's bear hug was soapy. "Not in this family."

A small smile dimpled Toni's cheek.

"That's better," said Brian. "Now let's go and catch TV in Aunty Kelly's room."

ALEX WAS EXHAUSTED. He watched but didn't see the eight o'clock evening news. Panic cruised the edge of his consciousness. The world headlines atrophied and died. He reached out to touch Pam, but she wasn't there. He'd been unaware of her leaving and wondered where she was but had no energy to find out. He pulled his hand over his face and blocked out the newsreader and the events of the day. Depression was outstripped his medication; the abyss waited. Pam had asked him to tell De Bruin that he was battling, but he hadn't. De Bruin would probably increase the dosage of his medication and he hated the side-effects that such a change would bring.

· · ·

"YOU LOOK as tired as Kelly. Do you want hot chocolate?" Pam's question startled him. He hadn't heard her come back. "I'm making some for the kids; they're all in Kelly's room and I think we could do with an early night too."

"Sounds good. What about Toni and her pregnancy? Have you spoken to her?"

"A little. I'll take her to my gynae," said Pam. "Get things sorted."

"No." Alex pulled away. "She's not having an abortion." He might have had to order a hit on Stelios to keep Toni alive and safe, but it had tormented the life out of him. He wasn't a murderer; there would be no abortion.

"Of course, not; it's illegal," said Pam.

"I know that, but England is a short trip away and I'm telling you now that that's not going to happen. *Thank God Stelios had done a runner, because if he hadn't, he'd be dead right now.* Bile rose in Alex's throat, he swallowed it, but the guilt stayed and burnt.

"Relax, Alex. She wants to keep the baby, but she'll need regular check-ups and all that jazz."

"Thank God. I thought you'd…"

"What?" Pam's face was flushed. "Encourage her to get rid of it? You should know me better than that."

Alex held up his hands, willed his legs to stand. "I do and I'm sorry. Don't look at me like that." Fuck, he was going to hurl. His pills weren't helping and his breathing was ragged. "I'm going to bed."

"We need to talk about this."

"I can't."

"It's important, Alex."

"I said I can't. Goodnight."

"Bugger off."

Pam's anger stung, but he walked away, desperate to stay ahead of the encroaching panic.

JASMINE FLOATED through the open bedroom curtains, its sweetness overlying the smell of vomit. Soft, silver light from a full moon fell onto the carpet and across the bed. Fully-clothed, Alex clutched a pillow to his stomach, his six-foot frame curled in the foetal position facing the large window. Hot chocolate splashed into the saucer as Pam plonked it on the bedside table and reached for the lamp switch. Alex stayed her hand and stopped her switching it on, but moon-light picked up the frown between his eyebrows, she caught the tightening of his lips, smelt bile. Concern brushed away the anger from her eyes.

"Have you been sick?" she asked. "Did you tell Doctor De Bruin how you're battling?"

"No."

"I'm going to phone him."

"Don't do that."

"But you're slipping, Alex. I thought the therapy was working. You seemed to be getting your old self back."

Alex turned to face her. "Well, I hate to be the one to tell you, Pam, but I haven't got anything back. It's the pills. They make me sleep; they keep me calm, they plonk my one foot in front of the other and they fooled you. When they wear off I either feel like death or my heart pounds and I'm terrified."

"I'm sure he can do something. He taught you how to breathe and that helped; you haven't had a panic attack for a while."

"Four days. Not even a week. Big deal. So I can breathe, who the hell can't?"

"Please let me phone him."

"Let it go."

"Alex."

"What?"

"You're giving up."

"Is that what you think?" Alex glared at her. "Well, I'm not. I just know he'll increase the meds and I don't want to take more of the fucking stuff. End of story."

"Stop shouting at me."

"Don't nag."

"Oh shut up."

PAM STORMED INTO THE BATHROOM, shoved the plug in the bath, opened the hot tap full blast and shook a vigorous measure of camomile essential oil over the water. The recommended three drops were no match for her anger. Undressing, she caught sight of herself in the wall mirrors. Steam softened her reflection, but not her tight mouth or the fury in her eyes, but Loretta's lingerie got ten out of ten. Hiding and exposing just enough bare flesh, the black lace underwear measured up and looked fantastic. It was capable of seducing a mega-depressed husband, but she ripped it off. There would be no bra and panties parade for Alex tonight. The combination of his depression and stubbornness was impossible to beat and she was too livid to try.

20

P am pleaded with Alex to take De Bruin's advice and stay home for a few days; give himself time to get used to the medication, but he had tender documents to complete and a looming deadline. She didn't understand and he didn't have the energy to discuss it further. Tenders were his responsibility. She glared her disapproval, called him a stubborn idiot, fed him multivitamins that turned his pee bright yellow and held back on a good-bye kiss when he dragged himself and his grey, gaunt face to work.

AT THE OFFICE, Steve ground out butt after cigarette butt in a mass-grave of filters and sneaked glances at his partner when he thought Alex wasn't looking. Contrived casual inquiries on the tender's progress, offers of help and limitless refills of coffee belied his worry and Alex grafted for three, long caffeine-twitching and chemical-coated days before slipping the completed forms into their large, buff, self-addressed envelope. Steve clapped. "You deserve a French Dunk at Marc's. My treat," he said.

"Thanks, but I'll pass." Alex ran a hand over his face. He had no appetite. Not for food or life. Not in a single dramatic moment, but drop, by unnoticed drop, it had leached from his being. He was empty, but not hungry; parched, but not thirsty. Steve played castanets with his car keys. "Come on," he said. "We're talking Marc's French Dunk. Hot, fresh bread, thin beef strips."

"Yeah, I know, and great gravy. But I'm buggered."

"No kidding. You look like shit. I'd better have a word with Pam."

"Forget it. She's fed up with me, wants me to talk to De Bruin and maybe increase the medication."

"And you said?"

Alex shrugged. "Man, I hate the pills."

"Know what I think?" Steve didn't wait for an answer. "I think you should come and play tennis and drink beer with me."

"So you don't agree with her?"

"Hey, man, I'm not going head to head with Pam, but I know what your problem is."

"What?"

"You worry too much."

"And you wouldn't worry if your daughter..."

"I'm talking about other issues besides this stuff with Stelios. You worry about the business, the staff, your wife and kids, my wife and kids, my divorce. Hell, everything. You even worried about De Bruin and computerising that question- naire of his."

"Okay, okay. What's your point?"

"Seriously, Alex, I can't worry and whack a ball at the same time. I'm whacking a shit-load of balls lately. You need to do that too."

"What? Whack a ball?"

Steve grinned. "Something like that. Go fly your model aeroplanes. You used to enter competitions. You taught Brian and Pam's brother to fly."

"Haven't touched a plane in ages and Kevin's in Cape Town. He flies with a club down there."

"And Brian?"

"He's pretty good. He's got a few gliders, and especially loves the slope-soarers."

"When did you last throw a plane off a slope?"

"More than a year ago; when we went with Eric and took Kevin. Brian flies with Eric most Saturdays at the local field."

"Why with Eric? Why not with you?"

Alex shrugged. Guilt slipped into the mire of nothingness that surrounded him. He shifted and looked away. "I've just got no interest," he said.

Steve's frown pulled his brows together. "You need to pull your finger out, man," he said. "Go flying with your kid. Have fun and get rid of all this shrink crap."

Steve's solution was simple and it tempted Alex. No therapy, no pill dosage to bugger around with. Pam wouldn't approve, but, what the heck, he was already in trouble with her.

"I'll give it a try," he heard himself say, as he picked up the buff envelope. "I'll post this on the way home," he said. "You still paying for the French Dunks?"

"Sure."

"Let's go then."

MARC'S WAS ROWDY. The noise and the people scratched Alex's nerves. Forcing cheerfulness, he wrested control, smudged the wet chalk scream from the blackboard of his mind and sank his teeth into the dipped roll, cracking the crisp outside crust, filling his mouth with fillet steak and herb gravy. His brain registered cardboard and no amount of chewing changed the message. His tongue rolled the food from one cheek to the other, but his throat refused to swallow it. Steve downed two beers and cleared his plate, mopping up the last drops of gravy, sucking his fingers and burping in appreciation. He lit a cigarette and raised his glass.

"Cheers. Here's to my soon-to-be-single status and your successful tender."

"Amen," said Alex. He forced his Adam's apple to work and swallowed the food. It was a small victory, but he couldn't face another bite; he declined a Dom Pedro and pushed back his seat, leaving the diner with the important envelope and a luxury doggy-bag for Mickey and Bella.

THERE WAS no air-conditioning in the post-office and the still,

hot air numbed the queue inside. Sloppy, slow and conde-
scending, the counter assistants served the customers,
handing out stamps and change and taking payment for telephone accounts. The panic came without warning. It flipped
Alex's stomach, pulled the beige post office walls together
and pushed the air from his lungs. Sweat beaded his forehead. His heart raced and he searched for an escape, but a
long row of sane people stood between him and the door, and
a vice squeezed his chest. The doctors were wrong. This was a
heart attack. He was going to die. His wet palms wrinkled the
envelope. Shit, he'd ploughed through the paperwork and
produced a bloody good chance for Powertronics to nail the
contract; he had to get it registered. He closed his eyes.
Doctor De Bruin's Afrikaans-infected English filtered through
the red spots behind his eyes.

*Breathe in, Alex. Hold it. Breathe out. Again. Slowly. And again;
slower. Good.*

Alex visualised the leather couch, the comforting room. The
mantra droned on.

"NEXT," Teller three called.

Again. Breathe in.

The tap on Alex's shoulder went unnoticed as his diaphragm
rose and fell under his flat palm.

"Next." The irritated voice demanded action and the queue
shuffled. *And out.*

"Hey, man," a sharp prod in the back. "Stop whispering to
yourself. You're next."

· · ·

EVEN HEART BEATS. Dry hands. Alex turned, victory curling his lips. "Thanks," he said.

The prodder nodded and avoided eye contact and Alex took his growing manic smile to Counter 3 where it bounced off the assistant's dour face.

Too bad.

Alex grinned and grinned and waited for the registration slip.

He'd stopped a panic attack in its tracks. He'd done the impossible and it had gone unnoticed in the trapped post-office heat. He felt good, really good. Shit, man, he *felt*; that in itself was amazing. His wide smile raised a few eyebrows and whispering behind palms, but he didn't care; he wasn't embarrassed. He'd breathed his way out of a panic attack, managed it all on his own, no psychiatrist or doctor in sight. Pocketing the registration slip, he decided to drop in at Central Hobbies and Toys, the perfect place to find his equivalent of Steve's tennis racquet. It was time to whack his way back to life.

BLACK FOAM LINED the slick aluminium case and cradled the latest radio transmitter in the perfectly fitted cut-out. Alex tweaked the sticks. Left, right, up, down; the smooth movements impressed him and he imagined his model glider receiving and reacting to their commands and flying in a clear sky. His old radio was adequate, but Brian shared it, and, if they were going to fly together, they'd need to have two. Alex splurged and added a huge teddy bear for his unborn grandchild to the expensive purchase. Steve's plan wasn't coming in cheap, but this light-hearted moment was priceless. Shit, he'd controlled the panic, something worth celebrating; he was euphoric, keen to spend and the salesman gave him his undivided attention and a hefty slip. Alex signed and loaded his credit card with at least six months' worth of shrink's fees. Steve's game-plan was on.

"Wow." Brian was impressed with the new radio. "Did you get a good price for your old one?"

"No."

"How come? It was still cool."

"And it's yours."

"Gee, thanks, Dad." Brian's blue eyes shone.

"Have you got some money saved?"

Brian nodded.

"Good, you'll need it for servos for the new slope-soarers."

"What new slope-soarers?"

"The ones we're going to build."

"Really?"

Alex nodded. "Really. Fancy that, do you?"

"Hell, yes. How about Eric and Kevin? Let's build them each one as a surprise; Kev promised to come up for one of his vacs," said Brian. "Will Ma be okay about the radio?"

"I'm banking on it. Where is she?"

"At the hairdresser."

. . .

Alex poured over plans with Brian and they selected one to build. He was eager to get started. It was a good feeling; one he hadn't had in ages. He'd blown the budget; replaced De Bruin with a transmitter and embraced Steve's theory. It was time to put the teddy bear on Toni's bed, scratch in the workshop for materials and get started on the slope-soarers. His biggest problem was Pam. He had to convince her that Steve's plan was the way to go. He hated the pills; they made him groggy, his limbs heavy and he'd conquered a panic attack. He could beat this bloody depression. Sure, Pieter had taught him the breathing techniques, but now he had them taped, and buying the radio had given him a lift and he was keen to tackle slope-soarers. Steve's advice was a whole lot more attractive than endless therapy, but Pam was stubborn. Would a defeated panic attack win her over? It had to, he wasn't going back to the shrink and the medication and that was that.

21

"Nothing like a bit of pain to spice things up." Raymond winked at Pam's refection in the salon mirror. "Can't say it turns me on," winced Pam, as the crochet hook hit her scalp and yanked a long strand of hair through one of the tiny holes of the opaque rubber cap. Forced down tight on her head, it sprouted a waterfall of thin locks. Her passport described her hair as 'fair', but, in truth, the waterfall was drab mouse and, draped in the pink, back-to-front protective cape, she resembled a wild, moulting troll. But Raymond was changing that, transforming her dull tresses into a swinging, highlighted, honey-blonde bob.

HE PULLED a brush across the cap and through the mousy waterfall. The rubber muffled the dragging bristles and reminded Pam of being underwater. "Let's try a couple of shades lighter today. Get you spruced up and sexy," he said.

"I'm easy."

"Music to my ears. My place or yours?"

"How about here?"

"Kinky."

Flirting with Raymond was fun and a tad dangerous. They shared a peculiar familiarity. Not a friendship or an acquaintance, but an intimacy born of regular shared snippets of each other's lives. He wasn't gay and he didn't walk or talk funny. With deep dimples, a dark moustache, and Hawaiian shirts, he was a local version of Magnum PI and Pam knew that he was not-quite-yet-divorced from his wife, an events co-ordinator, had two boys and coached soccer.

"With or without the rubber?" He tapped the cap, consulted her colour chart and mixed the potion for today.

"How about with or without a granny?"

He raised his eyebrows and addressed her reflection. "You?"

"Yep."

"My God. You a granny? I don't believe it. I gather Toni's pregnant?"

Pam nodded.

"Is she going to marry that older guy, what's his name – Stelios?"

"He's in Greece."

"When's he coming back?"

"He isn't. He's skipped the country."

"Threatened to kill him, did you?" Raymond teased.

God, he was so close to the truth. Pam shivered and pulled the troll cape close.

"Not quite," she said, but the memory of the insane conversation in James's office, Toni connected to the world of criminals, protecting her, taking care of Stelios, and her temptation to do so, echoed in her mind.

"Didn't get a chance to. I found out that he's a criminal, and now he's on the run and he can't come back here."

"Bloody hell, what's he done?" Raymond applied bleach.

Pam closed her eyes to the faint ammonia fumes coming from the chemicals smeared on the cap on her head and told him about Toni's disappearance, calling in the police, the discovery of Stelios's criminal record. She told Raymond the facts, but kept the fear, rage and hopelessness to herself. Emotions weren't part of the salon sharing experience.

"You're kidding me. A drug-dealer," said Raymond. "What happened then?"

Ding-dong. The salon bell called his attention to the front desk and he smiled and waved in a grey-haired matron.

"Damn, my three o'clock shampoo and set has just arrived. You'll have to fill me in later." He caught the eye of his apprentice. "Put my lady under the lights, please."

BLEACH COOKED under the infrared lamps and Pam's stomach churned under the cape. The timer tinged. Neat rows of curlers covered the head of Raymond's three o'clock appointment and Pam was escorted back to the washbasin. Hot water flowed over the cap and strong hands yanked it off, applied tint, shampoo, conditioner and wrapped her hair in a towel. The three o'clock matron was moved and popped under the dryer and Pam took up the chair in front of Raymond's mirror again.

"So, what next?" Raymond combed and snipped, his hands working fast. "Where did you find Toni?"

"In the Transkei. Stelios shipped her home." Pam recalled the sick relief of seeing her daughter and the shame of scooping all their money together and giving it to the black women who'd watched out for her. Their protection had been priceless.

"When did he skip the country?"

"Just before his appeal for the drug conviction came up. He'd told Toni he'd never go to jail."

"Does he know she's pregnant?"

Pam closed her eyes, unable to block out the image of Toni's brown nipples in Loretta's Lingerie Shoppe. "She says she told him and that he dumped her." Relief. Sadness. Toni loved Stelios. Pam loved Alex; she felt the weight of her daughter's heartbreak, but thanked God that Stelios had run off to Greece and left her behind.

"Bloody hell. What does hubby say?"

"He's okay with the baby but let's just say Stelios is lucky not to be here." Pam shuddered and faced the truth. Alex would have found a hitman and kept Toni safe. Goddamn it, if he hadn't, she would have.

"Is he still having those funny attacks?" asked Raymond. He blow-dried and smoothed her hair and she wished she had a brush that untangled thoughts.

She nodded. "Sometimes."

"And?"

"And what?"

Raymond caught her eye. "What you doing about it?"

"I kind of forced him to see a doctor."

"Good."

"A psychiatrist."

"Oh." Raymond wound her hair too tight around the brush.

"Ouch."

A slight smile for an apology, but Pam smarted.

"Just because he's going to a shrink doesn't mean he's crazy."

Raymond held her eye on the mirror. "Hey, I understand. Just because I'm a hairdresser doesn't mean I'm gay."

Pam had the grace to blush.

"Is the shrink helping?"

"Not yet. I want Alex to step things up, but he won't."

"I can relate to that."

"But, I think he needs to."

"Face it, Pam, a shrink isn't cool. Take my advice and don't go on at hubby unless you want to lose the whole bang shooting match." Raymond held up a hand mirror and showed her the back view of her hair. A curtain of blonde highlights caressed her shoulders. "Like it?"

"It's lovely," she said. Raymond was right, Alex never responded well to nagging, but she wasn't happy with his roller coaster moods and expected speedier progress. She sighed; at least he was seeing De Bruin. She was tired of thinking about it.

"Worth the pain?" Raymond's eye twinkled under an arched brow.

"Yes, well worth it." Pam smiled and swished her hair. He'd given her a male point of view and she decided to take it and let Alex call the shots. For now.

"You look good, but," he touched her jaw, "this is so tight it doesn't do justice to my work. Lighten up. How about having coffee with me?"

"How about I pay and make my next appointment?"

"Brushed off again."

"Can't jeopardise our relationship, my hair needs the best hairdresser in town."

"Flattery, always flattery," said Raymond as they walked to the front desk. "Six weeks from now?" Raymond pencilled in her next appointment.

"Sounds good."

He kissed both her cheeks and held her hands a second too long. "Bye, Pam, take care."

"You too."

Ding-dong. The door swung closed and Pam headed for her car.

SHE REVERSED and her highlighted hair swung across her shoulders. *Bet he'd love the black lace numbers from* Loretta's. The brash, unexpected thought startled her. *What the heck?* She was losing her mind. Move over Alex and make space on the couch. Flirting with Raymond was a game, picked up and left at the salon door, a harmless habitual boost to the ego, but the underwear was for Alex, wasn't it?

22

P am dumped her handbag on the telephone table in the entrance hall and slipped off her high-heeled sandals. Sweat from her hot, bare feet left evaporating prints on the cool tiled floor. She didn't register the early evening TV talk show, the sad ballad on the kitchen radio, or Mickey and Bella barking for supper; she'd tuned into the unexpected. Alex's animated voice. Following it, she found him in the workshop with Brian. He'd left for work that morning as depressed as a sunken *soufflé*, his face gaunt and grey, and Pam wasn't prepared for his wide grin and solid kiss. "Hi. You look good. Your hairdresser's done a good job."

"Thanks," Pam's cheeks flushed as she remembered her lewd thoughts of Raymond and his anticipated reaction to the underwear she'd bought at Loretta's Lingerie Shoppe. Alex's smile lit up his eyes. She'd forgotten how it could do that. Brian beckoned her to the workbench.

"Come and have a look at Dad's new radio," he said. It lay in the aluminium case, tucked into the foam cut-out. "And he's given me his old one and we're going flying together on Saturday," Brian flipped the instruction manual.

"You are?" Pam looked at Alex. Where was the morning's gloom, why was he so bright?

"Yep, we're building slope-soarers like this," he unrolled a blueprint and smoothed out the drawings of a fuselage and wing section. "It's called an Act and we're going to make four, one for Brian and me, and a surprise for Kevin and Eric."

"They'll be thrilled," said Pam.

"Especially Kev. Your baby brother trashed his plane last weekend."

"I'll have to teach that uncle of mine how to fly," grinned Brian. "Oh, Uncle Eric phoned for you, Ma."

"Did he leave a message?" asked Pam.

"No, but he said to get back to him before supper."

"Remember not to tell him about the plane," said Alex. "Why are you staring at me like that?"

"You haven't noticed my hair in ages."

"Really?"

"And when last were you in the workshop?"

"Can't remember, but I'm here now." The smile crinkled his eyes.

"What happened today?" Pam keep her tone light, she didn't want to harp, but she was unable to reconcile this enthusiastic Alex with the whacked-out man who'd kissed the air between them and headed off to Powertronics this morning. "What changed you from sorrowful Sam to happy Harry?"

Alex held up his hands. "I had a panic attack."

"At work?" asked Pam. Raymond had advised her not to 'go on', but his salon wisdom had no place here. "I knew it was coming. I'm phoning Pieter De Bruin."

"Hang on, let me finish," said Alex, but Pam brushed past him and Brian went off to his room.

"I'm not listening; your doctor needs to know what's happening."

Alex caught her arm and turned her to face him. She tried to pull away, but he held firm. "I wasn't at work," he said, "I was in the post office when I had the attack and guess what? I squashed it."

Pam eyes searched his. Had she heard right?

"And what's more, I have witnesses."

"What do you mean, witnesses?" asked Pam. Alex shrugged, a sheepish look on his face. "Well, people stared at me. I jabbered to myself and practised how to breathe the De Bruin way."

"And?" Pam raised an eyebrow.

"It worked." Alex snapped his fingers. "Like that."

"Like that?" Pam imitated his snapping fingers.

"Well not that quickly, but I got it under control, and man, it felt good. And then I bought the radio and felt even better." There it was again, that smile, so familiar, so welcome. It dared her to believe, to hope.

"I'm getting back into flying," said Alex. "I know the radio is expensive, but I figured that sharing one with Brian would be awkward. Here, try the sticks, feel how smooth they are." Pam waved away the invitation. The radio held no interest for her but his unexpected enthusiasm did.

"I'm glad you bought it, really, and I bet Brian is too…"

"But?"

"I still think we should contact the doctor, tell him you had an attack," she said. Alex shook his head.

"Steve thinks…"

"What? What does Steve think?"

"That if I get involved in flying, switch off and relax completely, I'll be okay without him."

"The psychiatrist? Alex, are you serious? I thought you liked him."

"I do, De Bruin's a great guy, but I hate the pills, and you've said yourself that I need to relax."

Pam nodded. "Yes, but…"

"Let me try."

Pam hesitated. He hadn't been this alive or happy for so long; death was absent from his eyes, life filled his voice; her husband was back and she didn't want to spoil it, but his good spirits were so sudden. How could she know if she could trust them?

Model the underwear, the old Alex will love it.

Her brain was up to tricks again but this time it was fingering her husband, not her hairdresser, and the idea, though whacky, had merit. Sexual desire was an excellent barometer of wellbeing and she had imported French lace equipment to test it.

"Okay," she said. "If you feel as good as this tomorrow we'll give it a try. Deal?"

"Deal."

"I'd better return Eric's call. I left work early and there may be a problem."

"What's for supper? I'm starving."

"How about taking the kids and fetching Chinese takeaways?"

"Consider it done."

BRIAN AND KELLY went with Alex, but a late afternoon attack of morning sickness had Toni on her knees in the bathroom, hugging the toilet bowl and Pam heard her retch as she dialled Eric's number. Poor kid, loving Stelios had come at a high price and she was paying daily with loneliness and draining nausea. Joan Martin, Pam's gynaecologist, was taking care of her and had discouraged any form of medication. Instead, she recommended frequent nibbling of dry biscuits and ginger ale. The flushing toilet, declaring nausea victor of the day, distracted Pam and Eric's voice startled her.

"Williams here."

"Oh, hi, Eric."

"Pam?"

"Yes. Sorry, I was miles away. Brian said you phoned. Nothing serious I hope."

"Are you sitting down?" Pam's heart sank. Toni came out of the bathroom, she waved and mouthed 'hello'; the freckles sprinkled on her nose were stark against pale skin and dark shadows circled blue eyes. Pam returned her silent greeting.

"What's the problem, Eric?"

"Who said there was one?"

"You did."

"No, I didn't. I asked if you were sitting down."

"Exactly. Spit it out."

"All our samples are approved. We've got the orders."

"For the gas arrestors?"

"And the capacitors."

Pam gasped and Eric laughed. "I told you not to worry, didn't I? How's that husband of yours?"

"Delighted with himself. He breathed himself out of a panic attack today."

"Great stuff."

"But he wants to stop seeing the doctor."

"And what do you say?

"Well, he's in such a good mood and Steve's convinced him

that getting back into flying is a healthier way to get rid of depression than pills and a shrink."

"I tend to agree with that. Avoid doctors and hate pills myself, but Alex seems to be improving and Steve's not thinking too straight, what with the divorce and all. Are you going along with it?"

"If he's still okay tomorrow."

"Okay then. Anyway, get yourselves to The Prawn Palace. It's time to celebrate."

SLOW MIDWEEK NIGHTS ensured empty tables at most restaurants, but The Prawn Palace wasn't one of them. They didn't take bookings, but excellent service, ambience and the best seafood in Johannesburg drew willing patrons to their thirty-minute queues and hefty prices. Funds were tight at Direct Technologies and Eric, Maggie and Pam worked long hours and scratched the coffers for meagre salaries, but tonight they relaxed and ate a delicious hole in their budget. Executing the large orders for gas arrestors and capacitors would push their three-man company to the limit, but they banned problems from the table and settled the butterflies in their stomachs with celebratory champagne. Excitement bubbled in their voices as they tucked big red serviettes onto their laps and attacked their piled plates. They drizzled lemon butter over snowy white rice, tore off pink shells and dipped sweet prawn flesh into pore-invading garlic and peri-peri sauces. Heaven.

"Here's to Porsches," toasted Eric.

"Mauritius," added Maggie.

"Holiday homes," Pam clinked the raised glasses.

"A Lear Jet," finished Alex and they burst out laughing. Eric caught Pam's eye and gave her a slight nod. Alex was his old self, aiming higher than any of them, as he always had.

THE MEAL WAS wonderful and back home the champagne and the last *Dom Pedro* diminished Pam's inhibitions. Black panties clung to her swaying hips as she stepped it out, Christy Brinkley style, on the bedroom carpet. A little tipsy, she giggled and twirled, slipped a bra strap off one shoulder, pouting and winking at Alex.

"Nice, very nice." He clapped and she blew him a kiss. He crooked his finger, beckoning her to him. Her hair swung on her shoulders as she sauntered over to him. Pulling her to him, he slid a hand into the delicate lace cup, scooping her soft flesh and teasing her nipple. His lips pressed intoxicating kisses on her neck. The test was going well. *He scored a definite A.* He tilted her face, looked into her eyes, unclasped the bra and dropped it on the floor. His hardness excited her. He kissed her, his tongue finding hers. She groaned. *Make that an A+.* Pulling away he slid the panties, inch by skin-tingling inch, down her legs. *A distinction; no need for the shrink and get these damn things off.*

Pam launched them and they parachuted down, covering an assortment of small bottles on Alex's bedside table. Through clear glass and flimsy black lace, two weeks of anti-depressants, tranquillisers and sleeping tablets peeped at the entwined naked bodies. Later, much later, Pam drifted off to sleep. Alex had passed with flying colours and proved he didn't need De Bruin or the meds, but the test was flawed, as she and Steve, whacker of tennis balls, were to find out.

23

S teve had to phone Pam. His hand hovered over the telephone, but he redirected it to the Marlboro packet. He pulled out a cigarette, tapping it on the desk before lighting up, filling his lungs with smoke and exhaling a long, grey-tinged sigh. Across the office, Alex's chair was empty, his working papers, pencils and pens strewn on the floor. Steve smoked slowly, down to the filter tip, lit a second cigarette from the glowing end and searched for the right words to tell Pam that, after only two weeks, his suggested 'cure' for Alex had bombed. His brain came up with 'Hello' and/or 'Hi Pam'. Pathetic, but what excuse did he have for steering Alex away from the shrink's couch to a flying field? Arrogant meddling came to mind. He ground out the butt. Pam was going to kill him.

THE PHONE on Alex's desk phone rang and gave Steve a reprieve. He walked over and lifted the receiver.

"Hi, can you pick up supper on the way home?"

Shit, it was Pam. He cleared his throat and settled for "Hi, Pam", followed by a feeble, "It's Steve; how's Kelly? Alex told me she's on show at the hospital."

"Oh, hello Steve, I guess I dialled your number by mistake. Kelly's fine, but you know her, she hates it when immunologists come here and run tests on her. I'm taking the kids to visit her this afternoon to cheer her up. Can you transfer me to Alex?"

"No," said Steve. "I'm sorry. You were right, you are right, I mean you dialled the right… hell, I shouldn't have…."

"What are you going on about?"

Steve hesitated, "Alex isn't here right now," he said.

"Darn. When's he coming back?"

"Well, er, Pam," Steve swallowed. "I was about to phone you. He's in Riverside Clinic and he needs pyjamas and stuff."

"Riverside Clinic, the psychiatric hospital?" The rising alarm in Pam's voice increased his discomfort and he fumbled in his pocket, but his smokes were on his desk and that was a planet away.

"Why's he there? What happened?"

"He kind of collapsed." Steve stretched as far as he could, his fingers waggling and grasping thin air for the cigarette packet.

"Collapsed? Do you mean fainted?"

Steve gave up on the smokes and dropped into Alex's chair. "Well, no, he sort of hugged himself and said, 'It's not a heart attack, it's not a heart attack'. I sure as hell wasn't convinced because he looked real sick, his skin was grey and sweaty and I wanted to call an ambulance, but he got all agitated, swiped all his stuff off the desk then he, you know, collapsed and just sat there staring at nothing."

"So why didn't you phone me?"

"I did, but Maggie said you'd left early to go to the bank on your way home, so I got hold of De Bruin and he arranged to meet us at Riverside. He seems like a really good guy. He said... Heck, Pam, I know you weren't happy that Alex stopped seeing him and I feel lousy, but..."

"Just tell me what he said."

"That it's dangerous to stop taking the medication suddenly. Shit, I've stuffed up the works and pushed him back into depression. I'm sorry, Pam, I just wanted to help him," Steve paused. *Why had he interfered?* "I thought he was just worried, you know, stressed-out. Something a bit of fun could fix."

He waited. She was going to give him what for and he didn't blame her; he should have minded his own business. Silence. Fuck, she was livid, too angry to speak to him. He shifted his weight; his mouth was dry. "I was dead wrong, Pam."

"So was I." Pam's voice was flat, weary. No trace of anger, no accusation, no absolution. Nothing. She didn't say goodbye, but the dead line pronounced him guilty, a know-it-all-jerk, responsible for Alex's breakdown.

PAM REPLACED THE RECEIVER. *So much for the black underwear test.* Her head throbbed, a 100 kg dumb-bell lay on her chest and a lump lodged in her throat. Her hands shook as she checked the contents of Kelly's pink bag. Clean pajamas, a new puzzle and the schoolbooks she'd asked for. The tissues were missing. *Alex isn't better. Never was. And I knew it, I saw the signs.*

LAST WEEK he'd started tossing and turning again, waking her at three-thirty every morning. She'd headed for the kitchen, made them warm Horlicks, forced a yawn and pulled up the blanket of denial. "Let's get back to sleep," she'd said, squeezing her eyelids together, shutting out his pale face and the truth.

PAM PICKED up Kelly's bag. "Bring some tissues, Toni," she called. "Brian's waiting in the car." *Poor Steve, bet he got a real shock.*

"Here you are," said Toni, "and here's Kelly's favourite photo of Mickey."

Pam tucked them into the bag. "Thanks. Let's go."

IN THE CAR, Pam turned the key half-way and stopped. She had to swing by Riverside and drop off the overnight bag she'd put together for Alex, but the kids didn't know about his collapse and the mental hospital was unknown territory; a place forced upon her, one that disturbed her, one she resented. It was not a good idea to take the children there.

"I think you two should stay home," she said.

"Why?" asked Toni.

"I'll take you to see Kelly tomorrow," said Pam.

"But I've got extra shorthand tomorrow afternoon." Toni pulled a face. Morning sickness had clashed with her matric exams and killed her chances of a University pass. Northern Commercial College had gained a pregnant wannabe fine arts student, but nausea distracted her from dictation, and retching in the ladies' toilets on the second floor kept her from attending sterile secretarial classes. Catching up the missed lectures took care of her spare time.

"We'll go in the evening," said Pam.

"I'll be too tired." Toni rolled her eyes. "Why can't we go now?"

"Come on, Ma." Brian folded his arms across his chest. "She's expecting us. She gets bored in hospital and she's not sick this time."

Argumentative kids were the last straw. "Don't give me any lip. You're staying here and that's that."

Toni nudged Brian, but they didn't move.

"Now, do what I say and get out of the car." Pam's voice shook.

"Ma, what's wrong? We thought Kelly was okay." Toni's concern for her sister doused Pam's anger. The children weren't to blame for Alex being in the mental hospital or her fear and frustration. Lashing out at them was wrong. "Kelly's fine."

"So why can't we visit her?"

Pam smoothed her skirt. What excuse could she give them? None. Lying wasn't her style and besides, Toni was on her way to being a mother herself, and Brian was fourteen going on forty, and he was about to do his usual thing and argue with her forever. They would cope.

"I have to stop in at Riverside Clinic. Dad's there."

"The mental hospital?" Brian's eyes were wide with disbelief. "Why?"

"He had some sort of collapse at work. Steve phoned Doctor de Bruin; apparently he has patients in there."

Brian touched her shoulder. "Don't you want us to come with you?"

Pam patted his hand. "No, Brian, not this time."

"Okay then." Quick to give Riverside Clinic a miss, Brian opened the door. "Give them both my love."

"Mine too," said Toni. "Tell Kelly I'll see her tomorrow and, Ma, take it easy."

As Pam drove away she tightened her grip on the steering-wheel. "Keep calm," she said out loud. "This is not a repeat of last November's nightmare. Yes, Alex and Kelly are both in hospital again, but this time Kelly is fine and I know that Toni's safe at home and that bastard, Stelios, is in Greece." Pam nodded to herself. "Okay, so she's pregnant, but I don't have to go looking for her in Hillbrow." Another nod relaxed her grip and she scanned the road ahead for signs for the clinic. Up there, in white, a large arrow and Riverside Clinic painted on a green background, showed the next turn off to the left. Following the arrow, she drove down a quiet residential street and into the hospital grounds. Alex was inside this foreign place; it intimidated her. She scanned the windows, imagining rows of soulless eyes watching her from padded cells, arms strapped to untrustworthy bodies. The hairs on the back of her neck bristled. She told herself that it was nonsensical fear, garnered in dark cinemas and from watching Hollywood horror movies, but she shuddered, took a deep breath and counted to ten before she walked in.

24

In best-selling psychological thrillers, the serial killers are invisible in their ordinariness. They work at regular jobs, pay bills, shop and mingle with sane folk, when they aren't hacking up and packing body parts. *Like that good-looking guy chatting up the pretty receptionist. He could be luring her to her death with those exotic flowers.* Pam's paranoia crawled all over her. She struggled to collect her common sense as she willed her feet to approach the desk.

"Excuse me, I'm looking for Alex Richards," she said.

"Who's his doctor?" asked the receptionist.

"De Bruin," replied Pam.

The young woman ran a slim finger down a typed list. "Ah, here we are," she smiled, and her even white teeth and dimples turned her pretty face to lovely. *The psycho with the flowers had good taste.*

"Duncan's delivering these anthuriums to your husband's ward, he'll take you there, won't you, Duncan?"

"Sure." Pam's psycho scooped up a vase of blood-red anthuriums. "This way," he said. The receptionist gave her an encouraging smile and flapped her hands in the direction of his back and embroidered jacket and Pam gave her a sheepish smile before following the deliveryman from Exquisite Blooms to Ward D.

SISTER MURRAY SIGNED for the flowers and tucked her pen next to a pair of scissors and thermometer in her breast pocket. "Your husband's sleeping, Mrs. Richards," she said, "but I'll take you to him." Pam's high-heeled sandals resounded in the silent wake of Sister Murray's white leather lace-ups. She followed her into a side ward where Alex lay on a single bed; his fully-clothed body facing the window. Afternoon sunlight filtered through blue curtains, casting bruised shadows on his still form. "He's sedated," said Sister Murray, placing a chair next to the bed. "Sit yourself down, Doctor will be here soon."

"Thank you." Pam sat with her back to the window and faced her husband. *Dear God he looks dreadful.* Bloodless lips, drained, unhealthy grey skin, hollowed cheeks and ringed, closed eyes. Her nails dug into her palms and she hooked her sandals around the legs of the chair, anchoring the overwhelming urge to run back to the time before Toni's drama, to the time when she and Alex were an ordinary couple rearing a regular, happy family, far away from this ward and this frightening place of the mentally ill.

"You look pale," said Sister Murray, "and Duncan mentioned that he thought you were nervous. Can I get you a glass of water?"

Pam shook her head. She was a neurotic mess and Duncan and Sister Murray knew it. How humiliating. "No, thanks," she said. "It's just that I've never been in a... well a..."

"Mental hospital?"

Pam nodded. A smile turned up the corners of the Sister's mouth and she winked at Pam as she left the ward. "No need to be nervous," she chuckled. "You're safe here with me; they keep all the real crazies locked up in the basement."

ALONE IN THE SILENT WARD, Pam fidgeted in her chair and glanced at her watch. *Where is this doctor? I can't sit here forever. I must get to Kelly by three.* Alex stirred, his hand reached for, but missed his face, and fell back onto the bed. His eyelids stretched to open, but drugs glued them shut. He frowned and Pam picked up his hand and squeezed it, but it offered no response. It lay in hers, unaware of her fingers laced in his and the touch of her skin. It took nothing and offered nothing. It saddened Pam; it irritated her too. "For Pete's sake, Alex, wake up. Fight. Come on, pull yourself together."

"YOU ASK FOR THE IMPOSSIBLE." The words, spoken as if read from a script and laced with a guttural Afrikaans accent, caught Pam off guard and she jumped.

"I am Doctor Pieter De Bruin." He extended a large hand, keeping his arm soldier straight. "I apologise for startling you. We have spoken on the telephone. You are Alex's wife." He was well over six foot and Pam stood to greet him. A thickened waistline, faint lines around the eyes and a receding hairline pegged him as in his late thirties.

"Yes, I am," she said, embarrassed at being overheard. "You must think I'm daft talking to Alex when he's like this."

"Daft?"

"It's an English expression meaning, you know." Her index finger drew circles in the air at the side of her head, "Crazy."

"Ahh, yes; my speciality," he said.

"I'm sorry," Pam's cheeks burned. "I don't mean to be derogatory and really, I don't usually talk to Alex like that. I don't know what's come over me."

"I do," he said. "Come, let us talk. We can use the ward next door."

THEY SAT ON THE VISITORS' chairs placed on either side of an unoccupied bed. Precision-tucked corners of folded-down laundered sheets waited for its next patient and eavesdropped on their conversation. De Bruin leaned back in his chair. Behind John Lennon glasses, his brown eyes held hers. "You are angry," he said.

"Pardon?"

"And resentful." A manicured finger stroked his moustache.

"I'm not."

"No?"

Pam shook her head. "No," she repeated. "I just want him to wake up. I want him to be himself." She bit down the turmoil inside. "And I've also got to get to another hospital."

"Kelly, I assume?"

"Yes, I suppose Alex has spoken about her." Pam understood now. Alex had told his De Bruin that he thought she was angry, and now she was stuck with 'the angry wife' label.

"He has, but only a little. He told me that she has a chronic condition and that you have two other teenage children and a grandchild on the way."

"That's right. And did he say that I was angry?"

"No, but these are immense responsibilities, Pam."

"I guess." *If Alex hadn't said anything, what was this man getting at?*

"And you are facing them alone."

She was unprepared for the compassionate hand he placed on her shoulder and tears pricked the back of her eyes. Alex lay next door. His inert body was the price of her stupidity and that dumb underwear test. Why had she dropped her guard, along with the black bits of lace from Loretta's? Because he'd controlled a panic attack? No, it was his laughter. It tangled her common sense and his optimism swept lingering strands of doubt to far corners of her mind. Full of his old self, he had lightened her heart, built model gliders with Brian, bought Mickey Mouse emblazoned T-shirts for Kelly and stretched a canvas for Toni. The picture of a happy man; a healthy man. It was an illusion and she had been stupid enough to believe it.

The tears spilt and Pam dashed them away with the back of her hand. "Okay, Doctor de Bruin, you're right, I'm angry. I could have prevented this."

"Please call me Pieter. But I disagree with you. Do not blame yourself."

"But I do. I was a fool and I thought he was well, that he could stop seeing you, but I should have insisted."

"Therapy must be his choice, not yours."

"He was his old self for a while, then he started waking early again and became withdrawn and I told myself he'd be okay." Pam bit her lip. "I wanted him to be okay."

"You are not responsible for his decision. You have your own to make. Living with a depressed person is difficult. Yes?"

"Sometimes." Where was this heading?

"You must find a way to handle it as you have done with Kelly's illness."

"But this is different. He's my husband, not my child. I can't treat him in the same way."

"Of course, not. You have a difficult challenge and I would advise that you practise compartmentalisation. Keep him in one, Kelly in another, your work in another, and so on. Keep them separate and attend to them one at a time. That way you will survive. I have prescribed different medication for Alex; it will suit him better, but it takes three weeks before it becomes effective."

"Three weeks?"

"Too long?"

Pam nodded.

"And you must learn to be selfish. Carry on with your life and distance yourself from the depression. The compartments I spoke of will help. His depression has trapped you and that is why you are resentful."

"All this is easier said than done."

"I know, but it is important. At the moment, Alex is stable, but I would like to keep him sedated tonight. He can go home tomorrow and he has an appointment to see me next Thursday as usual."

Pam checked her watch. She had wanted to be here when Alex woke up, but Kelly would be waiting.

"Go to Kelly," said De Bruin.

Pam hesitated.

"I will take good care of him. Trust me, I am a doctor," he smiled, and Pam caught the flicker of mischief in his eyes and smiled back.

"A good one I hope," she teased.

"I am not a merely a good one. I am a gifted psychiatrist."

Pam laughed. "And a modest man."

BEFORE LEAVING, Pam checked in on Alex. He was still sleeping. *Alex and his depression are inseparable; one and the same. How the hell do I distance myself from one and not the other?* She finger-raked her hair. The split ends cried out for Raymond's scissors. De Bruin was spot on; she was angry. Angry with herself and angry with Alex, and resentful and trapped and, if she didn't hurry, she'd be late for Kelly.

"I must go," she whispered, kissing Alex's grey cheek. "I love you and I like your shrink, but he's given me a huge challenge and I'm not sure I'm up to it."

25

P am jolted from deep sleep to full alert, adrenaline shooting through her and raising the hairs on the back of her neck. She sifted the night noises of the house. Something was wrong. There was a muffled noise in the entrance hall. Shit.

"Did you hear that, Alex?" she gave him a good shake, but he didn't twitch an eyelash. Her next shake was harder, but she kept her voice low. "Alex, wake up." Zero reaction. Cursing the magic of his sleeping pills and shoving her feet onto the carpet, she grabbed the long, heavy torch and pepper-spray from the bedside table and inched her way down the passage, past the children's bedrooms, and pressed her ear against the closed wooden door at the end. The muffled noise was Toni's voice. "...can't help it, Stelios."

Stelios.

"Please don't fight with me."

Glued to the spot, Pam listened to Toni sniffle and blow her nose. *She's crying. That bastard. I'm going to grab that phone and make him sorry he ever messed with her.*

"I'm sorry. I know your Uncle George told me to use his telephone, but he's too far from the college."

What the hell?

"It's okay, I checked and everyone's asleep."

Wrong, mother dear is wide awake.

"Don't say that Stelios, my folks have been great, and I don't want to hurt them. They're going to be really angry."

Damn right. About what?

"Yes, the nursing home and everything's arranged. I do love you and I'll come with the baby, I promise."

Shock belly-punched Pam and she sagged against the wall. *Toni's going to run away to Greece.* The exposed secret dumped Pam's latest happy family fantasy into the rubbish bin, on top of the shattered illusion of Alex's good health. She gagged on the stench of her self-deception and faced reality. She couldn't trust Toni or Alex's stability; both were erratic at best. She rubbed the goosebumps on her arms and hugged herself. *Losing her daughter and grandchild was unthinkable, but how could she stop it from happening?* Uncle George's inconvenient telephone and Toni's bad checking had forewarned her. It was her one advantage and she turned from the closed door and crept back to bed, but Toni's secret was too heavy to keep and she shook Alex hard, feeling she had to get it out, but he slept on and only the walls heard her anguish as she tossed and turned until day pushed aside the darkness of the night, but not her mind.

"MORNING, PAM." Eric looked up from the Monday newspaper, and, fluttering her nails in greeting while talking on the phone, Maggie set off her charm bracelet and marked the start of a new working week.

"Hi. Good weekend?" asked Pam, taking her seat at the assembly table and steeling herself for boredom. She appreciated the improvement of Direct Technologies' bottom line, but the connectors engaged none of her brain cells and a long day yawned ahead.

"Great," replied Eric. "Is Alex still in hospital?'

"No, both he and Kelly are home again and he went to work this morning."

"So he's okay then?"

Pam waggled her hand. "So-so, he's hanging in there. I suppose we can't ask for more."

"But you'd like to?"

"You bet," she said.

"Me too. I miss my friend." Eric's words touched her and she had to turn away.

SHE THREADED a length of cable through a header and crimped it closed. She packed the completed connector into a box, picked up another piece of cable and repeated the procedure. Maggie updated stock cards, Eric read the business section of the morning paper and Pam's fingers set up a smooth rhythm, but her mind clicked into worry mode. Click. Alex. Click. Riverside Clinic. Click. Pieter De Bruin. Click. Last night's telephone call. *No don't go there. Listen to De Bruin and compartmentalise it.*

ERIC FOLDED THE NEWSPAPER. "Archbishop Desmond Tutu is making life difficult for us," he said. Pam dropped a connector onto the slate floor. "Sorry, I was lost in thought," she said. "You said something about Tutu?"

"He's calling for trade sanctions against South Africa. We could have big problems with our European suppliers. We should meet them, talk to them face to face, people are more inclined to make a plan and help you if they know you personally. Any chance of us managing the cost of a trip, Pam?" Eric took off his glasses and twirled the arms. She shook her head. "You know there isn't," she said. They'd discussed Direct Technologies' funds. They all knew that they were shorter than a hooker's skirt. Forward cover for the foreign currency to meet the last big orders had committed them to the hilt. Eric was fully aware that the cupboard was empty with not a crumb in sight. *Why wouldn't he accept it and stop asking her stupid questions?*

"Pity. We really should go, you know. It's important; if we have trouble delivering the capacitors we're sunk."

Pam's head spun. Eric wasn't exaggerating, but her mind had run non-stop last night, turning Toni's secret over and over and she was on edge, and now the head of the Anglican Church was piling on extra pressure and threatening the survival of their little company.

"We could see our arses," Eric's whining threw her switch.

"There's no bloody money and you know it. And that's that," she said.

His mouth dropped open and Maggie looked up from the stock cards. Pam put her hands over her face, regretting and ashamed of her sharp tongue. Maggie pushed back her chair. "Stop nagging, Eric," she said. "Give me a chance to call our suppliers before your pessimism has us all in the gutter, but first, let's have coffee. Can I get a rusk or something with yours, Pam?"

Pam peered out from her fingers. "A slug of patience and humour," she said.

Maggie gave her a smile that said she understood and went to the kitchen. Pam pushed back her hair and caught Eric's eye. "I'm sorry Eric. I had a bad night and I took it out on you."

"Alex?" Eric leaned forward, arms folded on his desk. Pam walked over to the picture window and stared at the pool and the Kreepy Krauley chugging on its endless journey, swallowing debris and pulsating in the sparkling water.

"Yes and no. I overheard Toni talking to Stelios late last night. I thought things were over between them; that he was out of our lives. Naive of me, hey? Well, it seems that I was greatly mistaken and she's planning to run off to Greece when the baby comes."

"Crikey. What did Alex say?"

"Absolutely nothing. Thanks to De Bruin's excellent sleeping pills, he slept like the dead and I don't want Toni to know that I know so I didn't tell him about it this morning because I know he'll take it up with her, but frankly, I don't know what to do."

"Don't stop her. Let her go."

"What?" Pam stared at Eric. Had he lost his mind? "Stelios will break her heart."

"It's her heart and her life."

"But what about the drugs? He's a dealer, for God's sake. You know she'll be in danger. She's only seventeen. How can you say it's okay to let her run off and live with a criminal? And what about the baby? Stelios is not father material, now is he? Wouldn't you stop her if she was your daughter?"

Pam held his eye and Eric was the first to look away.

"Morning," said Steve, as Alex hung his jacket over the back of the chair. "I didn't think you'd be in today."

"I escaped from the loony-bin yesterday." Alex tried to make light of his embarrassment. "Thanks for getting me there."

"Hell, I was only too pleased to hand you over; besides, it's the least I could do. De Bruin kind of said the attack was because you'd stopped taking the pills and guess whose stupid fault that was?" Steve's grin took care of the awkwardness. "Anyway, coffee's made. Help yourself."

"Thanks. Want a refill?" asked Alex.

Steve shook his head and held up his mug, the inevitable cigarette locked between his fingers. "Second one already."

The rich aroma of Steve's excellent percolated coffee filled the small staff kitchen. Alex reached for his sludge-green mug. It was a gift from Toni and her first attempt at throwing on a pottery wheel. Starting out as a cylindrical vase for Pam's long-stemmed roses, it had suffered and almost collapsed under the uneven pressure of Toni's fingers, and saved by her teacher who had cut it down and shown Toni how to smooth the lip, pull and attach a handle, and *voila,* it had survived as his coffee mug.

ALEX FILLED it and took it back to the office. A plastic packet sat in the middle of his desk. "What's this?" he asked.

"Your stuff," said Steve. He looked away and took a pull on his cigarette.

Alex emptied the contents. His stationery fell out, tumbling across the smooth wooden surface. "Shit." He remembered breaking out into a cold sweat, his heart thudding faster and faster as De Bruin's breathing exercises failed and the panic that had smothered him before he'd swept everything off his desk and onto the floor.

"Who picked it up?" he asked.

"*Moi,*" Steve swirled his coffee.

Alex cleared his throat. "I owe you one, man. I lost it there."

"Forget it. De Bruin seems like a good guy and it looks like he sorted you out."

Alex nodded. Chemicals swam in his blood, his head was fuzzy and butterfly wings fluttered in his stomach, but the abyss was at arm's length. He was sorted, for now, for this moment.

"Good. We've got work to do." Steve rubbed his hands together. "We landed that tender. You did good, partner."

Alex fingered the small bottle in his shirt pocket and the pills rattled against the glass. He would cope, from one dose to the next, he would cope.

"Back on meds?" asked Steve.

"Yes."

Steve wagged his cigarette at Alex. "Take my advice," he said, "stick to them this time."

26

L ike a mosquito, Toni's one-sided telephone conversation buzzed in and out of Pam's thoughts as she assembled connectors and wrote up the company's books. *I can't do this compartmentalising crap.* Working through her index book, Maggie phoned the suppliers and Eric, ignoring her instructions to piss off, drummed his fingers on his desk, hovered in the office, frowning and chewing on his glasses, and getting up their noses like the smell of a wet dog.

AT FOUR-THIRTY MAGGIE capped her pen. "You can relax, Eric. Most of our suppliers say they'll continue to do business with us for as long as they can."

"How long's that?" asked Eric.

Maggie sighed and rubbed her neck. "I don't have a crystal ball, Eric, but our immediate orders are covered."

"Do you think they'll trade via the back door if need be?"

Maggie shot him an exasperated look. "How the hell should I know? Anyway, for now, we don't need a back door. I told you; we're okay for the moment."

Eric shook his head. "It's not good enough," he said, "we should meet with them."

Pam bit her tongue and looked heavenwards. She understood his concern, but he wasn't listening to Maggie, and Tutu's call for sanctions was just that, a call, not yet taken up by the world against their Apartheid country. Maggie shook her head.

"It's good enough for today," she said. "I'm done in and you're behaving like a child nagging for a toy in the supermarket when you've been told there's no money. For God's sake stop it and do something useful like pouring us all a drink."

Eric looked from one irritated face to the other, pushed his glasses onto his nose and stuck his hands up in surrender. "Fine. Okay. Gin and tonic for you, Pam?"

She scraped her hair back from her face, wound it in a red elastic band and secured it at the base of her neck. The style, or lack thereof, did nothing to lift her spirits and she felt like a dowdy frump. "Not if I can twist Raymond's arm this late in the afternoon. I must get my hair done," she said, as she dialled the hairdresser's number.

THE SALON'S tape-recorder was set on low, background volume and Chris de Burg serenaded his "Lady in Red" and Raymond's firm fingers massaged her head. Overlapping circles, deliberate and slow at the base of her neck, small and tight on her temples and forehead, smoothed the rag-tag thoughts of Toni and Alex and worked conditioner into her wet hair. A smile played at the corners of her mouth, her head tilted backwards into the basin. "But you're not as good as Mavis," she said.

He switched off the hot water feed. Jets of cold stung her scalp and paid her back for the tease.

"Not fair," she gasped.

"All's fair in my salon, especially when I have no staff and it's after five," he laughed, wrapping a dry towel around her head and leading her to the mirror.

"Sorry I phoned so late," said Pam, "and thanks for staying open for me."

"For you, darling, anything," Raymond smiled at her. "Besides, you sounded desperate." He scooted into position behind her, removed the towel and held up a wet strand. "Will you look at these split ends?" he scolded, catching her eye in the mirror. "All thanks to the elastic bands I see you've taken to wearing."

"Like you said, I was desperate."

"And elastic bands are the answer?" Raymond asked.

"No, you are."

"I've been telling you that for years." Raymond grinned.

"For my hair, Raymond," laughed Pam. "You're the answer for my hair."

"No question," said Raymond, brandishing a wide-toothed comb and tilting her head down. Her hair squeaked as he parted and pinned it into sections. "But my talents are not restricted to hair," he said.

"I'm sure they aren't." Pam's voice was light, but she remembered her last appointment and the crazy thoughts she'd had on the way home about him and the black underwear that she'd purchased at Loretta's Lingerie Shoppe and she was glad he couldn't see her face and embarrassed blush.

"Now, let me fix this damage," he said.

CUT, wet hair fell to the floor and piled up between her high-heeled sandals and his black boots. Without restraint, Raymond sang along with Chris, his tuneless voice lagging a full beat behind the singer's. His hands guided her head back up. "Can't sing," he said, flashing his Tom Selleck dimples at her reflection.

"You don't say," Pam grinned back.

"Short enough?" he asked. She nodded and he swopped the scissors for a round brush and switched on the hair-dryer.

"How's the family?" she asked.

"Signed the divorce papers, got shared custody of the kids."

"You okay?"

"With the divorce? Yes, but I wish we'd worked out the marriage for the kids."

"How are they taking it?"

"They seem okay. They've got used to us leading separate lives over the last few years now. It's not like we did it this overnight, but still…And your family?"

"Fine," said Pam, but the lie hooked her back into last night. *Toni's going to run away again.*

She studied herself in the mirror. A muscle twitched at the corner of her mouth, but it was the only sign of the turmoil broiling inside.

"What? No drama?" teased Raymond. "Hubby's behaving?"

"Hubby? Oh, yes, I mean no." Alex was the lesser story of her day, but she shivered as she remembered the narrow hospital bed and his sedated body curled in the foetal position. "He collapsed at work and had to be taken to hospital."

"I knew it. Drama. Is he still in there?"

"In hospital? No, he was only there a couple of days, but he's back to seeing his psychiatrist again."

"Good, that's what you want, isn't it?" he sprayed his work into place.

She chewed her lip.

Raymond whipped off the shoulder cape and brushed stray cuttings from her neck. "Well, it is, isn't it?" he asked her reflection.

Her throat was tight. She thought it was, but with De Bruin and therapy came tranquillisers, anti-depressants and sleeping pills and no midnight hero for the likes of last night. "His pills get to me, but yes, it's what I want." Her answer didn't cover all the bases, but the salon was not the place for deep emotion.

"That's good then." Raymond held a mirror behind her head showing off his work. The perfect cut hung in a smooth line to her shoulders. "Like it?" he asked.

"It's lovely, thanks," she said and flashed a smile. She picked up her bag, pulled out her diary and dragged her thoughts to the present, anchoring them in the moment. "Six weeks from now gets us to…"

"Hey, not so fast, you haven't had a cup of coffee and it's part of the hair experience here."

"But Mavis has gone already."

"There's a café next door. They make better coffee than Mavis."

Alex slept through everything. Everything. Damn him.

"Okay," she heard herself say. "But we'll have to be quick. I've got to pick up Brian."

Raymond's grin was wicked. "Right, madam, one quickie coming up."

27

Raymond was right; the café's coffee was better than Mavis's but not good enough to linger over. It was his charm that kept her at the table. His wicked humour evicted her troubled thoughts like errant tenants, dumping them on the pavement outside the café, and she found herself laughing at his jokes.

"You do a very good impersonation of the Pink Panther. You should be on the stage."

"And you should have coffee with me more often." He slid his hand across the table. It stopped a millimetre from hers. Traces of tint lodged beneath his short nails. He held her gaze and touched her fingertips. "Do you like theatre? I'd love to take you."

PAM'S HEART thudded in her chest. This was serious flirting, not the 'teasing in the salon along with your hairdo' variety. She held her breath. He picked up her hand and brushed it with his lips. It was the whisper of a kiss, but it seared her skin and turbo-charged her hormones. They raced out of control, trampled logic, by-passed intelligence, scrambled her brain cells and registered the flecks in his eyes. Palest gold on brown velvet. She felt dizzy as he tilted up her chin and bent his head towards her. His eyes closed, his lashes were long and straight, his warm breath mingled with hers. He was gorgeous and he was going to kiss her. What would it taste like? Should she kiss him back?

This was dangerous

She was married.

His lips parted slightly. He leaned in closer.

He smelt like Alex.

ONE WHIFF of Old Spice Aftershave swept aside her hormone storm and Pam, wife of twenty years, mother of three teenagers, two girls and a boy called Brian, jumped up and knocked over her chair. Raymond's eyes flew open, his kiss airborne.

"Oh my God." Pam picked up the chair, grabbed her bag and scratched for her car keys. Raymond stared at her. "What's up?" he asked.

"It's Brian. I've forgotten all about him. I must go. I'm sorry, Raymond."

SHE RAN from the coffee shop. It was dusk and the light was bad enough for her to switch on the car's headlights. She should be home by now. How could she forget her child? What had come over her? Why had she accepted the coffee 'date'?

DAMN, Pieter De Bruin was right. She was angry, very angry, and her anger had flared up in the salon. Had she gone for coffee to get her own back on Alex? For his bloody depressed comatosed body not investigating the strange noise last night? For her thudding heart? For hearing Toni's secret plans? If she was looking for revenge, she was being irrational. After all, she'd begged him to go back to the psychiatrist, knowing full well that the medication was part of De Bruin's package. She had no one but herself to blame for Alex doing sweet bugger-all, but she had wanted to shake him so hard that his teeth would fall out.

"DISTANCE YOURSELF," De Bruin had told her at the Riverside Clinic and she'd looked at Alex's exhausted, sedated body and thought that would be impossible, but here she was, a few weeks into Alex's treatment, so distanced from him that she'd put her lips out for a smooch, and, if Raymond hadn't splashed Old Spice onto his shaved face that morning and the kiss had connected would her revenge have stopped there? And when would she have remembered Brian? God, she was a dreadful wife and mother.

THE ALFA'S headlights captured Brian and his doubles-partner, Gary, waiting outside the school gates. They lounged against the fence and chatted, Brian bouncing his tennis racket against knobbly knees and Gary's takkies kicking the pavement, loosening and spraying showers of tiny stones. Pam hooted and swung the Alfa into a parking space. Flipping open the boot, Brian dumped his gear inside and climbed into the passenger seat.

"Hi. Can you give Gary a lift?" he asked.

"Sure," said Pam, glad that he hadn't asked why she was late.

"Thanks, Mrs. Richards," said Gary, folding a replica of Brian's gangly body into the back-seat.

"How did the match go?" she asked

"They took the first set, but then Gary served like a pro and we got a love game and they died fast, hey Gary?"

Gary grinned at Brian. "*Ja*, we hammered them. Two sets to one."

"I'm starving," said Brian. He opened the cubbyhole. "Ahh, munchies. A Lunch Bar and a Kit Kat and a bon-bon. What'd you want?" he asked Gary.

"Lunch Bar."

Brian handed it over, peeled the red wrapper off a Kit Kat, ate it, two fingers at a time and gave the bon-bon to Pam. She popped the chocolate-coated toffee into her mouth, chewed and listened to them gloating about the match, but their pride could not wipe out her embarrassment or guilt. She couldn't go back to the salon and face Raymond, not after running out on their coffee 'date'. And what was she going to tell Alex if he asked why she was so late? That Raymond had almost kissed her? That she'd almost kissed him back? That she'd forgotten Brian? That his bloody depression and sleeping pills were to blame?

SHE PULLED into the dark garage and breathed a sigh of relief. Alex wasn't home. His empty parking space covered her delinquent tracks, the flirting and near kiss. Brian climbed out, pulled his tog bag from the car and hoisted it on his shoulders.

"Where's Dad? Do you think he's okay?" he asked. Concern pulled his brows together and Pam's relief evaporated.

Has Alex collapsed? Had Steve tried to contact her? Was De Bruin attending to him at the Riverside Clinic?

Pam had no idea where Alex was, but she put on a reassuring smile.

"He's fine," she said. Brian shouldn't be worried about the whereabouts of his father, but the chaotic midnight trips to hospital emergency rooms and Alex's stay at Riverside were shared family memories, slotted into their minds and as indelible as birthday celebrations and Christmas holidays at the coast.

"HE's PROBABLY WORKING LATE as usual," she said, and Brian nodded and headed towards the kitchen. She'd smudged his anxiety, but hers latched onto the package insert of Alex's new medication. Drowsiness was one of the listed side-effects.

He's had an accident. He's fallen asleep at the wheel. His car's a write-off and he's lying somewhere, unconscious. He's dead... Will you SHUT UP?

She clambered from the car, catching a high heel in the hem of her skirt. Hopping on one leg she freed her shoe, whipped off the other one and hurried barefoot after Brian.

BARKING A WELCOME, Mickey and Bella scooted around their legs, pawing the air and begging for tickles. Pam's hair fell forward as she bent down and petted them, and she took the moment to compose her face and hide her worry from the children. Toni waved a vegetable knife in greeting, tipped tomatoes and thin slices of cucumber from a chopping board into a bowl of torn lettuce. No sign of secret calls to Stelios or plans to go to Greece showed in her smile.

"Hi, food's nearly ready," said Kelly. Under her watchful eye, lasagne bubbled and browned under the grill. It seemed that supper, unlike Pam, was under control.

"Hi, girls," she said, draining the urgency from her voice and dropping her sandals under the counter. "Any messages?"

"Two. Dad phoned hours ago, and said he's going to be late," replied Toni "They got the tender and they're all going for drinks."

Alex was partying, not dying.

Pam hugged her tight, "Thanks for getting supper ready."

"Careful, Ma, you're squashing the baby," grinned Toni. "Anyway, I only made the salad."

"Grab some glasses, Brian. Let's celebrate Dad's tender," Pam felt lightheaded. Alex was safe. "Pour a little wine for us, but just a cooldrink for you, Toni. How's my grandchild today?"

"Behaving. I've only been sick three times since this morning. I can't wait to feel it kicking."

"Me neither," said Kelly, placing the steaming pasta on the counter. "Grub's up, but please let's stop calling your baby 'It'."

Brian heaped his plate. "So, what do you think we should call it?"

"Dinks," said Toni, her eyes soft, "when I talk to it, I call it Dinks."

And you're taking Dinks to Greece. But not yet. Pam raised her glass, "To Dad landing the tender and little Dinks," she said.

"The tender and Dinks." They chinked glasses.

"What was the other message?" she asked, loading salad onto her fork and popping it into her mouth.

"Your hairdresser phoned," said Toni.

Pam concentrated hard. If Toni could hide secrets behind a normal face so could she. She didn't choke, but her cheeks warmed a little and she tossed back a swig of Nederberg Stein.

"Apparently, you left in a hurry and didn't make another appointment, so he's booked your normal six-weekly, whatever that is."

It was Raymond's way of telling her that he'd wiped today's 'date' from the slate, the *status quo* had been restored and she could return to the salon without embarrassment.

"That's great," said Pam.

"But he did say that if you want to see him before, just phone."

He'd left the gate open to play.

"I won't," she said, closing it. Alex was back in therapy, giving her what support he could, doing his best. It wasn't enough, but she couldn't ask for, or expect, any more. Fun dangled beyond the gate, but she dared not step through it.

28

Celebration of the tender was well underway and rolling on its own energy. Steve eyed the pyramid of empty beer cans, held his with both hands and placed it on top. Lingering fingertips balanced it and he stepped back. The stack wobbled and the staff of Powertronics took bets on it falling. Odds were that it would, but it remained standing and Steve gave a victory bow and unzipped another Castle. Holding his breath, young Andrew from the test bay added his can to the unstable structure, but it crashed to the floor and proclaimed Steve the champion beer-can balancer. Alex was sober. Abandoning the flat remains of his nursed beer on the table he moved to the fringe of the party. Steve's tricks and excellent hosting skills would cover up his early departure. A full day at work and a few party hours were pushing De Bruin's new prescription to the limit. It needed tuning and claustrophobia picked at the edges of the chemical Band Aid. He was coming unstuck and it would be hours before the party ended. Many hangovers would head straight to the office coffee pot tomorrow. He was the first to leave and not a minute too soon. The black abyss clawed at him, dragging him to that helpless pit and he forced his legs to run to his car.

It was ten-thirty. Pam would be up when he arrived home, but his unfocused mind forced him to travel in the slow lane of the double-carriageway. His grip on the steering-wheel was tight. Congested city blocks gave way to scattered suburbia. Confident drivers passed him on the right and he swore in frustration as their lights vanished into the distance. He used to have that confidence, that power, that energy and excitement. He'd turned into a bloody geriatric. No wonder Pam looked at him as though he was a stranger and wore that smile, the over-bright one that she pinned on her face when Kelly was gravely ill. She was dead scared, out of her depth, pretending like hell that everything was fine, but how long could she put in the effort? How much time did he have to kick this depression in the butt and get his life back? Not much. She was patient, but she must be pissed off, hell, he was pissed off; these sessions with De Bruin better work and fast, before that fragile smile of hers cracked and she gave up on him.

Nearly home, only five kilometres to go, but the traffic merged into single file and blue lights flashed up ahead. He worked the brakes, joined the snake of red tail-lights and checked the time. Damn. It was later than he thought. He poked the car's nose out of the queue and pulled it back. A bloody road-block. He was stuck. Responding to heightening political unrest across the country, the police searched for illegal weapons and arrested people, mostly blacks, who did not carry valid identity documents. Why tonight? Torch beams waved random vehicles to the side of the road. The traffic crept forward; stopped; crept forward. Alex's hands started to sweat and he wiped them, one at a time, on his trousers, filled his lungs with air and opened the window. He exhaled slowly, but his heart raced and that damn void of nothingness pressed in.

"Your ID please, sir."

A flashlight waved him over. Panic ripped off the plaster. Hell no, not now. He couldn't breathe. Home, Pam and pills were ten minutes away. He pulled his blue ID book from his wallet and handed it over. The photo was checked against his face, the pages thumbed, his driver's licence found.

"Do you have any weapons? Guns, knives?" asked the cop.

Alex shook his head. "No."

"Step out and open the boot."

Alex's legs refused to move, sweat stuck to his forehead and his mouth was dry. "I can't," he rasped.

The policeman's heeled boot dragged a straight line in the dirt. "*Kom*. Walk here, sir," he said.

"I'm not drunk, believe me," said Alex, his heart thudding. "I wish I was."

The cop stuck his head through the window, his face a few inches from Alex's. His nostrils quivered. "Breathe out hard," he ordered.

Breathe - the magic word.

There was a paper packet, an emergency panic-killer as De Bruin called it, in the cubbyhole. He'd get it out, shove his nose and mouth in it as his shrink had taught him and breathe in and out for a couple of minutes. It would take the edge off, reverse the rush of fear. He turned away from the cop, leaned across the passenger seat and sprang the latch.

"STOP."

Alex swivelled back and stared down the barrel of a gun. Adrenaline shot his hands up to the roof. "DON'T SHOOT," he yelled.

"OUT."

"I can't breathe." Alex gripped the door for support and obeyed. The cop kept him in the gun's sight and slid into Alex's warm seat. He swiped his hand through the cubby-hole, spewing the brown packet, a tube of humbugs, a Dire Straits tape and the car's service record book onto the floor. He climbed out, leaving the mess where it lay.

"I thought you were reaching for one of these," he tapped his gun.

"I told you, I don't have one," said Alex.

"*Ja*, well…" The cop shrugged, handed back the ID book, strode over to the verge. Alex's body slumped back into the car. He picked up the brown paper packet, breathed into it until his heartbeat slowed, then crumpled it and flung it at the windscreen. "Bastard," he shouted out of the window, but the cop didn't hear him as the next pulled-over car churned up gravel and a cloud of dust.

IT WAS past eleven when he hurried into the house, shushing the dogs and shooing them back to the girls' bedrooms, but soft light escaped from the open main bedroom door and lit his way up the passage. Pam was propped up against a continental pillow, a book resting in her lap. "Hi," she said. "How was the party?

"Steve was on top form," he said, as he sat down on the side of the bed and slid off his shoes. He was more than ready for a bath, pills and bed. "I like your hair-cut," he said.

"Thanks. And you? Were you also on good form?" She scanned his face. It was a habit she'd developed since the Riverside Clinic episode and was one he didn't like too much. He kissed her cheek and smelled toothpaste.

"I got stuck in a road-block." He pulled off is socks. "It was a bit like being stuck in a Black Adder skit; totally absurd, you'll laugh when I tell you about it."

Pam gave a little stretch and closed her book. He'd passed her inspection and he loosened his tie.

"I was pulled over. I wasn't feeling too good and I remembered the packet in the cubbyhole and tried to get it, but this paranoid cop thought I was going for a gun. Next thing I know he's got his gun stuck in my face. I nearly shat myself. Imagine getting shot for a paper packet," he gave her a grin, unbuttoned his shirt and walked to the bathroom.

GUSHING water and wool carpeting hid Pam's footsteps. She stood in the doorway, arms folded. "What was wrong?" she asked.

"Huh?" He dumped his clothes on the side of the laundry basket and shook a generous helping of blue Radox salts into the hot water.

"What was wrong? You said you weren't feeling too good," she said, her eyes wide with worry. He should never have told her that part. It was the point at which she'd stopped listening to his story. She'd missed the funny side; he made a note to keep his big mouth shut in future. He turned back to the bath. "It was nothing," he said. "Go back to bed."

But Pam put down the loo seat, pulled up her feet and hugged her knees. "If it was nothing why did you need the packet?" she asked. His muscles across his shoulders tensed. He sank into the water and closed his eyes, shutting out her concern and pinched face. He didn't want to talk about the clawing fear, the exploding panic and the rest of the nightmare. He was beyond rehashing it. "What was wrong, Alex? Why won't you tell me?"

His jaw twitched. He should have stayed at the bloody party.

"Alex?"

She wasn't going to stop, was she? He sat bolt upright, water streaming from his back. "There's nothing to tell, okay?"

"No, it's not okay, I worry about you."

"Well don't, I'm fine." Alex soaped the facecloth. God, he was tired. He was ready to swallow his pills and put an end to the day, but an angry flush was spreading over his wife's cheeks and her eyes blazed.

"Really?" she said. She turned on her heel and strode from the room. Shit. She wasn't finished with him.

HE SCRUBBED his skin until it glowed and itched. He soaked in the deep water. The chemical barrier was running out and he wasn't up to Pam's grilling. He turned on the hot tap. Water gushed into the tub, steam misted the bathroom mirror and he lay back in the bath, but the persistent abyss yawned. He filled his head with thoughts. Work, Steve, the party, Kelly and her puzzle, Brian and the planes, Pam and her new hair-cut, Toni and that Greek sod. Anything and everything squirmed, and darkness overwhelmed him. His pills would sort him out, but they were next to the bed. Surely, she would be asleep by now?

FAT CHANCE. She sat on the edge of the bed, the pill bottles rattling in the fist that she shook at him. "If you're so fine what are these for? Fun?" she asked.

He held out a prune-puckered hand, his lips tight. "Give them to me, Pam."

She shoved them at him. "Well, it was no fun when you were dead to the world last night," she said.

"There's no pleasing you, is there?" Alex said through clenched teeth, "You wanted me to go back to the shrink and I did. Now I'm back on these pills and you want fun." He shook the night's dose into his palm, jabbed out a small blue tablet and showed it to her. "This is a sleeping pill; sleeping pills make you sleep. There is no fun. Do you want me to take it or not?"

Pam bit her lip; her eyes glistened. "Take it," she said. He swallowed the whole chemical cocktail and climbed into bed, turning his back to her. He hated it when she cried and couldn't deal with it now.

"I thought I heard burglars last night," her voice cracked and slugged a belly-blow. Burglars were his department not hers. He was a useless shit. He turned to face her, but her back was turned to him. He touched her shoulder; it heaved as she took a deep breath. "But it wasn't burglars, it was Toni. She was talking to Stelios on the phone and I heard her tell him that she'd take the baby to Greece."

Fuck. Another belly-blow.

"Is she mad? I thought that bastard had dumped her. Did you talk some sense into her?" he asked.

"No. She doesn't know that I know." Pam reached for a tissue and blew her nose. Alex flung back the duvet. "It's time she did."

"What are you doing?"

"I'm going to have it out with her."

"Don't." Pam grabbed his wrist. "It won't help and she needs her sleep."

"What she needs is to grow up and think about her baby." Alex shrugged off Pam's hand.

"It's Dinks."

"What's dinks?" Cotton-wool filled his head. The sleeping pill was kicking in and Pam wasn't making sense.

"Kelly said the baby needed a name and Toni said that, when she talks to it, she calls it Dinks, so she does think of it, Alex, more than you imagine and I'm sure she loves it."

"Well Dinks deserves a good home and I'm going to tell her that that fucking drug-dealer sure as hell won't provide one." The words slurred and slipped off his thickening tongue.

"Confronting her won't do it," said Pam, her voice was muffled, coming from a distance. His system was shutting down. It cancelled the order to his legs; he could not stride to Toni's room. He had to sort this crap out.

"I'll get hold of James."

"What for?"

"Help." The last tentacles of consciousness dragged the word from his lips and he slipped into the black sea of oblivion.

29

Alex woke early. He hated waking up. He kept his eyes shut tight as dawn wriggled through the curtains. Unrelenting cold dread and Toni slithered through the residue of sleeping pills and settled in the pit of his stomach. His fears ballooned as he remembered Pam telling him that she'd overheard Toni talking to Stelios and had stumbled on the plans they had for her to run away when the baby was born. Shit. If she got to Greece they'd never see her again. She'd be living in the dangerous world of a wanted criminal and would be dependent on him. She'd land up in jail or dead. Jesus Christ, what the hell was he going to do? He remembered thinking of a plan last night, but what was it?

Pam fidgeted and he willed his body to turn over. Her face, drawn and pale was close to his. He reached for her, wanting to hug the worry from her eyes, but his limbs were slow.

"I don't think James can help," she said.

"What?"

"Remember last night? You said you were going to get hold of him." Her tired, exasperated voice welcomed him to a new day.

Ah yes, that was it. James, he was going to see James.

"It's a waste of time." Her logic dismissed his plan and his desire to hug her faded fast.

"He doesn't have a magic wand and if he says anything about..." Pam shuddered.

"About what?" It was too early for games and the sedatives lingered in his blood, blunting his brain, hampering body movement.

Pam shot him a look. He was too slow on the uptake for her. "you know, us sorting out Stelios."

Sounds of retching came from the children's bathroom. "Is that Toni?" he asked.

"Yes. Dinks has her up and hanging over the loo at sparrow's every morning."

Alex lay still, listening to his daughter heave.

SHE WAS SEVENTEEN, pregnant and she called his unborn grandchild 'Dinks'. Hell, she was just a kid. His kid. He couldn't stand by and let her run away to the arms and life of a criminal. The toilet flushed, the bathroom door clicked open and Toni's slippers flapped as she went back to bed. He'd fucked up. Left it too late to get rid of Stelios and now, thanks to his moral high ground, the bastard was safe and sound in Greece and seducing Toni yet again. Murder is irrevocable. The stain would be on his soul forever, but to hell with his soul, what about the lives of his daughter and grandchild?

"This time I will," he said.

STEVE SUCKED on his cigarette and shook his head as Alex dialled the lawyer's number and held the receiver to his ear. "Hell man, you don't want that shit again and, believe me," smoke streamed from Steve's nostrils, emphasising his point, "I don't want it either."

"What choice do I have? It's my kid and her kid's life we're talking about here and you should have seen Pam's face when she told me about the phone call; she's terrified."

"Hang fire, man, Toni's staying put until..."

"Griffiths." James' curt greeting cut in and Alex waved down Steve's reasoning.

"Hi, James, can you talk?" he asked. Steve got up and left the office.

"Pam overheard Toni talking to Stelios last night and... Hell, I need to see you."

"I'm in court all day. Bring lunch to my desk at twelve-thirty. A toasted ham and cheese, white bread, with pickles and chilli sauce, from Pete's Deli and don't be late."

Alex pitched up with the order. "Thanks for seeing me," he said, as James peeled off the greaseproof wrapping and sunk his teeth in, taking a large bite. "You mentioned Toni and Stelios," he said, mopping chilli from the corner of his mouth. "I gather that, even though he fucked off to Greece, he's still an issue?"

Alex nodded. "He's in contact with Toni. Sounds like they've made plans and she's running to Greece after the baby's born and taking it with her."

"When is your grandchild due to arrive?"

"I'm not good with that stuff. Pam's been taking Toni to her gynae and I think around August, September." Alex cleared his throat. "When he sent her back from the Transkei, we could have... you know... made him disappear, but I hesitated and he skipped the country. If I have the chance again..." Alex ground to a halt, embarrassed, unable to look James in the eye.

James shook his head. "Fucking impossible. As long as he stays in Greece he's safe."

Fear, like acid, burned in his throat. Pam was right. James had no magic wand.

"But we can make it fucking difficult for her to leave."

Alex swallowed. "How?"

"I'll get hold of Bezuidenhout. We'll stop her getting another fucking false passport. Bring me her real one and I'll lock it up for safe-keeping."

"Thanks James."

James looked at him, his face grim. "You'd better start praying that she comes to her senses, because that's all I can offer and let me tell you it's fuck-all."

30

B rian was in a hurry. The team was having an early morning tennis practice in preparation for the afternoon match against St David's and, before Pam pulled up the handbrake, he jumped out of the car, popped open the boot and grabbed his school and tog bags.

"Hold it," called Pam. "Remember, Kelly's having her injections this afternoon. I'll get back as soon as I can to fetch you. Just wait for me at the gate."

"Aw, Ma, you were late last time." Brian hoisted his tog bag onto his shoulder.

Guilty as charged. I was late, very late. I was dilly-dallying with Raymond and I forgot you.

"Okay then, I'll get Dad to pick you up."

"Great," he shouted, as he disappeared into a sea of grey pants, skirts and white shirts; the jostling vigour of high school. Pam turned to Kelly.

"If we get finished early at the hospital we'll go shopping for your jeans," she said.

"Ma." Kelly rolled her eyes. "You know I can't walk with those golf balls on my legs."

"Damn, I wasn't thinking" said Pam, but she was thinking and she wished she could stop. Turn off Alex, Toni, Stelios, Dinks, find the exit to the labyrinth of her mind.

"How about shopping tomorrow then?" she said.

Kelly nodded and opened the car door. "Okay."

"Bye," Pam pecked Kelly on the cheek. Its warmth brought her skittering thoughts to a halt and she caught her daughter's hand. It was also warm.

"You feeling okay?" she asked.

"Why?" Kelly tossed back a question and pushed Pam's hand from her forehead. "You're fussing," she said. "I'm fine; it's just hot in the car."

But it wasn't; the air-conditioner was doing a good job.

"No school for you. I'm taking you to Doctor Frank," said Pam.

Kelly sighed. "But on Saturday the Australian doctors said I was okay."

THAT WAS TRUE. For two days the immunologists visiting from Australia had scrutinised Kelly's skinny body, scarred lungs, clubbed fingers, thrush-coated mouth, nails, hair and skin. "You're looking good," they said, and meant it.

· · ·

PAM FROWNED. "I KNOW, SNOGGUMS, BUT..."

Kelly's jaw was set. "I've got a maths exam and it counts towards my year mark."

KELLY LONGED FOR ACADEMIC COLOURS, but frequent bouts of pneumonia and hospital stays held them out of reach. To catch up, she had put in hours of extra lessons and studying until she fell asleep over her books. For the last three years, pride and sadness had burst Pam's heart as Brian, shy and gangly, had climbed the steps to the stage to accept his rewards for obtaining an overall year mark of above eighty percent. Kelly, missing her colours by one measly percent, had clapped harder than anyone else; her dreams dashed and lost to illness.

KELLY'S immune system guaranteed hurdles ahead and the school year was young. Missing today's maths exam would jeopardise her chances and could rob her of the opportunity to achieve colours yet again. Pam touched her daughter's hand. *Warm; definitely a temperature.* Stifling her inner responsible voice, she opened the door. "Good luck," she said, and Kelly's wide smile was her reward; but worry rode with her to work.

ERIC WAVED as she parked under the Syringa tree, her tyres crunching and popping the berries that covered the concrete driveway. He was packing boxes into his car, wearing his Thursday fashion-statement. Pressed suit pants, no socks, rubber-soled sandals and a brown dustcoat over a crisp, blue-striped shirt; his clothes and white skin elicited wide grins from his fellow deliverymen. *Baas* they called him as they waited with him in the queue at the client's Goods Receiving Depot, and laughed at the jokes he told in *Fanakalo*, a bastard language born in the gold mines, belonging to no one and everyone. And, when nature called him to the 'Whites-Only' men's room, they kept his place in the line and took care of his laden trolley.

"Morning, Eric," said Pam, peering into his car. Boxes filled the back and front passenger seats. His leather shoes, the toes stuffed with rolled socks were shoved into the door pockets and his suit jacket and tie hung on a hook, in readiness for a business lunch.

"The car's pretty full. Early start?"

Eric fitted more boxes into the boot, closed it and climbed into the driver's seat. "Yes, but not as early as Alex. He stopped in on his way to work."

His words pulled Pam to attention. "Why?" she asked.

Alex hadn't said he was coming to her office, not that they'd said much of anything to each other since James had proved her right and had given them 'fuck-all'; his words, not hers, to help keep Toni in the country. Locked in a bad dream, they saw the fear of losing her in each other's eyes and turned away. It was heavy on their marriage; too heavy to give it a voice and this morning they'd hardly kissed each other goodbye when he took Toni to college.

·   ·   ·

"WHY WHAT?" asked Eric

"Why did he come in? Could he drive? Was he having a panic attack?"

"No, none of the above." Eric started the car, putting it into reverse gear. "Brian sent him. He's on the bum for some of my favourite red paint; wants to spray a glider with it. See you later."

OF COURSE, the four gliders that Brian and Alex had started building the day he had conquered the panic attack in the post office and passed her stupid underwear test. One of the planes was a surprise for Eric, and Brian was finishing it off. Pam breathed; Alex was fine.

HIGH HEELS HOOKED on the bottom chair rung, coffee mug in hand, Maggie fed yellow tape into the telex machine. It clicked and clattered, deciphered the punched holes and sent Direct Technologies' order for capacitors to their German supplier.

"Hi, Pam," she said, waving the mug in the direction of a tray, littered with crumbs, croissants, butter, jam and grated cheese, sitting on the despatch table. "Help yourself."

"Thanks, I will," said Pam. "Just got to phone the hospital first." She dialled and Sister Armstrong in Ward 385 answered the call.

"OF COURSE, I'll arrange for Doctor Frank to pop in and examine Kelly while she's having her injection this afternoon," she said. "Better to be safe than sorry with my favourite patient. The immunoglobin is already in the fridge and poor Beth has drawn the short straw again and will be giving the injections."

PAM REPLACED the receiver and stared into space.

"What's up with Kelly?" asked Maggie.

"She's running a slight temperature."

"Alex didn't mention it earlier."

"He doesn't know; I only noticed it when I dropped her at school this morning. I should have taken her straight to Doctor Frank. There's no such thing as a slight temp when it comes to Kelly, but she has this maths exam today and you know how she is."

"Stubborn comes to mind," smiled Maggie. "Now grab some breakfast, compliments of your hubby. He popped in for paint and brought the croissants, not that he ate anything himself. This new stuff with Toni and Stelios has knocked him. I bet you're glad he's back with the psychiatrist."

Pam clapped her hand to her mouth. "Oh no, Alex's therapy session. I told Brian that Alex would pick him up. Darn, I forgot it's Thursday just like I forgot Brian last week."

"You forgot Brian?"

Pam buried her fingers in her hair. "I kind of got involved with Raymond and lost track of time."

"What do you mean - involved?

"He took me for coffee. Mavis wasn't in the salon to make some for me."

Maggie's fine brow arched. "You went with Raymond, our flirt?"

Pam nodded. The tape twisted and the telex gargled to a stop. Maggie unplugged the machine.

"Well, don't just sit on the details, let me have them," she said.

"Strictly between you and me? Not even Eric?"

"Welcome to the confessional." Maggie's spread arms embraced the multipurpose family-room office.

MAGGIE MADE A GOOD PRIEST. Her grey eyes showed no emotion or judgement as she listened without interruption as Pam told the tale of the 'date'; the airborne kiss, Brian stranded outside the dark school and the guilt that had niggled her in the middle of the night as she lay next to Alex's drugged body.

"What do you say to that, Maggs?" asked Pam. "Am I losing it?" Maggie patted Pam's shoulder and rose to the challenge of psychologist.

"I'd say you're ripe for an affair."

"Rubbish."

"I'm serious. You're right there facing all sort of weird nonsense, but for heaven's sake," Maggie rolled her eyes, "you can do better than a hairdresser."

Pam laughed. "You're a first-class snob, Margaret Williams," she said. "But you're wrong about me. I love Alex. I'm not up for an affair."

"No? Face it, Pam, Alex is bloody hard going right now. From where I sit, you need a break and that makes Raymond dangerous. Dear Lord, I'll have to find you another hairdresser."

31

Kelly's grin curled around the thermometer clamped between her teeth. "I nailed the exam," she said. Pam patted her daughter's thin hand. It was still warm and she'd heard her cough a few times on the way to the hospital. "Good for you," she said, as Beth squeezed the plunger and forced the last of the immunogobulin through the thick needle.

"There, Sweetie; done till next month," said Beth, patting a sterile gauze square on Kelly's golf ball lumps and blotting up the leaking excess liquid. She took the thermometer from Kelly's mouth and Pam leaned forward in her seat.

"A tad above normal," said Beth, shaking the mercury back down into the bulb.

Pam frowned.

Beth's fingertips rested on Kelly's wrist and counted heartbeats. "A little fast, nothing drastic but I've paged Doctor Frank as you asked, Pam."

Kelly sighed. "You're fussing again, Ma," she said

"Maybe."

"I need to get home, Ma. I've got a science project to finish."

"We're not going anywhere until Doctor Frank has checked you out," said Pam, as she folded her arms ignoring Kelly's miffed face, sat back and waited for the paediatrician.

WHITE COATS FLAPPING, Doctors Simmonds and Clegg, the visiting Australian immunologists, followed Doctor Frank into Ward 385. They were excited. He'd told them that Kelly Richards was running a temperature and that her mother had phoned and asked for a consultation. It was an opportunity to observe Kelly's lazy leucocytes and incomplete immune system in action, but their buzzing anticipation irritated Doctor Frank. He'd treated Kelly since she was a spunky two-year-old with a five-year life expectancy, arranged her trip to the NIH and watched death reach for her many times during her sixteen years. He had no logical answer for her survival, but, if asked, he would say that she was a miracle; a stubborn miracle with a fiery will to live, whose strong family and intuitive mother anchored her to this earth. Pam's gift was uncanny. It was as if she was plugged into Kelly's system, scanning it for fluctuations. Her ability to detect danger awed him. Her call meant trouble and, without hesitation, he had ordered chest X-rays.

SISTER ARMSTRONG MOUNTED the black plates onto the light box. Clear lungs caged in white ribs. No opaque spots. Doctor Frank smiled.

"No evidence of pneumonia," he said taping Kelly's leg. "I see you've had your injections." He picked up her chart. "Let's see what's what here."

"Beth said nothing drastic," Kelly piped up.

Pam kept quiet, but the furrows between her brows told him that she wasn't convinced. He flipped through the graphs.

"Beth could be right," he said, handing Kelly's file to the scientists. Clegg leaned towards Simmonds. "Pity," he whispered.

The word bounced off the polished Marley tiled floor and Kelly's eyes dropped. Pam's cheeks flamed and she turned on him.

"Excuse me," she said. "Did I hear you say 'pity'?"

Clegg took a step back. "Sorry," he said.

"Sorry isn't good enough," spat Pam. She pointed at Kelly. "My child missed two days of school for you and your research. You examined her from back to front and inside out. Did you by any chance find her deaf?"

"No. Look, I'm really sorry," Clegg held up his hands.

"What you are is bloody insensitive and rude."

"Calm down, Ma." Kelly pulled at Pam's arm, her eyes behind pink-framed glasses wide with embarrassment and looked to Doctor Frank for support, but he folded his arms and glared at Clegg. Pam never lost her cool and her outburst had surprised him, but she was doing an excellent job of expressing his own feelings and he was not about to intervene.

"You studied her, but you never once saw her as anything

except a specimen, a bunch of cells that don't work properly. Well she's a person; she has feelings and damn good hearing and I'll thank you to remember that before you open your mouth in future."

"Yes, Ma'am," Clegg all but stood to attention and saluted, "it's just that we kind of hoped… I mean we thought she was sick and…"

Pam stood up and Kelly cringed, and Doctor Frank saved the brilliant scientist from burying himself in Pam's ire.

"Let's have a listen to that chest of yours, young lady," he said. Kelly breathed in and out, in and out. Doctor Frank closed his eyes and moved the stethoscope inch by slow inch over her chest, his brows drawn together in concentration.

There it was. Pam's intuition. A rumble on the right side. Drat.

"In the bronchial tubes," he said, moving aside, allowing Clegg and Simmonds the chance to listen.

"Hear it?"

Clegg nodded. "It's pretty faint, but it's there," he said. His back was to Pam and he gave Simmonds the thumbs-up sign. Doctor Frank shoved his balled fists deep into his coat pockets. It would not be proper to punch a visiting immunologist in front of a case study, but he sure as hell wanted to.

"I'm afraid that Beth is wrong, Kelly," he said. "You've got bronchitis."

"But I can go home?"

He ruffled the light brown curls that barely hid the bald, dry fungal patches. "You need antibiotics," he said. He loathed prescribing them. They accelerated fungal growth and, within a day or two, the patches would spread to her forehead, the thrush in her mouth would thicken and her tongue and lips would crack and bleed.

"I can take pills at home," she said, her eyes pleading with him.

"I'd also like you to start physio."

"Mom's good at that; she'll do it," she turned to Pam. "Won't you, Ma?"

"Sure."

It was his call. He weighed up the gamble. Pam would pick up any change, good or bad in Kelly, but intravenous antibiotics worked quicker than pills and Kelly turned sour fast. She'd wrong-footed him before, landed up in oxygen tents and added more than a few silver hairs to his head.

"We'd like her to stay," said Simmonds and his colleague nodded. They were keen to run more tests, feast on Kelly's bronchitis. Pam shot them a shrivelling glare. Their appetite for information embarrassed him. It was insatiable. Pity.

"I'll let you go home, but if you aren't better in forty-eight hours you must come back in," he said.

Kelly grinned. She lifted her legs off the bed and stood up.

"Thanks, Doctor," said Pam, as she tucked her hand under Kelly's elbow, ignoring the Australians and helped her hobble from the ward.

. . .

SHE CHECKED her watch as they waited for the lift. Brian would be expecting Alex to pick him up, but Alex was at De Bruin's. She was going to be late collecting her son again, but this time she wasn't flirting with Raymond and she could tell him why.

ALEX'S APPOINTMENT was always the last one on Thursday and the psychiatrist and patient had fallen into the habit of lingering in the comfortable consulting room. After the formal hour session, they'd opened their lives to each other. Therapies founded by Jung and Freud, ethics and business, religion and death, Alex's model aeroplanes, Pieter's opera collection, they spoke of anything that was of importance to either of them and today was no different.

ALEX'S ENERGY level registered zero. Crossing his long legs at the ankles and smoothing his moustache, Pieter settled back into the wingback chair and listened as Alex updated him with Pam's growing fear and irritation, Toni's uncovered secret and his latest attempt at keeping her safe. De Bruin asked the occasional question and, in answering, Alex found that his anxiety lessened. Steve was right. Toni wasn't going anywhere right now.

"I've got time to make a plan," he said.

Pieter nodded. "One that does not involve murder and destroy your soul," he said.

Alex wasn't sure that he had a soul, but De Bruin was confident that it existed, and the subject sparked one of their debates. Alex was energised by the time they shook hands outside the consulting rooms, climbed into their cars and headed home.

HE PLONKED his car keys and Eric's tin of paint on the workbench. "What's that smell?" he asked, wrinkling his nose. Brian grinned. "Sweat. I played a hard game this afternoon."

"Win?"

"Yep."

"Great, but you sure can do with a shower," Alex picked up a fuselage. "It's looking pretty good," he said, his palm registering its weight. "Just a tad heavy."

"It's Eric's plane. Do you think he suspects that we're building one for him, Dad?"

"Nope. He gave me the paint without question because he's used to you bumming stuff for your planes." Alex squinted down the body, turning it this way and that. It lined up straight and true. He traded the fuselage for the wings, ran his hand ran over them, his fingers hunting down rough spots.

"So," asked Brian, biting on his thumb as he did before a tennis match. "Is it okay?"

Alex nodded. He was proud of Brian. He'd done a great job.

"I reckon Eric's got a mean surprise coming his way."

"Thanks, Dad," Brian grinned. "The plans were pretty difficult to follow and I did a bit of guesswork here and there, but I can't finish it. I'm not that good at spraying."

"I'll help you do it," Alex heard himself say and realised that he wanted to. It was a good feeling. Brian shook the tin. "Can we spray it tonight?" he asked.

"What about your homework?"

"Done. Check with Ma." Brian was keen.

"Okay, I will." Alex smiled. "Where is she?"

"With Kelly. She's hitting that yucky stuff off her ribs."

Alex's good feeling vanished and he handed the glider back to Brian.

"Catch you later," he said heading for Kelly's room.

CLUP, clup, clup. He hated that sound. He waited for Pam's voice. It followed on cue.

"Cough," she said.

Kelly obliged and the sound of her efforts stayed his hand on the door handle. Poor kid. As soon as he thought it, he pulled himself up short. Kelly loathed pity. She was a good kid, no, scratch that too, she was a great kid and she deserved more than his sympathy. What she deserved was his strength and it was time to curl the corners of his mouth into a smile, swing open the door and walk in.

MICKEY JUMPED off the bed and danced on his hind legs, demanding his usual attention and Alex obliged. Tickled and patted, the dog hopped back to his spot next to Kelly's feet, did a quick circle and flopped down. She was lying, face-down, a pillow stacked between her tummy and the mattress.

Pam straddled the back of her thighs, hands cupped. Clup, clup, clup. They thumped the thick towel, folded and draped on Kelly's bare back.

"Cough," said Alex, pulling a bunch of tissues from the box next to the bed and handing them to her. Kelly's eyes smiled hello. She covered her mouth with the tissue and spat. Ugh, he remembered that the NIH had taught them to examine her sputum.

"Yuk," she said looking at the pale-yellow streaks. He turned his head away, his eyes settling on the desk by the window and Kelly's new puzzle. The pieces were sorted, the four corners and straight edges in place, the rest spread out in groups of matching colours in the upside-down lid.

"Hi," said Pam, not missing a thump. "We have a touch of bronchitis."

"So I see. How're you, Kelly?" he asked, and her reply was as reliable as tomorrow's dawn.

"Fine thank you, Dad, and you?"

"Fine too."

Dear God, how he wished that were true for both of them; but he was on uppers, downers and sleeping pills and taking up space on Pieter De Bruin's couch and Kelly was never fine, never would be fine, not for one single day of her life and that was the fucking truth.

"HEY, Dad, I did good in my maths exam." Kelly's bright smile and Pam's smug one pushed back the dark thoughts.

"That's my girl," he said. He pulled up a seat at the puzzle and, with each placed piece, he vowed that he would be fine. Kelly and his family deserved it.

32

K elly peeled open the tissue. Clear, priceless spit clung to it. "You don't have to thump me anymore, Ma," she said. Mischief spread over her face. "Shame, I feel sorry for the poor Australian doctors, they'll be disappointed by this."

Pam kissed Kelly's bare back and handed her a T-shirt. "I'll phone Doctor Frank and tell him to convey your sympathies and wish them a good trip home."

"I'M MORE than happy to do that," laughed Doctor Frank. He heard the lightness in Pam's voice and Kelly and a yapping dog in the background.

"We still need to listen to her lungs."

"Can my gynae do that? My other daughter has an appointment with her today."

"That'll be fine," he said. "I er, I heard, you're going to be a granny?"

"Did Kelly tell you?"

"No, she told Beth and Beth told me. Anyway, congratulations."

"Thanks. You won't believe how many people avoid the subject."

"Well it seems that Kelly can't wait to be an aunty, but apparently she's not going to change any dirty nappies."

Pam laughed and Doctor Frank thought that she sounded more like the Pam he'd come to know. He was worried about her.

BETH HAD ALSO TOLD him that Kelly's sister had run away with her boyfriend and come back pregnant, and that the boyfriend was in trouble with the law, a drug-dealer or something equally sinister and that he'd skipped the country. If all this was true, the Richards family was dealing with abnormal stress and it explained Pam's display of anger in front of the scientists. It was out of character. But where was Kelly's dad in all this? He had not seen him visit Kelly during her last two hospital stays. Why? As Kelly's doctor, it was none of his business if her parents were having marital problems, but these would impact on her. He didn't want to poke his nose in, but she had carved a place in his heart and he decided to cross the paediatric line.

"ABOUT THE SPECIALISTS, Pam; they deserved your dressing-down, but it's not like you," he said.

"I know and I'm tempted to say I'm sorry, but..."

"No, no, they deserved it, but it's more Alex's style and I haven't seen him lately. I don't mean to pry," he said, pausing before he invaded her privacy. "But he always visits and builds puzzles with her... and I wondered, you know... why he hasn't been."

There was an awkward silence. It had been a mistake to bring up the subject and he wanted to take his words back. What if they had separated and Alex wasn't living at home? Beth hadn't said anything, but it was possible.

"He was also in hospital. He thought he was having heart attacks. It turns out that he's clinically depressed."

Her explanation was to the point, but the short, sharp sentences betrayed her worry.

HE'D WITNESSED depression's destruction up close and it was the last thing the Richards family needed. "Is he having treatment?" he asked, keeping his voice calm.

Pam's hesitation was expected.

"Yes, he's been seeing a psychiatrist, Pieter De Bruin."

Doctor Frank breathed a sigh of relief. "I can vouch for De Bruin," he said.

"You know him?"

"He treated my nephew." Doctor Frank remembered Ian's breakdown; the horror of a shattered young man with haunted eyes and shuddered. "I highly recommend him."

"Did your nephew have depression?"

"The Military called it post-traumatic stress. That's Pieter De

Bruin's speciality. Ian was up on the Angolan Border when he tried to take out his officer and commit suicide in the camp."

"That's dreadful; I'm sorry. Is he okay now?"

"He hasn't had a nightmare or a fight in six months and he's holding down a steady job," he said.

"Alex is up and down like a yo-yo. It's encouraging to know that he's in good hands."

The relief in her voice validated his interference.

"These things take time," he said, wishing he could tell her that the road ahead was easy. "Please ask your gynaecologist to phone me when she's checked Kelly out."

"I will and thanks for telling me about Ian. I can't tell you how much it helps."

"Take care Pam." He hung up and, staring at the framed degrees on the opposite wall, he thought about Kelly, the stubborn toddler who was now a determined young woman. Over the years she'd had stretched his skills to the limit, spending her last birthday in hospital, pale and hollow-eyed, in the oxygen tent. Alex had sat vigil with Pam, his hand holding hers, squeezing it when Kelly groaned, drawing his wife close when the crisis had passed and holding her as her pent-up tears soaked his shoulder.

HAVING WITNESSED Ian's breakdown and watching it toss the young man into a whirlpool of emotions, sucking his loved ones into a vortex of confusion, Doctor Frank understood Pam's unusual behaviour and was relieved that Alex was in the care of a good man. He'd never seen Alex cry. Young Ian hadn't either, not until De Bruin had unlocked his tears and pulled him back from death.

THE GYNAECOLOGIST GAVE Pam the thumbs-up sign. Kelly's lungs were clear.

"Your turn, Toni," Joan Martin patted the examination bed. Kelly had warmed the sheets, but Toni gasped as the stethoscope touched her tummy.

"Listen," Joan handed her the earpiece.

Toni held her breath.

"Can you hear it?"

Toni eyes were wide. "Is that my baby?"

"Yes, it is," laughed Joan. "But I don't know where you're hiding it. Your stomach's still as flat as a pancake."

"Have a listen, Ma."

Pam hooked the instrument in her ear and her throat caught as she listened to the miracle of her grandchild's heartbeat. Was it a boy or a girl? It didn't matter; she already loved it.

"Gimme, gimme, let Aunty Kelly have a turn," begged Kelly.

"Wow, that's fast."

"Remember that's a baby you're listening to," said Joan.

"We're calling it Dinks for now," said Kelly. "Toni hasn't chosen a proper name yet."

"That's cute. You can get dressed Toni. Any questions?"

Toni twisted a strand of hair in her fingers. "Not really, but when I think about the birth I get scared."

"Every mother-to-be does," Joan patted Toni's hand. "But I'll take good care of you and Mom will be there too. Are you still getting sick?"

"All the time, but, like you said in the beginning, I don't want to take anything that could harm Dinks."

Joan patted her hand. "You're through the first trimester. It's safer now and I can give you a script."

"I'd rather not," said Toni. "Dinks is special."

YET YOU'RE MAKING plans to run away and take Dinks with you to Greece.

PAM TURNED AWAY before Toni saw the knowledge in her eyes. Beating nineteen to the dozen, Dinks's heart had touched her own and released a flood of pure, overwhelming love for her unborn grandchild. *Dear God, we've got to stop her.*

ON THE WAY HOME, they picked up Brian and stopped at the CNA to buy a name-your-baby book. The children pored over the pages looking up the meanings of their own names, laughing at Humphrey and Elvira, feeling sorry for anyone stuck with parents who'd called them Egbert. Their chatting pulled Pam from her troubled thoughts and into the fun, but they considered her suggestions too old-fashioned for Dinks and, by the time they'd pulled into the driveway, she hadn't added a single name to the list of favourites written on the back page of Kelly's Zulu book.

"Write down Dimitri," said Toni.

The fun vanished for Pam.

Brian pulled a face. "What kind of name is that?" he asked.

"I like it," said Toni.

"Poor Dinks," said Kelly as she wrote it down, but she stuck a huge question mark next to it. The muscle at the base of Pam's skull knotted and kick-started a headache. She knew that name, seen in James's office, written in bold, black felt-tip on the front cover of the court record of **Stelios Dimitri Panos, Case 26/689/85,** Dinks's father and the author of her nightmare.

33

She pulled into the garage and parked next to Alex's car. What was it doing there? He'd told her not to expect him for supper? Why was he home? What was wrong? Whatever it was she had no energy to deal with it and her feet dragged as she followed the chatting children into the house.

Mickey and Bella's customary welcome hammered and hurt her head. "For God's sake, sort those dogs out," she snapped. The girls threw each other a 'what's got into her' look, scooped up their pets and headed for the safety of the kitchen where they raided the fridge, opened Cokes and switched on the kettle. The zipped cans and bubbling water ricocheted in Pam's head as she went in search of her husband. She needed to find him in one healthy goddamn piece, hand over the kids, their tennis matches, injections and gynae check-ups, crawl into bed, pull up the covers and tell the world to go and crap on someone else.

"Tea's ready, Ma," called Toni.

"I'll be back in a moment," said Pam, she was thirsty and tea before handing over to Alex sounded like a good idea.

But where is he?

The phone rang.

"That'll be for you, Pam," Alex called from their bedroom. His voice was irritable and croaky. He sounded full of flu, but not down in the dumps. The hammering in Pam's head eased a little and the noisy kitchen slipped into a comfortable background hum. Depression hadn't driven him home.

"Some guy's been phoning and asking for you all afternoon. He refused to leave a message or his name."

A guilty hand flew to her hair. It must be Raymond calling to confirm her appointment, but why hadn't he left his name? She should have listened to Maggie, her priest and psychologist, and phoned the salon to cancel it, but she hadn't, neither had she stopped the memory of his airborne kiss from weaving through her thoughts like a purring cat. Alex sounded suspicious, but there was nothing to be suspicious about, was there? She steadied her breathing and picked up the receiver.

"Hello."

"Is that Pamela Richards?" Relief flooded her. It wasn't Raymond. "Yes." She frowned. Alex had said this guy had been phoning all afternoon, but she didn't recognise the toffee-nosed, posh accent.

"Who is this?" she asked.

"Do you wear a size 32B bra?"

Good grief. An upper-crust pervert.

"Who the hell are you?"

"Well, do you?"

His nerve kept her ear glued to the phone.

"Who wants to know? What business is it of yours?" she asked.

He ignored her. "Did you buy a bra from Loretta's Lingerie Shoppe in March?"

"I might have."

She'd buried the black French lace number with knickers to match, in her underwear drawer after Alex's collapse and Steve taking him to the Riverside Clinic.

"Well, if you did buy a bra from Loretta's and you do wear a size 32B then you've won Triumph's competition 'Romancing in Rio.'

"Excuse me. Did you say I've won a competition?"

"If you bought..."

"Yes, yes, I did and I do wear a size 32B bra."

"Then congratulations. Your prize is a ten-day trip to Rio for two people in July, all expenses paid and accommodation in a five-star hotel."

She was stunned. Her headache disappeared.

"Thank you, thank you, thank you," she gabbled. She was thrilled and excited.

"My pleasure, Pamela Richards. Triumph's marketing division will be in touch shortly to make the arrangements."

Bikinis, suntan lotion, famous beaches and revelry beckoned. She'd won the perfect escape from the insane pressures of their lives.

"ALEX," she yelled as she ran down the passage to the bedroom. "You're never going to believe this."

"Well, who the hell was he?" croaked Alex as she plonked down beside him. He looked miserable. Tissues plugged his red nose. She checked his eyes. They were flu flat and streaming, not depression dead. Good, she was *au fait* with snotty noses and aching joints. It was fake heart attacks and a lifeless body slumped in a chair that threw her. Rummaging in the pedestal drawer she found a bottle of Vick's Nasal Spray and handed it to him. He ditched the tissue plugs, squirted his nostrils and sniffed hard. She would mix him a hot toddy, heavy on healing whiskey, unearth throat gargle and feed him mega-doses of vitamin C and gallons of liquid. Guaranteed, he'd be sneeze-free in no time.

"Good heavens, I don't know, he didn't say, but he did say that I've won a trip to Rio. We go in July. Isn't that fantastic? When's Carnival time? Kelly and Brian will be on school holidays and I think Kevin has varsity vac. I'm sure he'll come and stay with the kids and I'll take Toni to Joan Martin for a check-up and sort Kelly's injection out before we go. They can muddle on without us for ten days. Eric and Maggie will keep tabs on them."

"Whoa, take a breath. How did you win this trip?"

"I'm not quite sure but, remember the black bra I bought a while ago?"

"The one you flaunted after our celebration of Eric's order?" Alex gave a pained smile.

"Yes, anyway," she waved her tipsy modelling memory aside. "Somehow buying that bra put my name into a competition and I won. Isn't that fantastic?"

"I don't see how we can go," said Alex.

"You're kidding me" Pam stared him in disbelief. "What's stopping us?"

"Everything you just mentioned." Alex ticked his fingers as he reeled off his reasons.

"Kelly, Toni, your business, my business. We can't offload our bizarre family responsibilities; it's just not right. The time is wrong; it's impossible."

"Oh, don't be so bloody negative, Alex," Pam folded her arms tight. Her hands wanted to slap his damned fingers. "Where's your spirit of adventure? The time is right. We need a break. We need to go away and lick our wounds and relax after the Toni and Stelios saga. We need some time alone; just the two of us."

My recently-divorced hairdresser tried to kiss me, which is flattering, and I wanted him to, which is unsettling, and I haven't cancelled my next appointment, which is downright dangerous. We need this.

"Can't you see this prize is heaven-sent?"

"I remember the bra," said Alex, a shadow flitting across his face. "And I also remember feeling so good that I stopped taking my pills, and I also remember crashing and landing up in the loony-bin. Do you remember that?"

"Yes, but..."

"And then there's Toni planning to run away to Greece."

"Only after the baby is born," Pam argued.

"You sure about that?"

Pam crossed her fingers. "Yes," she said. She'd won a trip; she smelt freedom and they were going to Rio.

"And Kelly?"

Pam shot him a scathing look and lifted her chin. Kelly squeezed her heart. Kelly's courage, not her illness, defined their daughter. "You can't use Kelly as an excuse. She'll read us the riot act if we don't go because of her and you know it."

Alex examined her face. Determination flushed her cheeks and her eyes flashed. "What about our businesses?"

"We're not indispensable, Alex, and it's only for ten days."

"And what's your answer for me?"

"You?"

"Yes, me. I'm on all these bloody pills and seeing a shrink."

"But you're getting better."

"The truth is that I'm just glued together. Sometimes."

"I'll think of something, trust me."

A trace of amusement crept into his eyes. "I'm sure you will, but I'm warning you..."

"We'll work around it, we've got time; we're not going tomorrow."

"You're very persuasive," he said, unfolding her arms. "And very pretty."

He held her hands and pulled her to him. She breathed in Vicks Vaporub and Old Spice aftershave and searched his eyes.

"You angling?" she asked, surprised; his meds screwed his sex-drive: whether it kicked in or not depended on the chemical cocktail of the day.

"Yep. About time too don't you think?"

"The kids..."

"Close the door."

She closed it as quietly as possible.

"I don't want your flu," she said.

"I won't kiss you," he said.

But he did, many times, in many places. Today, the drug cocktail was perfect.

34

Devoid of her make-up and bracelet, Maggie sat at the telex machine, feet shoved into high-heeled mules, hair in electric curlers, boobs wobbling against the satin of her turquoise dressing-gown as she thumped the keys.

"Morning, Maggie," Pam waved as she headed for the dining-room to collect a chair for the day.

"Oh, my God," said Maggie, "is that the time already? I haven't even brushed my teeth. Eric left early for that break-fast seminar you booked him into and I came in here and got stuck into telexing and following up deliveries with our suppliers."

"I thought it was important that he attend," said Pam, setting the chair straight and hanging her bag over its back. "The Reserve Bank's tightening up on foreign exchange control and I'm hoping that the financial gurus have a few tips for us."

Maggie hammered the keyboard. "How are we supposed to

run an import business in this country with Tutu yelling for sanctions and the Government tying up the money? I could do with a bit of good news, I really could."

Pam smiled. "Well, I've got some."

"Ah-ha," said Maggie, looking up, trusting her fingers to find and strike the correct keys.

"I won a trip to Rio."

Maggie's fuchsia pink nails hung in mid-air. "Honest?"

"Yep and I've got these to thank for it." Pam put her hands to her chest.

Maggie stared.

"Your wedding and engagement rings?"

"No, not them. These," Pam cupped her breasts. "My charlies."

Maggie laughed. "You're having me on."

"Scout's honour, I'm not."

Maggie stood and adjusted her dressing-gown, re-wrapping the satin fronts, right over left, tightening the belt and settling her hourglass figure back on the chair. "Spill the beans, girl," she said, pulling curlers from her hair.

Pam's own shock, intrigue and delight crossed Maggie's face as she listened to the tale of Alex's annoyance, the unnamed stranger and his bizarre questions.

"So, you see, my 32Bs won me a trip."

Maggie's curls bounced as she laughed. "So, Lucky Tits, when are you going to do this Romancing in Rio thing?"

"In July, but Alex and I haven't finalised it yet," said Pam, a small frown wriggling between her brows. Yesterday's chemicals had facilitated perfect late afternoon sex, but, during the night, depression had barged into their happiness, kidnapped her sexy husband and left that all too familiar slumped body in her bed. Today Alex's eyes were dull. He was down and avoiding the subject of Rio.

"Is the prize open-ended?"

"No, we have to go sometime in July. I guess we'll fit in with school and varsity holidays. I'll ask Kev to come up from Stellenbosch and stay with the kids, but would you also keep an eye on them, Maggs?"

"Of course."

Pam picked up the nano-second of hesitation.

"But?"

A shadow flitted across Maggie's eyes. "No buts, but, look... Does Kevin know about Toni?"

Pam flip-flapped her hand. "So, so. He knows that she's pregnant and that Stelios buggered off to Greece, and I guess he thinks, as I did, that all the drama is behind us, but don't worry, I'll get him up to speed with Toni's new secret plans."

"No, no, don't do that, "said Maggie. "You'll put the fear of God into him."

Pam's shoulders slumped; she understood why Maggie had hesitated.

Maggie was scared and who could blame her? Of late, the Richards' family, once boring in its ordinariness, was unpredictable and too volatile to pass onto friends or baby brothers. Her joyful anticipation shrivelled.

"Alex is right. We can't just up and go. There's just too much responsibility."

Maggie tossed her curls. "I can handle responsibility."

"The likes of Toni, Stelios and Kelly? All of them? Altogether?"

Maggie sat still and a hollow ache filled Pam, as her trip slipped away.

"Well, yes," said Maggie. "I'll admit, I'll be praying like hell that nothing happens while you are away and I'm sure nothing will, but you and Alex must go."

It was unfair to ask such a favour of Maggie and Kevin.

"Don't sweat, Maggie. Alex isn't keen to go," said Pam. "Anyway, the more I think of it, the more complicated it seems. I'd worry all the time about the girls." Pam swallowed her disappointment and reached for the cashbook file.

"Then make him keen," said Maggie, her grey eyes serious.

"But the kids..."

"Leave them to me. I believe in my bones that this trip was meant to be. You guys need time out and besides, I don't like this thing between you and Raymond."

"What thing? I've told you there's..."

Maggie stood up, hands on hips. "Look me in the eyes and tell me that you're not feeling trapped in your marriage, tired of running after and worrying about everyone, fed up with the whole bang-shoot."

"I'm not."

"Pardon?"

"Well, just sometimes," admitted Pam. Maggie had hit a soft spot. Raymond offered fun and freedom and her responsibilities and Alex's depression were heavy.

"I'd say most times and playing games with Raymond is dangerous."

"You're making something out of nothing."

"Am I?"

Pam's cheeks flushed.

Maggie wagged a finger. "See, I'm right," she said, gathering up her curlers. "And the Man Upstairs," she looked at a space way beyond the ceiling, "has sent you a marriage-saving gift. Give thanks, get Alex on the plane and stop lusting after our hairdresser."

Pam opened her mouth to argue, but Maggie held up a hand full of clips.

"I'm going to get dressed," she said. "And you're going to Rio." She spun on her heels, fluffing the feathers on her slippers and marched out.

Forty minutes later she emerged, make-up flawless, a riot of glossy, black curls framing her face and trickling down her slender neck. Red lipstick matched the belt and candy stripes of the big shirt top that fell to her hips. Casual navy slacks and sling-back shoes completed the fashionable, carefully casual, look. She took up her seat, fed yellow tape into the telex machine and slipped into sergeant-major role.

"You'll work on Alex and put Raymond straight, no pun intended," she said, giving her partner the no-nonsense eye.

"You know Raymond's straight," Pam laughed. "But I'll try and get Alex on the plane."

ERIC RETURNED AT LUNCHTIME, dropping an absent-minded kiss on Maggie's Coty Peach blushed cheek.

"How did the breakfast go?" she asked.

He grunted and dropped his briefcase on his desk. Pulling out the high-backed chair he sat down with his back to the window.

"We're in trouble," he said, and his downcast voice raised the hair on Pam's neck. She turned to face him. "They're talking about cutting import permits," said Eric.

"That's ridiculous. The quotas are stingy enough as it is." Maggie's grey eyes flashed.

"When?" asked Pam, biting her lip. "Our big shipment of gas arrestors from *Sun Trading* is due to arrive soon and it'll pretty much take care of our Yen permits."

"The guys reckon about next week." Eric rubbed his hands over his face. "We're in shit."

"What's wrong with this Government? We work our tails off, get a fantastic order book and they kill us with red tape." Maggie voiced Pam's fears. Without valid foreign exchange permits, Direct Technologies was out of business. She looked around the converted family room, imagining it without packing-boxes, shelves, files - a dead company, buried by politicians.

"We've got permits for Pounds, Deutschmarks, a few thousand Dollars and loads of Pesetas," she said.

Eric shook his head. "Our client only approved the sample gas arrestors from Japan and Spain. Seeing as we're out of yen, we'll have to bring them in from Spain, but I'm not happy to place the order on Rogaf. We sent them a million telexes before they understood us and sent the darn things."

"But they are approved," Maggie emphasised.

"Yes but - believe me, girls, I'm not nagging - if we have to rely on Rogaf I'll have to go to their factory and check them out. I promise I'll make the most of the ticket and touch base with as many of our suppliers as possible. How about it?"

"Pam?" Maggie threw her a 'what-do-we-do-now' look.

"Guess we'll have to find some cash," sighed Pam. "I'll visit Don Pearson and ask for an increase in our overdraft."

"He'll love that," said Eric, mischief sparkling in his eyes. "He's got a soft spot for you."

"Nonsense," said Pam. "His daughter is pregnant. She's unmarried and at university, and he knows about Toni, so we talk about our kids."

"And that's why he pops in here with all kinds of stuff for

you to sign and drops off our cheque books? Bank managers don't usually make house-calls."

"I'm with Eric on that one," said Maggie. "And I think it's great. Wear something a little distracting when you go."

"You're both mad," said Pam.

"Pity Rogaf isn't in Brazil," said Maggie.

Eric's brows pulled together. "Why Brazil?"

Maggie's dimples danced. "Pam's going there. She won a trip to Rio, thanks to her tits."

35

I nspector Bezuidenhout stood under the front door light and listened to the dogs sniffing inside. He hammered home the brass lion's-head door knocker and the high-pitched yapping set his teeth on edge. He had little time for small breeds. He understood that their sharp hearing made them good watchdogs, but give him a proper dog, like Digger, any day. Digger was the cross-bred Boxer that Hettie had rescued from the SPCA a few years back.

SHE'D PUT a leather collar and a red bow around the dog's neck and given it to him, along with a Gary Player golf-shirt, for his birthday. Golf was too expensive for his pocket. He'd never swing a club or walk a green, but the shirt flattered his ample stomach and he wore it to the dog-training lessons. Digger hated the lessons and, when Ignatius pulled the shirt over his head and whistled for him, he dived under the couch and hid away. At the field, he all but dislocated his master's shoulder as he strained at the end of the leash to get at the snooty, obedient thoroughbreds. Lessons over, he bounded after, and into them, then, turning his attention to the large grounds, he earned his name. He dug holes everywhere. Big holes. Holes bigger than the terrier whose mistress fell into one of them, twisted her ankle and complained to the teacher. They were asked to leave before he learnt to 'heel' or 'stay' which suited him just fine, and now, when his master donned the red golf-shirt and hooked him up to the leash, Digger loved taking him for a run.

"QUIET YOU TWO. Mickey, Bella, come here." A husky voice subdued the yapping and Bezuidenhout felt an eye examining him through the spy-hole. His visit here wasn't necessary; he could just as easily phone James Griffiths with his report on Monday morning, but Pam and Alex Richards deserved to hear what he had to say first-hand. He squared his shoulders and tucked the Tupperware container under his elbow. Returning it gave him an excuse for being here, one that would allay any suspicions that might pop into Antoinette's head if she saw him. He glanced at his watch. It was almost seven-thirty and Hettie would soon be home from her Friday evening Bible class.

SERVICE to his community defined him; not the political policing of the day. He hated hounding the black people and jailing anyone without a trial; it made him feel dirty and kept him awake at night. It wasn't honest police work but ferreting out the supplier of Antoinette Richards' false passport was.

HE DIDN'T like James Griffiths either. The lawyer was short on pleasantries and his over-use of the 'F-word' offended him, but he had to admit that he commanded attention. Striding past Sergeant Coetzee's windmill-waving arms, he'd entered Ignatius's out-of-bounds office, closed the door, handed him a business card and launched into what he called 'the matter at hand'.

"Inspector," he said, as he paced back and forth in the small space. "I am the Richards' lawyer. I'm here to inform you that, unbeknown to Antoinette Richards, her mother has recently found out that she's back in contact with that motherfucking drug-dealer, Stelios Panos," he paused, maintaining eye contact with Bezuidenhout, before continuing. "I see you remember him. Nasty piece of work. The silly girl plans to run off again, this time to Greece. I am in possession of her legal passport so she will need a fucking false one and another one for her child to accomplish this feat."

"Her child?" asked Bezuidenhout. Antoinette didn't have a child.

"Correct. She is pregnant. The fucker left her with the proverbial bun in the oven and she is planning to leave with it when it is born. I'm here to get your word that the police will find Stelios's purveyor of false identities and that they will make sure that he or she will not be able to supply her with another."

"I do not like your tone, Mr Griffiths. Are you insinuating that we are not doing our job properly? I take offence to that. We have already identified him. I am a professional and I get results."

"I'm glad you do and I'm more than pleased with your fucking reaction; it's exactly what I'm looking for."

· · ·

THE FRONT DOOR opened slightly and Bezuidenhout shifted the Tupperware box from his right to his left hand. His unfamiliar bulk sparked another barking attack from the two dogs locked in the girl's arms. She was as tall as Antoinette, but pale, matchstick thin and fragile. She reminded him of the see-through bone china cups locked in Hettie's display cabinet. Deep blue, almost violet eyes, assessed him from behind thick glasses and she did not invite him in.

"I'm Inspector Bezuidenhout," he said.

The ghost of a frown flittered between her brows.

"I'm from the Randburg police station."

The frown disappeared as she smiled. "You're the policeman who found Toni. I'm her sister, Kelly. Please come in." The dogs struggled to get free and she pushed the door open further with her elbow. This must be the child who had been in hospital when Antoinette went missing. She must have been very ill; she was skin and bone. Hell, man, some people just had no luck.

"Pleased to meet you. Are your parents at home?" he asked.

"Yes, in the family room," she said. " Come this way." Her jutting hip closed the door and she put the dogs down on the floor. They sniffed him out, scooting around his ankles, almost tripping him up as he followed her past the half-moon table. A bowl of roses, a pile of travel brochures and a framed photo of three kids, smiling and hanging upside down from a jungle gym, sat next to the telephone. Bezuidenhout recognised two of the children as Antoinette and Kelly. The third was a boy, whose boyish features were all but lost in the youth slouched on the couch next to Mr Richards, watching television.

. . .

WHEN HE CAUGHT sight of Bezuidenhout, he sat up straight, as though caught in some act of wrong-doing. It was a knee-jerk reaction; one which the police uniform never failed to illicit and it amused Ignatius. Alex Richards stood and extended his hand. "Good evening Inspector," he said. "This is my son, Brian, and of course, you already know Toni." His eyes darted from Bezuidenhout to his daughter and back again and Ignatius understood the slight shake of his head, He was not to mention the lawyer's visit to the Station. He returned it with the slightest nod; Pam and Alex's secret, about Toni's secret, was safe with him.

"Hi," Brian gave an awkward half-wave.

"Hi," Toni's smile was guarded. She sat with her feet tucked under her bottom and rolled a Brazil travel guide in her hand.

"Evening." Bezuidenhout inclined his head and Toni unfolded her legs, placing her feet, prim and proper, on the floor. Her tracksuit showed no sign of her pregnancy. If anything, she looked as if she'd lost a bit of weight.

"Have a seat." Alex waved him to an empty armchair.

"Thank you." He lowered himself into the seat and stood up again as Pam came in with a loaded tray. She stopped short. Milk sploshed from the full jug onto the embroidered tray-cloth.

"What a surprise," she said, setting down the tray. Her eyes asked for news but begged him not to tell her anything in front of Antoinette.

"We finished all your biscuits and I'm returning the box," he said, tapping the plastic lid. Pam smiled. "I wondered where it had gotten to, but you shouldn't have gone to all the trouble to bring it back."

"No trouble," he said.

"Sure?" in a single word she asked a multitude of silent questions.

"Absolutely none."

"Join us for coffee," her warm smile thanked him. "I'll get another cup from the kitchen."

"I'll get it, Ma." Toni put the brochure on the table and scooped up the ugly one of the two yappers and hurried from the room. From the back he could see that her waist had thickened and he'd bet she was having a boy. Hettie said boys were carried in the back.

DESPITE HIMSELF, he admired Antoinette's loyalty to her Greek boyfriend. It frustrated the hell out of him. It was misplaced, caused heartache and had closed his case of abduction, but it ran in this family. Look at the parents. Flung in their faces, Toni's false passport and membership card to 'Idols', the most raided nightclub in Johannesburg, had shattered them, yet, here they were, standing by her and her pregnancy and going all out to keep her safe. Not many parents did that. He was drawn to this capacity to love and forgive; it was a rare commodity in his world.

THE COFFEE WAS GOOD, but Hettie would be home by now and he refused a second cup and handed the Tupperware box to

Pam, making sure she felt the envelope stuck underneath, and followed Alex to the door.

"Planning a trip?" Bezuidenhout pointed to the brochures on the telephone table.

"Pam won a trip to Rio."

"Congratulations. I've never won anything. You must be excited."

Alex's shrug told him that the man was in no hurry to pack.

"Is the family going?"

"No, it's just for the two of us."

Bezuidenhout nodded; now he understood the lawyer's visit even better. Alex was scared to leave Antoinette, worried that she would do a runner to Stelios. His news might help to change that. "Your lawyer was at the station."

Alex nodded. "Is that why you came here?"

"*Ja*, I'll be reporting back to him on Monday, but I thought you would like to hear the news before then, there's a copy of the Death Certificate for Lance Redman stuck under the Tupperware Box. He was killed in a drive-by shooting on the Easter weekend."

"Who's Redman?"

"Antoinette's contact for fake passports. We had some luck with Redman being taken out by his own kind. We've opened a murder case and Stelios's uncle is part of our investigation."

"You mean…?" Alex's brain made sense of Bezuidenhout's tale and relief spread over his face. Bezuidenhout nodded.

"Redman is dead and Uncle George is in trouble. Believe me, Mr. Richards, Antoinette will find it bloody difficult to get a passport and run off to Greece."

"Thank God."

"Let me know when you go to Rio and I'll check in on the family while you're away." "Thank you, I appreciate it and I know my wife appreciates it." Alex held out his hand and Ignatius shook it. He was glad he wasn't in Alex's shoes. He must be dead scared of living through the nightmare of a runaway child again.

"It's my pleasure, sir."

BEZUIDENHOUT STEPPED out into the autumn evening. A chill wind had swept in while he was inside and he pulled his collar up to cover his ears. He was drawn to this family. He'd told Hettie about the courage and love that knitted it together, and how the father of Toni's unborn child tethered it to the dangerous underworld of drugs. He would keep an eye on the children and ask Hettie to pray to her God for help. He wanted to keep them safe.

36

P   am took Maggie's advice to heart. She went all out to tempt Alex. She searched the display racks at the travel agents, collected brochures on Rio and passed them on to him, but her agitation grew as he shuffled and reshuffled them before laying them aside like a bad hand of cards, promising to look at them later. He never did. His avoidance and lack of enthusiasm licked the icing off her excitement. She swallowed her disappointment, but it churned inside and she turned again to Pieter De Bruin for advice.

"He won't talk about it," she told the psychiatrist.

"He fears it."

"Why? I thought that, after the nightmare we've been through with Toni, he'd welcome a chance to escape and he's working under such pressure that a break will do him good," she said.

"You call it an escape," said Pieter. "But you do not understand. He can leave his work and family responsibilities behind, but not the depression. It will go with him. It is heavy baggage and he is not ready to carry it. He will collapse. To a degree, the medication is working. I am sure that you will agree that he is functioning, but the crucial balance of the correct dosage is not always there. It will kick in and synchronise his body and mind and then he will be ready to go, but that will take time."

"How much time?" she whispered.

"I cannot say."

She cried inside, but she understood what he was saying. She'd glimpsed that crucial balance.

IT FLOATED like a seashell in the shallows of a spent wave. It tantalised and coaxed and convinced her, time and again, that Alex was whole and recovered, but, just as her hands reached to scoop it up and touch its beauty, a wave of panic sucked it back, tumbling and smashing it as Alex sank back into the dark abyss, leaving her alone and weeping on a desolate beach of despair. The glimpses, the hope, the illusion, the devastation and the bitter disappointments all confirmed Pieter's assessment and she faced the facts. Alex was not ready to go to Rio.

Triumph sent a letter of congratulations, asking her to contact them with dates for the trip. They wanted to arrange a press release and hand over the prize, but she couldn't ask Alex about it, and slipped the letter into her handbag. She shoved the brochures in the drawer of the bedside pedestal, behind a pile of old birthday and Christmas cards and the family Bible that had belonged to her Great Grandmother. She shut the drawer on the promises of carefree days, powdery, soft beaches, swaying umbrella palms and exotic delights. They were out of sight, but they grew and festered in her mind and she itched to pull them out. A second letter arrived from Triumph.

They were writing, they said, to remind her about the trip she'd won and asked her to contact them with her details as they wanted to finalise the tickets and arrange a press function to hand over the prize, asap.

Her lips set in a firm line. As her gran would say, they must think her right odd. Regular people don't need reminding that they've won a trip to Rio. Whether Alex was ready or not, she had to tackle him and fix their departure date and, after supper tonight, was as good a time as any to do so.

She cooked his favourite curry, but he toyed with it, eating very little, offering a busy day as an excuse for not doing it justice, however his gaunt face told her he was battling and that she shouldn't bother serving the fruit salad and ice cream for dessert. Furthermore, if she was wise, she would defer the Rio discussion to a better time.

SHE SIGHED and scraped his barely-touched meal into the rubbish bin, dumping the plate into the sink. "And when, pray tell, will that be?" she asked her reflection in the kitchen window. Alex's lack of appetite sapped her energy. She leant across the sink to draw the curtains and a Kombi, painted in swirling psychedelic colours, pulled into the drive-way. Who on earth was this? She was not in the mood for company. The van sputtered to an oil-leaking halt, the doors slid back, and her spirits lifted. It was Valentino and a bunch of the kids from the art school.

. . .

"You've got company, Toni," she called, watching them haul boxes and packets from the dilapidated interior. Toni opened the front door and ran to the van. Hugs and kisses, ohhs and ahhs were exchanged in the driveway and they made their way inside.

"We'll clean up, we promise, Mrs. Richards," they said, as they spread themselves, chocolate cake, sausage rolls, crisps, beer and Cokes around the family room. They tied a bonnet on Toni's head, a bib around her neck and sat her on a large, white ceramic potty. Self-portraits embellished it and Pam thought that one day, if these talented kids fulfilled their dreams and became famous artists, it would be a very valuable collector's piece for her grandchild.

Valentino, and his older brother, Daniel, the owner and driver of the Volksie bus, carried in a huge box wrapped in baby paper and covered with dozens of bows. Valentino flipped back his shoulder-length hair, opened his shaved arms and embraced the room. "It's from all of us," he declared.

"Definitely gay," Alex whispered to Pam.

"Who cares? He's a damn good friend to Toni."

She sounded tetchy and she'd been preoccupied at supper. He had the feeling that she wasn't happy with him but couldn't work out why. Must be because he hadn't eaten much of his supper; everything had been okay between them when he had left for work this morning.

"What's wrong?" he asked.

She put a finger on her lips, her eyes telling him to be quiet. Maybe it wasn't him, but one of the kids.

"Is Kelly okay?"

She nodded, her lips pressed together.

"Then what's up?"

"Later," she held up a hand. "Toni's opening her present."

YEP, he was in trouble. Why and how deep he didn't know, but he was obviously going to find out later. He shrugged, there was bugger-all he could do about it right now. Sipping Coke straight from a can, he found a seat on the other side of the room and turned his attention to Toni's bubbly eccentric friends. Their clothes were not carbon copies; each one flaunted his/her own style. They were extreme, daring, glamorous, flamboyant, anything but ordinary and their confidence electrified the air. Unlimited energy and freedom was theirs and they were exploring worlds far different to Toni's, yet here they were, keeping a pulse on her life, letting her know that, pregnant or not, she was forever a kindred spirit. He watched her wipe away a tear with the back of her hand, give a shaky grin as she picked off the bows, one by one, and peeled back pieces of sticky-tape. She was opening the present as slowly as she could. It made Christmas and birthdays last longer she'd told him when she was little. His throat ached.

"LET me help or we'll be here all night," said Brian, his hands reaching for the wrapping-paper, but Toni gave them a stinging slap. Kelly tucked her hands safe under her armpits, but her foot tapped the tiled floor as her pregnant sister stripped the box naked and Daniel read the printing on the sides.

"A three-in-one pram. Wow," he said, giving Toni a grin and a thorough once-over. "These guys must really like you. They tell me you're pregnant, but where are you hiding the baby?"

"Right here," laughed Toni, pointing to the small bulge pushing against the waist of her red dungarees. Valentino's hand flew to his cheek and he stepped forward, his eyes wide with wonder.

"Oh, Precious. Can I feel? Does it move?" he asked. Toni nodded. "It feels like a flutter, like a feather tickling me on the inside and I've heard the heartbeat," she said.

Everyone lined up to touch her tummy, Daniel too. He was last in the queue, but Toni stiffened as he put out his hand and Pam sat up straight. Unlike the others, he was not an old, familiar school friend. She liked Valentino and this was his brother, but he'd never sat in a class with her daughter, never painted and sculpted nudes in her company, and the look in his eye was that of a 'straight' healthy male who found her Toni attractive. Daniel pulled his hand back and Pam relaxed, but throughout the evening she caught the smiles, shy on Toni's part, downright bold on Daniel's, that flashed between them. He seemed a nice enough guy, but Pam was wary of the young man's attention. She'd misjudged Stelios and he'd put them through hell. The nightmare of Toni, missing, and in danger, haunted her and unforgettable heartache skewed her objectivity and raised her suspicions, but a thought wriggled into her head. If Daniel and Toni hit it off, all the secret plans to run off to Greece would disappear and they could get back to being a regular family again. The twisted thought had appeal. How else would they stop her going? Bezuidenhout had told Alex that it would be difficult for her to get another forged passport, but he did not say it would be impossible. What chance did Daniel have with her?

STELIOS HAD BROKEN her heart when he ditched her, saving his neck from a prison sentence by fleeing to Greece, but Pam had overhead her planning to take the baby and go to him. Toni was lonely, cut off from her old friends and not fitting in at the secretarial college and the baby was growing inside her and tightening the blood-knot with its father. Was all forgiven? Could it ever be?

DAMN. Daniel was not a quick-fix answer to Toni's situation, but, when Pam overheard him asking if he could pick Toni up after college the next day and saw her nod in reply, she crossed her fingers. Maybe, just maybe, a miracle would happen and Daniel would steal her daughter's heart.

IT WAS past midnight when the art kids hopped back into Daniel's van. The Richards' family waved goodbye until the kombi reversed out of the drive, swung into the main road and vanished from sight. Back inside, the family room felt like an empty theatre after a sparkling performance. The stage was empty, but the magic lingered. Alex's bedtime pills were long overdue and his nerves twitched, but, as the evening's scenes replayed in his mind, a soppy smile crept across his face and he helped the kids tidy up. He plonked the large, white potty into the three-in-one pram and Toni wheeled it to her bedroom. Her sister and brother followed, chatting as they made their way to bed. He closed the windows, checked the locks on the doors and carried the large, empty box and torn wrapping paper to the kitchen.

PAM PULLED a small pot of steaming milk from the stove. "Horlicks?" she asked. Her back was stiff, her lips twitched and she gave herself that familiar silent nod. She was rehearsing a speech. The evening's show wasn't over. He was about to find out the reason for her earlier displeasure.

"No thanks," he said. Whatever she wanted to say would have to remain a secret until tomorrow. "I'm bushed and going to bed."

He bent to kiss her. She averted her face. Not a good sign.

"I got a letter from Triumph this afternoon," she said, swishing the milk back and forth.

"Who is Triumph?" he asked. He had to get to the bedroom and the pills he should have taken two-and-a-half hours ago.

"The bra people," she said, slapping the spoon on the counter. "I won a trip, remember?"

"Of course, I do." The kitchen was shrinking; he had to escape. He couldn't talk about the trip, her prize or anything to do with Rio. She threw him a look and he stood still.

"The PR department want to book the tickets and hand over the prize, but I need dates from you." She poured the milk into the mug, stirring in a teaspoon of sugar. He ran his hand over his face, wiping sweat from his forehead and avoiding her eyes. The walls pressed in. "Just give me time to think about it."

She dumped the mug onto the counter. Horlicks splashed onto the Formica and she grabbed a dishcloth and mopped it up. "What do you have to think about? Pick a date, any date, in July, I don't care what it is."

His throbbing temples scrambled his thoughts. Her cheeks flamed. He tried to speak, to plead his case, but the words stuck to his dry palate. Tears glistened in her eyes. She was disappointed, frustrated, but he couldn't give her dates, not tonight. He walked away.

"Thanks for nothing." The dishcloth whizzed past his head and hit the wall. He didn't look back.

37

"Ma? Ma, are you up?" Kelly's anxious voice called through the bedroom door and woke Pam. Filtering through the curtains, the morning sun bathed the bedroom in light too bright for six-thirty. A quick glance at the clock had her flinging back the duvet and peeling off her pyjamas.

"Coming," she called, diving into the cupboard, grabbing clothes, pulling on underwear and a white, cotton-knit top. She shook Alex's body. "Get up." He grunted. Swallowed late, his sleeping pills were still on duty and his body sagged into the mattress. She gave him another rough shake. "It's after seven." She zipped herself into a black skirt and charged for the bathroom, scrubbed her teeth, pulled a brush through the tangles in her hair. Dark circles ringed her eyes and fretful sleep dulled her skin; she shuddered. She looked dreadful and there was no time for make-up. Kelly and her science project were due at school in twenty minutes.

• • •

ROTTEN GUTS WAS Brian's name for her model of the digestive system and it counted for fifty percent of her term mark. He'd engineered the stomach and anus valves, securing them in a shallow box that looked like a lidless coffin.

PAM SLAPPED on moisturiser and Alex's reflection materialised next to hers in mirror. His drained eyes avoided hers. His jaw was clenched. His silence cemented last night's fight into the morning rush. She turned on a bare heel and flounced out.

THE CHILDREN HAD FINISHED their breakfast and cleared away the dishes, but open cereal boxes, milk and sugar cluttered the counter. Pam was going with Maggie to *Makro,* the big discount store, to do the monthly stationery shopping for Direct Technologies. She shoved her feet into comfy walking flats, threw a fistful of Coco Pops into her mouth, switched on the warm kettle and spooned instant coffee into two mugs. Toni was retching in the kids' bathroom and she heard Alex knock on the door.

"We're late, Toni," he called.

The toilet flushed and the kettle boiled. Pam crunched dry cereal and cold-shouldered Alex as he fumbled in the fridge and downed his first pills of the day with water straight from the bottle. Last night's quarrel screamed over their studied silence. She slid a mug of coffee in his direction.

"Thanks," he mumbled. He gulped down the hot liquid, slung a tie around his neck and tied his shoelaces. Kelly rushed into the kitchen, her face a picture of agitation.

"Hurry up, Ma," she said, scooping the lunch-boxes off the counter. "Brian's already in the car. He's put our school bags and the model in the boot."

Pam whipped up her bag and glanced in Alex's direction. His gaunt face locked out the chance she threw at him. No travel dates. Bugger him. She pushed past without kissing him goodbye, pecked Toni on the forehead and followed Kelly's skinny legs to the garage. Brian and Kelly swopped a 'what's up with her' glance as she slammed the car door shut, rammed the gearstick into reverse and shot out of the garage.

"MA." yelled Brian.

DORIS JEFFREY'S REFLECTION, hair swinging in a damp pony-tail, filled the rear-view mirror. Adrenaline shot through Pam's body and her foot floored the brakes. Brian's head jerked forward, and Kelly screamed. The car screeched, swerved and missed Doris. Face pale, her neighbour made the sign of the cross, kissed her fingertips and sank to her knees. Pam jumped out of the car and knelt over her.

"Are you okay?" she asked.

Doris nodded. "I'm fine," she gasped.

"You sure? I'm sorry… Oh my God, what a fright, I didn't mean to…"

"I'm fine, really, just give me a minute then I'll hop over the fence, go home and have a lie down. You'd best be on your way. Your kids are late for school."

Sitting on her heels, Doris waved her back to the car, pulled a cross and chain out of the top of her sweatshirt and held it, in a tight fist, to her heart.

SWEAT GLUED Pam's hands to the steering-wheel. She'd almost killed her friend. What the hell was she doing getting so angry with Alex that she couldn't think or see straight? It was stupid. Hadn't Pieter told her that Alex wasn't capable of coughing up the damn dates? The sooner she listened to what he had to say and accepted it the better. She wiped her palms on her skirt, gave the kids a reassuring smile and eased into the street.

THE SCHOOL GROUNDS WERE EMPTY; assembly was over, and first period had already started. The Alfa's squealing brakes echoed in the quiet street as Pam pulled to a stop at the main gate.

"I'll help Kelly; you get to class," she instructed Brian. He unloaded the boot, handed Kelly her bag, grabbed his own and ran. Kelly hefted the bag and hurried on and Pam picked up the science project. Balancing Rotten Guts on her hip, she trotted after her daughter.

Fitting herself and Rotten Guts through the door of the science laboratory was not easy. Twisting and turning the bloody thing at all angles, Pam succeeded in getting the top half in, but the mid-section got stuck in the door-frame, and the bottom half remained in the corridor outside the class-room. The students and Mr Johnson swivelled their heads in her direction and Kelly rushed over. "Don't break it," she said, crawling out into the passage. Carefully, she pushed and Pam pulled, but it stayed stuck until Emma, Kelly's best friend, added a bit of weight to Kelly's push and Rotten Guts popped from the door-frame. Amid tittering, the three of them found space between the other models and propped it against the wall. Effort and embarrassment burnt their cheeks. Mr Thompson turned back the cuff of his sleeve and looked at his watch.

"I'm sorry; it's my fault that Kelly's late," Pam mumbled. "Please excuse her."

The class registered her unkempt hair and sweat-streaked, soap-dried face. They stared and Kelly squirmed.

"Sorry, Snoggums," Pam whispered in Kelly's burning ear as she beat a hasty retreat.

AT WORK, she kept last night's quarrel to herself, applied make-up to conceal the dark circles under her eyes and finger-combed her hair into a ponytail. Raymond would have a fit if he saw the red elastic band. She banished Rotten Guts, Alex, Triumph and Rio to the back of her mind, but they snuck out, trawled *Makro's* towering aisles and spoilt the monthly shopping spree with Maggie.

REPLENISHING stationery supplies was an excuse to escape their tedious office duties. A feast of non-essential office snacks and bargains raided from the special offer bins took up most of the trolley space and made dents in their personal credit cards. Girl fun, they called it, but today Pam's false smile made her cheeks ache, while Maggie dilly-dallied and found the buy of the day. Wedging her toes under the thin straps of a pair of black patent stilettos, Maggie secured the ankle-straps and waggled her feet.

"Look you, now there's gorgeous," she said, her Welsh lilt and tinkle of silver charms grabbing Pam's attention. "And here's a red pair in your size. Try them on, go on. Today they're half-price." Dangling from Maggie's index finger, glossy red patent clashed with her *Revlon's* pale ginger nail polish and tempted Pam, but her appetite was too jaded to put the sandals on. She took them and dropped them into their trolley, on top of two giant packets of peri-peri peanuts.

"They'll fit," she said, and, ignoring the 'what's up' arch of Maggie's groomed eyebrow she led the way to the tills and drove them back to the office where they unpacked the Alfa's boot. The *Makro* experience came without shopping bags, and, balancing their purchases in their arms, they staggered to the front door and Eric's latest 'Tit Memo'.

HE'D WRITTEN the first one when she won the prize and today's was written on a small piece of paper torn from the spine of Maggie's notebook and tacked to the wooden door. Maggie squinted at it. "I can't see a thing without my glasses. Can you read it?" she asked, hugging lever arch files, two reams of A4 white paper, two boxes of 24 Mars Bars and Peppermint Crisps, a giant packet of cashews and the black patent stilettos to her ample breast. Equally laden, Pam peered over Maggie's shoulder and read the note aloud.

· · ·

*T*o: *Big Tits and Lucky Tits*

From: No Tits

Gone to collect the cable shipment at customs.

GOOD NEWS - WE GOT THE GAS ARRESTOR ORDER FOR DECEMBER.

Bad news – Pretoria won't increase Yen permits - we must place on Rogaf. I must to go to Spain.

LT - GOOD LUCK WITH DON. WE NEED MONEY.

NT.

"Nothing like a bit of pressure," said Pam, thinking of her 3 o'clock appointment with Don Pearson and the wobbly balance sheet she was taking to him, but she returned Maggie's grin; it was a great order.

"I reckon this calls for celebration," said Maggie. Juggling the shopping, she unlocked the door and kicked it inwards. "How about queuing at The Prawn Palace this evening, say around seven?"

Pam hesitated.

"Something wrong? I knew there was. You couldn't get us out of *Makro* quick enough. Is it Alex?" Not so long-ago Maggie would have asked if it was Kelly, but Alex's depression had stolen prime spot in the never-ending deluge of bad events.

"We're sort of not speaking. Triumph wants to arrange a cocktail party and press release and hand tickets over to me, but last night Alex side-stepped the subject of dates as usual and I lost my cool, so honestly, I don't know how he is."

"Look, I don't want to interfere, but what about asking Eric to talk to him?"

Pam waggled her hand.

"No. It won't help," she said. "Pieter tells me that Alex simply can't face the whole idea of travelling right now." She tossed her head and swallowed the lump that was so often in her throat these days. "So, I'm just going to phone Triumph, give them any old dates in July and hope to hell he comes right by then." She opened the cupboard under her desk and packed away the tally rolls. Keeping the 'what if he isn't' thoughts at bay, she stowed the envelopes and lever arch files, tore off a sheet of kitchen paper from the holder fixed above the dispatch counter, wiped her hands and smoothed her skirt over her hips.

Maggie headed for the bar fridge under the components' assembly line. "Of course, he'll be okay by then and we'll celebrate Eric's order another time." She moved beer bottles, making space for the boxes of chocolates. "Peppermint Crisp?" she asked, biting off a piece before handing Pam the foil-wrapped bar. "Mmmm, heaven," she said. "But come on, try on your shoes before you go to the bank and bring us back some cash."

"Some cash?" Pam snapped her fingers. "Just like that?"

"Sure, Don likes you. Turn on your charm, smile sweetly and ask nicely," Maggie teased, but Pam chewed chocolate and her bottom lip.

THE FACT WAS that the balance sheet was weak, and the cash flow was an aneurism ready to burst. Handling their biggest order to date via telex with Rogaf was too risky. One interpretation error, one late delivery and Direct Technologies was dead. The visit to Europe was no longer a matter for heated discussion. Eric was right; he had to go to Spain.

SHE PULLED off her flat shoes and wriggled her hot feet into the stilettos.

"What do you think?" she asked, flexing her ankle.

"Fantastic. They look like stilettos should look, high and sexy. They match your nail polish perfectly and they're just what I had in mind when I said you should wear something distracting to the meeting." Maggie gave her a thumbs-up, a black-lashed wink. "Now, give me swinging hips and a trial slink around the office."

"You're not serious?"

"Don't be such a fuddy-duddy. I guarantee they'll brighten Don's day more than those dull figures you've put together. As my Grandmother Gwyneth used to say, a man is no match for a woman's charms, well, what she actually said was, 'a stiff cock has no conscience' and those shoes are designed to turn a man on."

"You're outrageous," laughed Pam.

"That I am, now, hip sway, please."

Pam pranced across the slasto floor, rolling her hips as instructed.

"Well, look at you," said Maggie, clapping her hands together. "Born to slink." She opened her desk drawer, pulled the stopper from the neck of a bottle of Chanel Number 5, dabbed it behind Pam's ears, the inside of her wrists and elbows and the back of her knees, gathered up the reports, handed them to Pam and propelled her strutting partner out of the office.

38

His fingers had touched every hair on her head, but for a split-second Pam didn't recognise the tall man in a grey pinstriped suit coming out of the bank and giving her a Colgate toothpaste smile. He laughed as she returned it with a vague twitch of the lips. "It's me, Raymond," he said. "What are you doing here?"

"Asking for a loan." She felt a warm blush move up her neck. He looked good. Too good for innocence, Maggie would say.

"Me too. My accountant said I needed money to pay my taxes so here I am all dressed up in my begging gear. Like it?"

"Very smart." Pam kept her voice light, but her pulse quickened. "Did they work? Your clothes? Did you get the money?"

Raymond nodded, stroking the suit's lapels. "A treat," he said. He gave her hair the once-over. "Looks like I've got a bit of work to do on Friday," he said, pulling car keys from his jacket pocket. Gold flecks danced in his eyes. Did he know that she noticed them?

"Friday?" she feigned surprise.

In spite of Maggie nagging her to avoid temptation and find a new hairdresser, Pam hadn't cancelled the appointment she'd circled on her calendar five weeks ago. Raymond gave her a lazy smile.

"I have you booked as my last appointment," he said. Her mouth went dry, her skin tingled and a thousand butterflies flapped their wings in her stomach. She felt like a school-girl, excited and giddy. It was a dangerous, carefree feeling for the mother of three teenage children whose husband of twenty years was a depressed stranger. She could see Maggie's fierce grey eyes and wagging school-marm finger and heard her telling her to run, but she drank in the heady, sparkling moment and filled her lungs with electrified air.

"Date?" Raymond's question clamped her raging senses. This game had to stop. It was dangerous. His was a busy salon and she was one of many clients, she could bluff her way out.

"I cancelled, didn't I?" she asked, her eyes wide with false innocence. The flecks danced in his eyes.

"No, you didn't. I thought you would, so I've checked your appointment regularly. It's still pencilled in my book."

He'd go to Rio in a flash. Nothing wrong with his crucial balance.

The blush flooded her cheeks. *Dear God, she was comparing him with Alex. Her Alex who was doing his best to kick depression in the butt and get their life back on track.*

"Look, Raymond, I can't..."

"Sure you can," he grinned anyway, I asked Mario to keep your coffee warm."

"Mario?"

"The guy who owns the café next to the salon. See you." He waved and headed to his car before she could protest further.

EFFICIENT AIR-CONDITIONING inside the bank cooled her flushed face and raised goosebumps on her arms. She found an empty chair to sit on outside Don's office, took a few deep breaths and tried to focus on the figures she'd prepared for him, but running into Raymond had sent her arse over kettle, as her gran would say. She would also say, "Nip this in the bud, my luv."

But he looks bloody fantastic in a suit.

Her own crucial balance capsized in a sea of tantalising thoughts.

PENELOPE SINCLAIR-SMITH stuck her head out of the door next to Don Pearson's. She wore a powder-blue twin-set and a string of pearls that could have come out of Pam's great aunt's jewellery box, and her hair was the same pink-rinsed grey, waved and kiss-curled into shape, framing an unlined face. Pam admired her smooth skin, the result of a lifetime spent sheltered under bonnets and sun-hats, but not the thin, tight lips that had never licked a smile.

"Come in," said Penelope, her sharp eyes cataloguing Pam's dark roots, bitten thumb-nail, cotton top, black skirt and red stilettos.

"But I've got an..." Pam clutched her papers.

"I know - an appointment with Donald. Well, he's gone home.

Gastric flu or food poisoning, I'm not sure which, but it requires urgent visits to the bathroom and I'm standing in for him for the next few days."

"Oh," Pam's heart sank, but she obeyed, entering Ms Sinclair-Smith's office and taking a seat in the visitor's chair.

The elderly woman had opened Direct Technologies' bank account, dotting the 'i's and the 't's in triplicate on all the forms, especially the suretyships and insurance for their inadequate overdraft. She was astute, due to retire and single, her life given to a bank that had denied her the manager's desk and fostered her meanness.

SHE SAT OPPOSITE PAM, her back to the large window that framed a sea of yellow car-ports in the parking-lot. Tortoise-shell framed glasses hung from a chain around her neck and rested on full bosoms, perfect pillows for the snuggling grandchildren that she'd never had. She held out her hand for the papers and, settling the glasses on her nose, peered through the bi-focal half-moons, scrutinising the figures, asking more probing questions than Don usually did and making copious notes in a neat, economical script. Pam smiled and fawned, presented a copy of Eric's new order, said it wasn't included in the figures presented, emphasised its high profit margin and the positive effect it would have on the predicted bottom line. Penelope's

raised hand cut short the sales pitch. She tapped the papers tidy and let her glasses fall back onto her breast. It rose and fell as the hum of late banking business filtered through the door and intensified the silence within. Pam pushed her knees tightly together and willed herself not to fidget. Ms

Sinclair-Smith controlled the silence, the overdraft and Eric's trip.

"I'm afraid we cannot help you. Your company looks too risky."

"But the new order really makes a huge difference."

If only Don were here. He'd look beyond the slither of Direct Technologies recorded in the black and white cash-flow and see their vibrant, ambitious company. He'd help it survive.

"We're only asking for..."

"I know, more money; but let's face the facts. As importers, you are at the mercy of our volatile rand and a world threatening sanctions on South Africa."

"Exactly." Pam sat forward, her palms turned up, open, imploring. "That's why we need the money. We need the money to go to Europe and verify our suppliers' support, especially those in Spain."

Ms Sinclair-Smith's thin mouth twitched, her eyes locked onto Pam's shoes. "I remember wearing heels like that," she said. "They're killers." She stood up and handed the papers back to Pam. "It is impossible for us to increase your overdraft at this time."

PAM all but snatched the sheets from the spinster's hand and strode from the office. Trapped inside the revolving door, she seethed. Her efforts had been as wasted as Penelope's billowing breasts. *How dare that woman smirk at her shoes?* Shrivelled ovaries and spite, not the company's figures, had denied Direct Technologies the increased loan. Pam pushed her weight against the door handle, but it was as stubborn as Alex's depression and resisted her attempts to speed it up. Forced to wait out the door's slow turn, her brain threw up a solution to Eric's nagging, but she didn't like it. Alex's crucial balance kicked in and out; giving her hope; snatching it away; tarnishing the excitement of winning the trip. She was beaten. To hell with her dreams; the prize was Eric's ticket to Europe.

39

T he air-conditioner in De Bruin's office lifted and waved the half-pulled tissue on the coffee table. An antique inkwell sat next to the tissue box and a prism paperweight tossed jewelled colours onto Pieter's anchored notebook. Alex glanced at the large face of the railway clock. Thursday's session was drawing to a close and his body was behaving normally, no racing heart, no clammy hands, no need to practise breathing. There was only ten minutes to go and he was eager to slip from official to friendship time, pick up where they'd left off last week and chat about Jung's *Answer to Job* and Pieter's diagnostic questionnaire. His programmer had given him a list of questions to ask the psychiatrist and he would enjoy the role-swapping.

"How do you feel about Pam winning the trip?"

Pieter's question came from left field and slammed into the soft underbelly of his tranquillised emotions, dragging out the buried fear and exploding it. He folded his arms tighter across his chest and held his breath. Pieter stretched out his long legs, crossed them at his ankles and stroked his moustache in slow, smooth sweeps, from the middle to the clipped edges. Alex shot a look at the railway clock; six minutes left. His head spun. Pictures from Pam's brochure collection crowded in: The dazzling beaches, Sugar Loaf Mountain, Carnival, headdresses, centrefold perfect bodies and tiny bikinis. Any normal male would be on the first flight to Rio.

But he wasn't any normal male. He was a fucking scared dickhead sitting on a shrink's couch.

Through clenched teeth his mouth spat out a reply.

"I wish she hadn't won the damn thing."

Pieter gave a slight nod but remained silent.

Shit, the truth was out, he might as well expand on it.

"Every day I force myself to get out of bed and go to work. I want to tell you that without the pills I wouldn't manage. I go from dose to dose and sometimes I take them before time. And the emptiness... That fucking hole, it lies there... All the time, waiting for me to fall in. How the hell am I going to go to Rio? Shit, what if I have a panic attack on the plane, or in bloody Brazil? Hell. No man, I can't. I just can't go."

Pieter shook his head. "You have not answered my question, Alex. I asked you how you feel."

Alex stared at Pieter. He hated those words. He'd told Pieter hundreds of times that they irritated the hell out of him. He never knew what to say or whether he was giving the right answer. Pieter never told him. From the middle to the clipped edge, Pieter stroked his moustache and waited. Relentless. Okay, tell him.

"I'm scared. Scared shitless."

De Bruin threw back his head and laughed. "That is most descriptive. You are learning to express yourself and I am very proud of you."

"Yes, well," Alex shrugged, shifting in his seat. "Pam isn't. She's pushing for dates and I can't give them to her. She's pissed off with me and I don't blame her. I'm pretty pissed off with me too."

Pieter steepled his fingers, tapped them against pursed lips. "You have exposed your fear, expressed it, now you must face and conquer it."

Alex snorted. "Oh yeah? And just how do I do that?"

"With a 'trial' journey," said Pieter, indicating inverted commas in the air. "And your passion for aeroplanes."

"You're kidding me, what passion? I started building a couple of slope soarers with Brian, but since the Riverside Clinic episode, I hardly join him in the workshop and the poor kid has landed up making them more or less on his own."

"But you did start them and you have helped him; trust me, your passion is there, but like a warrior's sword plunged into a dying body, it is held in a sheath of depression. We will extricate it, wield it and destroy your fear." Pieter's theatrical words, gift-wrapped in his guttural Afrikaans accent, tugged a dry smile from Alex.

"And how exactly do we extricate this sword?" he asked.

"Take those new gliders to the mountains in the Eastern Transvaal. Have you not told me that it is magic to fly there?"

Alex gave a hesitant nod. "I did, but it takes a couple of hours to get there."

"And that makes you nervous?"

"Yes." This time his nod was firm. Kaap se Hoop was four-and-a-half long hours away. His medication worked ninety percent of the time, but the volatile remaining ten percent ripped him into a million crazy pieces.

"I see, but it makes you less nervous than thinking of Rio."

"Maybe, but... Look..."

"I would like to teach you visualisation. First, we will start with your normal relaxation exercise. Make yourself comfortable."

"I really don't..."

Pieter waited. Alex shifted an inch backward in his seat. A trace of amusement snuck into De Bruin's voice.

"Ahh, Alex, you can do better than that. Lean back. That is better. Now, close your eyes. Drop those shoulders and unclench your fists. Good, breathe as you do to calm the panic."

Slow, steady breaths sucked out the fear. Pieter was right. The journey to Kaap se Hoop did not scare him as much as Rio; there was no airport, no crowds, no queues and no claustro-phobic overseas flight. Just a car drive to a mountain and a slope.

Pieter's voice floated in. "Now, picture yourself getting ready to go. You are making an early start, walking out of your front door."

Alex's mind clicked into the scene.

His footsteps crunched on the bricks outside the door.

"You are carrying suitcases." Pieter added the props.

Heavy, tan leather cases pulled his elbows straight. He loaded them into the boot. Autumn nipped the tips of his ears and fingers and he pulled up the collar of his navy windbreaker. The red fleece lining hugged his neck.

"The children are excited and waiting." Pieter cued in the cast.

They argued. No one wanted to sit in the middle of the back seat. Morning sickness drained Toni's face and Kelly's skinny body screamed for a pillow-padded corner. Brian got the middle spot.

"But it's not my turn. It's not fair," he whined, but he climbed in, scowled at the girls and settled into a sulk. Alex slipped aeroplane wings into a harness slung from the roof of the car.

"Pam climbs into the car, she is impatient to go."

The safety-belt clicked as she strapped herself into the passenger seat, wedged the cooler-bag and padkos into the space in front of her feet and closed the door.

"You settle into your seat, turn on the ignition."

The engine purred. He checked his shirt pocket for his medication. NO PILLS. He shoved his hands into the back pocket of his jeans. NOTHING.

The visualised picture shattered.

"Shit, I can't do this."

Alex stood up, ran his hand over his neck and peeled the collar from his sticky neck. He unbuttoned and rolled up his shirt cuffs, yanked the pulled tissue from the box and wiped his forehead dry.

No place was safe, panic-free. Not Rio, not Kaap se Hoop, not the trusted shrink's couch.

"It will get easier," soothed Pieter.

"Like when? Man, I freaked out there. I'm sweating like a pig."

"I promise. It will get better and a journey to the mountains will speed up the progress."

"Hell, I don't know..."

"I would like to come and see you fly," said Pieter.

"You would?" Hope flickered in Alex. If Pieter accompanied him and kept the dreaded ten percent chemical lapse at bay, maybe he could drive to the Eastern Transvaal, extricate the bloody sword, kill his fear and get his act together.

He'd told Pieter that Pam was pissed off with him because he couldn't give her dates for Rio, but it was worse than that. His depression was chipping away at the foundation of their marriage. His panic attacks, mood swings and seclusion strained the love from her voice, polished her smile brittle-bright and stopped it reaching her eyes. Their marriage was cracking; he had to prop it up. Pam loved the mountains and she'd jump at the chance to spend a weekend there.

"Seriously, you'd like to come?"

"Of course," said Pieter. "I cannot resist the rare and potent force of magic."

40

Alex's car swung into the driveway spewing up dust which swirled and settled on the broad agapanthus leaves and white Shasta daisies flourishing on Frans's well-tended pavement. Parking next to the Alfa he turned off the engine and sat in the car, ignoring Mickey and Bella's barks. He was eager to give Pam the good news, to try and put things right between them, but she hadn't kissed him goodbye this morning and, after twenty years of marriage and goodbye kisses he knew the score. He was in trouble. Would Pieter's idea of a 'trial trip' curl her tight lips into a smile?

And if depression strikes?

The thought slapped him.

Shit, what then? The trip would be a disaster; he'd never get to Rio. Pam would never forgive him.

He climbed out of the car and let himself in.

· · ·

"Mickey. Bella. Shut up."

"Toni sounds cross," he said, scooping up the yapping dogs. "Where is she? Let's go find her."

She was sitting at the dining-room table, leaning forward, scowling at a small notebook and chewing the top of a sharp pencil. Tucked behind her ears, her hair fell to her waist. It shone brightly, like it had when she'd sat at his mother's feet, cuddling Anna, her First Love doll, and counted the slow stokes of her Gran's silver hairbrush. Long before she reached one hundred he'd have to pick up her sleep-warm body and carry her to bed.

Toni's hand rested on the small bulge of her pregnant stomach. His mother's words and knitting needles echoed in his head. "She's not the first unmarried girl to get pregnant and she won't be the last. Forgive her and get on with it," she had said, casting off a matineé jacket. Click-click went her needles, pulling one spaghetti-thin stitch over the other, and he'd almost done what she said. He'd forgiven Toni for being pregnant, but not for running away. Her deceit lay like a stone in his heart and ate holes in his soul. Every so often he'd catch Pam flinch, wrap her arms around her chest and blink away unbidden thoughts and know she felt the same, yet, somehow, she'd managed to open her heart to Toni and withhold none of her love. He couldn't do that; he had to protect himself. When Toni was missing, he'd swallowed De Bruin's pills and slept at night, but Pam hadn't, and her swollen red eyes and gaunt face tore him to pieces. It was her wretchedness and Kelly and Brian's tight faces that morphed his fear and pain and changed it into anger. Waiting for the Transkei bus, he'd planning her punishment. No movies, no parties, no friends. NO FUCKING STELIOS and, if she didn't obey him, a bloody good hiding and a trip to the welfare court. And then he'd seen her in the throng of black women and he'd loved her and given thanks to a God he wasn't sure he believed in.

SHE LOOKED up from her books and smiled. "Hi, Dad." He put down the dogs, but the weight of lost innocence stayed with him.

"Hi. Where's your Mom and why such a worried face?" he asked.

"She's in the veggie garden. I wrote this in class and I can't make sense of it."

Alex looked over her shoulder. "What on earth...?"

"It's Pitman's, Dad."

"What?"

"Shorthand. I hate it."

He stared at the mess and his grip tightened on the back of the chair. Art flowed in her blood. Line, shape and colour defined her, not these squiggles and dots. This was not what he wanted for his daughter, but she'd run away, failed Matric and he knew she was planning to run away again to that piece of scum in Greece. He, Pam, the kids – his family - would not survive another terrifying episode. Maybe, just maybe, Pam's hopes would come true and Toni would get to like Valentino's brother, Daniel and Stelios would be history.

And pigs might fly.

. . .

Toni pulled a face. "And I also hate dictation, but Ma says it's useful stuff and I'll get the hang of it."

Never. He had to keep her in South Africa. "Do you know what I think? I think you should go back to school next year, get that University pass, do a Fine Arts degree, go into fashion design or architecture, anything you want to."

Tears sprang into her eyes. "But everything's changed, Dad. The baby..."

"We'll help with the baby."

"It's not just the baby," she said, her voice thick. "Everything's changed."

"Give it a try," he said. "It's possible to change it back, Toni."

He heard the lie. It wasn't possible to change it back. He loved her, but his pain and anger stained the present and bled into the future.

41

Row by row Pam worked the vegetable patch, yanking out the weeds, shaking soil from their tangled roots and flinging them into the wheelbarrow. Sweat stained the underarms and back of her T-shirt and she dashed her tears away with the back of her garden glove, leaving muddy tracks on her cheeks.

Stop it. You're always bloody crying. It's boring. What's done is done.

She'd swung by the school on her way home from the bank and picked up the kids. Kelly was excited, bubbling over. Mr Thompson had entered her digestive system project, aka Rotten Guts, into the Inter-Provincial Science Fair in September. Kelly was explaining enzymes and proteins, but, although Pam was thrilled for her, she only half-listened while her head and heart examined the idea that had flashed into her mind as she'd fumed in the bank's revolving door. Her heart said it was a bad idea. It longed for escape, romance and thrills. It ached to go to Rio with Alex. Her mind didn't agree. It pointed out that, right now, Alex had zilch inclination to see Sugar Loaf Mountain or dance in the Rio Carnival. Taking him to Rio would be like dragging a dog to the vet. His bum would be on the floor and the trip would be a pain in the butt. Her mind won. She would get Eric that ticket to Europe.

SHE BLINKED BACK HER LOSS, mopped the sweat from her forehead, shoved the hand spade into the ground and stood up, rubbing her back. Thank goodness Frans was due back from his three-week annual holiday next Monday. Not that she expected him back until the Wednesday. It was his habit to return a day or two late, clear his throat and deliver his excuse.

"Aarh-em. The taxi, maa. The taxi, she never come. I wait and wait. No bus, no taxi, nothing." She would give him a 'Really? I'm not stupid' look and threaten to fire him if he did it again and he'd grin, knowing she understood the love he had for his family and that he was late because he had left them at the last possible moment. He'd deliver a parting "Aarh-em" and the ritual would be over until his next weekend off.

HIS MEALIE PLANTS were now knee-high, straight and strong, the tiny ears of corn peeking out from the space between the stalks and bent leaves. Soon he would harvest and sell them at the Zionist Church and his fellow worshipers would pay willingly for the Cokes he stored in the cooler-box they'd given him for Christmas. Weeds strangled her tomatoes, smothered her carrots and choked her green peppers and snap peas, but they didn't grow in his patch. They destroyed her hope of a good crop, much like Penelope Sinclair-Smith had almost destroyed the future of Direct Technologies. No further money was forthcoming from the bank, but Pam had put her idea into action and had secured the funds to go to Spain from Judith Anderson, Triumph's PR lady, who, after two reminders, was delighted to hear from Pam.

"Can you attend a prize hand-over cocktail party next week Tuesday, Mrs Richards?" she had asked.

Do you really want to do this? Think carefully before you do.

"Hello, Mrs. Richards, are you there? Hello?"

"We can't... I mean I ...I can't go," she'd whispered.

"Pardon? Mrs. Richards, did you say you can't go?"

"Yes."

"But why?"

The words tumbled out.

"I really do want to, but I can't, my husband isn't well. I don't know when he will get better, if ever, and my business partner needs to go to Europe, but the bank won't increase our overdraft and we need the money."

"Oh, my dear, you do sound upset."

"I'd like to cash in the prize, please."

"I'm afraid you can't. The rules of the competition are very clear, and the prize cannot be converted to cash. Listen, I would like to help. Let me speak to my boss and see what can be done and I'll get back to you."

PAM GRABBED the hand fork and shoved it into the soil. Damn Penelope. Damn Alex. Dammit. Dammit. Dammit. The rough wooden handle burst the blister in the palm of her hand. Shit. She pulled off her gloves and rinsed her hands under the garden tap, cooling the flaming skin and flooding the mint bush growing in the zinc bucket beneath. She turned off the tap as tightly as she could. It dripped, as Frans had often told her it did, but she wasn't used to Alex not fixing things around the house and kept forgetting to call in a plumber. She tugged at the mint, pulling off a few sprigs. Finely chopped and soaked in boiling water, with a dash of vinegar and a teaspoon of sugar, it would make a perfect sauce for tonight's roast leg of lamb, not that she had the appetite for it. Through the open kitchen window, she could hear Epol pellets pinging into the dogs' stainless-steel bowls and Kelly's deep voice as she instructed Mickey and Bella to stay away from each other's food. It was time to leave the garden and fix the vegetables and gravy. She tried giving the tap another turn. She turned it as tight as she could. It dripped. For Pete's sake. She picked up a half-brick and clouted it.

"Must you attack everything?"

She spun around and the teasing smile faded from Alex's face.

"What's wrong?" he asked.

"Nothing."

"You've been crying. Your face is all streaky."

"It's nothing."

Guilt crept into his eyes. "Look, if you're still mad about this morning and Rio, I spoke to Pieter, and ..."

"It's not..." she choked back the insistent tears. "It's not Rio, well not only Rio, it's everything."

"Such as?"

You going AWOL, Eric's whining, Penelope Sinclaire-Smith's spite, Kelly's illness, Toni's pregnancy, Brian's sport, tight budgets, never-ending bills, the dirty laundry, our life.

Rio.

"What's everything?"

She wiped her hands on the back of her shorts and sifted her thoughts. Alex was seeing Pieter every week, swallowing handfuls of pills, forcing himself out of bed and never missing a day at work. How could she tell him she was fed up to the back teeth; tired of coping on her own, that she missed him like crazy? She couldn't.

"Eric landed a huge order for gas arrestors."

"Well, that's great, isn't it?"

"Yes, but we only have permits for Pesetas, so we had to place our order on Rogaf in Spain, but they don't understand English. We obviously can't afford to mess up, so we have to go to their factory, but we don't have the money."

He shrugged his shoulders. "That's easy to fix. Get an increase on your overdraft."

"I've already tried that. No luck." She bit her lip to stop it quivering.

"Okay, listen, in six months Powertronics will be in a position to lend a bit of cash."

"We can't wait that long." She bent to hide her tears, gripped the tap and tried forcing it closed again. "Fuck."

"Here, let me do that." His firm twist did the trick. "There. I'll fix it properly on the weekend. What you need, besides my muscles, is a bit of magic and we might just find some in the Eastern Transvaal."

His lopsided grin was engaging, but it annoyed her. "What on earth has the Eastern Transvaal got to do with cash-flow?" she asked.

"Nothing, but some time ago I told Pieter about flying on the slope."

"And?" She stripped the mint leaves from their stalks.

"He'd like to go there. Today we spoke about my fears and Rio and he suggested a 'trial trip' to the Eastern Transvaal to sort out my head and get me on the plane. So, how about booking rooms for us and the Williams' at the Valencia? And maybe I'll be able to give you those dates for Triumph when we get back?"

He pushed the wheelbarrow to the small compost heap. She stared at his back, unable to believe what he was saying. She felt cheated.

TRUE TO HER WORD, Judith had reported back. "Good news for your company. Triumph will hand over a 'Romancing in Rio' voucher to you at the cocktail party, but the sponsoring airline has agreed to let you exchange the full value of the prize, accommodation included, for air tickets to any other destination or destinations, of your choice."

"That's fantastic. I'll give you my partners' details as soon as we've worked out an itinerary."

"Mrs. Richards, I'm afraid you don't understand. Unfortunately, the tickets are not transferable. Only you and your husband can use them."

HE TIPPED out the wilted weeds and sand. "You don't seem too happy," he said. "I thought you'd love to go to The Valencia?"

"Of course, I would."

He propped the barrow handles against the wall and turned to her. "I promise I'll do my level best to get to Rio." His eyes held hers, and, in their depths, beyond the fear she saw his love for her, and it made her sad.

"But this morning you..."

"Can we get past this morning and try to get to Rio?" he asked.

She stared at him. "No. I told Triumph we couldn't go."

"Well then phone them back and tell them that we can."

"I can't. I did a deal with them. I exchanged the prize for the business trip to Europe."

"That's great. I bet Eric's pleased. He loves business trips."

Relief flickered in his eyes and her sadness vanished. "You're glad, aren't you?"

Didn't he understand that she'd given up her dream? She kicked the tap. Hard.

"Look, I know you're disappointed," he said.

"Damn right I am."

"Hey, we'll still go to the mountains. At least you'll get away and, without an overseas trip hanging over us, there's no pressure."

"Really? No pressure? You'd better hope like hell that Pieter's idea works. We're not going to Rio, Alex, but the tickets are not transferable to a third party."

His face paled.

"We're going to Europe. Loads of countries in Europe."

"Jesus Christ."

42

The beat of *Tainted Love* thundered and shook the night club's walls. Mia Napoli was hopping. On a platform above the dancefloor, the DJ danced to the music. Spinning around, whacking his hips from side to side, back and forth, arms waving in the air above his shaking head, he lived each beat. Breathless, Toni sank into a corner booth, flipped her hair behind her ears, zipped open a Coke, tilted her head back and took a long swig. Daniel's mouth moved, but the music drowned out his words. She leaned closer to him.

"Can't hear you," she shouted.

"I said, I've been asking you forever to come out with me," Daniel yelled back. "I'd almost given up. What made you say yes this time?"

Toni turned away from him, her fingers fiddling with a strand of her hair.

"Well?" he shouted.

Toni pointed to her ears. "Can't hear. Come on, let's dance, I love this one."

WRIGGLING into a space between the Friday night clubbing bodies, they danced and whistled on the crowded floor and shouted for more when the DJ faded out *Forever Young*. The opening soft chords of Joy Division's "Love Will Tear Us Apart" pulled the kaleidoscopic figures into each other's arms and Toni blushed as her tummy bulge touched Daniel and he drew her closer. "I'm glad you came," he said.

"Me too. I haven't danced in ages."

"I mean... I really like you."

Toni pulled back. "Even though I'm pregnant?"

Daniel nodded. "So, what's the score with you and Stelios?" His eyes scanned her face.

"We're over," she said, but her chin pinched.

"Really? Valentino warned me that you still have the hots for him."

She tossed back her head. *Did she?"*

BRIAN AND KELLY had heard her shouting and crying on the phone. She'd slammed down the receiver, tears running down her cheeks.

"He asked me if Dinks was his!"

"Who?"

"Stelios, he was on the phone. We've been making plans for when the baby is born."

"You're running away again." Kelly had turned and left.

"Shit, Toni, I think that's a bad, I mean, a really bad idea. Man, if you knew what trouble you caused the first time… Heck, I was scared, Kelly was scared, and you don't want to know about Mom and Dad. I had tennis to keep me busy, and I kind of shut it off, but, jeez, once was enough."

"I'm not running away again. Not after what he's just said. I never want to see him again, and he's never going to see Dinks."

"I am so pleased to hear that, and so will everyone else"

"Please promise not to tell anyone. Mom and Dad will have a thousand fits, and I don't want them to know I was even thinking of going to Stelios. Promise?"

"Okay, but I must tell Kelly, or she'll never speak to you again,"

Daniel looked into her eyes.

"Last time I spoke to him, he asked me if I was sure that the baby was his. Believe me when I say it's over - it's over."

Daniel squeezed her hand. "Do you love him?"

"He is the father of my child."

"I know that, but do you love him?"

The light strobes crossed her face, fracturing her features, but not the sadness he saw in her eyes. She bit her lip and nodded and his heart sank. Joy Division faded out and "Don't Stop 'Til You Get Enough" assaulted the slow-dancing couples, swinging them into a fast dance, but Daniel kept Toni close to his chest. He liked that she'd told the truth, admitting her love for Stelios. Her answer did not make him happy, but he hated girls who played games. "So why did you say yes when I asked you out this time?" he asked.

"You really want to know?"

"Yes."

"Because my mother told me to. You just kept on and on and she felt sorry for you."

"Oh," he groaned.

"But that's not the only reason. I think I like you too."

"ALEX, take your pills and go to sleep," said Pam.

"I'll take them later. She'd better be home by twelve."

"She will be. Just go to bed, your pacing is driving me mad."

He lasted until eleven, scratching her nerves like fingernails on a blackboard with every glance at his watch.

"What time do you have?" he'd asked for the hundredth time.

"For heaven's sake, the same as you. Eleven. Will you please just relax?"

"I can't. It's the first time she's been out on a date since she ran away. I like Daniel, but she's pregnant, and... Shit, if he's taking advantage of her situation, I'll..."

"Oh, please, give it a rest," sighed Pam.

"What do we know about him?"

"Come on, Alex," she snapped. "We've known his brother since Toni started art school and we know his parents. They are nice people. In any case I think he really likes her; he phoned four times before she agreed to go out with him."

"Exactly. Valentino's harmless, but Daniel's not a queer and I'll bet he's trying his luck with her right now."

"You're being ridiculous, he's a nice boy."

"Is he? I remember you lobbying for Stelios too. I said he was too old for her, but you..."

"Okay, okay. I was wrong about Stelios, but you're being neurotic and the fact that she's out with someone besides Stelios should make you happy. I hope Daniel steals her heart; that they fall in love and..."

"Live happily ever after?" he snorted. "Have you forgotten who the baby's father is?"

Pam glared at him. "Of course, not, but you are so bloody negative."

"And you," he said, pointing a finger at her, "are so naïve. You don't get it, there is no fairy-tale ending here. Toni's pregnant with a fucking criminal's baby, he's never going to let go of that, not for Daniel or anyone else and we'll never be rid of him."

"Oh, shut up," she shouted. "Take your damn pills and go to bed."

SOUND TRAVELLED WELL in the slumbering suburb and Pam

heard Daniel's Kombi change gears as it turned at the corner of their street and again as it crawled up the driveway. She checked the bedside clock radio. *Five minutes before curfew, a good sign.* Next to her, Alex, who had told Daniel to have Toni home by twelve, snored and twitched in his drugged sleep.

The Kombi's engine shuddered and stopped, switching every nerve in Pam's body onto red alert. She closed her book, switched off the light and lay next to her husband. He grunted and laid a heavy arm across her stomach; she turned onto her side, her back curved against his chest. His breathing raised goose-bumps on her back and shoulders. She pulled up the duvet and lay still. Mickey scratched at Kelly's bedroom door and Bella yapped in the entrance hall. Pam heard the van's doors open and close; the squeak of Daniel's shoes, the click of Toni's heels as they walked to the tiled porch and the clunk of the rubber doorstop. Toni whispered and Bella stopped barking.

Silence.

Pam's body tensed. Daniel's footsteps did not return to the van. Had Toni invited him in? Were they making coffee? They were too damn quiet. Her legs screamed to kick off the duvet, march down the passage and see what they were getting up to, but she forced her body to stay in the bed next to the comatose Alex. His paranoia seeped into her. Toni was a vulnerable, lonely, pregnant teenager and Daniel was a healthy straight male. He'd phoned and phoned, asking her to go out and she'd said no. Suspicion crept into Pam's head and twisted the paranoia into a riot of insane thoughts.

Why had Toni changed her mind? Because she'd spoken to Stelios. They were using Daniel to lull her and Alex into a false sense of security while they plotted her escape to Greece. His Uncle George had found another forger. Toni had another passport. Any day now she'd be gone.

THE LATCH on the front door clicked. Daniel's footsteps squeaked back to the Kombi. The van door creaked open. Pam shifted her tense body and Alex rolled over to his side of the bed. She longed for her husband, unscarred by depression and her daughter untouched by Stelios. A shudder racked her body. She longed for the impossible. It was gone forever.

43

J oseph was Frans's cousin and Direct Technologies' two-days-a-week gardener. Yesterday he'd given the lawn a crew-cut, trimmed the edges razor-sharp, turned over the flower beds, hosed down the driveway and washed the tiled patio. Done for the day, he'd hung his khaki overall on a hook inside the garage, checked out his smile in the cottage-pane size mirror stuck above it, tucked in his pressed white shirt and straightened his snazzy tie.

"I come back next-of-next week, medem."

"See you next week," Maggie had handed over his wages.

"Ja, that's right, next-of-next week. Thank you, medem." Folding the notes in half and in half again he'd buried them in a pocket of his dry-cleaned trousers, tipped his trilby at her, fluttering the guinea-fowl feathers stuck in the hatband, and sauntered to the corner to chat up the living-out maids waiting at the taxi rank.

. . .

THE SPRINKLER CAUGHT Eric's eye. He dropped his briefcase back onto the desk. "Dammit, I forgot to move that bloody thing and I've got to pick up the samples from

Rogaf at the post office for my nine-thirty appointment."

"Go or you'll be late," said Pam, shooing her hands at him. "I'll sort it out."

"Thanks, LT," said Eric, grabbing the briefcase, shoving his arms into his jacket sleeves, pecking Maggie on the cheek and, with a quick "See you later, girls", hurried out of the office.

Pam dragged the sprinkler from the rose garden to the centre of the lawn, positioning it so that the spraying circle did not touch Joseph Masango's pristine patio. It was peaceful in the garden. Thin, white clouds stitched the blue sky and beckoned Pam to pull up a chair, tilt her face to the filtered sun and savour its caress, but a mug of half-finished first-of-the-day coffee and her open cash-book waited on her desk. Maggie's voice cut through the swishing sprinkler and her words jerked Pam's head in the direction of the open office window.

"I am absolutely certain that Pam cancelled her appointment with you, Raymond."

Pam's breath caught in her chest.

"I see. Well, now, there's foolish," tutted Maggie in her best Welsh.

Pam bent the hosepipe onto itself, cutting off the water supply to the sprinkler, her ears tuned into Maggie's one-way conversation.

"Not that it's any of my business, mind, but I've been a client of yours for more years than I care to remember, and I don't appreciate you trying to kiss my friend."

Bloody hell. Maggie was way out of line.

"It'll be against my better judgement, but I'll give her the message."

PAM FLUNG DOWN THE SPRINKLER. It fell on the grass, spraying water in all directions, soaking her as it squirmed and squiggled to right itself. She shoved back her wet hair, whipped off her shoes and stomped barefoot back into the office.

"How dare you?" she hissed.

Maggie's eyes grew wide. "Pardon?"

"I heard what you just said to Raymond. I told you about the coffee 'date' in strictest confidence. I even asked you not to mention it to Eric and here you go blabbing to Raymond himself."

Maggie pulled herself up to her full five foot four inches. "You said you had cancelled your appointment."

"I did not say anything of the sort."

"Well you said you would."

"I did not. You told me to, but I didn't."

"You're playing with fire and you know it."

"And, as you so rightly told Raymond, it's none of your business."

Maggie's stuck her hands on her hips and leaned forward,

her nose almost touching Pam's. "Oh, but it is," she said. "I introduced you to him and I feel responsible for this... This... Nonsense."

"God, I feel so embarrassed. How could you tick him off like that?"

Maggie wagged a pale pink fingernail, the charms on her bracelet clanging and clunking. "I'm trying to stop you ruining your marriage."

Pam's fists thumped the desk. Coffee jumped out of the mugs. "I'll thank you to stay out of my marriage."

Maggie ignored Pam. "Alex is really trying; doing what you asked him to do. He's seeing a shrink every week, taking you to the mountains and your favourite hotel. Now's not the time to go messing around with Raymond."

"Bully for Alex and I am not going to mess around with Raymond, as you put it," Pam drew a breath. "And I am going to his salon to get my hair done."

"Really? Just that? Raymond's a big flirt."

"He's always been a big flirt and you've always known it."

"But he's never taken his flirting outside of the salon before."

Pam rolled her eyes ceiling-ward. "He didn't take anything outside of the salon. He took me for coffee because Mavis wasn't there to make me some."

"And then? He tried to kiss you and you almost let him. You told me so."

"God, I wish I hadn't said a word."

"And you were so smitten that you forgot Brian."

The truth zipped Pam's mouth, but she glared at Maggie.

"Surely you'll feel awkward going back to the salon?"

"Oh, I do now, now that you've given him what for."

"Then cancel."

"No."

Maggie returned Pam's glare. "You fancy him, Pam, that you do, but you're married to Alex and that, in my books, is trouble. What's more, he's planning another date."

"No he's not."

"Then why has he given you the last booking of the day?"

"How do you know that?"

"Because he told me to tell you so." Maggie snatched up the receiver and shoved it at Pam. "Cancel."

A blush spread up Pam's neck and burned her cheeks. Did he have another date in mind? And, if he did, would she go?

She grabbed the receiver. "Tell you what, just to please you, I'll get an earlier appointment. Does that meet with your approval?"

Maggie threw up her hands. "No it does not, but I'm done arguing with you. Go if you must."

44

S tanding in the salon doorway, Pam felt more awkward than she thought she would. Butterflies flapped in her stomach leaving her feeling nauseous. Maggie was right; she should not have come. Her brain searched for a perfect excuse to flee, but a coiffed client came out and held the door open for her and Raymond caught her eye. He waved a tail-comb in greeting and the butterflies flapped their wings faster and faster. She twiddled her fingers in a coy response and walked in.

Raymond's young apprentice-cum-receptionist, Kate, smiled and flashed silver braces. "Hi, Pam," she said. "Take a seat at the basin, Mavis is waiting for you and Raymond's nearly finished."

Combing his client's brown fringe into place, Raymond smiled at her reflection in the mirror. His dimple cut into his chin and her legs turned to jelly. Maggie's finger wagged. *Get out now.*

"I'm afraid that I can't stay," she stammered.

Raymond winked. Maggie's wagging finger disappeared and rational thought bolted off like a horse without a rider. Giddy and breathless she went to the basin and gave her blushing head over to Mavis's legendary scalp massage.

"I bring coffee, milk and one sugar," said Mavis as she delivered a shampooed and conditioned Pam to Raymond's workstation.

"No need," he said. "Pam and I will grab one later at the café, won't we?"

Pam felt her head nod.

He fastened the black cape at the back of her neck and his warm fingers lingered at the top of her spine as he draped a fresh towel over her shoulders and tucked it in. In the mirror, his gaze held hers, the gold specks danced in his eyes and a smile curled the corners of his lips. Her mouth went dry. Her cheeks were hot, and her restless fingers fiddled with her wedding and engagement rings. This was wrong. She looked down at her plain court shoes.

"So, did you get the loan?" he asked, combing her wet hair. He must be able to see that her neck was on fire.

"Pardon?" she mumbled.

"Did you get the loan that you were hoping for when I saw you at the bank?"

"Oh, the loan. No, no I didn't."

"Why not?"

"Why not?"

She was repeating his questions like an idiot.

"Yes, why not?"

Under the cape, she turned and turned the rings on her finger.

"Well, the guy I usually see was sick and his stand-in didn't like my company's balance sheet, or me, or my shoes."

"I loved those shoes."

Her heart thudded and she stopped turning her rings.

"You did?"

Was that her voice?

"They were red patent leather, three, no, almost four-inch stilettos, a single strap across the toes. Right?"

"Right. I'm impressed."

"I hope so, but I didn't like the perfume you were wearing. Chanel No. 5 it was."

Her heart sank and the rings burned her finger.

Stand up; walk out. He's a big flirt. You don't wear Chanel, he's mixing you up with someone else he's flirting with. Alex will get better; Toni's dating Daniel; Stelios is in Greece; Kelly isn't in hospital; Brian is the greatest kid in the world. Raymond is trouble. You don't need him.

"My first girlfriend wore it, so does Maggie. I thought it was a bit heavy for you.

Of course, you'd worn Maggie's perfume that day.

"But I like how you smell today."

"I like how you smell today too." The words popped out. Why on earth had she said that?

Because it was true. He grinned at her reflection. "The saleslady said it's a new line of aftershave guaranteed to make me irresistible. Is it working?"

"I... er... I..." Like gold chains thrown carelessly into a jewellery box, Pam's thoughts tangled and knotted and rendered her silent. He reached for his scissors.

"I'll take that as a yes. Have you got to fetch anyone for anything today?" he asked, holding her gaze

Say yes.

Her eyes were bright; her skin glowed. "No."

He tilted her head down and snipped off the tired dead ends of her hair, her common sense and her roles of wife and mother and God, she felt alive.

45

"Did you say that Act is mine?" asked Eric, pointing to the plane on the dining table.

"Yes," said Brian.

Eric beamed. He pulled out a chair, sat down and put his can of Castle beer next to Toni's Pitman's shorthand book. He propped his elbows on the wooden top, rested his chin on his locked fingers and gazed like a lover at the model glider, assembled and lying on the linen runner. Three other gliders were stacked against the wall, their wings already slotted into the fuselages and widespread.

"Do you like it, Uncle Eric?" asked Brian. "We had trouble finishing it. The plane's a bit heavy; the paint was too thick, but it's your favourite colour."

Eric rubbed his hands together, picked up his glider and cradled the fuselage in his palm. Slowly and gently he stroked his fingers over its smooth surface and sighed. "It's beautiful, Brian. Now I know why you came in that morning and bummed my paint, Alex. I love it. Man, am I going to have fun at the slope."

"Me too," said Brian. "We made four. One's for Kevin; he's coming with us to the slope."

"He's motoring up from Cape Town. Bringing his plane, the Gentle Lady, and a surprise," said Alex.

"Hope the surprise is a new design."

"Could be. It'll be fun to see what he does with one of these Acts."

"I'll say. That Gentle Lady of his is slow and these babies are bloody fast." Eric grinned and balanced the glider by its wings on his fingertips. "The centre of gravity is spot on. She's perfect. I don't know how to thank you guys."

"Don't thank me," said Alex. "Brian pretty much built them by himself. I kind of deserted him. He did a great job."

Brian beamed. "I was worried that you would find all the faults and hate it. I've never made a plane from start to finish, let alone four, but, Dad started them. I just took over because he was sick."

Alex shrank from Brian's words and Eric caught his friend's grimace. "I like the white stripes on top," he said, draining the last of his beer. "Good taping job, Brian, she's a real pretty plane. I can't wait to fly her. Think you're up to challenging me and your Dad?"

"For sure. I'm going to fly the fastest, right next to the cliff-face."

"Did you hear that, Alex?"

Alex gave a smile and nodded.

He had been sick when Brian made the four Acts *and he was still sick. What if Pieter's plan failed? What if he had a panic attack or, worse yet, the goddamn depression hit big time and they were stuck on the slope?*

He wiped the sweat from his hands onto his jeans.

"He thinks he can outfly us," said Eric.

"He's no match for us old guys," said Alex, plunging his hands into his pockets to hide their trembling.

"Oh yeah? Just watch me. Mom will capture my victory on her camera," said Brian.

"I'm not so sure about that," said Eric. "Maggie tells me they're going to laze around the hotel on sun beds in the gardens, sip gin and tonic, read books and catch tans."

"Don't worry, Uncle Eric, they always come up on the first day and that's the day I'm going to beat you."

Eric grinned and dismantled the Act, tucking the wings, fuselage and tail under his arm. "Thanks again for this," he said. "Tell Pam I said hi. I picked up a small capacitor order today and wanted to check if she'd paid for the last shipment, but not to worry I'll chat to her at the office."

"She's at the hairdresser," said Alex.

"Raymond?"

"Yes."

"I thought I heard her and Maggie say they were changing hairdressers."

"Pam never mentioned it. I used to think he was gay, but I believe he's been married and has kids."

"Could be."

Alex shrugged. "Who knows?"

PAM DID. She flipped her newly-trimmed hair away from her face and reached across the café table for the sugar, but Raymond caught her hand and held it in his. Her heart raced, her breath stuck in her throat. He turned her hand over and traced the lines on her palm, one by one, his feather-light touch scorching her flesh.

"Anyone ever read this?' he asked.

Unable to speak, she shook her head.

"See this line here? It's your loveline. It's deep, indicating meaningful relationships of the heart, but, look, it's broken in three. Three loves maybe? Interesting." He looked into her eyes. She could not move or resist when he reached for her other hand. "And see these tiny lines at the base of your pinky finger? That's the number of children you'll have. Also three. Guess you haven't got any *laat lammetjies* on the way. Palms are fascinating, don't you think?"

"I've never given them much thought." She tried to think further than her burning hand and his warm, dry one holding hers. He kept his eyes fixed on her and laced his fingers through hers. A slight squeeze. Her fingers squeezed back. Pam, mother of three, wife of Alex, floated off and watched this smitten woman and this man with gold flecks in his eyes, sitting as close to each other as they could without attracting anyone's attention. She forgot her coffee. It cooled as they whispered, hands touching, and the air between them ignited. Bright and thrilling it crackled and made her feel delectable and desired. As their coffee was refilled they laughed, at what she could not say, but she saw the unhappiness in his eyes when he said he wished his sons were living with him and not his ex-spouse and he listened when she said she missed Alex. They made a pact not to speak of their partners again.

"NEXT THURSDAY?" he said, and every cell in her body tingled. She nodded.

"Grand. It's a date."

His words stung the smitten woman. God, what would Maggie say? She'd accused her of fancying Raymond. She was near the mark, but the kids had a better expression for what she felt. She had the hots for him.

"Oh shit, you're right, it will be a date. Look, Raymond, maybe I..."

"Don't back out, please," he said. He kissed her fingertips and she melted. "I know just the place; out of town, on the banks of the river."

"How far is it?"

"About a half an hour away, far enough not to bump into anyone you know."

"Crickey, I hadn't thought of that."

"Don't look so scared," laughed Raymond.

"But what if someone does see us? You're kind of single, but if Alex..."

"Shush, no partners, remember?"

"Yes, but..."

"No buts, please, just come. Wear dark glasses and a wig if you're really worried. I've got a red one in the salon. I'll draw you a map. It's dead easy to get there - you'll love it, it's romantic, food's great and we'll have fun, I promise."

46

"Do you have change for ten bucks?" asked Alex. He reached for her bag and Pam's brain scrambled for an explanation of what he would find inside.

"I've got an early morning appointment in town and I'm out of parking money," he said, handing her the bag. She breathed and gave thanks to God, Alex's mother, or whoever it was who had taught him his respect for privacy. The contents of her bag remained her secret and she did not have to lie.

She hated lies and had arranged lifts for the children without resorting to them but explaining away a red wig tucked next to her cheque book would change that. Scratching in her purse she found five twenty-cent coins and gave them to Alex.

"Thanks," he said, handing her a ten rand note in exchange. She couldn't take it.

"Keep it," she said, putting the purse back into her bag and pressing the stud closed.

"No, take it."

"I'll have it," said Toni, plucking it from his fingers. "Come on, Dad. Bye, Ma, see you later. Daniel said you asked him to pick me up and invited him for supper."

"Tonight?" asked Alex. "I'll only get in late. It's Thursday, my day for seeing Pieter."

"I thought that was off this week. Seeing as Daniels's coming with us to the slope on Saturday I thought he should get to know us a bit better," said Pam, hitching the closed bag to the safety of her shoulder.

"But Pieter's checking me out before we go."

Toni sighed. "Shall I tell Daniel that dinner's off, Ma? Will you fetch me?"

Pam shook her head. She'd arranged Toni's lift with Daniel because she couldn't fetch her today. She was having lunch with Raymond. She waved her fingers.

"No, no. Come home with Daniel and don't worry, we'll have curry and eat in relays."

"Curry sounds good," said Alex, picking up his lunch-box.

"Let's go, Ma," said Kelly. "No time to yak about supper now, we'll be late. Bye Dad." Brian shoved his tennis racquet into his tog bag and raised his hand in farewell. "Later," he said, and headed after Kelly in the direction of the garage. Pam planted kisses on Toni and Alex's cheeks.

"Bye. Tell Pieter I'm looking forward to seeing him at the slope."

●　　●　　●

Parking at the office, Pam checked her face in the rear-view mirror. High colour flushed her cheeks and her blue eyes sparkled. Dammit, she looked as excited as she felt. Maggie would take one look at her and know that she was up to something. She broke out in a sweat.

SHE WAS UP TO SOMETHING and if Maggie found out that she was having lunch at a country restaurant with Raymond she'd kill her, or worse yet tell Eric, who would tell Alex.

Oh God, what then? Guilt pummelled the excitement and churned her stomach. She clapped a hand over her mouth and ran into the office.

"Are you okay?" asked Eric.

"My, God you look pale," said Maggie." Can I get you some water?"

Pam waved their concern aside, ducked into the toilet and hurled her breakfast into the bowl. Propping herself up at the wash basin she flushed away the half-digested Rice Krispies, rinsed out her mouth and splashed water on her face.

"Cancel lunch," she told the pale face in the mirror. Water hissed in the pipes and filled the cistern. She shook her head. "No," she said. "Just calm down; it's only lunch with your hairdresser."

Back in the office, Pam gave a worried Eric and Maggie a weak smile. "Just a bit of an upset tummy," she said, hooking her bag over the back of her chair and giving the clasp a quick check. It wouldn't do for Maggie to spy the wig and start asking awkward questions. She felt weak, a bit giddy, and not sharp enough to come up with plausible answers.

"Let's tackle the list of overseas suppliers that you think Alex and I must visit; see how many countries are involved and tell Pieter. Going to the slope is his idea, but he thought it would get Alex ready for a holiday in Rio, not a business trip across Europe."

BY ELEVEN O'CLOCK two further potent jolts of excitement clashed in her stomach and sent her back to the bathroom. *This is madness; call the bloody thing off.* The face in the mirror was a mess. She'd hate Raymond to see her like this. She nodded. She was not going to go to the country restaurant; there would be no lunch date; not today. Her stomach could not handle the thrill. She made it back to her desk and studied the list of five suppliers and three countries. "Do you think we need to add the French cable-connector people?" she asked.

"I'm not sure, but I don't like your frequent trips to the loo, think you need to write the rest of the day off," said Maggie.

"No, really, I'm fine; just give me a minute or two."

"I insist."

"Me too," said Eric, "But, hey, you'd better be okay by Saturday and the weekend at the slope. Go home. Get your stomach sorted out."

GOING home was not going to fix her stomach; she knew that a quick call to Raymond and cancelling lunch would. Her hand reached for the phone. She wouldn't even have to speak to him, the receptionist would answer and she'd ask her to tell him she had an upset tummy. It was the truth and, what's more, it would stop whatever it was that was going on between them. He'd give up on her and she'd be forced to find another hairdresser. There would be no further emotional clashes wrecking her guts, no further divine tingles, no brown eyes with gold flecks to gaze into. She turned from the phone and picked up her bag.

"Okay. See you guys on the mountain," she said.

THE VOMITING ATTACKS had muddled her brain. When they had been at Mario's café, Raymond had drawn a map to the restaurant on the back of the serviette, but she'd given it back to him.

"I'd hate someone to find it. Besides, it looks pretty straight forward. I'll get there."

"Sure?"

"Sure."

She remembered that he'd marked the turn-off at the third dirt road from the garage; but had it been a BP or a Total garage? And should she turn left or right onto the dirt road?

"I should have taken the damn map," she muttered. Her sweating hands slipped on the steering wheel; a garage, but no dirt road up ahead. Damn. She glanced at her watch. Bloody hell. She was going to be late and Raymond would think she was standing him up and leave. She raked her fingers through her hair.

Oh No. Her hair. She'd forgotten to put the wig on.

"Okay," she spoke to the empty car. "Stop at the garage, pin up the hair, pull on the wig, fix the face and get directions."

. . .

THE ATTENDANT WAVED her to the petrol pumps.

"Please let him know where the restaurant is," she prayed, unsure that God would consider helping her, seeing as His views on adultery were a definite no-no.

"Do you know how to get to the restaurant, The Two Willows?" she asked.

"Yes, *medem*, my son works there. His name is same as me. Amos."

"Great," Pam was relieved; perhaps God was okay with just a date. "Will you draw me a map? Where's the bathroom?"

He nodded and pointed to the open door at the end of the building and gave her a key to the restroom. When she returned to the car, face fixed and red wig in place, he wouldn't give her the cash slip with the map that he'd drawn on the back. She tried to take it from him.

"No," he said. "This for the lady with blonde hair."

"I am the lady with the blonde hair," she said.

"*Aikona*," he said, folding his arms across his chest.

"I am; look," she said, pulling up one side of the wig.

"*Haw*, why you do that?" he asked.

Because I'm tired of being me.

"For fun," she said.

His eyes narrowed.

"The map," she said.

He hesitated, then gave it to her and watched her swing onto the road, his face a picture of disbelief.

TRUE TO AMOS'S MAP, the BP Garage and a dirt road came into view. The oval sign at the corner said *Two Willows* and the arrow under the name pointed to the left. She shifted down a gear, reducing speed and turned the Alfa onto the graded road. It went on and on and on. She checked the cash slip. Dirt road, the sign for Two Willows, a bridge. *Where's the bridge? How far up the road?* Oh dear Lord, she was thirty minutes late. Would Raymond still be there? The dirt road shook the Alfa. A bend, a river. Ah yes, Raymond had said that the restaurant sat on the banks of a river. Another oval sign. Amos's bridge, a blue plumbago hedge. There it was, dead ahead, the thatch roof of a Cape Dutch building, a willow tree at either end of its wide-open porch, a raked gravel drive. And Raymond.

HER HEART LURCHED. He stood at the bottom of the stone steps. He waved at her and her hormones screamed. She parked, kicked off her sensible work courts and wriggled her bare feet into the red stilettos. He opened the door and laughed.

"I really didn't think you'd come in disguise," he said. His offered hand enveloped hers and squeezed it. She squeezed back, locked her shaking legs together at the knees and swung them out of the car.

"The wig's great, but no one else has those big blue eyes. They're a dead giveaway."

"Oh, my God," her hands flew to her face, checked her head. "I've left my dark glasses in the toilet at the petrol station."

"Never mind, our champagne's waiting."

No. She had to get them back; the kids had clubbed together and had bought them for her last birthday. She always squinted in the sun, and, at the slope tomorrow, everyone would notice that she wasn't wearing them.

A waiter appeared, popped the cork and poured gold liquid into long-stemmed flutes. Raymond handed her a glass, his fingers lingering on hers. She glugged down a mouthful of bursting bubbles; her skin sizzled from his touch, but her brain told her to grab the waiter before he bowed and left.

If he was Amos's son he could phone his father, ask him to find her sunglasses and then she could pick them up at the garage on her way home.

"To us," said Raymond.

"Yes, to us," she said. " Just give me a minute," she called to the waiter. "Excuse me"

"*Medem?*"

"Is your name Amos?"

"Pam, what are you..."

"I'm sorry, Raymond, Amos's father, also Amos, was the attendant at the garage."

"What? You've lost me."

"The garage where I left my glasses."

"Amos is by reception, *Medem*," said the waiter.

"Thank you," she turned back to Raymond. "Please excuse me. I must sort this out. I'll be right back," she promised.

"Take your time," he said, but as he tossed the full flute of champagne down his throat she knew she'd better hurry, which she did, and the flecks danced in his eyes and he smiled when she told him that Amos had phoned his father and her sunglasses were at the garage and she was hungry and ready for lunch. His fingers touched hers as he handed her the abandoned flute of champagne. His knee pressed against hers under the table in the dining-room, his moustache tickled her lips when he kissed her, and, after dessert, his hand on the small of her back, felt right as he walked her back to the reception and his voice excited her as he booked a table for the following week.

ALEX SLIPPED OFF HIS SHOES, swung his legs onto the soft leather and laid his head back on the pillow. His arms lay straight by his side.

"You look like one of the toy soldiers I had as a boy. They stood at attention on the chest of drawers in my bedroom, waiting for me to line them up for battle. Relax, Alex, I am not going to send you to war."

"Oh yeah? Then what do you want me to lie here for, Pieter?"

"I am going to teach you how to control your nerves. I am going to teach you self-hypnosis."

Alex sat up. "Forget that. I'm not going to do stuff at the click of your finger."

Pieter laughed. "You will be the hypnotist, not me. You will control your own thoughts; stop your panic before it overcomes you. Learn this technique and you will have a formidable weapon with which to fight your depression."

"I don't see how. Hypnosis is a whole load of hocus-pocus rubbish."

"Would I recommend you learn rubbish? I am surprised at you. I did not expect you to judge a therapy out of hand. I know you as a man with an open mind and I thought you were ready for it. Self-hypnosis is simple, but powerful. Learn it and you will travel well."

"Look, all I know about hypnosis is that someone takes control of another person's mind and gets them to do all sorts of crazy things that they normally wouldn't do."

"Do you think I would recommend that?"

"No, but..."

"Good, I would not."

Alex closed his eyes. He was tired, tired of having to find new ways to fight, tired to the bone, he didn't want to learn another technique.

"I promise you, you will be in my debt eternally for teaching you this."

Alex sighed. "I'm so sick of..."

"I know."

"How long does it take to learn?"

"It depends. It really is a knack, like finding your balance on a bicycle."

"By the time we go to the slope?"

"This Saturday? No."

"By the time we go fly out?"

"That is my goal."

Alex sighed. "You do know that Pam's got us going all over Europe?"

Pieter nodded. "I do, she phoned and told me."

"You mean she phoned to ask if you thought I was up to it."

Pieter shrugged. "You know Pam."

Alex bit his lip. "I can't put my finger on it, but for sure I'm not in her good books lately."

"Are you in her bad ones?"

"I don't know. I can't read her."

"Your depression is hard on her too."

"I know, I've thought about that and, in the beginning, I think it was that, but now I get the feeling that she's, I don't know, sort of there, but not there. She's Pam, but she's not, if you know what I mean."

"This condition does alienate people. I think it will be good for her to talk to someone. I will phone her."

"God, no. She'll know I've been talking to you about her. She'll give me hell."

"On a scale of one to ten how different do you find her?

"Seven plus."

Pieter raised an eyebrow, pursed his lips and stroked his moustache.

"That different? I think we had better step up your therapy, starting with self-hypnosis."

Alex knew that, when Pam smiled at him, it did not reach her eyes. When she touched him, it was without caress; when she kissed him, it was without passion; when she lay with him, it was without her soul.

He had to get himself back. She was living with, but not liking, the person he'd become. He swung his legs back onto the couch, wriggling his toes in his socks. "This had better be good. "I need a miracle."

"I am offering self-hypnosis. Are you ready to begin?"

"I have to be."

47

Their departure for Kaap se Hoop, early on Saturday morning, was not as Alex had visualised it in Pieter's consulting room.

Firstly, the kids didn't fight. Brian and Kelly had the whole backseat to sprawl out on and Toni caught a ride in Daniel's van.

Alex had been wary when Daniel had asked if he could tag along, but Pam had given him one of her 'for heaven's sake' looks.

"Dump the paranoia," she said. "Be happy that here's a nice guy who's okay with Toni's pregnancy and likes her enough to spend a whole weekend with her crazy family on the top of a mountain, flying model gliders. I just hope the wind blows otherwise he'll sit there bored, doing bugger-all."

Secondly, he didn't panic. He fiddled in his shirt pocket and his pill bottles were there. He shook them and they rattled a chemical melody of tranquilisers, anti-depressants, mood equalisers and sleeping pills.

Thirdly, Pam didn't squeeze in packets full of food and drink onto the floor in front of her seat. Except for her handbag, the space was empty. No dried *wors*, Fizzers, Bacon Kips, marshmallow fish, Sparkles, chewing gum, cashew nuts, Simba Chips, Mint Imperials, Lemon Creams, Nik-Naks, Cokes, Cream Sodas, Fanta Oranges, wafer biscuits or chocolate digestives. Nothing.

"Where's the *padkos*, Ma?" asked Brian.

"There isn't any."

"Not even biltong?"

She shook her head.

"How come?" asked Alex.

Her family's stunned faces stared at her, waiting for her reply. Nothing but the truth came to mind. Thoughts of Raymond had kidnapped and filled her mind and she'd forgotten.

"YOU'RE JUST TEASING us about the *padkos*, aren't you, Ma?" said Kelly.

Again, Pam shook her head.

"Mrs. Richards," said Daniel, "I've got a six-pack and Cokes in a cooler-bag and a packet of peanuts in the cubbyhole; you're welcome to them."

As one, the family turned and stared at him. Toni's folded arms covered the tiny bulge of her tummy.

"You don't understand, Dan. Mom packs the best *padkos* ever. We never go on a trip without it or John Denver. I made a copy of his tape for us, but I was going to get stuff from Ma to eat in the van."

"It's sweet of you to offer, Daniel, but keep your cooler-bag, we'll stop and get some cool drinks and crisps on the way."

"You got nothing for the slope either?" asked Brian.

"No, sorry."

"I can't believe it," said Alex. "You do know that we are going to go straight up to the mountain?"

"Well now we'll have to stop at the hotel for something to eat," said Pam.

"But that'll take ages. We planned to meet the Williams' and Kevin at the slope at about ten."

"So, we'll be late. I was too busy to shop for *padkos*."

"Why didn't you say so? I would have got it."

Pam turned on him. "Because I forgot, okay?"

"But..." Alex shook his head as if to clear a puzzled thought.

Anger and guilt scrambled together, and Pam glared at him. "You manage to forget your keys, appointments, wallet, pills," she said, climbing into the car.

"Okay. Don't go on."

"Well, just this once, I forgot the *padkos*."

"I get the message. It's my fault that we've got no food for the road." Alex yanked open the car door. "Let's get this circus on the road. Keep up with me, Daniel."

"Yes, sir."

. . .

SUBURBIA GAVE WAY TO PLOTS. Plots rolled into farms. Farms stretched to the horizon. Morning dew glistened and dripped from the pink, blue, white and mauve petals of the cosmos bushes that crowded the verges. Alex fixed his eyes on the white lines painted on the tar for miles ahead, but his mind was twisting and turning a picture of Pam's flushed, bright red face before she'd ripped into him. He understood that she was busy; admitted that he forgot stuff all the time, but the force of her anger belly-belted him and the whole business of her forgetting the *padkos* was exactly what he'd tried to explain to Pieter.

HATING BEING APART, they'd married two years before he finished his course at University. Scraping together enough money for petrol and basic food, they'd commemorated his graduation with a three-day holiday in a two-man tent in a caravan park off Durban Beach, but Pam had shoved packets into the Beetle.

"What have you got there?"

"Everything. Simba chips, a box of Nutties, Romany Creams, marshmallow mice, Wilson's toffees, Cokes and Minute Maid Orange Juice, Chappies bubble-gum and Mint Imperials and biltong."

"We can't afford all that."

"It's called saving months of empty Coke bottles. I took them to the café last night and exchanged them for *padkos*. Don't you think that the start of a journey is like us, special and a cause for celebration; a feast?"

"Even if I didn't, you've made sure that we've got one."

"And I always will."

TODAY, there was not a single packet at her feet. It was not her anger that made him grip the wheel and grind his teeth. She'd forgotten the *padkos*. She no longer thought that they were special.

FROM BEHIND HER sunglasses Pam stole sideways looks at the tight line of his mouth, the frown furrowed between his eyebrows. She turned on the radio, fiddled to find a music station. He grimaced at the static and she turned it off and pulled down the sun-visor, and the mirror caught Daniel's van a short distance behind them. Toni was talking to him and he was smiling.

At least they're enjoying themselves, thought Pam, turning her attention to the back-seat where Kelly sat staring out of the window, her fist clutching the gold cross of her necklace and tugging it back and forth tight across her chin. Brian was looking at the floor, chewing his bottom lip. Like ice water, guilt sloshed in her stomach. The kids hated friction between her and Alex and she was the one to blame for the tense mood in the car. She wanted to delve into packets of food, pass delicious snacks and drinks to the kids and Alex, and wipe away the questions she'd seen in his eyes. She wanted to plonk her feet on the dashboard, stick on the John Denver tape and laugh at their hysterical attempts to sing along to the slightly stretched, over-used tape. She longed to sink into the comfort of their family history but, how could she? She'd lunched with Raymond and was planning to do so again. John Denver and his songs stayed in the cubbyhole.

ALEX DIDN'T SAY A WORD, but Pam's ear could hear his brain whirring and trying to make sense of her forgetfulness. How could she be so stupid? Her mind was a mess. For some obscure reason, she had packed Loretta's black lace number into her case, but nothing, absolutely nothing for the family to eat. Alex had questions running around his head and she had no good answers for them. She couldn't tell him about Raymond and why she'd forgotten the food. Her excuse that she had been too busy sounded lame, even to her ears. Would future dates with Raymond cause her to forget Kelly's doctor's appointment or Toni's gynae check-up? God, how was she going to carry this weekend off? She heard Pieter's voice counselling her at the Riverside Clinic, showing her how to survive Alex's breakdown. "Compartmentalise," he had said. "Put Alex in one, Kelly in another, work in another, and so on."

IT WAS GOOD ADVICE; she had survived then, and she would now. As they pulled into the half-way petrol station, she put Raymond, the café, Two Willows and their date together into a compartment and turned to her family.

"I've been thinking. We can still go straight to the slope," she said. "I'll quickly go and find a telephone in the office over there and organise to pick up a picnic basket on from The Valencia. I'll have them pack in some of their special home-made pies, a cheese platter, fruit and stuff. How does that sound?"

"Yum, Ma," said Kelly.

"Good. Does anyone want anything else?" She gave Alex a 'let's make up' look. "What about you, Alex?"

"No. I think you've got everything covered," he said.

"Banana bread, Ma," said Brian. "Oh, and wind; please order the wind."

48

Not a whisper of a breeze hung in the pristine air when they arrived at the slope. Kevin was standing at the edge of the steep cliff, pointing down the cliff-face to the mud huts of the African village, nestled on the banks of a lazy river, in the valley below. His arm was draped over the tanned shoulders of a dark-haired girl who wore an oversized pink T-shirt, white Bata takkies without laces, and the shortest blue denim shorts that Pam had ever seen. They'd already claimed their piece of *veld* and littered it with brown and orange floral fold-up chairs, a blue zip-up cooler-bag, bulging leather holdall and red-checked picnic rug. The unassembled parts of Kevin's Gentle Lady were spread out on the rug, the wings hidden and protected under yellow towels. Hearing Alex's car, they turned their backs on the ring of mountains curving around and cocooning the village. Kevin wagged his finger.

"You're late," he called, as Alex pulled onto the slope and parked a short distance from their marked spot. "We said ten and it's now ten-thirty."

They all climbed out of the car and joined Kevin and the dark-haired girl at the edge.

"You're late," he said again, a wide smile spreading over his face. "Must be a first for you, hey, Alex? But you still got here before Eric. We saw his car going around one of the bends, way down by the forest. What happened? Are you not allowed to pop pills and drive like a bat out of hell?"

"We had to stop at the hotel and get food. Pam forgot the *padkos*."

Pam felt the colour rise in her cheeks.

KEVIN ADORED Alex and had done so ever since Alex had taught him to ride a two-wheeler bicycle. He'd give her what for if he knew about Raymond. Alex was his hero forever and he'd never understand how lonely she was, or her urge to escape from the wreckage of her husband's depression. The abyss had stolen his sparkle, laughter, strength, love, caring; everything that made up the Alex she'd fallen in love with and married, and had left this lifeless man in his place.

"IT'S my fault we're late," she said.

"Never mind," said Kevin, picking her off her feet and swinging her around. "Man, it's good to see you."

Pam laughed. "Put me down," she said. Kevin did as he was told and half-shook hands, half-hugged Alex. They patted each other on the back.

"Seriously, Alex, you're okay?" Kevin searched his brother-in-law's face.

"Sure." Alex patted his shirt pocket. "Just as long as I take these. How's varsity?"

"No, man, fine. Perfect, in fact." Kevin pulled the dark-haired girl close. "Meet my surprise - this is Natalie, she's a law student and madly in love with me, aren't you Nat? This is Alex, my big sister, Pam, and my cuzzies, Kelly and Brian."

Natalie gave them a coy Princess Di smile. "Hullo," she said. "I've heard so much about you guys."

"Oh, no," Brian rolled his eyes in mock horror. "Bet Kevin told you that we're his crazy family. He tells everyone that."

Natalie giggled. "Actually, he did, but he said 'nice' crazy."

"Well, that's true," said Kelly, "but don't worry, Dad's brought along his psychiatrist. That's him over there driving behind the Kombi and in front of the Williams'."

They waved at Pieter.

"Good morning," he called. The tyres of his green BMW's wheels crunched dry grass stumps as he parked and climbed out of his car.

Pam gasped. He wore a purple, floral artist's smock. Full gathers hung from his broad shoulders to the middle of his thick, pale thighs. His long legs separated the hem of the smock from his rolled-over ankle socks, broad feet and clod-hopper rubber-soled leather sandals. With his feet astride and his chest puffed out like a pigeon, he surveyed the scene, pulled on a wide-brimmed pointed straw hat and snapped the elastic band under his chin. "It is magnificent here," he said.

Brian elbowed Kelly. "I can't see his pants, can you?"

Kelly giggled behind a cupped hand.

"Shush," said Pam, her eyes wide.

Natalie whispered. "Wow, he's got really long legs. He doesn't look a bit like a psychiatrist."

Pieter opened the boot and bent into it. The smock rode up his back as he pulled out boxes. Another elbow dig from Brian. "Hey, Kelly, dig those short running shorts. Really shiny."

Pieter looked over at Pam. He held up his hand, his thumb and index fingertips touching and forming a circle. Everything is okay, it said, I am in control. Relax; the weekend and Alex will be perfect. Pam nodded and turned to Natalie.

"Oh, but he is," she said. *He would understand her loneliness and why she wanted to have lunch with Raymond.* "And believe me, he's the best. Did you warn Natalie about the wind, Kevin?"

"Yes, I told her that if there isn't any, we can't fly and we'll all be bored out of our minds, but she came anyway."

"I've got exams coming up, so I brought my books. I'll be fine."

Brian rolled his eyes again. "Oh, no, not another study freak."

"He's referring to me," said Kelly. "I've also got my books."

"Catching up on school work?"

"Yes."

"Kevin said you were in hospital and that your sister is preg..."

"Shush, Nat." Kevin nudged her.

Kelly laughed. "It's no secret, Kev. Toni is pregnant. I hope Daniel's van didn't shake Dinks up too much."

"Who are Daniel and Dinks?" asked Kevin.

"We call the baby Dinks and Daniel is kind of Toni's new boyfriend," said Brian. Kevin looked at Pam and made a puzzled face.

"I thought you told me you'd overheard her making plans to go to Gr..."

Pam shot him a quick look, but Brian caught it.

"You think she's going to Greece?" he asked. "Well, I don't know when you overheard her, but she's not going. Ask Kelly. We caught her crying and Toni told us that Stelios had asked her if Dinks was his baby. Man, when she stopped crying she went ballistic. She never wants to see him again and she's never going to let him see the baby. Not ever."

"What a bastard. If I get my hands on that bloody Greek I'll kill him." Alex's lips set into a thin line.

Kelly glared at Brian. "You and your big mouth, she asked us to keep it a secret, but you've just told everyone."

Pam was furious. "How dare he ask her that? What kind of girl does he think she is? She loves him; she'd never..."

Kelly flapped her hands. "Shush, she's coming over. Please, you don't know anything."

Pam and Alex exchanged looks. So help them they'd kill him. Kelly elbowed Brian.

"What? Now everyone knows," he said. "No one needs to worry about her going to Greece anymore."

"But we promised," said Kelly. "Please don't say anything to her about it."

Alex threw up his hands. "Okay. Okay."

"Shit, poor, Toni, I won't say anything," said Kevin.

AN ACHE SETTLED IN PAM. Toni wasn't going to run away to Greece and she longed to kiss her daughter's life better, wipe the slate clean of Stelios, but the child she carried was his. Whether they liked it or not, Dinks bound them forever and Stelios was a dangerous man with lethal contacts. Toni was too young and naive to realise what power he had. His cruel words must have broken her heart, but she'd chosen not to seek her mother's comfort. She was no longer her little girl with a grazed knee, a broken doll, a lost necklace, but a young woman facing a difficult road and Pam had to respect her privacy.

"I won't say a word," she said.

TONI WAS CHATTING with Eric and Maggie and Daniel's arm was around her waist. Had she told him that Stelios had broken her heart? Had he understood her pain, held her tight and kissed her better? With all her being, Pam hoped he had.

Kevin grabbed Natalie's hand. "Nat, meet my arty cousin, Toni, and this is Eric and Maggie."

Natalie smiled her Princess Di smile again. "You're late," she said, mimicking Kevin, who grinned like a Cheshire cat. Pam and Maggie exchanged strained smiles. Things hadn't been the same between them since Pam's last appointment with

Raymond and Maggie's pinched face had not encouraged Pam to tell her about the forthcoming lunch date. The secret lodged itself in their friendship, like a stone in a shoe and made it an uncomfortable fit.

ERIC WALKED TO THE EDGE, pulled a blade of grass from the *veld*.

"Where's the wind?" he asked, as he shredded it and tossed the pieces into the air. There was not even the slightest hint of a current to keep them up and the pieces floated down and disappeared back into the dry earth. "Nothing," he said.

"It'll come," said Brian

"*Jeez*, I hope so."

"Have faith," said Pieter as he joined the group.

ALEX INTRODUCED HIM TO EVERYONE. Eric's handshake was quick, his eyebrow rose, and he glanced away from the shrink's hidden shorts, flamboyant shirt and religious words. Alex's mouth tugged in amusement before he turned his attention to an iron stake which he hammered into the ground, attaching a long ribbon of pink single-ply toilet paper to it.

"What is that?" asked Pieter.

"Our windsock," said Brian. "Do you like it?"

"I do. It is most creative," said Pieter. "A good invention."

Eric's shrug dismissed Pieter's flowery speech. "'*n Boer maak 'n plan*," he said.

. . .

HEFTING a Turkish rug on his shoulder, Pieter carried it to a level spot and unrolled it, covering the grass stubble with faded jewel colours. Taking out a pile of books from his canvas rucksack he placed them on the fringe and stood back, hands on hips, taking stock.

"One last touch," he said. He walked to the car and pulled out a box of cushions.

Eric's eyebrows arched higher as Pieter threw them onto the carpet and spread his arms wide.

"There," he said. "You are waiting for your wizard, the wind, and Brian has said it will come; meantime," he paused and bowed, "I give you Istanbul."

49

The pilots busied themselves, assembled their gliders, testing the servos and transmitters, readying the planes for flight. Kevin was the group's novice flyer and Alex helped him test his equipment. Taking the transmitter box, he walked away, working the sticks, sending signals back to the receivers of Kevin's new Act.

"Okay," Kevin shouted, each time the ailerons or flaps screeched and responded to the signals received. His transmitter passed the range test. Work on the planes was soon done. They were ready to fly, but the dead air kept them earthbound. The pilots gathered at the edge, gazing down into the valley, willing the wind to sweep through the sparse bush and rush up the rugged cliff-face. Pieter walked over to join them. Eric took one look at his long, bare legs and straw hat and gave him a wide berth, but the shrink ignored his discomfort and stepped into his space, bombarding him with questions and adding to his frustration.

• • •

PIETER WAS FASCINATED WITH EVERYTHING. What he knew of slope-soaring was second-hand, gleaned from Alex in endless hours of therapy sessions. Being here gave him a peep into his patient's passion. Building and flying model gliders was a significant part of his life and, since the onset of his depression, often dragged him back from its relentless power. Such passion impressed Pieter and stirred his curiosity and he hoped to see its power at work this weekend. He ran large, manicured hands over the fuselages, felt the sharp leading edges of the wings and listened to the communicating tweaks between servos and receivers.

"Let me help," he said.

Alex handed him yellow tape and scissors. "Stick a strip here and here, where the wings meet the fuselage."

It was a simple task, it required no experience or technical talent, but, after his third futile attempt, Pieter laughed and extricated his fingers from a sticky, tangled mess. "I surrender," he said. "I am clumsy. I am not an engineer or mechanic but, I am a gifted psychiatrist."

"Well *ja*, no fine," Eric grunted.

Pieter's self-praise and Eric's irritation made Alex laugh. "Believe me, Eric, he's not just big-headed, he's bloody good."

"But you do not think so, Eric?" Pieter watched Eric shrug.

"May I ask why not?"

"Well, let's face it, you've treated Alex for months and he's not..." Eric pulled a stick of grass from a clump at his feet.

"Yes?"

"Well...Look... He still gets depressed and I think he should be better, that's all."

"Aw come on, Eric," said Alex. "Don't you remember Steve taking me to the loony-bin; Pam rushing me to the hospital with 'heart attacks'? Shit, I was a mess."

"Sure I do, but you're taking a million pills and hell, man... I don't know."

"Listen, if it wasn't for Pieter I wouldn't be on this slope today."

Pieter held up his hands. "Please, gentlemen. Alex, Eric is angry that I have not cured you, not so, Eric?"

"Well, yes, I guess I am."

"And you did not know that you were angry. I told you, Eric, I am good at this."

"So, I'm angry; so what. If you're so good you can change that."

"How?"

"By fixing my friend."

"I intend to; he's my friend too."

WHILE NATALIE and the children sat with them, Maggie chatted, but when they drifted off, leaving the two women alone, she shifted her fold-up chair so that her back was slightly turned towards Pam and became silent.

"Maggie, I know that you..." The words dried up and clogged in Pam's throat. She hated the tension that lay between them.

"You don't know anything."

"Maggie, please."

Maggie's shoulders stiffened. "Let's not talk."

"You don't understand."

"No, I don't."

Pam hated this. Maggie had shared her life; the good and the bad, for eighteen years; holding her up when Kelly, face blue, lungs starved, lay in the oxygen tents, holding her close and clapping when Alex was away in Ireland on business and Brian walked onto the school stage to accept his first academic colours. Holding her tight when she wept and worried and looked for Toni. Maggie was her best friend, her true friend. She knew everything about her, but now she wouldn't even look at her.

"I've had lunch with him." The secret was out.

Maggie swung around. "There's bloody daft, you are."

"I know." Tears swam in Pam's eyes.

Maggie turned her chair around, pulled a tissue from under her bra strap. "You're a sorry mess, Mrs. Richards," she said.

"I know." Pam took the tissue and blew her nose.

"And what's wrong with me," said Maggie, "that I'm still sitting here?"

"Thanks."

They stared at each other. Their shared years had changed them. Their faces and bodies were now a bit saggy and thickened in places and the flimsy friendship of two new, young mothers had become a sisterhood. The charm bracelet jingled as Maggie reached over and patted Pam's hand and lifted her heart.

"Maggs, he's booked another lunch."

"Not another word. I know you want so hard to tell me about it, but I don't want to know anything, do you hear?" said Maggie.

"Okay, but what if..."

Maggie held up her hand. "No. Just go away. Do that picture-taking thing that you always do here at the slope. Let me get on with my book. I will not listen to another word on this."

50

Dismissed by Maggie, but relieved that they were on speaking terms once more; Pam put Raymond into his compartment in her mind and fetched her Pentax from the cubbyhole in the car.

There was no wind.

With the exception of Maggie and Pam, the group made aeroplanes from pages torn from Brian's school jotter and soon the air was full of paper darts and laughter, as they competed with each other for the longest flight and Daniel's packet of peanuts. Pam walked to the edge and the stark beauty of the steep cliff face caught her breath. She squeezed and clicked, squeezed and clicked the shutter, capturing the clasping roots of stunted shrubs on jagged rocks, the short, flat-roofed trees forcing their trunks through the grey, granite mountain face, the thatched roofed village nestled far below and the brown children playing on dirt roads seldom travelled by cars. It was a perfect slope. The contours of the surrounding mountains curved and caught the merest snitch of wind and the plateaux was a smooth, tailor made landing-spot for the gliders, but without wind the perfect slope was useless and the assembled planes lay dead on the ground. The pilots made small talk and waited. Pam snapped their frustration. The toilet-paper ribbon hanging from its stake, puddling, lifeless, on the dry, brown *veld*. Kevin, tearing the paper into pieces, tossing them up into the air. Pink loo confetti floating back to earth and settling among the sleek planes. Eric, licking his forefinger and waving it in the windless air. Alex's frown, his stride to and from the cliff face. The majestic mountains protecting the village. She clicked the shutter and captured magic on film.

BRIAN CARRIED his Act to Pieter's carpet, kicked off his Hi-Tecs, stuffed his socks into the toes, sat down cross-legged and pulled off his baggy sweatshirt. It roughed up his hair and rumpled his black T-shirt as it rode up his back. A quick shrug of his shoulders and the fabric fell back into place. His fingers raked the hair off his face and he wiped his hands across his chest, dragging sweat across the word AVIATOR, printed in white on the front. He pulled the Act onto his lap, resting it across his knees. Pam twisted the lens, brought the furrow between his brows and the freckles dusted on his nose into focus. Click.

He looked up.

"Go away, Ma. You're a menace with that camera." She squeezed the shutter again, freezing his cheeky grin, blue eyes and the sun in his hair. "Enough. Go. Get the wind."

"Sorry, can't do that," she said. She pointed the viewfinder at Kelly, Toni and Daniel. They were standing at the edge, looking over the valley, Daniel's arm across the back of Toni's waist and hers across his and Kelly's. The arm-chain made a good photo. Pointing to The Valencia's picnic basket, Toni whispered in Daniel's ear and he nodded and walked over to it and hefted it onto his shoulders. His thumbs-up sign to Toni, his ready-to-please smile and the clear sky backdrop made another good picture, as did her girls. Left alone, they faced each other, smiles on their faces and Kelly rubbed the small bulge of Toni's tummy.

She heard the shutter and scowled. "Ah, Ma, I look fat. Go. Take some pics of the love-birds."

Kevin's head was touching Natalie's as they gazed into each other's eyes, hands and fingers entwined. Her suntanned legs were pressed against his and they didn't hear her shoot their photos or the empty click when the spool ran out. Pam wound it off, popped it into a canister, returned to her chair next to Maggie's and inserted a new 36-reel into the Pentax.

"This lot's getting impatient," she said.

"Especially Eric," said Maggie. "I can see him getting antsy. I'd better give him something to eat before he throws his plane off. He's ready to do it, wind or no wind." She closed her book and rummaged around in Eric's large toolbox. "Ah, dried *wors*," she said, pulling out a brown, fat-stained, paper packet. "This will keep them busy for a while."

Eric chewed on the dried sausage and washed it down with a Coke from Kevin's

cooler-bag. He wiped his mouth with the back of his hand and looked up into the sky. "Where's the frigging wind? I heard that a bunch of people came here last week and had the best flying ever."

"Kevin said they phoned him and got him really excited," said Alex. "Just as well he brought Natalie. *Kafuffling's* been keeping him occupied, but Pam should get a photo of that scowl on his dial; he's looking pretty fed up right now."

"Me too," Eric bent down and picked up his Act.

"Hey," Maggie shouted, pointing a perfectly painted nail at him. "Just leave that plane right there; wait until the wind comes."

"And if it doesn't? We've come all this way to fly. I can't sit here all day."

"Eric." Maggie shot him a look, her grey eyes turning charcoal. "Don't be getting daft."

"Okay," growled Eric. He walked over to Pieter's carpet and chatted to Brian.

Pieter produced a chilled bottle of Johannesburger and goblets and poured the wine.

"Just a little for the children," said Pam, "and none for Toni and Alex."

Pieter smiled and handed everyone a glass. "One will do them no harm. I would like to propose a toast," said Pieter. "To my Istanbul, this mountain and its magic."

"Here, here."

They raised their glasses.

"To your Istanbul," said Eric. "But I've got to tell you that there's no wind, so there's no magic."

"Of course, there is," said Maggie. "Stop moaning. Just look at the magnificent view and try one of the meat pies, they're delicious." Maggie brushed pastry crumbs from her chin and the corners of her mouth with a linen serviette. Eric grunted, but helped himself to one. Pieter opened a small book and settled his long body against a pile of cushions. "You are right, Eric, there is no wind, but on this slope and in these pages there is magic. Let me read to you."

"What's the book called?" asked Brian.

"It doesn't matter."

"Is it any good?" asked Eric.

"Very. One of my patients wrote it. You will not be disappointed. Come, everyone, take a pillow. Make your bodies comfortable, close your eyes if you want, let your mind engage with the words and wander into their world."

"Group therapy, hey, Pieter," said Alex, propping his head on green and orange patchwork.

Eric settled on the edge of the carpet.

LOUNGING LIKE SULTANS, they drank white wine, picked at the remnants of The Valencia's picnic and listened as Pieter's Afrikaans accent enriched his patient's words. They resonated and rustled the stillness of the mountain.

"I heard the voice. Like a lover's, it was at once innocent and seductive, soft and ripe. It lured me to a secret place of exquisite joy and sorrow."

Eric moved his purple pillow closer but kept his eyes open. The story unfolded, captivating them all. The wind, or lack thereof, dwindled in importance as the words cast their spell.

"...my heart is shredded, but I am blessed; I am a child of the free." Pieter closed the book. "The End."

"Ah gee," said Kelly.

ERIC WAS the first to stretch. The edge lured him from enchantment and he yearned to fly. His model was ready. He picked it up, ignored Maggie's look and sauntered over to the edge. Kevin followed suit. Below, leaves dangled on dust-cracked bushes. Nothing stirred in the valley; children slept in the mud huts, cool and out of the mid-afternoon heat.

"This is it. The wind's never going to come," he said to Kevin.

A look and a slight nod passed between them. They raised their right arms, their brand-new Acts poised in their hands.

"No." shouted Maggie.

Alex jumped to his feet. "Kev. Stop."

They flung the models. Kevin's Act nose-dived, picked up speed and headed for the ground."Shit," he yelled. "Help. Somebody. Help."

Alex grabbed the box out of his hands and pulled on the sticks. Kevin, hands clasped behind his head, held his breath. "Can you bring it back?" he asked.

"No fucking chance. Just watch it. See where it lands."

ERIC'S PLANE WALLOWED, dipped, stalled. Sweat broke out on his brow and he worked the transmitter sticks. The glider raced for the ground. He fed in up elevator, the Act climbed, levelled out, but there was nothing under its wings, no wind, no thermal. It stalled and dived out of sight. Splintering branches echoed up the cliff. His eyes searched the clump of bushes growing on a ledge a hundred feet below, but he couldn't see his plane.

"Bugger it." He put down the transmitter and glared at Maggie. "Don't," he said.

"Don't what?" she glared back.

"Don't say anything." He hitched up his pants and started the climb down.

IN THE DEAD AIR, Kevin's Act fell like a brick. It headed for a boulder. Alex gave the sticks a sharp pull and the plane veered off to the left, slowed down, levelled out and landed on a flat outcrop, not far from the village.

"Gee, thanks," said Kevin.

Alex handed him the box. "Didn't you hear me yell stop?"

"I just got tired of waiting and Eric threw his."

"Eric's got more money than sense," said Maggie, her hands planted on her hips. "And I'll have something to say when he gets back."

"You always do, Maggs." Alex smiled. "We can't help ourselves, we come here to fly. Kev, your plane's at the bottom. I'll drive down with you, but the road is far from the landing spot and you've got a long way to walk."

"I'd better say goodbye to Nat."

51

T he wind came at dusk.

It stretched and yawned in the thatch-roofed village. Picking up speed, it rustled through the pine forest, tore at the shrubs clinging to the rock face and roared up the slope face at 25 kph, whipping the pink toilet roll ribbon upright. At ninety degrees to the *veld*, their makeshift wind-sock decreed the slope perfect at last.

"Oh no. I've just taken my plane apart," said Brian. Requiring repair, Kevin and Eric's planes were already packed away in their cars. Alex grabbed his Act. Standing at the edge, he balanced it in his right hand and pointed the fibre-glass nose directly into the wind. He slung the harness of the comput-erised transmitter box around his neck and his fingers hovered over the smooth sticks, poised to take instant control. Depression fled in the wake of adrenalin. It flooded every cell in his body, priming him for the moment of launch. Excited, the pilots gathered close to him. Locked into his energy, they stood, tense and still, the wind stinging their faces. With their hands shoved deep in their jacket pockets, they willed him to throw the plane.

His mouth and throat were dry. Intense concentration contained his anxious excitement. His mind was sharp, his thoughts clear. He lined up the flight in his head, visualised the air speed, the currents, the force beneath the Act's wings, his fingers on the sticks, controlling its every move. His nerves were raw, alive. He stepped back on his right leg, drew back his right arm, arched his back and threw the plane, javelin-style, into the air. It soared upwards, ripping through the sky. Reflexive grins spread across their faces. Alex was one with his plane, feeling the power of the wind lifting the wings, the warmth of the dying sun on the fuselage. A rush of good air tweaked the adrenalin in his veins. *Man, this was fun.* He applied feather-light pressure to the sticks, trimming in the down-elevator. The model responded. It flew faster, up and away from him, keening as its wings cut the sky. Riveted, the pilots watched the fibre-glass model ride the wind, harness the power and become a deadly missile. It sped along the edge of the cliff face at 80 kph. Alex worked the sticks. At his bidding, the Act braked, banked, screamed, turned and whizzed across the valley.

Standing next to Pieter, Pam saw the thrill of flying steal the flatness from her husband's eyes and unlock his prison of depression. His face came alive. Her heart raced and she nudged Pieter. His smile and imperceptible nod of his head acknowledged the metamorphosis.

"Does he not look magnificent?" he asked.

"Oh, yes," she said, unable to contain her joy. "To be honest,

I'd given up hope of ever seeing him like this again. I tried to accept the depressed man he'd become."

"Did you succeed?"

"I was too lonely without him." Thoughts of Raymond leaked from his compartment in her head. His theatrical imperson-ations, his air-borne kiss, his jokes, his laughter, his hand holding hers.

She bent and rubbed her calf, letting her hair fall to hide the blush rising on her cheeks.

"No, I didn't succeed." The whisper caught in her throat and whooshed her shame into the wind.

"Did you try my advice?"

She nodded at the memory of Raymond's foot travelling up her shin, his hand holding hers, his kisses drying on her fingertips, his moustache scratching her chin, his lips pressing against hers, his voice booking their next date.

She kept her head down. "Yes, but the compartment game is pretty complicated," she said.

"Well, I do not think that you will have to do it for much longer. Look at Alex."

One glance at her husband and Raymond vanished.

Alex focused on the sleek red and white glider. The wind blew his black hair back from his face and slapped his clothes to his body, outlining his long legs, flat stomach, broad shoul-ders and the chest she laid her head on whenever her world fell apart. The dying sunlight outlined his strong jaw, his confident stance. Her throat ached. She watched him. This was her Alex. Her eyes drank him in. He stood at the edge, his movements on the transmitter sticks deft. He was in full control, zoned into the thrill and she loved him.

"Wow, that looks good, Dad," shouted Brian, the wind whipping his words upwards.

Alex pulled the transmitter strap off his neck, nodded and handed his son the box. Brian pushed the Act into a dive, reined it in, flew it almost out of sight, brought it back to the cliff face, it screamed, braked, turned, circled.

"Yikes, it's fast."

"It's getting dark, bring it in."

"No, the first flight is yours," Brian returned the box. "You do it."

Alex grinned. The tricky light was against him, but he milked the last flying minute from the dying day, then, with a touch of his finger, he slowed down the Act, flew it smooth and straight to the landing spot and applause.

"Wonderful. Wonderful. I am proud of you, Alex," cheered Pieter.

"Great flight," shouted Eric. "What a fantastic plane, you sure hyped the competition, but watch out for me tomorrow."

Alex shot Pam a smile. It was almost shy, as if he was unsure that she'd return it, but she beamed, and his eyes sparkled as he dismantled his plane. Her heart thudded; she was lightheaded, breathless and she yearned to touch him, for him to touch her. She'd forgotten how good that felt.

"Do you agree that bringing him here was a stroke of genius?" asked Pieter.

"God, yes."

"I can see why you wanted him back."

"But," she hesitated, Pieter waited for her to go on and doubt crept into her voice. "Is he here to stay?"

Pieter put his arm around her shoulder and hugged her. "He will be shortly. Can you wait?"

Alex had asked her that too.

SHE'D BEEN Toni's age, working at her first job and living at home with her parents in Cape Town. She was 'going steady' with Alex and, when her folks retired to the living room after a Sunday roast, they were left alone doing kitchen duty. Their fingers had touched, lingered, and their bodies brushed and pushed against each other.

"You smell good."

"It's Elizabeth Arden's Blue Grass."

Flicking the dishcloth over his shoulder, he'd drawn her to him, encircling her waist from behind, his hands locked over her belly button, his hardness pressing into her. Leaning back against his chest, she'd closed her eyes, her toes melting as he kissed the crook of her neck.

"I want you, Pam."

"I want you too."

"I must go to Jo'burg."

"What? Jo'Burg. Why?"

"I've got to get a good degree and Wits is the best university in the country. I want to give you everything."

"I don't want everything. I just want us to be together."

"We will be. I promise."

"But Johannesburg is one thousand four hundred kilometres from Cape Town. How long will this degree take?"

"Four years."

"That's ages," her voice caught in her throat.

" Don't cry. Please don't cry. I'll write every day and come back at the end of each semester. I love you, Pam."

"I love you too."

"Will you marry me? Can you wait?"

THE SUN WAS SINKING behind the surrounding mountains. The red-washed sky held the night at bay, and the planes were packed into their cars.

"I love him. I have always loved him. His depression blinded me, but he is the man who makes me whole. I can wait."

THEY LEFT no trace of their day on the slope and, by the time that they packed the planes, food, chairs, books and Pieter's Istanbul into their cars, stars studded the sky and a full moon filtered through the tall pine trees, throwing ghost shadows on the dark forest roads. In the Richards' car, the radio-face glowed, outlining Alex's profile. His deep-set eyes concentrated on the twists in the dirt road and faint snores from the back seat told Pam that Kelly and Brian were sleeping. She reached into the cubbyhole and took out the John Denver tape, popping it on, turning the volume down so as not to wake them. The opening notes of "Sunshine on my Shoulders" kissed the night.

"I'm sorry about the *padkos*," she said, putting her hand on his thigh. It was too familiar to her to send an electric shock up her arm, but it felt right, like she was back home, safe, after a perilous journey.

"That's okay. The hotel put together a good picnic," said Alex, covering her hand with his.

She ached inside; she loved him so.

The drive back to the hotel seemed to take forever and, what with a day filled with planes, wind and flying to talk about, dinner took an eternity to complete. By the time goodnights were said in the corridors and their bedroom door was locked, she was more than ready to don the black lace bra and panties and have her husband peel them off.

52

The sun caressed her. She woke slowly, lingering in that sweet place where dreams and reality touch and blur at the edges.

"Thank you. Put the tray here on the grass." Maggie's voice and the clink of coins on metal eased her eyes open.

Her sunglasses cut the glare, but not the brilliance of The Valencia's gardens. Tall trees and yellow-striped umbrellas dotted the endless Kikuyu lawn, providing shade for the sun-screened bodies reclining on thick, cushioned sun-beds. A riot of red, pink, yellow and orange hibiscus bushes surrounded the deep end of the swimming pool, their flow stemmed by stately agapanthus and lemon marigolds. Any self-respecting cat would envy her yawn, arched back, taut arms and pointed toes, as she stretched and swung her feet off the lounger. Grass blades pricked her feet as she slotted the lounger into sitting position and took a sweating glass from Maggie.

"Cheers," she said. They chinked glasses, sloshing ice and fizzing Tonic Water.

"Ah, G and T, the best habit you've taught me," said Pam, reclining on the cushions and dunking the lemon slice with Sugar Pink painted fingernails. "How long have I been sleeping and where are the girls?"

"About an hour and at the horses. Toni might be too pregnant to ride, but she couldn't stay away, and she dragged Kelly with her. Is she over the morning sickness?"

"Not a chance; she hogs the bathroom all the time."

"Oh dear, I can see that she's not put on any weight. I like her new lad."

"I like him too. I'm not sure he's her lad, but the kids say that Stelios had the audacity to ask her if Dinks was his and Toni went berserk, so Daniel's got a chance."

"What a bastard. How dare he?"

"That's what I said. Anyway, she's through with him, touch wood; won't let him have anything to do with the baby."

"Good for her. Thank God he's out of the picture."

"I hope so. I'd like to think that if he came back she wouldn't do anything stupid."

"Like you?"

"Are you referring to Raymond? I thought you didn't want to talk about him."

"I don't. It just popped out, but now that it has, I'm going to stick my neck out and tell you that a second lunch is madness; the next date will be in the bedroom."

"No it won't."

"Have you lost all your common sense? I wish I could stay out of it," sighed Maggie. "But you and Alex are our friends, if you mess up..."

"But, I won't," laughed Pam, tipping her face to the sun, savouring its warmth, the pampering of lush surroundings, the decadence of sloth. She tasted the joy of new beginnings and her lips curled into a smile.

Maggie wagged a finger. "I'm serious. I do not find the idea of your date with our hairdresser funny. You're going to destroy your family, mark my words."

"I won't Maggie. I promise."

"Don't promise, just stop, that's all. Stop seeing Raymond."

"Okay."

Maggie's finger hung in mid-air.

"Well there's a turnaround for you."

Pam's laugh came from her belly. "It is isn't it? I love the slope. I love the aeroplanes. I love this place and, yesterday, I found out that I'm madly in love with Alex. You can stop worrying, Maggie."

53

Back in the office on Monday, Maggie worked on the list of suppliers that Pam and Alex were going to visit, adding products, physical addresses, telephone and fax numbers.

"There you go," she said, handing a sheet of A4 paper to Pam.

"Now let me get Raymond on the phone for you and you can tell him it's over," she said, picking up the receiver.

"No, Maggie, don't. I can't do it over the phone. He deserves me telling him face to face. I'll do it on Thursday."

"You're not still going to have lunch with him, are you?" Maggie's hands flapped and fanned her face. "Oh, you are getting my knickers into a right knot, you are. Look, I know you're back into Alex, but Raymond's still Raymond, the good-looking flirt."

"You don't need to worry, Maggs, I won't let our good-looking flirt talk a hole in my head."

"But you might. What if Alex slides back? I really think you should tell Raymond now."

"I expect Alex to slide back as you put it. I can't shoo away his depression, neither can he, but he's working on it, and, more importantly, you're right, I am back into him."

Maggie's charms jiggled and clanked. "Well, go. Get this face to face stuff over now, today. I can't sit here waiting till Thursday."

"You want me to end it now, in his salon?"

Maggie picked up the phone. "No, I'm going to tell him to meet you at the café next door. Just get out of here."

Pam's heart refused to slow down as she walked past 'their' table and took a seat at the quietest spot in the cafe. She smoothed her skirt, propped her elbows on the table and balanced her forehead on the tips of her steepled fingers. God, how was she going to tell him? What would he say? He'd coloured her world, infused it with fun and somehow that had given her the lift she'd needed to stay with Alex, hoping for him to get better, giving her the strength to accept his depression and love him again.

Her mind tried out a few phrases. *It wasn't working. It wasn't his fault. She hadn't planned it. It wasn't fair.*

"*Medem,* would you like to order?" The waiter handed her a menu. How long had he been standing there? Her stomach felt icky and she needed to pee. Raymond walked in, scanned the room. She waved. He didn't smile.

"Hi," she said.

"Hi." He pulled out a chair, handed back the menus. "Two coffees, one black, one white with cold milk, please, Isaac."

"Yes, Mr. Raymond." The waiter disappeared. She searched for words, gentle words, special words. Any words. She bit back tears. She wasn't here to make him feel sorry for her, to forgive her because of her tears. He reached for her hand.

"I know why you're here," he said.

"Maggie?"

"Yes."

"Damn her. I told her that I wanted to tell you myself."

"She's a good friend, Pam. She's only looking out for you."

"I love him."

"She said so. What she said was that you'd never fallen out of love with him, but that you'd found out that you loved him this weekend. It was all a bit Welsh, just like Maggie, but I got the message. But we're here now and we agreed not to speak about our partners, remember?"

She picked up the serviette and blew her nose. "I am sorry, you know that, don't you?" she said. He held her hand, without squeezing it, without lacing his fingers through hers. He touched her wedding ring, twisted it round her finger.

He looked sad. "I do." he said. She pulled the red wig out of her bag and handed it to him.

"Keep it, "he said. "Wear it sometimes and remember us."

"I will, "she said.

.   .   .

BACK AT HOME, she wrapped it in a hotel-issued shower cap and tucked it, together with the memories she had shared with Raymond, into the empty make-up case that lived in the darkness of her vanity bag and gently zipped it closed.

AUTUMN GAVE way to winter's chill. It snuck in one evening when Kelly and Brian were in their bedrooms studying for exams and Toni was at the movies with Daniel. It gave Pam the excuse to light a fire and sneak in a cuddle with Alex. Her love for him was in top gear. In its newness, she found hope and dreams for their future. Not that she had shrugged off the power of his depression. It had scarred her, driven her to the brink of adultery and it still held Alex in its palm, but he was no longer crouched in its clutched fingers. He'd pried them open and his progress sparkled in her eyes and lightened her step as she carried the tray, laden with a pot of coffee, two stemmed glasses, sugar, whiskey and cream, from the kitchen to the lounge and set it on the coffee table next to a pile of magazines. Bella circled a spot on the carpet and flopped down, resting her head on her front paws, watching as Pam lined the grate with newspaper balls and placed logs on top. At the strike of the match, the little dog's ears pricked up and, before the flare tasted *The Star*, she jumped up on the couch. Pam pushed down the plunger, trapping the coffee grounds under the mesh, called for Alex and shooed Bella back onto the floor.

"IRISH WHISKEY. WHAT'S THE OCCASION?" asked Alex.

"Us," said Pam, patting the seat next to her. "Come. Sit."

Alex did as he was told and Pam snuggled into him, resting

her head in the crook of his neck where it met his shoulders. She breathed him in. The smell of Old Spice caressed her and her newfound hope. It nurtured her dreams. He lifted her chin with his index finger and turned her face to his. She closed her eyes and he kissed her full on the lips. She only pulled back when he flicked his tongue into his mouth.

"The kids are still up," she said. She enjoyed his hand touching and creeping up her thigh, but she pushed it away. "Later."

"Promise?"

"Only if you pour us a couple of great Irish whiskeys, run me a bath, scrub my back and give me a massage."

"Consider it done." He poured coffee to within a half-inch of the rim of the glasses, dribbled cream from the back of a spoon, slipping white blankets on top.

"For you, Madame," he said, as he wondered, not for the first time at the change in her. She smiled, talked and touched him, not as if it was her duty, but as if she wanted to. It had started that night at The Valencia, when she'd come onto him. Black underwear, perfume, suspender belt; man, the whole works. Overcoming the calming effects of his tranquillisers, she'd seduced him good and proper.

LAZY BLUE FLAMES curled around spitting logs, orange fire danced in the grate and smoke ghosts escaped up the chimney. He watched Pam take a sip of her Irish and lick away a cream moustache.

"First class," she said.

"Guess we're on for later."

"Guess we are," she laughed and handed him a copy of the modelling magazine, *Silent Flight.*

"I found a fabulous flying holiday in Devon in there and Maggie has left us free time to fit it in. here's our itinerary." She tossed him a sheet of paper covered in orange highlighter.

"Everyone in Europe is listening to Tutu and his anti-apartheid sermons and Maggie had to do a lot of talking. Those highlighted in orange agreed to see us; the rest said no. Have a look."

He couldn't. He stared at a spot on the carpet.

"Imagine if Loretta hadn't entered me into that competition."

"I wouldn't be here, shitting myself," he blurted out. "Maybe you should go alone. I'm not up to it."

Pam's brows pulled together. "Alex, I watched you fly on the mountain; you were in complete control. You can do this."

"I don't think so."

"Just have a look. Please."

His heart was thumping. Her eyes pleaded.

"Show me," he said.

"Here are the pictures. Don't you just love the Dover cottages and the cliffs coming straight up from the sea? You'll be flying from the top of them."

He tried to concentrate. Panic rushed in.

Focus. Focus.

"It's a bit expensive, but you'll love it, Alex, and I think we should fit it in when we're done with Maggie's list. We'll need a bit of R & R by that time, don't you think?"

Oh, shit, is this Maggie's list? Fuck. England. Spain. Germany. France. Portugal.

"Are you kidding me? Five countries?"

Pam leaned over and touched his arm. "Don't fret; it's really only four. Ignore France; they said no."

His head spun, the orange highlighter blinded him.

"In three weeks?"

"I know it's a bit crowded, but Maggie had to fit everyone in, and guess what?"

"What?"

"Most of them are sorting out accommodation for us."

Shit. He didn't even know where they would be staying.

HIS PANICKED BRAIN could not work out whether fear or frustration clouded Pam's eyes. "Look, I'm bushed, I'm going to turn in."

"Alex, please," her hands reached for him. "Everything will be okay."

SHE WATCHED him leave the room, his shoulders sagging, his feet dragging, and her heart sank. The schedule was too much and the promise of flying off the Cliffs of Dover had disappeared in his panic. Her frustration and the lounge walls closed in on her. She had to get out of the house.

IT WAS FREEZING OUTSIDE. She pulled her jersey sleeves down, covering her hands with them and hugged herself. Her sobs took her by surprise. Her shoulders shook, her back sagged against the rough wall. She slid down and buried her head in her arms. She fisted her mouth, fought for control, tasted blood and salt.

What were they going to do? Alex needed more time, but the flights were booked, monies paid, meetings arranged. Would she manage by herself?

The front door swung open and Alex's knees clicked as he knelt next to her. She picked up the front of her jersey and blew her nose on the soft wool. He put his arm over her shoulder and pulled her close. "I didn't mean to freak out."

She sniffed and buried her face in his chest. "I know."

"It's just that Maggie's list shocked me."

"If you really can't manage we'll make other plans."

"I'm adding another country to the list."

"What?" she pulled back and searched his eyes. "Are you kidding me?"

"I remembered my business trip to Ireland, how beautiful it was, how I missed you, how I wanted you there. Now we can go together."

"Alex, that would be wonderful."

"I'll do all the stuff Pieter's told me to, but I can't guarantee anything."

She threw her arms around him.

"I'd be lying if I did."

"That you would, so don't, but that's okay, and thank you."

54

Toni was in the examination room putting her clothes back on and Joan took up the seat across the desk from Pam.

"I shouldn't be telling you this," she said, leaning forward in her executive chair. "But I've thought and thought about it, and decided that, if this was my daughter and grandchild, I'd want to know."

"What's wrong? Is it Toni, or Dinks, or both?"

Joan shook her head. "No, they're in perfect shape." She hesitated. "I hate breaking patient confidentiality and, believe me, I wouldn't do it if I didn't think that there was a good chance that Toni might not be here when you get back from Europe."

Pam's body sank against the chair. Joan poured her a glass of water from the carafe on her desk.

"Here, drink this. You're as white as a sheet."

Pam took a sip, but it turned her stomach. Joan picked up Toni's open file.

"Toni told me that she didn't care that you hated the baby's father; that he'd had to go to Greece without her because he wasn't going to go to jail for something he didn't do."

"That's rubbish; he's as guilty as sin. I read the transcript of his trial."

"She said she was at the trial and that he was framed. She loves him and she said that nothing would stop them being together again. I must say I believed her and I'm worried that she's going to run away again while you're gone."

"When did she tell you this?"

"Not long after you first brought her here."

Pam felt giddy with relief. That was ages ago. Things were different now.

"Don't worry, she won't do that. She might have loved him then, but he's history now. According to my kids, she went berserk when he asked her if Dinks was his. She'll be here when we get home."

PAM FELT SURE OF THIS, but, as they drove away from the gynaecologist, a thread of suspicion slipped into her head. Toni seemed happy and Daniel more often than not joined the Richards family for supper and took her out on weekends. But was it all a con? Did Toni still have plans to run away? Was she in touch with Stelios? In and out the thread went, weaving fear. Toni had loved him, run away with him and she was having his baby. Reason stayed the needle. Stelios was out of the country; Toni's passport was in James Griffiths's safe; Ignatius Bezuidenhout had told them that the forger was dead and Kelly and Brian had said the relationship was over.

"I'm going to breast-feed for the first three months," Toni's bright voice broke into her thoughts. "Jean said it boosts the immune system and to do it if I can, but I think I'll get Dinks on a bottle by January. I'm planning to go back to school next year. What do you think, Ma, will you help me?"

"Of course, I will. It's a great plan. I love it and Dad will too. We'll do anything to make it come true."

What a joy it would be to look after Dinks, but she knew that love never quite died, that it flared on the top of remote mountain slopes, that Daniel did not yet hold the core of Toni's heart. There was a chance, albeit a small one, that Toni would disappear while they were overseas. She couldn't take that chance.

PAM SAT on the side of the bed, her face pale. "I can't get on the plane," she said, her shoulders sagging.

"That's my line, don't steal it," said Alex, swallowing his pills.

"I can't face Toni running away again."

He pulled her down into bed, held her close to his chest. "Me neither. She's not going anywhere, not yet anyway."

"How can you be so sure?"

"Where's my wise wife? The one who told me that Toni was safe as long as she was pregnant?" He lifted her hair, nuzzled her neck. "You told me that Stelios was a selfish bastard; that he'd deliberately skipped the country without Toni because he didn't want to take care of a pregnant girlfriend, that he'd leave her here until the baby arrived. Well, he's still the same selfish bastard and she's more pregnant than ever."

"But I'm wiser, I'm not sure she'll be here when we get back."

"What about Kelly then? Are you sure that she won't get sick while we're away?"

"No, but Doctor Frank is here and I'm taking her for a check-up tomorrow."

"And that's all we can do for Toni. We'll get Bezuidenhout and James to check up on her."

"It's not the same."

"Sure it is. We want to protect the kids, keep them safe, keep them alive, keep them with us, but depression has taught me that we're not in control. All we can do is our best on the day, and that means that tomorrow we get hold of James and Inspector Bezuidenhout."

"And then?"

"Come Friday, we get on the plane and pray like hell that nothing happens."

SLEEP SLACKENED HIS BODY, his arm sagged on her waist and his hand let hers fall from his. She listened to the night sounds of the house and understood what he had said. Leaving the children was a risk, but risk coloured their lives; it sent Kelly to school, Brian to compete in tennis, Toni to love and fall pregnant. It frightened and excited her. It kept her awake.

· · ·

SHE WRIGGLED out from under Alex's arm, switched on the light and picked up her book, but she couldn't concentrate. After reading the same page twice and not remembering a single word, she admitted defeat, turned back the duvet, slipped her feet into her slippers, pulled on her dressing-gown and went to pack the kids' lunch-boxes for the next day. At the doorway, her hand found the switch and she flooded the kitchen with fluorescent light.

"Hi, Ma."

She jumped. "My God, Brian, what on earth are you doing here?"

"Couldn't sleep."

"Oh, *jeez*, it's my fault, isn't it? I shouldn't have given you that list last night."

How stupid of me to ask him to read it.

The list was for Kevin. It was full of telephone numbers of doctors, chemist, dentist, Maggie-private, Maggie-office, neighbour-Doris, schools, Steve-office, Steve-personal, Daniel, three weeks' worth of schedules for the kids, ante-natal and pottery for Toni, tennis, school and team and science project for Brian, medication, what to watch for and medical procedures for Kelly (2 pages), extra maths lessons and Interact meetings.

In black and white, the never-ending responsibilities were enough to give nightmares to a person twice his age.

"I'm sorry I gave it to you."

"What?"

"The list. Isn't that what's keeping you awake?"

"Well, it was a gospel, and it did kind of scare me, but Kevin and I will manage it. I really can't sleep because I'm too excited to. Kev and I are going to design a new plane for the slope, one that will beat the Act. I was just sitting here in the dark thinking about the wings when you barged in."

Pam ruffled his hair, made them cocoa, dismissed her neurosis and barged out.

55

Alex knew he'd have to get hold of James before the lawyer's day started. It ran on court time and, once in motion, legal matters buried him in paper and arguments. Pam had dressed and gone through to the kitchen and he could hear Kelly and Brian knocking on the bathroom door. Toni was, as usual, hogging the bathroom and hurling into the toilet bowl. He walked down the passage, told Brian and Kelly to use the *en suite* bathroom and added his own thump to the door. "Hurry up, Toni. I've got to be in town early this morning."

"But I haven't had breakfast yet," he heard the toilet flush, the tap open. "Joan said it's important for the baby."

"So is my appointment. Come to the car when you're finished here. I'll treat you to a toasted bacon and egg from the college tuck-shop."

Pam handed him a packed lunch. "James?" she asked.

He nodded. "Will you go to Bezuidenhout?"

"As soon as I've dropped the kids at school."

JAMES SHRUGGED his arms into his cloak and pushed back the sleeves. "To what do I owe the pleasure of breakfast, Alex?" he asked, biting into the toasted sandwich. "No, let me guess." He wiped crumbs and runny egg from his chin. "It's Antoinette, that fucking boyfriend, sorry ex-boyfriend of hers and your trip."

"How do you know?"

"I have eyes and ears everywhere and I wondered when you would get here. In the meantime, thanks to the drive-by shooting of one Lance Redman, I've had cause to liaise with Pam's Inspector Bezuidenhout and we've tied up Stelios's uncle in a legal knot of note. He's currently reporting daily to Hillbrow Police Station where his passport is under lock and key. I told Bezuidenhout you're leaving on Friday and he's arranged a tail on Toni and port authorities have circulated photographs of her."

Alex stared at him. "I…er… I don't know what to say, how to thank you."

"A rare fillet steak and an outrageously expensive bottle of red wine in a swanky restaurant when you get back will suffice." James collected an armful of files from his desk. "Tell Steve I'm working on his ex-wife and their offspring."

"Sure."

"Alex, understand that nothing's fucking fool-proof. I've done what I can, but Toni could still disappear. Now fuck off, I'm due in court."

· · ·

STEVE'S ASHTRAY WAS CLEAN. Open packets of Simba chips, Wilson's Toffees and Quality Street filled last Christmas's Baker's biscuit tin.

"What's all this?" Alex took off his corduroy jacket and hung it from the back of his chair.

"Doctor's orders. I've got to quit smoking."

"What doctor? You never go the doctor."

"Divorce stress, watching you, hell man, I'm only human." Steve unwrapped a toffee and popped it into his mouth.

"Have you tried whacking a tennis ball?" asked Alex.

Steve chucked a chocolate triangle at Alex's head. "Why so late?"

"Went to see James. Traffic crossing Johannesburg."

Steve's tongue worked at the toffee between his teeth. Shit, he hoped that it was a social call and not another drama in the Richards' household. He'd got used to Alex holding up his side of the business again and didn't want him back in the Riverside Clinic.

"And how was James?" he asked, although, having seen James last week, he knew the lawyer was fine and on form.

JAMES WAS REPRESENTING both Steve and Jean in the divorce, on the proviso that, 'they didn't haggle like fucking fishwives.' He was splitting their assets fifty-fifty and had called them to his chambers to discuss the kids.

"I insist that you resolve this matter in a manner which will leave the least scars on the innocent victims of your failed marriage," he said. "I would suggest that, as Steve was the one who left the marital home, the children stay where they are with Jean, and that she be given custody with weekends and alternative school holidays going to Steve."

"You can see them whenever you want," said Jean, shaking hands. It was a sweet deal and had worked well until last week when Jean had told him she was moving into her mother's house to nurse her through cancer.

"You've got to do something," he said to James. "Her mother lives in Port Elizabeth and I'll never see my kids."

ALEX TOOK a Bar One from the biscuit box. "James is okay. He said to tell you he's working on Jean and your offspring, but the gynae put the wind-up Pam, made her think Toni might do a runner while we're away. I thought it best to make him aware of the possibility, but he'd already contacted the police and airport security."

"He's good. Guess we've both got a fighting chance of spending the future with our kids."

Alex threw the chocolate wrapper in the wastepaper basket, picked up the phone and dialled Pam's office number.

"Damn. It's out of order," he said placing the receiver back on the cradle. "I wanted to save her the drive to the police station this afternoon."

"Don't sweat it. That Inspector likes her and he'll appreciate her visit."

"I bet he will."

56

Workers dressed in 'Municipality of Johannesburg' overalls were tiling the entrance of the police station. 'DO NOT WALK' signs were propped on the steps and cement dust crunched under Pam's medium-heeled, work courts as she entered the face-brick building and joined the queue of two people standing in front of the beige Formica counter. Sergeant Coetzee was on early shift desk-duty and she wondered if he would remember the day she'd barged in to report Toni missing, lost her temper, cried, blown her nose on paper from the men's toilet, discovered Stelios was a drug-dealer, fainted and driven with him in the police car to the cottage in Lanseria. She thought he would.

The queue moved up. The elderly man in front of her straightened his blue safari jacket, folded his arms across his chest and addressed Coetzee.

"My wife said I must come and report the theft of my car radio. *Maar,* look at this place," he said. "It's filthy."

"Sorry, *Meneer*, it's because of the renovations."

"*Ag*, that's an excuse, this country has gone to the dogs and the police along with it."

"Do you want to open a case, *Meneer*?"

"*Ja*, that's what I said."

"What happened?" Coetzee licked his pencil and slid carbon paper into place.

"My wife's sick and she sent me to the Pick 'n Pay to do her shopping. I parked in the disabled bay, but when I came out the side window of my car was smashed and the *bleddy* radio was gone."

Coetzee chewed his tongue as he wrote.

"When was that?"

"About eleven o'clock yesterday morning."

"Why didn't you come here then?"

"*Jislaaik,* don't you listen? My wife is sick. I had to take the groceries home and when I got there she told me to come and report it."

"When was that?"

"What do you mean when was that? You sound like a parrot. Here, just give me that paper, let me fill it in." He took a pen from his shirt pocket and pulled the forms across the counter from Coetzee.

"Don't forget to date and sign it, *Meneer*."

"I'm not stupid."

Pam glanced at her watch; it was nearly eight. Her desk waited. Creditors, bank reconciliation, invoicing, all had to be up to date before she left for Europe. She only had today and a few hours tomorrow morning after her appointment for a trim with Helen at Head Start, her new hairdressers. Doris from next door had recommended the place and Maggie had made a booking. "Just in case your fingers, accidentally on purpose, ring Raymond's salon," she said.

SERGEANT COETZEE CHECKED the form and gave it back. "*Dankie, Meneer*. The case number for your insurance is at the top."

"And that's it?"

"*Ja.*"

"I bet you do nothing about it. I'm glad I'm too old to be alive when we get a black president."

With a disgusted turn of his Grasshopper heels, the man left, and Pam stepped up to the counter.

"Hi, Sergeant Coetzee," said Pam.

"*Mevrou* Richards."

"You remember me?"

"*Ja*, of course, your daughter ran off with the drug-dealer who wore white shoes and skipped his bail."

"I'm impressed."

He blushed. "*Ja*, well. You remember where the Inspector sits?"

"I do."

"Good, he's expecting you."

"Oh, is he? Do you know why?"

"He just said he was."

THE DOOR WAS AJAR, and Pam knocked.

"Come in."

Ignatius sat behind his desk, his back to the burglar-barred window and he stood up when she entered. She noticed that his shirt buttons met without gaping.

"Hello, Ig, you look well. You've lost weight."

Bezuidenhout tapped his stomach. "Hettie woke up one day and said our *boeps* had to go. She put us on diet and used my credit card to buy us two pairs of fancy takkies and a stronger harness for Digger."

"Well, you look good."

"You too. Have a seat."

"Thanks," Pam smoothed her skirt, and sat on the vinyl visitor's chair. "Sergeant Coetzee said you were expecting me."

"*Ja*. When I returned your Tupperware, I said to your husband that I'd keep an eye on your family when you went overseas."

"Thank you, Ig, I appreciate it. I'm nervous to get on the plane and leave Toni. My young brother is looking after the kids. He knows what's happened with Stelios, but you know how it is."

"Unfortunately, yes, but me and that lawyer of yours have enlisted Dirk Swanepoel."

Pam's eyes flew open. "Dirk Swanepoel? Isn't he the guy from child welfare?"

"Don't look so scared, he's helped us a good deal. I notified him when Toni ran away and, more importantly, told him that the guy she was with was a wanted criminal. Anyway, I also told him that you and your husband are going overseas, and he's pulled some strings at Jan Smuts and Lanseria Airport and both airports have her listed as an accessory to him skipping bail."

"But she wasn't; she could be arrested."

"Only if she tries to duck, but don't worry, Dirk's on your side. He's just making sure she doesn't get out of South Africa while you are gone."

WHEN PAM ARRIVED AT WORK, Maggie was filing papers alphabetically into a lever-arch file.

"Eric's doing his Thursday deliveries and won't be back for the rest of the day," she said, punching holes and slipping sheets on the spikes. "He said we'll be at the airport at three o'clock tomorrow. How're you getting there? Is Kevin taking you?"

"No, Steve's taking us. Brian and Kelly have tennis and extra maths and Kevin will be rounding them up, and Daniel's fetching Toni from college. They're all going for pizza and a movie tomorrow night."

"Toni seems to like Daniel."

"I hope it's not a scam."

"What makes you say that?"

"In her first trimester she told the gynae that nothing was going to keep her from Stelios."

"But that was months ago. Things have changed."

"God, I hope so, and James and Inspector Bezuidenhout know we are going, but Maggs if there's trouble..."

"There won't be, now stop fretting," Maggie patted her arm and handed her the file. "Don't lose this, stick it in your hand-luggage just in case your baggage goes missing."

Pam fished out a copy of the list she'd made for Kevin.

"Trade," she said. "Brian calls it a gospel. Kevin has one, so has Joan Martin and I'll give Doctor Frank one this afternoon and James and Inspector Bezuidenhout have your list of our hotels."

"Covering all your bases?"

"Trying to."

"Are you coming in to the office tomorrow?"

"Not if I can help it, I'm due at the hairdresser at ten and colouring takes a while."

"He phoned earlier."

"Who?"

"Raymond. He said if you ever get tired of being blonde, or want a change, phone him."

· · ·

DOCTOR FRANK WAS RUNNING ten minutes late. Kelly took a Cadbury's Flake from her blazer pocket, untwisting one end of the wrapping.

"Want some, Ma?" she said, handing Pam the chocolate.

"Thanks," Pam took a bite, savoured the dissolving chocolate on her tongue. She gave it back to her daughter and scrambled in her bag for her current to-do notes.

Kelly shook flakes into her mouth and closed her eyes. "Mmm, delicious, hey?"

"Good for the soul but not my hips," said Pam, refusing Kelly's second offer as, clicking the top of her Parker Jotter, she ticked off mealie meal, dog food, treats for kids and Kevin, pay bills on spike, pay Frans, order meat, Toni - Gynae, Kelly - Dr F and scored three lines though Stelios - Police.

The red light on Mrs. Schmidt's telephone flashed. She stopped tapping the typewriter keys and peered over the top of the narrow lens of her glasses. "Mrs. Richards, you can go through, Doctor will see you now." Pam shoved the list into the side pocket of her skirt and tapped Kelly on the shoulder. "Let's go," she said and walked into Doctor Frank's consulting room.

"Hello, Pam. Hi, Kelly, how're you feeling?" he asked. Pam's smile made it hard for him to judge if the stress level in the Richards' household had improved since she'd told him about Toni's pregnancy and her husband's depression. He hoped that Pieter De Bruin was doing as good a job with Alex as he'd done with his Ian.

"Fine thanks," said Kelly. He stood up and walked from

behind his desk to the examination couch. Always dapper, he sported a red bow tie and, under his unbuttoned white coat, a grey striped shirt and charcoal trousers that skimmed his highly polished shoes.

"Get undressed, hop up and let's verify that, young lady," he said. Plain gold cuff-links peeped out from his coat sleeves as he rubbed and warmed the stethoscope on his lapel. Kelly took off her school blouse and stepped out of her skirt. She was thin, far too thin, as if she would disappear if he stopped watching her. He felt a surge of relief as she pulled her spencer over her head, exposing two slightly raised buds on her chest. Her breasts had started to develop again, an indicator of a good appetite and weight gain.

"Mrs. Schmidt tells me you're off to Europe, Pam."

"Three more sleeps," said Kelly.

"If you're happy with Kelly, we'll fly out on Friday night," said Pam.

"Aw, Ma, I'm fine. Tell her to stop fussing, Dr Frank."

He laughed, "Cheeky, hey. Well, let's see if you're right."

He breathed on the stethoscope, placing it on her chest. "Cold?" he asked.

"No."

"Deep breath," he said.

Her rib-cage expanded. Good. He shifted the stethoscope a little to the right. "Again."

She filled her lungs with air. Good. "Again."

One deep breath at a time he examined her whole chest. He

moved around to the other side of the bed. "Right, now for your back," he said, repeating the procedure. Her lungs sounded clear. Good.

"Okay, nearly done. Lie down."

Kelly lay back on the narrow bed. Her panties hung off jutting out hip bones, stretched from one to the other like a trampoline over her sunken stomach. He wound the stethoscope back around his neck, placed his left hand, palm down on the top of her chest, and, with the finger-tips of his right hand, double-tapped the knuckles on his fingers. Tap tap. Tap tap. Tap tap. The hollow echo delighted him. He nodded and Pam's manicured hand gave Kelly's a squeeze.

"Well, this time, Kelly, you are right. Everything is clear. You may get dressed and Pam, you can stop fussing, she's fine to go."

"Oh, the children aren't going; it's a business trip for my company."

"In that case, tell Alex that I'm at the other end of the phone if he needs me."

"Thanks, Doctor Frank, my brother is coming up from Cape Town to look after the kids, and he'll be relieved to hear that."

"Your brother's baby-sitting?"

"Yes and my friend Maggie is around for back-up."

And what about Alex? he thought. *Was he sick? In hospital? Unable to look after the children? Not responding to De Bruin's treatment as well as Ian?* He didn't want to pry, but he felt compelled to ask, "And Alex, how is he doing with De Bruin?"

"You were right about Pieter; he is an excellent psychiatrist. Alex is making progress and he's coming with me."

"Ahhh, I see, a sleeping partner."

Pam laughed. "Not quite. I won a bra competition and landed the job of going to meet Direct Technologies' suppliers."

"A bra competition?"

"I bought a bra and won a trip to Rio."

"Really? How amazing. I've never won anything, let alone a trip to Rio, but Mrs. Schmidt said you're off to Europe?"

"The sponsors let me swap it. So, instead of one airport stop, it's grown to eleven."

After two years of therapy, Ian wouldn't cope with such a gruelling schedule.

"That's a lot of travelling, Pam."

"I know. Alex wishes that my sales partner could go, but that's not possible. I can tell you what the company has in the bank, but I know nothing about electronics and Alex is an expert, so he's coming along to do the talking."

"That'll be a first, Ma," grinned Kelly. Pam pretended to smack her. "No more cheek from you today," she said. Kelly got dressed, pushing her arms into the blazer that Pam held ready for her.

"I'll leave a copy of the itinerary and all the contact details with Mrs. Schmidt on our way out," said Pam.

"Bye, Kelly. Enjoy the trip, Pam."

"Thanks. See you when I get back."

Kelly wriggled her fingers in a goodbye.

DOCTOR FRANK SMOOTHED the creases of Kelly's fragile body from the sheet, puffed out the indent of her head from the pillow and stood on a crumpled piece of paper. He flattened it out and ran his eyes down a list. It was long and had fallen out of Pam's pocket.

He rang for Mrs. Schmidt. "Is Mrs. Richards still here?" he asked.

"Yes, I'm organising Kelly's next appointment with her."

"She's dropped a list of sorts; it looks important, please come in and fetch it for her."

He twisted the cap off his Sheaffer fountain pen and, for a second, before writing "Have Fun", he wondered why "Stelios-Police" had been ruled- out three times over. It seemed she'd dealt with them good and proper.

57

M aggie and Eric scanned the international check-in counters.

"Oh my God," said Maggie clapping her hand over her mouth. "There they are at the SAA counter. It's opening and they are first in line. Alex is shoving the suitcases along with his foot."

"Ahh yes, I see him, but where's Pam?"

"That's her, next to him; she's fishing for something in her bag."

"*Jeez*, what's she done to her hair? She looks like my granny."

"She's seen us, she's waving the tickets. Come on, Alex needs a hand with the luggage. Wipe that gormless look off your face, stop staring at her and don't say a word. Got it?"

"Yes, Boss."

Maggie tugged on a smile. "Hi, guys, all ready to charm our suppliers?"

"I wish," said Alex, hefting a case onto the scale. Eric tore his eyes away from Pam and patted his friend's back. "Here, let me get that. You okay, got your stuff for... you know?"

"Under my anorak," said Alex tapping his chest.

Maggie pushed a small CNA packet into Pam's hands.

"No time to wrap it. You know us, always too rushed."

"Thanks, Maggs." Pam started to open the packet.

"No, keep it till you get on the plane. It's just a little something to keep you occupied in those quiet moments that you pencilled in on the schedule."

"The ones you rubbed out and filled in with another business appointment?" Pam grinned and slipped the packet into her bulging shoulder-bag. "What are you staring at, Eric?"

"What have you done to your hair?" he blurted out and Maggie shot him a glare.

"It's my new stylist's idea. She said short, permed hair would make me look ten years younger. What do you think?"

"I, er... Well, what a difference a hairstyle makes."

"Eric."

Pam laughed. "It's okay, Maggs, I hate it too and Alex burst out laughing when I came home. As soon as I get the boarding tickets Eric and Alex can go for coffee, while you and I buy some straightener, find a sink and fix it."

"I've no idea what possessed you to go to her," said Alex. "That Raymond guy always made a good job of your hair."

Maggie didn't dare look at Pam. "It was my idea," she said.

"We've gone to him for years and it was time to try someone new."

"Well, thanks, Maggie, you changed my wife from a sexy blonde to... "

"My granny," said Eric.

"Shush you two. Come on Pam let's find a chemist."

"Please don't be long." Alex shifted from one foot to the other, sweat beaded on his top lip and he drew in a deep breath.

"You okay?" asked Eric.

"Feeling a bit claustrophobic. I'd like to go through to the departure lounge while it's quiet."

Pam smoothed the frown between his brows and handed him a tissue. He wiped his lips. "I'll sort my hair out in London," she said. "We can go through now."

"Thanks," he said, picking up their hand luggage.

"We'll say goodbye then," said Eric, shaking his friend's hand. "You take care."

"And don't worry about anything," said Maggie, her charms jangling as she gave Pam a hug. "Have a good time."

"And bring back lots of agencies," said Eric.

"Do you think they'll be okay, Maggs?" asked Eric as they headed to the car park.

"Hope so. Pam's tuned into him now, like she is with Kelly and she told me that Pieter added something called a beta-blocker just in case."

"I was talking more about them and, you know, their marriage and stuff. Alex told me he thought Pam had had enough of him."

"When did he say that?"

"Just before the slope weekend. He was worried and so am I."

"Eric, I could have fixed her hair in twenty minutes, but she went straight though because she could see that he was anxious."

"So?"

"She's getting on a plane looking like your granny. Doesn't that tell you that she loves him?"

"Guess it does." He nudged her in the ribs. "Would you do that for me."

Maggie laughed. "Not a chance."

A FEW STRAY passengers wandered around the departure lounge. Wings Café was almost empty, and it was easy to find a table in the corner overlooking the tarmac. Waiting for their coffees to cool, they watched the planes. Some were being directed to parking spots, others opened their bellies to the catering trolleys and forklifts that filled them with food and baggage, preparing them to carry hundreds of people on long flights.

"To US," said Alex, raising his cup to Pam. "I never thought we'd make it."

"But we did," she said.

"I started getting jittery out there. Sorry that you had to leave your hair."

"Don't worry, you'll be fine, but you'll have to help me straighten it."

"My pleasure. Let's see what Maggie gave you."

Pam took the CNA packet out of her bag and read the Post-it sticker attached to it.

"To Lucky Tits, From Big Tits & No Tits".

They both laughed.

"It's a diary," said Pam, flipping the pages. "Maggie's written on the fly-leaf."

"Read it."

"We want to hear all about it. Even the naughty parts."

Alex grinned, and Pam scrambled in her bag and found a pen.

"Right, Alex, give me the opening entry."

He pursed his lips. "Okay. It's July 15th, 1986 and I'm sitting in a café at Jan Smuts Airport with the woman I married twenty years ago. I'm still in love with her. She's changed a bit; she's got a funny, new hairstyle, but that's okay, because I've also changed; I've got a bit of grey hair and depression and she's packed a shit-load of drugs for me." Alex paused.

Pam looked up from the page. "And? What about saying something about flying to Europe?"

He gave her a wry smile. "I'd rather not think about it. I'm going to struggle, I know it."

"You're scared?"

He nodded.

"Okay then. My turn." Pam spoke as she scribbled. "Are we ready for Europe? Is Europe ready for us? We don't know, but we'll figure it out as we go along, and, we promise, we'll fill this *'tit'* trip with as many naughty parts as possible."

THE END

ACKNOWLEDGMENTS

I would like to thank my late mom, who treasured my early stories and poems. My husband, who encourages me to follow my dreams, and my children, who cheer me on.

My writing group, especially Laurence Cramer, for his mentorship and Janita Lawrence, for holding my hand and clicking me into the age of technology. My proof-readers, Gill Thomas, Mary Fairon and Meryl Skinstad, for finding promise in the first draft.

My editor, Catherine Eberle, for correcting the tenses and pulling the manuscript into shape, my cover designer, Erika Bester, for visually capturing my story, and my proof-reader, Paul Swallow, of Hirundo Rustica Author Services, for his invaluable input.

ABOUT THE AUTHOR

Shirley Goodrum lives in Hartbeespoort, South Africa. She bakes stories and brownies and watches magnificent sunsets.

Printed in Great Britain
by Amazon